P9-EMJ-736

"In *To Hold Infinity*, Meaney has achieved a cold fusion of post-cyberpunk tech noir with the expansive dreams of classic SF. The result is dark, complex, and glitters with brilliant strangeness.

"*Infinity* held me from the bullet-spray prose of its opening. I was immersed in Meaney's fantastic yet plausible future—a future transformed by technology, a future where even death isn't the end of the adventure, a future where the cool philosophies of the East have merged with Western science. But the whole is cemented together by the complex but very human bond between a mother and her son.

"John Meaney has rewired SF. Everything is different now."

—Stephen Baxter

"Reading John Meaney's *To Hold Infinity*, it's impossible to believe this is a first novel. Dazzlingly imagined and dazzlingly executed, it involves the reader in a future as real and vividly present as one of the novel's neural visions, and as original. Net Angels, Luculenti, Shadow People—this is a work of true uniqueness by a true talent. Wow!"

—Connie Willis

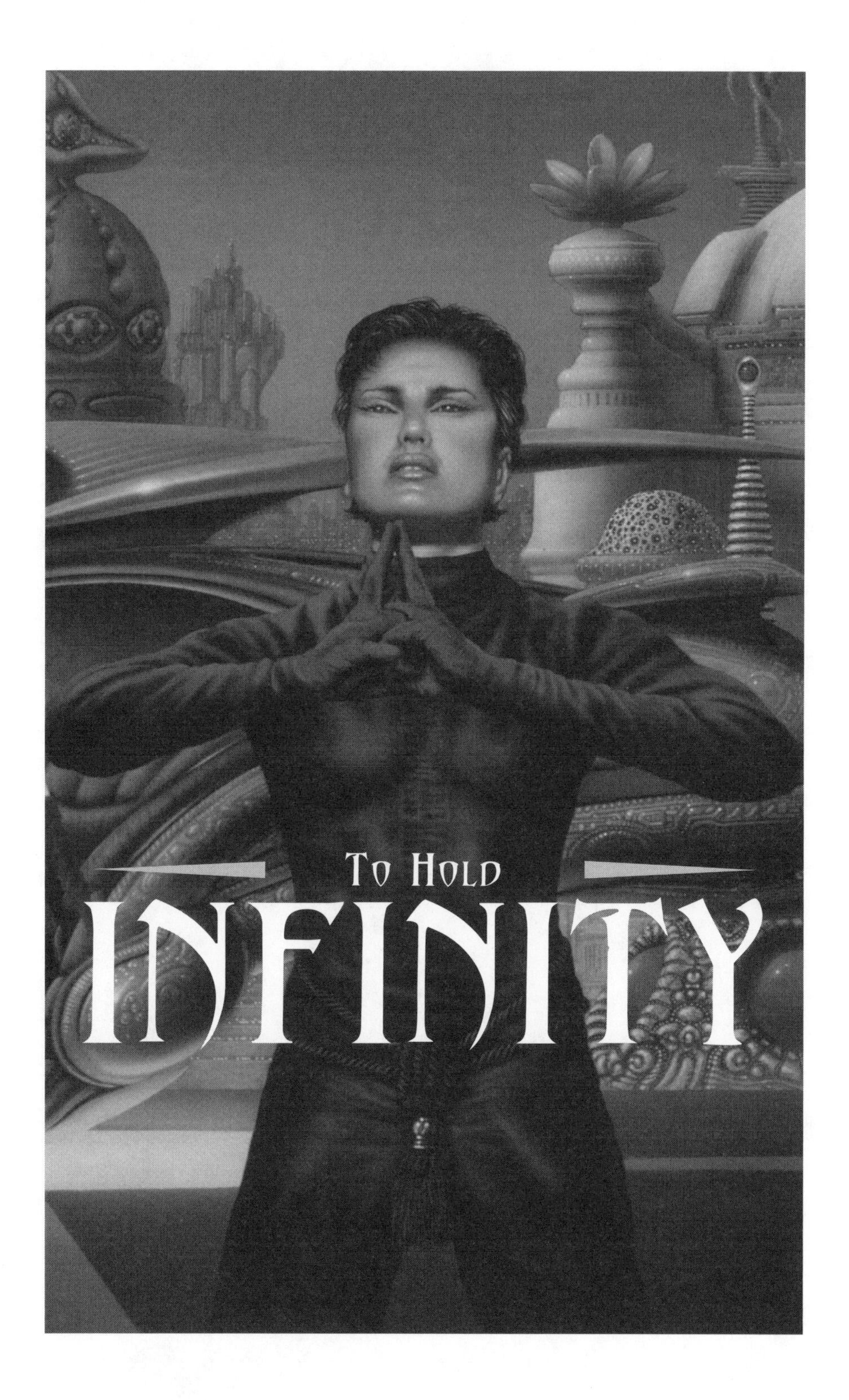
To Hold
INFINITY

Other Pyr® titles by John Meaney

Paradox: Book One of the Nulapeiron Sequence
Context: Book Two of the Nulapeiron Sequence
Resolution: Book Three of the Nulapeiron Sequence

To Hold INFINITY

JOHN MEANEY

an imprint of Prometheus Books
Amherst, NY

Published 2006 by Pyr®, an imprint of Prometheus Books

Inquiries should be addressed to
Pyr
59 John Glenn Drive
Amherst, New York 14228–2197
VOICE: 716–691–0133, ext. 207
FAX: 716–564–2711
WWW.PYRSF.COM

10 09 08 07 06 5 4 3 2 1

Library of Congress Cataloging-in-Publication Data

Meaney, John.
To hold infinity / John Meaney.
p. cm.
Originally published: London : Bantam Press, a division of Transworld Publishers, 1998.
ISBN-13: 978–1–59102–489–7 (hardcover : alk. paper)
ISBN-10: 1–59102–489–7 (hardcover : alk. paper)
1. Women biologists—Fiction. 2. Mothers and sons—Fiction. 3. Nanotechnology—Fiction. 4. Life on other planets—Fiction. I. Title.

PR6113.E17T6 2006
813'.6—dc22

2006016168

Printed in the United States of America on acid-free paper

Dedication

To the memory of my father,
Thomas Francis (Pat) Meaney,

And of the best wee Mum in the universe
Maimie Meaney, *née* Dullaghan,
immersed in infinity

Prologue

Flicker. Blindspin. Darkplunge. Golden light-fragments rip apart cobra's death-promise eyes. Laughter spirals. A muted discord: cymbals clash. Light, and light, kaleidoscopic fireworks burst above, below, drowning distant muttering.

Latch onto that. Ignore illusory cobras. The voice. Decode.

Tetsuo's fingers flicker in a manic dance of control gestures. Clammy sweat breaking out—ignore—and a huge fragment breaks loose, unfurls in golden sheets of holographic text.

[[[LogBegin: Module = Node75AG23: Type = PivotCentre: Axes = 6.

Concurrent_Execute

ThreadOne: <video> timestamp = 23091313:001, linkfile = call_logs/#78AF239

ThreadTwo: <audio> timestamp = 23091313:001, linkfile = internal.thislog

ThreadThree: <kinaesthesia> insert pending

ThreadFour: <proprioreceptive>, linkfile = *Creeping-Dread*

End_Concurrent_Execute]]]

[[[HeaderBegin: Module = Node98*34P9: Type = FlatText: Axes = 1

FARSTEEN: You bastard. I know. I know what you've been doing.

{UNIDENTIFIED}: Me? Surely you mean Rafael.

FARSTEEN: What's worse? That abomination, or your surveillance? My God, man! If he was only . . .

{UNIDENTIFIED}: You've played your part.

FARSTEEN: I knew I was selling to a middleman. But . . .

<<<Error condition: LUCFMT009867; diagnosis = Object fragmented. Error is fatal.>>>}}}

"Bloody hell."

It's a video-log, encrypted in Luculentus format, and Tetsuo has cracked just enough to scare him.

Clasping hands on the mound of his belly, he stares at the code fragments. They spark reflections from the glass desk, throw highlights across his burgundy silk kimono.

Rafael. The log mentioned Rafael.

Tetsuo minimizes the display, moving the shrunken image off to one side.

He reaches up to scratch his scalp, but remembers just in time. Gently, he touches the filigreed wire headgear inserted into his skull. Two days since the op. His hair an itching stubble, just starting to grow back.

And now this. Just when he has finally made good.

A chime: incoming realtime call. Sender IDs indicate Stargonier and Malone.

Damn. Another project slipping behind.

An external video view hangs beside him: his villa's white sweeping curves, the meadow and silver-dappled stream. Hot white sun, emerald sky. The beta moon's blue disk setting . . .

He shifts a peripheral display to strategy ware, and opens up the incoming call.

"Hi, Tetsuo."

Sylvester Stargonier's handsome profile. Beside him, a convoluted network diagram grows.

"Market forecast, with divergent contingency plans in the third tenday," Stargonier says, by way of explanation.

Elizabeth Malone's image: "Is the tech spec on schedule?"

Glowering hawk icon: the strategy ware notes her antagonism.

In a couple of tendays, when the mindware starts kicking in, Tetsuo will be able to hold his own against these Fulgidi merchants.

"Ahead of time," says Tetsuo. His palms are damp.

The strategy ware pulses: nine first-level outcomes. Second-level shifting too fast to read.

Win-win-win probabilities are in sharp decline.

"Here's the first design," Tetsuo adds, uploading.

"And the rest?"

Tiger, tiger, burning bright: a background icon. The ware is recommending a decisive attitude.

"Two days early," says Tetsuo, hoping he can make it true.

"Fine. Endit."

Malone's image disappears. Stargonier nods, and fades.

This is going badly.

The mindware isn't going to integrate in time for this project. Besides . . . he didn't deserve the upraise, in the first place. His family's association with the Pilots gave him an edge. And Rafael's sponsorship. Not his own pitiful talents.

A plaintive beep. His cracker ware has been busy, burrowing through near-sentient protocols and teasing out another shard of logcode.

Tetsuo gestures: go ahead.

A Luculentus appears, clad in green and burgundy. A LuxPrime courier.

"I'm Farsteen," says the image. "At least, a partial analogue. If I am online, the real Farsteen is surely dead."

Farsteen. The name from the video-log. Tetsuo glances at the log display, but leaves it minimized.

This is getting worse.

"I see you have been upraised. Perhaps the real Farsteen was in

Skein when you were presented. My congratulations, Luculentus Tetsuo Sunadomari."

Tetsuo's scalp crawls.

"I am damaged. Your biog-info was hard-linked to my framework. If you were not responsible for my death, then you are in great—"

The image shatters.

There is a distant crash of sound, like thunder.

An electronic wail splits the air.

"SecSys!"

A display opens at his command: across the meadow, black-suited, black-visored figures are running.

Running this way.

Tetsuo can only watch as his systems respond. Dark winged shapes—polyceramic smartbats catapulted from the house eyries—snap into formation and swoop, spitting toxins and screaming ultrasound.

The intruders brush them aside, and keep on coming.

Dry throat.

Tetsuo is frozen.

Five years on Fulgor. Five years of not hacking it. Drowning in the intense competition, on a world whose upper and mercantile classes drill their children relentlessly in the academic disciplines, in the hope of upraise to Luculentus greatness. He couldn't compete with his parents' brilliance on Earth, but this is worse.

But for one chance: the sudden demand for his mu-space tech speciality, Rafael's sponsorship, and the offworld quota, for upraising non-Fulgidi adults. His one chance of making it.

And now it's all coming apart. He saw a LuxPrime courier—the one in the log?—and heard the screaming argument with the proctor, and took that stupid chance. Just when things were going right.

Alarms squeal at a higher pitch, and the reek of smoke stings his nostrils.

Got to move.

He grabs a case of Luculentus-format info-crystals from his desk, and pockets them. There's no time to get the crystal he was working on. Though he was decoding from here, the crystal itself is still plugged into his bedroom terminal. No time—

Oh, no.

Mother. Perhaps he can get a message to her, before she leaves Earth.

He gestures for a holo-still: himself, long-haired, before the shaved skull and implants from the upraise op. Hand shaking, he indicates a monologue commencement.

"Mother. I'm looking forward to seeing you, but I have urgent business to attend to. Perhaps Akira can arrange for a later trip? I'll contact you soon."

His fingers twist, as though tying a knot, and the speech and image objects are linked.

He points. The message is sent.

It *must* reach Mother, in time to stop her leaving.

An awful tearing sound. Grasers splitting the ceramic armoured inner walls.

Gods. All this security. He never expected to use it.

He leans back in his chair.

"Backdoor."

For a moment, nothing happens.

"BACKDOOR! NOW!"

The chair's arms clasp him, envelope him. The chair whisks backwards.

The bottom drops out of his stomach.

Amber lights strobe vertically upwards, as he falls, encapsulated, through the drop-shaft.

Impact.

His teeth smash together. The burnt cupric taste of blood in his mouth.

His flyer's cockpit.

Above him, the cockpit's liquid bubble-membrane hardens. Ramjets roar, echoes crashing back from the cavern's walls.

In front, white lights suddenly arrow towards infinity, as the exit tunnel lights up.

His chair melds with the cockpit, and status displays spring into life.

All subsystems active.

An icon, glowing gold with outspread wings: a falcon.

Acceleration kicks him back as the lights race past. The flyer hurtles along its track.

Curving upwards, now, with the g vector tugging at his guts.

A speck of light.

Rocketing vertically. Combined accelerations pull him deeper into the control chair.

The speck is growing.

Hard to breathe.

. . . growing into a circle of greenish light . . .

He's yelling now, almost screaming.

. . . which is the sky, growing huge . . .

His eyes are squeezed almost shut.

. . . and bursting into being all around him, in a tear-blurred explosion of pale clear light.

He forces his eyes wide open.

Greenish skies, vanilla clouds.

Downward scan shows a tan plain, blotched with spinach-green, streaking past below. Kilometres flee beneath him, tracked by the broken cursor of his flyer's shadow.

The terrain's colours wash across the flyer's chameleon skin, as its smartatom processors furiously work to provide countermeasures to SatScan, orbiting high above the planet.

Distance covered: twelve hundred kilometres.

Ahead lies a bank of creamy golden clouds. The ground below is dark.

The flyer drops.

Acceleration grips his throat.

Going down, into darkness.

Now.

Diving into purple shadow.

Sheer purple gold-streaked rockface, the walls of Nether Canyon, streak past on either side.

Ghostly hand clutching a throat: the atmospheric-warning icon.

Ramjets howling, the flyer dives deep, far below the terraformed altitudes, into the region's hidden heart.

Into the hypozone.

Chapter One

Winter rain falling.
Icy thunder shaking cedars;
No baby cries.

Dark clouds, tinged with eerie yellow, rolled over Hokkaido's majestic peaks. The island sternly frowned upon the sombre, swelling Pacific waves. As salt spray spattered Yoshiko's face, her fingers tightened on the cold safety rail.

Ken's grave. She hoped the children—no, Akira was thirty-five, his wife the same—would they give Ken's grave the care it needed, while she was gone?

Oh, Ken.

She should have planted that micro-maple.

Wind buffeted her small body and she stepped unsteadily backwards, the wet deck slippery beneath her feet. Though she looked like a forty-year-old athlete—her age held at bay by *bushido* discipline and femtocyte telomere-repair—inside, her full sixty years lay heavily upon her.

"Mother?" Akira's voice was almost lost upon the wind.

He stood with Kumiko, his wife, dutifully behind the fluorescent orange holo-ribbon which demarcated the embarkation strip. Kumiko's porcelain-pale face seemed almost to float in the eldritch prestorm light.

At their feet, a harnessed lynxette crouched, tufted ears laid flat.

The other passengers, some thirty people, were shuffling across the metal deck towards the boarding-ramp. Above them, the silver-white orbital shuttle hovered, poised like a hawk above the restless waves.

"He didn't reply," said Yoshiko, "to my last h-mail."

"He'll be there. With acceptance tests and only one small gateway, the infoflow to Fulgor is massive right now. Personal h-mail has no chance."

Full connection of Fulgor's Skein to EveryWare—the interwoven NetEnvs of fifty worlds, including Earth—was imminent. In the skewed topology of commerce, Skein was fast becoming civilization's heart. It was technically superior, the heart of Fulgor's previously isolationist economy. Akira had explained all this.

"If you say so." Yoshiko's voice was soft.

Tetsuo. If you wanted to, you would surely have found a way.

The boarding chime sounded, oddly flat.

Yoshiko picked up her narrow carry-case from the deck. It was two and a half metres long, the one item she had not entrusted to a smartcart.

Akira and Kumiko bowed, the precision of that gesture a token of their love.

Yoshiko made her way to the other passengers.

Most were middle-aged Terrans, finely dressed in comparison to Yoshiko's plain jumpsuit. A few children. Among the crowd, a trio of tall, pale people—the tallest humans Yoshiko had ever seen—stood out. Silver light glittered from the fine headgear twisted through their hair.

Luculenti.

She wondered what they had been doing on Earth.

As she watched them—they appeared to be conversing without words, changing expressions flickering across their features—she wondered at their height and slender strength. Natural genetic drift, under offworld conditions?

Maybe. But Yoshiko's professional instinct was aroused. She suspected semilegal morphing femtocytes. Fulgor had only been settled for two centuries.

She drifted closer.

The Luculenta woman held her head close to her male companion. Yoshiko looked at her sculpted coiffure, interwoven with silver fibres. Did the headgear ever get caught in things? Did it hurt?

"—children's nexus ware." The Luculentus man had switched to speech. "A stability other cultures lack, don't you think?"

His patrician accent stiffened Yoshiko's spine.

"Awful conditions," the man added, looking around. "Local colour, I suppose."

The third of the Luculenti, a crimson-haired teenage girl, looked embarrassed.

"Temporary facilities, I believe," said the Luculenta woman soothingly.

Yoshiko smiled inwardly. Perhaps, truly, the outdoor platform and the long wait were not what a Luculentus was used to.

Everyone shuffled closer to the ramp. A child's laughter rang out.

Above, the sky was darkening quickly.

Suddenly, white and purple lightning spat, and the shuttle's wings flashed white. Torrential rain began to fall in silver sheets, crashing upon the metal deck.

There was a visceral crash of thunder.

Yoshiko took her place on the boarding-ramp's moving strip. She looked back through the near-metallic haze at Akira's forlorn figure. Kumiko must have taken the lynxette below.

The ramp lurched, and stopped.

Yoshiko grabbed for the rail but a strong young hand grasped her arm, steadying her. The Luculenta girl, crimson hair turned purple by the rain and plastered against her headgear.

"It's kind of fun, isn't it?" The girl shouted above the torrent's roar. "The storm, I mean."

Yoshiko looked around at the other passengers. Their shoulders were hunched, their faces pinched and miserable. The rain was implacable.

Yoshiko laughed.

"Yes," she said. "Yes, it is."

Until this moment, she had moved in a daze, coerced by friends and family to take this trip. They were worried, she knew, about the black depression hanging over her since Ken's death. But suddenly, right now, she saw that this journey was right. Something she had to do.

Buffeted by wind and rain, she walked up the stalled ramp with the Luculenta girl at her side.

At the hatchway, where a steward was ushering people in, she looked back. Akira was gone, and she felt the old darkness pressing at her again.

The hardwood sheath at her waist, tucked inside her jumpsuit, dug into her like guilt. The tanto dagger was legal. It was also the samurai woman's traditional suicide weapon.

No one bowed farewell to her.

Storm-rain fell, sweeping chaos across the deck, as pitiless and inevitable as death.

In the darkness, twigs snagged his headgear, and leaves scrunched under foot. His skin crawled. He pictured wriggling insectoids, dropping from the night-bound branches.

Forest. Wilderness.

Rafael Garcia de la Vega despised it.

He blinked his smartfilmed eyes twice, stepping up the gain. The moonlight scarcely penetrated the shadows. He double-blinked again, to extend the frequency range.

Tiny heat-sparks of life, everywhere. Rafael shuddered.

If Marianan were alive he could have done this remotely, through Skein—though he had not risked such a thing before.

But she was dead. Offline. If he wanted her, he had to have her physical remains.

His ankles ached.

Rustling sounds. Ignore.

He pushed through undergrowth, pulled aside a fernlike frond.

Sloping below, a long meadow, pale silver in the moonlight. Beyond, a crystal villa, its peach and orange radiance spilling out into the night. Faint strains of swirling music.

By the villa, a tower pointed like a bony finger towards the alpha moon.

Hidden by the hated forest, he crouched, afraid to leave its cover.

Marianan.

Down there, she waited for him. The sweet decaying fragments of her once-ripe soul.

Laughter rose inside him. What good was the game, without attendant risk?

He stepped out into the open.

Slowly, heart thumping, he moved down the grassy slope. Stars wavered and broke apart above him, their light scattered by his drifting smartatom film, his protection from SatScan surveillance.

Drenched with chill sweat, he stepped over a low stone wall, and crouched beneath ornate topiary.

Cut-off point.

He knelt, scanning with enhanced vision, slipping into control interface with the smartatom lattice hovering above him.

No scan-systems flared. No EM pulses tore his smartatoms apart.

The Ortegas were fools. This far from a city, and no security. Hardly a worthy challenge.

He slipped past a raven-shaped hedge. A woman's laughter rang out as he crossed a patio through a pool of light. He could hear men's voices, the clink of glasses.

Enjoy the party.

Something—

He stepped into darkness and froze.

Slowly, he raised his arm, activating the silver bracelet round his wrist.

A small feline shadow slipped across the lawn. A pet. A parasite. Rafael aimed the bracelet—then lowered it.

It wasn't worth spoiling this moment of communion.

A white marble archway led to the family shrines. They beckoned him, as surely as Marianan's pale flawless skin had attracted him in life.

He remembered: bare white shoulders, copper hair, amethyst-beaded headpiece, copper eyes. He had met her just once, at the Perigee Fair, and known immediately that she must be his.

But she had died, in a tragic flyer accident. No one had invited Rafael to the funeral.

No matter. She waited for him, still.

He moved, almost gliding, between two vast and overdecorated family mausoleums. Past a tasteless tomb, its passé holo hypersphere shining brightly.

Marianan's grave, he noted with relief, was simple and classical. A herb-scented candle—real, not holo—flickered before the shrine. Reflected flame danced upon the small crystal dome.

Rafael knelt on the damp-smelling soil. He lifted the dome, and reverently set it aside.

The cylinder, now revealed, was icy silver, trapped by moonlight and candlelight. Marianan's plexcore, offline.

The dead Luculenta's shattered soul awaited him.

Slowly, exquisitely slowly, he dug his fingers into the soil, and felt for the button's indentation like a lover's secret core.

He pressed inwards.

Inside the cylinder, unfocussed thoughts and memories burgeoned as the plexcore powered up. Though her fragile organic brain was decomposing with the rest of her bloated corpse, buried in the soil below, the torn half of Marianan's mind which lay not in organic substrates would soon be his.

Devoid of senses, remembering death, trapped within the activating plexcore, the half-sentient mind-fragments must be tearing themselves apart in pain and confusion.

Don't worry, my sweet. Release is at hand.

Rafael closed his eyes.

```
[[[(HeaderBegin: Module = Node 12A3.33Q8: Type
    = QuaternaryHyperCode: Axes = 256
    Concurrent_Execute
        ThreadOne: <rhombencephalon channel>.linkfile = Infiltrate
            .Alpha
        ThreadTwo: <intrapeduncular matrix>.linkfile = Infiltrate
            .Beta
        ThreadThree: <LuxPrime interface>linkfile = CodeSmash
        ThreadFour: <thalamic/cerebralmatrix>.linkfile = Subvert-
            Array
        ThreadFive: <superolateral net>.linkfile = MindWolf
End _Concurrent_Execute]]]
```

Shuddering, he loosed his vampire code.

Burning claws raked his brain, scraped his spine, hooked into his nerves and slowly drew them apart. He gasped and shivered at the cold wash of plexcore ware flooding into his cache, filling his torso-implants.

Too much. Keep control.

He had to contain the torn remnants of Marianan's mind, hold back from integration, until he was safely home.

"Tarfus?"

A deep shudder passed through Rafael.

"Come on, boy. Let's get you in for supper."

Control. Control, damn it.

The woman's voice was uncultured. Not Luculenta.

Calling the damned feline, as though it couldn't hunt smaller vermin by itself.

Rafael straightened up, forced a straight face despite the dark hunger roiling his guts, and stepped out into the light cast by a large window.

"Oh!" The serving-maid jumped.

The gold and purple feline in her arms spat, baring teeth.

"I beg your pardon," said Rafael, turning on his most disarming smile. "I didn't mean to startle you. I was just out for some fresh air."

"That's all right, sir," said the Fulgida maid, bobbing a short curtsy.

"I'm sorry." Rafael stepped aside, and gestured for her to pass.

Fulgida, not Luculenta. Without true Skein access, and the means to identify him.

As he waved the woman by, he aimed his bracelet, with its load of soluble toxic darts, at her throat.

The feline hissed.

"Be nice, Tarfus."

The maid's eyes were troubled.

"He's beautiful," said Rafael. "Gorgeous coat. And those eyes."

The maid blushed slightly.

She cradled the feline more tightly, and carried him into the villa.

"Good night," called Rafael softly, and lowered his arm, deactivating the bracelet.

His heart was pounding. Chaos was mounting, pulsing and burning, inside his implanted cache.

Control.

Trembling, holding his plundered soul-fragments tightly within himself, Rafael retraced his steps, past shrines and mausoleums, out into the dark and pregnant night.

Chapter Two

Falling mu-stars, black;
Cedars hide the lonely cat who
Cries in the night

Night's dark vault, a soft grey arch enclosing it: pale grey carpet arcing upwards to either side, narrowing to a ribbon's width above. A kilometre-wide window onto unwinking stars, the flat end of a great cylinder spinning in the void.

Ardua Station.

High above Yoshiko, the inner face was stippled with axial entrances, with radial elevators and crawling smartcarts. Access ways, progressively more utilitarian the closer they were to the zero-g spin axis, led to the busy interior.

Down here at the rim was tourist country. Exclusive boutiques beckoned quietly, offering jewellery and offworld exotica. Farther inside, garish holos advertised bars and clubs.

"Magnificent, isn't it?" the Luculenta girl said, gazing outwards.

"Yes," said Yoshiko, turning back. Stars and darkness wheeled majestically. "We're lucky."

To be here. To be alive at all, born of stardust, partaking briefly in the cosmic dream.

"We're just the tiniest blips in time," the girl muttered. "Transient dissipative structures."

Yoshiko looked at her, surprised.

"I'm sorry." The girl laughed. "I shouldn't be morbid."

No, thought Yoshiko. *That's the prerogative of those of us who are old.*

A memory flash: Tetsuo's halting h-mail, face oddly blank, apologizing for not attending his father's funeral. Business, crucial negotiations. Her own numb disbelief.

Nearly a year ago.

"—have introduced myself earlier."

"I'm sorry?" Yoshiko jerked herself back to the present.

"Vin," said the Luculenta girl. "Actually, it's Lavinia. Wretched, don't you think? My friends call me Vin."

"Sunadomari Yoshiko."

"Mrs. Sunadomari—"

"Please. Just Yoshiko."

Vin smiled brightly. "Thank you. Fancy a drink?"

"Yes, but—"

A smartcart rolled up, though Yoshiko hadn't seen Vin gesture for one. In Anglic and Nihongo, it offered refreshments, and Yoshiko chose Terran orange juice.

"You're from Nihonjin Columbia?"

"Yes. Vancouver, originally. Kanazawa prefecture. Then I studied in Quebec." Yoshiko sighed. "But I've lived in Okinawa now for, oh, many years."

Because it was your home, Ken, and I would have followed you anywhere.

"We saw a little of FedCan." Vin sipped from her glass. "Only a couple of days."

Yoshiko looked at her. "How many Terran languages do you know? Well enough to distinguish regional accents, that is?"

"All of them."

"I'm sorry?"

Vin ducked her head modestly. "It didn't take me long to pick them up."

"Good grief." Yoshiko set her glass down on a safety rail. "Are they all as bright as you, on Fulgor?"

"I guess so. The Luculenti, anyway."

"I see. And how many Fulgidi are Luculenti?"

"Point oh five percent of the population. Not many."

Yoshiko wondered how many Luculenti Tetsuo knew.

"My elder son lives on Fulgor," she said. "My younger son, on Earth, is paying for this trip."

"Kind of him."

Very kind, yes. But Yoshiko had seen the fear in Akira's eyes: the fear that, having seen Tetsuo one last time, Yoshiko would be ready for death herself.

Ah, my son. You know me too well.

"I've heard," said Yoshiko, focussing on the conversation for the girl's sake, "that Fulgor is a paradise."

"You need to visit other cultures, before you appreciate your own," said Vin, colour rising slightly in her cheeks.

They both remembered the remarks her father—if he was her father—had made back on Earth.

"In fact," Vin continued, "there's been a spate of violent deaths, suicides and maybe even murder, just recently, in the city nearest our house."

"Bad things happen everywhere, I guess."

"Not on the Fulgor I grew up on, when I was young."

Yoshiko looked at Vin's grave teenage face, maybe fifteen Terran years old.

Vin said, "We mature more quickly than Earthers."

Were my thoughts that obvious? wondered Yoshiko.

"So, is your son in business?"

"Mu-space comms," said Yoshiko. "Tech consultant."

"Oh, that's an active field right now. He should be OK."

Something in her tone made Yoshiko ask, "Is there some reason his work shouldn't be secure?"

Vin looked a little uncomfortable. "Fulgor can be a rough place to do business. Speaking of which—"

She held up a hand, as though asking for silence. A frown etched itself upon her young features, then cleared.

"Sorry," she said. "We have to take our comms opportunities when we get them. One of my corporations was in trouble, and I had to bail it out. Had to offload one of my smaller companies to do it, though."

"Oh," said Yoshiko, feeling stupid.

"Don't worry." Vin smiled brightly. "I'm sure your son is doing fine."

"I hope so."

"Er—Will you excuse me? I need to get back to my folks."

"Of course. Thanks for your company."

"See you later."

Vin walked into the nearest corridor. Yoshiko watched her go, then turned back to the great view window. The stars' motion was hypnotic, but—

Yoshiko did the calculation in her head. Ardua Station must be spinning fast, a revolution every forty-five seconds to produce one g at the outer hull. The night view was a corrected image, slowed down for the tourists.

Shaking her head, she turned away from the beautiful illusion, to the blatantly commercial façade at the station's core.

Rafael was all of them, simultaneously.

He felt the soaring pulse in Lydia's body as she/he leaped high—

Anya's pain, the blistered foot, the discipline which produced a perfect arabesque—

Every member of the chorus, movement flowing in perfect synchrony—

And, transcendent, the pattern of his own choreography—

With him, in Skein, he felt the dancers' soul-mothers, their appreciation and delight. Realtime holocams reproduced the crystal sphere in which the girls were dancing, a sphere rising through a clear green sea shot through with bright bacterial streamers.

Hard to hide his inner triumph, his awesome self-control. The intimate presence of Luculentae ladies was a vast temptation. He could plunder their minds and souls, every one of them, here and now.

Finale.

The crystal sphere broke the surface and split apart, opening like a flower, and Lydia sailed high above the kneeling chorus as triumphant horns heralded her leap into freedom.

. . . And Rafael blinked, dropping out of Skein, and his flyer's lounge—crystal chandeliers, luxuriant chaises longues—crowded into his attention.

There was a patter of applause as the Luculentae ladies, leaving Skein, rose to their feet in appreciation.

"Bravo, Rafael."

"Exquisite, *par excellence*."

Rafael rose from his couch and bowed. "You do me too much honour. Your soul-daughters performed magnificently."

"Rafael?"

"Yes?"

He received a <private send>; unmistakably feminine:

<<icon: leonine conductor, a baton of silver light>>
<<proprioreceptive: warm stirrings, speeding heartbeat>>
<<kinaesthetic: leaping, with arching back>>
<<visual: a shower of blood-red roses>>

"Ah, Rebecca."

"You were wonderful."

He replied with:

<<ideogram: RelaxedBeautyWithAwareness—beautiful-woman-reclines>>
<<touch: smooth, satin caress>>
<<audio_1: cascade of harpstrings>>
<<audio_2: waterfall, splashing>>
<<audio_3: monsoon rain>>
<<olfactory: exotic, musky fragrance, tinged with fruit>>
<<visual_1: one pink rose with thorny stem>>
<<visual_2: a droplet of blood, falling onto silk>>

"True beauty," he said, "is gracious with pale imitation."

"Sir." Rebecca curtsied, a hint of mockery in the gesture.

Some of the other Luculentae laughed.

Between Rafael and Rebecca a {public vision} appeared, visible to all:

{[Entwined hearts.]}
{[A balladeer crooning a lovers' song.]}
{[Angry hands loading an antique shotgun.]}
{[A red-faced Luculentus: a broad caricature of Rebecca's husband.]}

The image broke up like smoke and drifted into nothingness.

"Oh, no. Don't tell him." Rafael bowed to the Luculenta who had sent the {public vision}. Her name was Xanthia Delaggropos, a newcomer to this circle, and he liked her style. "I'll behave, I promise."

Xanthia nodded, a mysterious smile on her olive-skinned face, and turned to a smartcart for a drink, indicating her disinterest in continuing the game.

Rafael started to compose a flirtatious <private send>, then stopped. A singer and surgeon-programmer by primary professions, Xanthia had that rare extra quality—

Hunger was rising inside him.

He must be mad. Marianan's soul was frozen in his cache, awaiting release: with drugs and meditation he had fought down the urge to merge with her last night.

"If you'll excuse me." He cleared his throat. "We don't want your soul-daughters to drift away or drown."

[[Turquoise sea. A pale hand flailing desperately, then sinking out of sight.]]

[[Salty tang. Empty ocean waves.]]

"Let's hope not, Voretta," he said, recognizing her style, and smiled with apparent artlessness. He raised his hand in the privacy gesture, but received an interruption.

<<visual: linen-draped table, set for two>>

<<text: Dinner tonight?>>

"My pleasure," he said, though it might be considered a minor faux pas to respond verbally to a <private send>. His control was slipping, and that was partly Xanthia's doing, sitting there so calm and self-assured—

He forced his mind into low-level command interface.

[[[HeaderBegin: Module = Node12998.JH17: Type = Trinary-Hyper-Code: Axes = 64

Concurrent_Execute

ThreadOne: <rhombencephalon channel>.linkfile = FusionReacterOne

ThreadTwo: <intrapeduncular matrix>.linkfile = WingConfigure

ThreadThree: <thalamic/cerebralmatrix>.linkfile = ProcessFlight

End_Concurrent_Execute]]]

He reconfigured his delta wings, biting atmosphere, revelling in the airflow across his flight surfaces. The fusion reactor was his beating heart, pumping joyous power.

Silver-capped waves flew past beneath him.

Surface.

The water was an icy shock to his fuselage thermal sensors. He spread his wings, exhaling to decelerate, reversing thrust.

[[STATUS: (12.45, 44.88, 1, 3.7892, 5.73382, 2.300, 8.999, 0.001)]]

Bow wave decreasing. Velocity rapidly falling to zero.

Then he was at rest on the ocean, bobbing gently, his flyer's status a point in eight-dimensional phase space, nicely within the system-ok region.

[[[HeaderBegin: Module = Node00076.AA10: Type = Trinary-HyperCode: Axes = 0

Concurrent_Execute

ThreadOne: <rhombencephalon channel>.disengage

ThreadTwo: <intrapeduncular matrix>.disengage

ThreadThree: <thalamic/cerebral matrix>.disengage

End_Concurrent_Execute]]]

As Rafael's link with the exterior holocams faded, he caught a dreamlike image of nubile girls stepping gingerly from the opened crystal segments onto his smartraft, or diving adventurously into the ocean and striking out with athletic strokes towards the flyer.

He returned his attention to the flyer's lounge.

Voretta was watching him with expectant eyes.

<<audio: (softly) Tonight, Voretta, we shall celebrate.>>

A smile was her only reply. It was enough.

Chapter Three

Black shaded darkness.
Who hunts, emerald eyes gleaming?
Night holds him close.

A black hummingbird darted in front of her, startling Yoshiko. It hung in the air, wings blurred, drinking nectar from a crimson flower; then it flicked away, out of sight.

Joyous green life stretched all around her, beneath lighting panels replicating Terran daylight. They could shine more brightly, she knew, if oxygen demand increased.

She took a springy step onto a grassy path. This far up, centripetal acceleration was maybe two-thirds g. Maybe she should live in a space habitat.

Never to see Ken's grave again . . . Pay attention.

She should not be here. A smartcart, laden with pots of hybrid wheat, had passed her in a corridor. Unable to resist, she had followed it into an elevator, keeping to its sensors' blind spot—a trick Tetsuo had shown her years ago, with her own lab's smartcarts.

The smartcart's authorization had let her through the bio-area's scan-gate.

A wispy sensation on her cheek. She stopped, gently transferred a large brown spider from her shoulder to the nearest bush. Walked into its web. *Stupid old woman.*

From up ahead came faint strains of music, a melody she ought to recognize. Passing under a tree, beneath a scolding capuchin monkey, she pushed through foliage to a low cluster of white domes.

From an open doorway came a metallic voice—"*Rekka! Look out!*" —and the hissing sound of graser fire . . . or rather, holodramatists' conventional sound effect.

The stirring theme tune played.

A grin broke across Yoshiko's face. *Chandri, Space Explorer*, had been the boys' favourite hv serial. She remembered Tetsuo and Akira, glued to the view-stage.

From the doorway, she watched the terminal in the dome's shadowy interior.

The tiny figure of the heroine, Rekka Chandri, was bent over a biofact, evolving (in minutes, rather than days) a deadly variant of her remote-controlled beeswarm. Cannibalistic aliens (portrayed with horns instead of antlers, forestalling litigation from the real-life Haxigoji on whom they were based), threatened Rekka's camp, while her young side-kick fired warning shots above their heads.

Viewpoint shift: a blind Pilot, silver sockets where her eyes should have been, dropping out of mu-space and landing quickly, strapping on her ninja gear and leaping to the rescue—

Yoshiko laughed aloud.

There was a muffled curse, and the holodrama winked out.

"Lights."

A big square-jawed red-bearded man rose from a camp chair, and pushed back long red hair from his eyes. He tugged his blue jumpsuit into order. Behind him, on a workbench, lay a jumble of gene-splicers and ecomodellers and jury-rigged lash-ups whose purpose was hard to guess.

"Sorry, ma'am. Er—What can I do for you?"

"Pardon me, Mister—" Yoshiko read his name tag. "—Rasmussen. Don't halt the program on my account."

"Um . . . Well, I shouldn't have been watching it. But there's a punctuated evolutionary thread running on the biofact that'll take a couple of hours . . ."

"Especially on an old delta forty-seven," said Yoshiko, nodding at the plain black box beneath the workbench.

"We could do with a Gemini B-series, though reconfiguring for hypertetrahedral architecture can be a real bi—uh, bear." He stopped. "Guess you've worked with Advanced Thetas, then."

"I started on Beta thirties," said Yoshiko, showing her age. "Oemaru Bios was just taking off. I guess they're on the way down, now."

Rasmussen shook his head. "Damned marketing, that's the trouble. Everyone's switching to facet-driven free-pad systems, with the sexy NetEnv interfaces. Never mind whether they can actually do the job."

"Always quoting PIPS or EIPS ratings, while the Geminis are optimized for coevolutionary transactions. It's generations per second which counts."

"Damned straight." A grin spread over his broad face, and he held out a large callused hand. "Name's Eric. Nice to meet another Gemini bigot."

"Yoshiko."

They shook hands.

"You know," she added, "that it's field-upgradeable?"

"Yeah. Still can't get the budget. But I'll keep trying."

"Good luck." She looked at the terminal. "I should let you—get back to work."

He laughed. "I've seen it before. She gets rescued in the end."

"I know. My favourite was the Coolth story, where she met aquatic aliens who lived under a global icecap."

"And her ship was crushed, and she was trapped beneath the ice—"

"—And she reconfigured her own lungs with a reprogrammed portadoc—"

"—And aliens swarmed around, worshipping her—"

"—And their song split the ice."

Yoshiko sighed. "That was a while ago."

"Wasn't the music great? It seems like yesterday."

She guessed his age at thirty-five. Akira's age.

"Listen," she said. "I shouldn't really be here."

"I did wonder."

"I'm just a passenger, waiting for a mu-space ship, due in—" She touched a finger-ring, and orange digits formed in the air. "—thirty hours, or so."

"You've time to look around the rest of the bioarea, then?"

"Why, yes." Yoshiko smiled with pleasure. "I'd love to."

The refectory's hubbub almost drowned the sound system's lonely wail, about a drifting spacer, all alone in the dark and cold. Station crew were coming off shift, going on: hurried lunches, tech talk in unfamiliar fields which Yoshiko strained to get a sense of. Bleary-eyed breakfasts, relaxed dinners.

"You run overlapping shifts everywhere, then," she said.

Eric nodded. His counterpart, Jenna, had come on duty while he was showing Yoshiko the goat pens, two hours before his shift ended.

"Don't want people dog-tired if an emergency starts. Although—" He leaned forward and lowered his voice. "The station's way too old. Dangerous."

"What do you mean?" Yoshiko thought of hull explosions, bodies expelled into space.

"There's not enough p-suits to go round. Don't tell anyone I told you."

"What?" Yoshiko couldn't believe it. "If you think I'm going to— Oh, you bastard."

His roar of laughter caused half the crew to look around. No one complained. His big bearish chest shook with amusement.

"Had you there," he said, and swigged his ethanol-free beer.

"Very funny." Yoshiko smiled in spite of herself.

A beep sounded, and Eric raised his wrist. The image of Jenna, his colleague, grew above his commbracelet.

"Sorry, Eric. Could you come and lend a hand?"

"Sure. On my way. Endit."

Jenna's image disappeared.

"Want to come with me?" he asked.

She ought to be getting back to her cabin.

"If you wouldn't mind," she said.

Some of the crew members glanced at her curiously as they left together, embarrassing her. Thanks to her femtocytes and the *shugyo*—austere discipline—of her physical training, she could pass in low light for someone under forty. But she didn't feel that young.

She hoped Eric wouldn't get the wrong idea.

They took a fast-access shuttle-car, speeding along a crew-only tunnel, and got out by the bioarea. They walked through a membrane-lock.

Inside, Eric pulled a bicycle from a rack, and set it down in front of Yoshiko.

"Don't ask how long it's been." She took it from him. "But I can ride it, in two-thirds g."

He raised an eyebrow as she swung her leg easily over the saddle.

I'm more supple than you'll ever be, she thought, *though I'm nearly twice your age.*

He mounted his own bicycle.

"Ready?"

"Lead on."

"Oh, shit," said Jenna.

It was an apposite remark. On the examination table, a wobbly capuchin monkey had lost bowel control.

Eric resignedly plunged his hands into a bowl of smartgel, which slid up around his forearms, forming gloves. He began to wipe down the table.

While Jenna held the monkey, Yoshiko took the soporific delta-band from its forehead.

"Thanks," said Jenna.

There were sick goats in all three scan-units, which was why Jenna had given the monkey his exam in the old-fashioned way.

"Any time." Yoshiko wrinkled her nose.

"I can tell you mean that."

"Well . . ." Yoshiko looked at Eric, who grimaced. "Thanks for showing me round."

"You're welcome."

"Come back, if you can. We'd love to see you again," Jenna said, glancing at Eric.

Yoshiko cleared her throat.

"Right, then."

She left, waving farewell. Her bicycle was propped against the dome's exterior. She mounted quickly.

Pulse racing, she pushed off onto the grassy path and pedalled hard, digging deep and cycling fast, cycling the way she had when she and Ken were young.

Stuffed oiseaux d'or, on a bed of pilaf rice. Spiny pears. A spicy sauce.

Rafael speared one of the tiny birds, and popped it into his mouth.

"Delicious." He <sent>:

<<taste: soft, succulent meat>>
<<touch: texture of muscle fibres and tiny sinews upon his tongue>>

Voretta, using old-fashioned chopsticks, took a bird from his dish.

"Mm." She chewed slowly, eyes closed. "Stereo taste."

She was replaying Rafael's <send>, and enjoying it.

They were in his dining room, alone save for Voretta's grey-liveried servants, standing to attention near the walls.

"Did you enjoy today?" He raised a glass of crème de lothe, and sipped. "I thought it went very well."

"Next time," said Voretta, eyelids lowered, "we should collaborate. I've a feeling we might choreograph together very well."

"You may be right."

[[A couple—he in black coat and tails, she in a bright confection of a dress—danced a stately waltz.]]

The servants did not flinch as Voretta's [image], invisible to them, danced right through them, and faded.

Rafael passed a hand across his forehead. Inside, his cache was beginning to burn. Marianan's frozen mindcode, coming back to life.

"Are you OK?" asked Voretta.

"I'm fine. A little tired."

"It is getting late." Voretta raised a hand.

Her servants left the room, without a word.

Rafael barely saw them go.

"Voretta."

Her eyes were very big, and very dark.

[[Warms streams of golden light.]]
[[Rose petals falling, sweetly fragrant.]]

In private overlay:

<<visual: a thousand hands lightly caressing Rafael>>
<<touch: their fingertips against his skin>>
<<fragrance: a rush of pheromones>>

Rafael gestured, and orange flames rose in the hearth.

"My lady?" He rose from his seat, and offered his hand.

Voretta stood, elegant and proud, and she was almost as tall as he.

They kissed.

[[Explosion of fireworks.]]

<<kinaesthetic: freefall>>

<<proprioreceptive: conjoined, two bodies becoming one>>

Rafael's gentle fingertip degaussed her gown's mag-seam; the gown slid to the floor with a whisper.

His shirt fell away at her touch.

Her flawless body was clothed in [[luminescent white orchids]] which he kissed away, one by one. As the freeform floor shaped itself, rising up to support Voretta, his tongue left a <<visual: trail of dancing flames>> along the inside of her thigh.

<<audio: orchestral crescendo>>

[[Cannons, booming.]]

[[Burst of flaring light.]]

And she came with a deep sob of laughter.

Deftly, he led her back up the long slope of pleasure.

<<visual: endless glacier>>

<<kinaesthetic: flying free>>

<<proprioreceptive: engorged with blood>>

Voretta contributed <<visual: rainbows arcing overhead>> as she drew him deep inside her.

[[Endless soft white thighs.]]

He could do her now.

Really do her.

A [[kaleidoscope of swirling colours]] enveloped him, a [[rising drumbeat]] accompanying his nearing climax, but Rafael held back . . .

The fragments of Marianan, soft and warm, waited in his cache, yearning to be savoured.

Voretta . . .

Hold back. Hold back the moment.

Should he?

He could plunge into Voretta's mind, strip it apart, suck it into his own mind along with the sweet remnants of dead Marianan. Such a river, such a flood of ecstasy that would be . . .

Hold back.

He felt the near-overspill of his cache, a deep internal trembling, while [[fiery gold streamers]] of Voretta's [vision] poured through his shuddering body.

Control . . .

Watch it. *Don't let her see.*

He *was* losing control. Only microseconds left . . .

Marianan?

Or Voretta and Marianan, both?

Decide . . .

Practicalities: he would have to kill her servants, also, and find some way of wiping out traces of her visit here. Could he possibly get away with it?

A vision of proctors, hunting him down.

Decide now.

Voretta.

Marianan.

Damn it . . .

Marianan only, that was the way to go, but Voretta's eyes snapped opened as she gasped, and his own guard was close to dropping. He dared not let her see inside his mind, to see what he had done.

```
[[[HeaderBegin: Module = Node99Z8.53Y7 Type = Quaternary-
        HyperCode: Axes = 256
    Set priority = absolute
    Concurrent_Execute
        ThreadOne: <LuxPrime interface>.linkfile = CodeSmash
        ThreadTwo: <thalamic/cerebral matrix>.linkfile = PleasureOne
    End_Concurrent_Execute]]]
[[[HeaderBegin: Impromptu.Invoke = EXECUTE NOW]]]
```

Desperately, he drove into her pleasure centres—writing, not scanning—and [[black lace and overwhelming heat]] hailed their coming.

For a moment, he saw through her eyes <<video: Rafael's darkly burning stare>> and felt her <<proprioreceptive: heart pounding, almost bursting>> and <<audio: No, Rafael! Please, no!>>, but then he was in, wiping everything but pleasure from her mind.

Voretta cried aloud as she passed out and Rafael, triumphant, yelled as cached ware flooded through him and he became one with Marianan and all the dead Luculentae subsumed within his plexcores and he was the centre of the mighty universe and everything was his, forever.

Later, draped in one of Rafael's bathrobes, Voretta perched on a low couch, staring inwards with eyes like dead crystals.

Rafael toyed with a long-stemmed glass, waiting for her to leave.

"I . . . should be going," she said in a small voice.

Rafael put down his glass, and picked up Voretta's discarded gown from the floor. Her scent was still upon it.

"Thank you." She accepted the gown, and looked around vaguely. "Uh—"

"Use the bathroom through there," he said kindly.

Clutching the bathrobe's lapels high at her throat, she walked to the door, and stepped unsteadily through as it liquefied.

Rafael gestured, and the house system opened up a holo volume beside him.

Voretta's servants, in one of the drawing rooms. They looked up from the role-playing game they were engaged in.

"My lady will be leaving shortly," he said, and closed the display.

She did not reappear.

Hoping she had not been so inconsiderate as to do something stupid, he queried the house.

[[[HeaderBegin: Module = Node7*332: Type = Image: Axes = 4 Qry-Select = Voretta.Walking.0001]]]

It found her outside, walking down the broad steps, flanked by her tight-lipped servants. She had slipped out, past this room.

They boarded her flyer in silence.

It rose like an ungainly bird, then fled into the distance, gaining speed.

Rafael picked up his glass.

"To beauty."

He drank his solitary toast.

In her plain cabin, Yoshiko stripped off her jumpsuit and boots, down to her leotard, and ordered the bed to retract itself into the wall, making room.

"Command: music. Brahms, any piece. Lights at twenty percent."

As she began her warm-up, the rugged first symphony filled the darkened room. A more heuristic system might have sensed her mood, and chosen something lighter.

Neck rotations. Hips. As the music softened from *allegro* to *andante sostenuto*, she assumed a low straddle stance and held it for a count of two hundred. She lowered herself into a hurdler's stretch.

For forty minutes she worked, then knelt in *zazen*, meditating. Her heart slowed.

Still kneeling, she asked for a realtime comm to Eric Rasmussen, crewmember, and the terminal sprang to life.

A tousle-haired Eric appeared above the terminal.

"Hello—? Oh, Yoshiko."

In the image's background, a slender bare arm, and a woman calling, "Who is it, Eric?"

Yoshiko recognized the voice: Jenna.

"Sorry," she said, as the colour heightened in Eric's cheeks. "I didn't mean to intrude. Just wanted to thank you again, for showing me around."

"You're welcome, of course. I enjoyed it."

"Well—Goodnight."

"Goodnight."

Yoshiko waved the display away.

She knelt in the darkness, facing the blank wall, seeing nothing.

Chapter Four

Darkness in winter
Gleam, you stars, cold and icy!
Close lovers say No.

Hushed by anti-sound, enticingly lit, the little maze of quirky boutiques was an easy place in which to lose all track of time. Yoshiko, munching chocolate jantrasta, finally sat down by a fountain, and looked through the bag of drama crystals she had purchased.

"Bought anything nice?"

"Vin! How are you?" Yoshiko held up a crystal. "Rekka Chandri, Space Explorer. Don't ask. But have a sweet."

Vin shook her head. "We're eating soon. I was hoping you could join us. Maybe just for a drink?"

"I'd love to. Have we time for a few more stores?"

Vin smiled brightly. "If we go that way—" She pointed down a winding red-tiled corridor. "—We'll be heading in the right direction."

They walked past a Flaxian restaurant, boasting Sumtravnadni cuisine. A blimplike holo out front might have been the proprietor, or the plat du jour.

Vin wrinkled her nose. "I don't think I fancy—Hey, look. There's a Pilot!"

There was a crowd up ahead, but they parted to let the slight, black-jumpsuited man pass through. Quiet-looking. Nothing arrogant about him.

"Impressive, isn't he?" murmured Vin.

"They all are."

They watched until he disappeared into a side corridor.

Yoshiko let out her breath. "Perhaps we should head straight for your parents."

"Lori's my soul-mother. We are genetically related, but not closely."

"I beg your pardon."

"No reason why you should know." A slight frown creased Vin's forehead. "Septor's her consort."

To their left, a door-membrane bore an upward-pointing blue arrow.

"The restaurant's a long way round the rim," said Vin. "We'd save time going straight through, if you don't mind the g-shift."

"No problem," said Yoshiko, hiding her uncertainty.

"You're sure?"

Yoshiko nodded, and led the way through the membrane. A small spherical car was bobbing inside, waiting. She and Vin took facing cocoon seats.

Acceleration clutched her as the car shot upwards. Corridor entrances flicked past, then crew-access tunnels. The car slowed.

"We're near the spin-axis," said Vin. "Oh, listen."

Distant pipes and fiddles echoed, from the depths of a utilitarian tunnel.

"'The Rocky Road to Dublin,'" said Yoshiko, surprising herself.

The car began to turn over.

Yoshiko just glimpsed a rough holo—FREEFALL CEILIDH TONITE—before the car flipped completely, leaving her stomach behind.

She shut her eyes, and kept them shut until the car had finished dropping through all the levels.

"We're here," said Vin. "Are—?"

"I'm fine." Yoshiko climbed out, and forced herself to stand steadily. "Really."

"The restaurant's just along here." Vin's lips twitched. "These cars really give me an appetite."

"Septor Maximilian."

"Sunadomari Yoshiko."

They shook hands briefly, across the table.

"And this is Lori," said Vin. "My soul-mother."

Lori's handshake was firmer, her smile friendlier, than her consort's.

"So, what shall we have?"

They spent a few minutes over the menu icons, then silence settled on the table.

"Do you—?"

"Was your—?"

Lori laughed. "You first, Yoshiko."

"I wondered whether you enjoyed your trip to Earth."

"Too short," said Lori, glancing at Septor, who said nothing.

"Fun, though." Vin looked wistful.

Septor's voice was heavy with self-importance. "We made a point of getting to know Earthers of every social stratum."

Vin glanced up, as though there were something to be seen above Yoshiko's head, and reddened slightly.

"And some of them became our friends," she said harshly.

Septor laughed. The couple seated at the next table looked up.

"Indeed. It was interesting to see civilization's—" Septor's smile was mocking. "—*Our* civilization's precursors."

A human waiter accompanied by a smartcart walked up, and transferred drinks from cart to table.

"I'm glad you found Earth interesting, Septor," said Yoshiko. "I was surprised to hear Fulgor isn't as law-abiding as I'd expected."

"We haven't outgrown sensationalist NewsNets, that's for sure."

Lori leaned forward, placing a hand on Septor's arm while looking directly at Yoshiko. "Is this your first trip to Fulgor?"

"I'm going to see my son—"

A sudden hush descended upon the restaurant. Towards the rear, a privacy booth had unveiled. A lone Pilot stepped out, a formal black cape draped over her jumpsuit.

"Two in one day," breathed Vin.

A wave of silence travelled with the Pilot.

"She's coming this way."

The Pilot stopped at their table. In her taut olive-skinned face, her eyes—black-on-black Pilot's eyes—were glistening orbs of jet, totally sans whites. Shadowed pits, leading to unknown worlds.

"Professor Sunadomari." The Pilot bowed low. "I am Pilot Jana de Vries."

Yoshiko bowed in return.

"My commiserations," added the Pilot, "on your husband's death. He was a fine man."

Yoshiko's vision blurred with tears.

"Thank you."

After a moment, Septor cleared his throat.

"I say, Pilot," he began. "Could you tell me when we'll arrive on—?"

Golden fire coruscated across the Pilot's black eyes, flared brightly, then vanished. She turned her gaze on Septor.

The blood drained from his face.

The Pilot turned, cape swirling, and left the restaurant.

Vin stared at Yoshiko. "She *talked* to you!"

"It was kind of her."

Yoshiko dabbed at her eyes. Stupid to be affected like this, but it had been unexpected.

I miss you, Ken.

"You're acquainted with Pilots?" Lori asked, while passing a napkin to Septor, who mopped his now-damp forehead.

"Both my family and Ken's—he was my husband—worked on their programme."

For eight generations, on and off.

"Very impressive," said Lori. "Wouldn't you agree, darling?"

"Ah, yes." Septor took a deep gulp of wine. "Impressive, yes."

"Vin?" said Lori. "Perhaps you might invite Yoshiko to visit us, while she's on Fulgor?"

"Yes, please! Yoshiko, if you could come, that would be great!"

The pleading look in her eyes melted Yoshiko.

"I'd love to." She couldn't resist adding, "Do you think Jana will be piloting our ship?"

Vin snorted with laughter at Septor's expression, and even Lori's face was tight with amusement.

A mounted samurai horseman, his banner floating in an unfelt breeze, reared above Yoshiko's hand. One of her tu-rings was flashing high-priority red.

She looked around the departure lounge, but it was almost empty, an hour before transit.

The banner bore an incoming-mail icon. She pointed, and the horseman, one of her NetEnv agents, swirled and broke apart, then reformed into Tetsuo's familiar features.

"Mother. I'm looking forward to seeing you, but I have urgent business to attend to." His expression was blank, but there was an unsettling edge to his voice. "Perhaps Akira can arrange for a later trip? I'll contact you soon."

Yoshiko's thoughts were still whirling when the lounge began to fill. Eager passengers chatting brightly. Holiday atmosphere.

A migraine began to pulse over Yoshiko's left eye.

"Are you OK?" A man's voice. Crew-member's blue jumpsuit.

"I will be." She looked up. "Oh, Eric. How are you?"

"Er . . . Fine." Eric Rasmussen tugged at his beard, looking concerned. "Are you sure you're OK?"

"I had an h-mail from my son." The words flowed from Yoshiko without volition, surprising her. "I'm not sure he wants to see me."

"Did he give a reason?"

"Yes. Well, no. Not really."

He stared at her for a moment. "Fulgor's a big world. Plenty of other things to see."

"Yes, but—" Her shoulders sagged. "You're right. It seems stupid to turn round and go straight back to Earth."

Not to mention the insult to Akira, who had paid for the trip. And Tetsuo could hardly turn her away, once she was there.

"I just wanted to say—" Eric's voice trailed off. Unexpectedly, he grinned. "I'm glad you dropped in, even on our monkey business."

A smile tugged at Yoshiko's lips, despite herself.

Eric added, "You've brightened this place up, you know."

She had noticed it before, in the refectory: that damned twinkle in his eyes.

"I bet," she said, "you say that—"

"—to all the beautiful, intelligent scientists who wander by." Eric laughed. "Yeah, right."

Stop this.

Yoshiko shook her head, just as a low chime sounded.

"Time to board." Eric raised an eyebrow. "If you're going."

"I am. Thank you, Eric."

"Can I give you a hand with that—? I guess not."

Yoshiko hefted the narrow two-and-a-half-metre carry-case.

"You're a pole-vaulter?" said Eric. "No. Let me guess—"

"It's a naginata," she said.

"That's not rude, is it?"

"Not the last time I looked." She smiled. "Go look it up."

She gave a sketchy wave, and joined the other passengers crowded in front of the gate. Beyond, a white umbilical led to the waiting mu-space ship.

Her tanto, in its hardwood sheath, was in a pocket of her suit. Suicide weapon. On a sudden impulse, she called out Eric's name, and hurried back to him.

"Here," she said, holding out the sheathed dagger. "I won't be needing this."

He started to say something, smiling, then seemed to catch his breath. He took the tanto dagger from her without a word.

Tetsuo awoke slowly, eyes sticky with sleep, like a child. He turned his head, and sudden pain stabbed into his scalp.

"Damn it. Uh, command mode. Upright."

He groaned as his couch morphed back into a chair, sitting him upright.

Gingerly, he reached up, tracing the filigreed network of fine wire crowning his head, along to the scab-encrusted inserts into his scalp. Only the soft headrest and nervous exhaustion had allowed him to sleep at all.

"Daistral." His voice was a croak.

Still dark outside.

He rubbed his face. It was greasy with old sweat, rough with a stubble of beard. He felt awful, all the way through.

The console beeped, and extruded a tray with his cup of daistral.

He drank the steaming purple liquid gratefully. It washed away the fuzz from his gums, poured warmly into him, and cleared his brain.

Last night, he had polarized the cockpit bubble to black opacity. Maybe it wasn't dark outside.

He sat there, in his warm dark cabin, softly lit by indirect lighting, not wanting to see the world. Part of him wanted to call Rafael for advice, but Rafael might be part of the problem.

Tetsuo didn't need to access a crystal to recall the beginning of his partially retrieved info: the courier and some unknown other person. The courier he had seen at the Bureau? It could be. And then there was the mention of Rafael.

All of Tetsuo's troubles came flooding back to him. He was awake now, sure enough.

He sighed. "Clear membrane."

The cockpit bubble grew transparent.

Bars of roiling purple, interspersed with silver grey. High above, a fluffy-edged gap afforded a glimpse of greenish sky. All around, though, was bicoloured fog. Its purple and grey bands formed a strong Turing pattern, like the pelt of some strange striped carnivore.

Something moved. A shadow in the fog.

Tetsuo waited, but there was nothing more. His flyer's defences remained quiescent.

He finished his daistral.

After a while, a light shower of rain began to fall, spattering against the cockpit. Within minutes, it had washed the fog away. Then the rain, too, died.

The air was crystal clear.

The floor of Nether Canyon was a stippled expanse of rust-red and sugared-mint rock, glistening wetly in the morning sun. To either side, the canyon's immense walls rose up, sheer and vertical, for kilometres. The lime sky was a distant strip overhead.

As Tetsuo watched, a small family of semitransparent whirling propelloids—each the size of his fist—drifted slowly past.

The little group travelled onwards, parallel to the canyon wall. Tetsuo's gaze followed them until they were lost in the distance. Then he was alone, once more.

Chapter Five

Winter's early darkness,
Rain where trees are shaded,
Falling, always black.

A stately pavane of life and death: glycoprotein-analogues drifting laterally through a fluid mosaic of phospholipids and protein-like molecules. Yoshiko pointed at a twisted filament, and it grew large as the display zoomed in.

"Excuse me."

In a text volume, the relative atomic concentrations scrolled past, while graphs shifted in a third image. The primary display picked out a molecule and decoded it: hydrogen bonds in startling white, dynamic equations mapping field strengths.

"I'm sorry." A harried-looking woman walked right through the display.

Most interesting of all, the overall-properties map was highlighting a cohenstewart discontinuity—

"Wow!"

A small boy, carrying a toy spaceship and a bag of sweets, walked right through a blue alpha helix.

Stifling a sigh, Yoshiko gestured, and the display shrank to a tiny volume and froze. It had been taking her mind off other things. Perhaps she ought to reply to Tetsuo's h-mail, but what could she say?

"Put the sweets away, Jason." The woman was seeing to her son's seat harness.

The cabin was lavish, every couch equipped with terminal and drinks dispenser. There was nothing more an adult passenger could want. Holding the attention of a seven-year-old boy, though, was quite another matter.

An attendant appeared beside Yoshiko.

"Mrs. Sunadomari? This was sent aboard by a station crew-member. For you."

It was a small package, plainly wrapped.

"Thank you."

Across the aisle, the boy's mother looked exasperated.

"I'll be glad to get to the conference," she said. "When I'm working, I don't have people throwing tantrums."

Because, thought Yoshiko, *we adults are all so rational and well-balanced.*

The boy's face crumpled into tears. His mother looked stricken at the import of her words.

Trying not to think of Tetsuo and Akira at that age, Yoshiko killed her minimized display completely, and turned her attention to the package on her lap.

"Accept ident: input owner name."

A toy capuchin monkey sat up amid the tissue-paper lining of the opened box.

"Accept ident: input owner name."

The sound of crying had ceased. The boy, Jason, was staring at the monkey.

Smiling, Yoshiko leaned over, holding the monkey out to him.

"Perhaps he could ride on your spaceship."

Jason looked at the forgotten spaceship clutched in his hand, then up at his mother, with an imploring look in his eyes.

The woman nodded.

"Say your name," said Yoshiko, as he took the monkey.

"Jason Brown."

"Ident accepted." The monkey stood to attention. "Howya doin'," Jason?"

Jason giggled as the monkey performed a back-flip.

It was bad form, Yoshiko supposed, to give away a present from someone else. But she didn't expect to see Eric Rasmussen again.

"How can I thank you?" said his mother. "This trip's been hectic."

"I remember how difficult it can be."

"But it gets better when they're older, right?"

"Well . . ."

"That's what I was afraid of." She turned her seat, leaned across Jason, and held out her hand. "I'm Maggie."

"Yoshiko."

They shook, then returned their seats to the forward-facing position as a warning chimed.

"Sleepy time," said Maggie, taking a delta-band from the arm of Jason's seat.

"Not sleepy."

Yoshiko said, "It's a long flight. We need you to make sure the monkey's all right."

"Oh, OK. Better sleep."

He settled back, cradling the monkey. Maggie placed the band across Jason's forehead. Almost immediately, his eyelids fluttered and he slipped deeply into sleep.

"That's what makes it worth it," Maggie said softly.

A second chime sounded.

"Sleepy time." Maggie's grin was, for a second, identical to her son's.

"See you later."

All around, passengers were putting on their delta-bands.

An overhead display showed the station's coat of arms—its motto,

Per Ardua ad Astra—which was replaced with an exterior view of the station itself.

The station receded from the ship.

Most of the passengers were already unconscious, but Yoshiko still held her delta-band in her hand.

The display shifted to a sea of golden space, streaked here and there with crimson. Tiny black spongieform stars were riddled with holes, and encrusted with endlessly branching spiky protuberances.

Mu-space.

The display was a work of art. Literally so, for no normal human could see that fractal continuum for real, and survive.

If only I were a Pilot, thought Yoshiko, placing the delta-band on her forehead. *How wonderful that would—*

Suddenly, she was looking down at her body from above. Riding with the flow, used to meditation, she was not sleeping but drifting upwards, above the other passengers, and through the darkness of the mu-space vessel's hull.

If you could be here, Ken . . .

Then she was swimming in an amber ocean, where black stars sang and infinite whorls of energy smiled, and for a moment she was whole.

STATUS CHECK.

Tetsuo groaned, opening his eyes.

ITERATIVE DEEPENING CONCLUDED.

The tag end of some nightmare, red characters fading before his eyes. He rubbed them away.

Noonday sun glared on rust-red and green/white stratified rock-face.

Dozed off again. With no business meetings or design specs to finish, it was the first time in years he had gone back to sleep in the morning. He laughed, and stopped immediately, startled by the hysteria he heard.

At least the pain was gone from his scalp. There was a tightness in his chest, where the plexcore processor was implanted, but that was all.

What now? He checked his food inventory: four tendays' worth, for an average individual, according to the display. He factored in his stored biodata, and watched the figure drop below three tendays.

Patting his paunch, he realized he had to get offworld, as soon as possible. Or go to the proctors and come clean about the info he had stolen? They, at least, could protect him from attack teams.

He wondered if his unknown enemy had the resources to mount an aerial or orbital search.

There was an overhang up ahead. His flyer shuddered into life, and Tetsuo directed it slowly across the canyon floor, and settled below the overhang.

The flyer's smartskin blended immediately with the darker rock it now nestled on.

He ought to be happy to stay in here, in his cozy cockpit, but for some reason a desire to look outside took hold of him. Awkwardly, he shucked off his burgundy kimono. Tetsuo gestured, palms up, and the cockpit wall puckered and opened to reveal its contents. He pointed to a black jumpsuit, and the cockpit extruded a narrow arm, holding out the garment. Tetsuo took the jumpsuit, and quickly pulled it on.

He found a tub of smartgel and slapped some on his face. Immediately, it oozed across the exposed skin of face and hands, sealing it against the noxious atmosphere outside. He would still need a resp-mask. There was one next to the med-kit.

Blazing crimson.

Red light flashed across his vision and he dropped the mask, startled. What the hell was that?

The red light was gone.

The console's status displays all read normal. There was nothing outside but the deserted canyon. His flyer's cockpit was just as it had always been.

He picked up the resp-mask.

MASK.

The word disappeared. Hurriedly, he slapped the mask on. If hallucinogens were seeping into the cabin from outside, then this should protect him.

He took quick, shallow breaths. The mask's air had its usual stale taint, but at least it wasn't harmful. He looked around. No hallucinations. No bugs in the holodisplay.

"Command mode. Liquefy." The mask muffled his voice.

He climbed up onto his seat, and pushed through the cockpit membrane. It slid wetly across his skin as he stepped out onto his flyer's surface.

He walked across the delta wing, stippled red like the rock beneath, then dropped heavily onto the ground.

Wheezing already from the exertion, he moved away from the overhang. Out here, lighter peach-coloured rock swept in slabs across the canyon floor.

AEOLIAN SANDSTONE.

What? Tetsuo staggered, passing his hand before his eyes.

LE MAIN.

In katakana: TE.

"What's happening to me?"

HAND.

He whirled, but there was no one there. Whatever was happening, it was right inside his head.

Mindware.

Idiot. Of course, this was bound to happen. His plexcore was reaching out, through implanted comm-fibres and his own nervous system, trying to interface to his organic brain.

This was no time to be on his own, away from LuxPrime supervision and medical care.

Calmer now, he walked along the canyon floor, hardly seeing his surroundings. Dare he place a call to the proctors? Should he call a LuxPrime office? Rafael?

Sand scrunched under foot.

FOOTPRINT.

The imprint's outline was clear in the sand.

He was a thousand kilometres from the nearest terraformed region, far from human habitation.

FOOTPRINT.

Greensleeves.

Yoshiko, squinting, forced herself upright.

"Ladies and gentlemen, we are in Fulgor orbit. Transfer station docking in ten minutes."

To the soft strains of "Greensleeves," the passengers were coming awake. Yoshiko performed some neck rotations, and shrugged her shoulders to dissipate the tension.

"We're awake."

Yoshiko looked down at Jason's bright upturned face. He was still holding the monkey.

"Oh, God." Maggie rubbed her eyes. Her face was pale and drawn.

"Headache?" asked Yoshiko.

"Yeah. I hate this."

Yoshiko unfastened her harness, rubbed the stiffness from her legs, and crouched down beside Maggie.

"Give me your wrist."

"I've had acupressure before," Maggie said. "It doesn't—Ow!"

"Sorry."

"You didn't have to press so—Hey, the pain's gone. How did you manage that?"

"Just practice."

Jason looked up at his mother.

"She's a ninja," he said confidently.

Later, as they sat together in a drop-shuttle with a dozen other passengers, Maggie handed Yoshiko a crystal.

"In case we get separated later," she said. "I'm Maggie Brown, staying at the Primum Stratum conference centre in Lucis City. Give me a call, if you'd like to get together."

"I'd love to. My surname's Sunadomari. I'm . . . not sure where I'll be staying yet."

"This is Charlie," said Jason, holding up the toy monkey.

"Hi, Charlie." Yoshiko solemnly shook paws.

Maggie frowned. "Were you looking at cell membrane dynamics earlier?"

"Why, yes. Native Fulgor biochemistry."

"I'm a tech journo and writer. Are you any relation to Professor Sunadomari, from Sudarasys LifeTech?"

Yoshiko nodded. "That's me. How could you know my name?"

"One of the guys in my agency, Piotr Alexeievich, rehacked some of your papers as educational ware."

"My NetEnv agents handle that side of the business. Their algorithms are pretty sophisticated. I don't think I ever talked to your colleague."

"No loss. Isn't it a small universe, though?"

"It can be."

Outside, the alien view belied their words.

The shuttle dropped through copper clouds, passed over purple mountains bruising an ochre plain, and headed for the growing amber jewel that was Lucis City.

Chapter Six

Cries split the night.
Baby finds teddy and holds him.
No parent is close.

The woman was pale—even for a Luculenta—with flame-coloured hair and bright flashing eyes. Her elegant hands gestured animatedly as she talked to her shorter companion.

Rafael's pulse quickened, and he queried her identity in Skein.

[[Luculenta Rashella Syntharinova, ident 3α29Fδ7•ϵ {septΦΔ3}]]

He longed to learn more, but he could not enquire further without his interest being noted and logged. Sighing, he withdrew from Skein.

Crowds swirled past. The great hemispherical entrance hall was crowded, even though the conference was not yet in full swing.

He could still see her.

Rashella—ah, such a beautiful name—was taking a seat in one of the alcoves which ringed the hall. The other woman, to whom Rashella was talking, looked tawdry and insignificant, possibly an offworlder. But Rashella had that extra spark, the one shared by the intriguing Xanthia, and by Marianan, and by all his dead, fulfilled, sweet loves.

Voretta had been one of his almost-loves, good for slaking his physical desire—and, in this instance, for adding delicious spice to his intimate consummation with Marianan.

"I'm afraid I don't understand," the offworld woman was saying.

He had drifted closer to their alcove, almost without realizing it. He listened.

"Have you bought anything in Lucis City yet?" Rashella's voice was soft but clear.

"Er . . . yeah, some stuff."

"Check your account. Look at the currency translation function coded by each amount."

"I wondered what that notation meant."

"On Fulgor, every monetary transaction is context-sensitive, its value a coordinate in n-dimensional phase space, where n typically varies between two and four hundred."

"Oh, great. I'm trying to understand the economic implications of opening up EveryWare to Skein, and I don't even know what's happening when I buy a bottle of booze."

Rashella's laugh was a delight.

Unable to resist, Rafael stepped into the alcove, and gave a short bow.

"I beg your pardon, ladies." It was standard protocol to use mainly speech when non-Luculenti were present. "I haven't registered for the conference yet. Do you know where the trade fair stands are?"

"Level seven, hall beta," said the offworlder, while Rashella succinctly <sent> directions in a topographical knot.

"Thank you." He smiled at Rashella. "I am Rafael Garcia de la Vega."

"Rashella Syntharinova. And this is Maggie Brown, from Earth."

"You've come a long way, Ms. Brown."

"I'm a tech journo. Are you involved with the conference?"

"Ah, no. I just dabble." Rafael turned the full power of his gaze on Rashella. "I hope we'll meet again."

"Perhaps." Rashella inclined her head, the colour in her cheeks perhaps a little heightened.

"Ms. Brown." As Rafael bowed, he saw her catch her breath. From her pupil dilation, it appeared he had made a satisfactory impact upon her, as well.

He backed away gracefully, inordinately pleased with his performance. *Ah, Rashella.* To subsume a living mind like hers. She couldn't dream of such fulfilment.

He headed for the trade fair, dark plans crystallizing in his mind.

Tetsuo wasn't there to meet her.

The terminal complex was a jumble of amber halls, flowing corridors, without discrete levels. It was a three-dimensional maze, where a restaurant or store might bear any conceivable geometric relationship towards its neighbours.

Holo-ads splashed bright colours over a maelstrom of people. Yoshiko watched them, feeling lost.

Maggie had left immediately with Jason, heading for some conference centre, and the Maximilians must have taken a different drop shuttle.

And no Tetsuo.

Trailed by a smartcart carrying her luggage, she sat down at the edge of a waiting-area, and ordered orange juice from a dispenser. When she paid, one of her tu-rings flashed blue and green, indicating limited functionality. The other rings were dull orange. Quite inactive.

Even her NetEnv agents were inaccessible, unable to function in Fulgor's Skein.

"Excuse me, ma'am. Do you need help?" It was a big man, in a loose yellow outfit.

"Well—"

"I'm from the Happy Helix Eatery." He jerked a thumb behind him. "You looked a bit lost."

Yoshiko let out a breath. "I am. I guess I need a hotel. Are you a security guard?"

"Store monitor," the man said. "Now, see that silver device? On the pillar?"

Yoshiko nodded.

"Public access terminal."

The man showed her how to log on to Skein's public level. Yoshiko requested a realtime comm, and gave Tetsuo's full name and address.

The requested party was unavailable.

Yoshiko stared blankly at the low-res holo for a moment.

"Did you say you needed a hotel?"

Yoshiko jumped. She had forgotten about the "store monitor."

He showed her the options menu, and helped her book into a low-cost establishment right here in the terminal complex. The software was childishly simple to use, but Yoshiko said nothing as the man showed her how to download directions to the smartcart, so that it could lead the way to the hotel.

"Thank you," she said.

The man looked at her expectantly.

"What—?" she began, then saw the credit sensor at his belt, and extended her one functioning tu-ring. "Of course."

From the breadth of his smile, she gathered she had overtipped.

She followed the smartcart through a twisting maze of corridors to the hotel. The room was sparse but decent enough, and the smartcart parked itself in a small alcove.

After a while, she took mag-bands and a field generator from one of her bags, and performed a strength workout for twenty minutes. Then she stretched, showered, and ordered food. It arrived through a delivery membrane.

Then she lay on the bed, and stared wide-eyed at the ceiling, waiting for sleep to come.

She was on a new world. She had seen a spaceport terminal. A hotel room. And no sign of Tetsuo.

The auditorium was a dark cathedral. Rashella floated high above the floor, her face ghostly pale in the spotlight, her suspensor platform hidden in the darkness.

She moved like a hovering angel around vast holo graphics, pointing out white attractors tugging ellipsoids across coral surfaces of light.

Rafael had little interest in the content of her talk on macro-economic emergent phenomena, and her predictions of a boom in Fulgor's isolationist but rich economy once the Skein-EveryWare interface was truly opened. It was simple stuff, and most of the audience seated below the huge pulsing graphics were offworlders.

But her style of delivery was beguiling, and he watched until the lights came up and she invited questions from the audience. Then he slipped out into the entrance hall.

He stood behind a holo banner directing people to the trade fair. Tomorrow, he would have to return and look around it more closely, in the hope of picking up useful offworld tech. That was, after all, the way he had met Tetsuo Sunadomari—

There she was.

Rashella. Dark hair sprinkled with stars, as sunbeams from the skylights above sparked reflections from her headgear. Moving gracefully through the crowd, nodding to acquaintances.

She trailed hangers-on from the talk like a comet trailing dust. As she passed by a restaurant, then souvenir stores, she gradually lost her company.

Rafael hung back, not wanting to be seen near her.

He had never plundered a mind in Skein, in case LuxPrime AIs indirectly discovered his traces buried among the immense strata of audit logs. Instead, all his infiltration code revolved around the unaudited line-of-sight fast-comms used for [public visions] and <private sends>.

Farther back, but he could still see her lovely raven hair.

He closed his eyes—

[[[QryTrace(SND: ident = 3α29Fδ7, units = SI, ν = 3.247* 10^{14};
RCV: r, θ, Φ)
<<<MsgRcv LUCINT008339; cause = link established>>>
<<<detail is: r = 458.2, θ= 2.192, Φ = 0.002>>>]]]
[[[KinaesthesiaLink(QryTrace dynamic)]]]

—and shuddered slightly as the link was formed. Did Rashella, too, tremble at the unfelt touch of his mind?

He felt her, now, as part of himself.

Her motion tugged at him, and he followed.

The wild yet intricate death-sculptures from the Salmaegedon system occupied some thirty huge display cases, and Rafael followed Rashella's wandering motion through the exhibit. Shiny, delicately patterned carapaces of pink and grey, or white and silver dappled with black, were shaped into patterns of perspective which threatened to drag the mind out of its own perceptions, as though into another, starker, reality.

Rafael could have talked to Rashella about the exhibit. He knew of its mystery, of the constantly warring intelligent species with little apparent technology, who were to be found scattered among a dozen worlds orbiting Salmaegedon. Of their suicide pacts and self-mutilations, in what seemed to be a quest for beauty or enlightenment. This was a fascination which he and Rashella held in common.

He dared not talk to her again. Not here, where he might be seen and remembered.

Leaving now.

As he hurried to keep up with her, he caught the faintest edge of anxiety—his own, or her subliminal detection of the trace which linked them?

No matter. From the entrance hall, he took a different exit ramp, not looking in her direction, though her presence was like a clenched fist around his heart.

From the outside, the Primum Stratum conference centre was elegant, in an old-fashioned way. It comprised seventeen great round buildings, tiled in maroon and grey. They were flat-roofed, a collection of stacked cylinders of varying heights. Above them floated the wing-shaped hovering roof, a later addition, which today sparkled sapphire blue.

Rafael brushed past gawping tourists, and crossed a plaza. He hurried through a small arboretum.

There she was.

Past a motley crowd of non-Luculenti protestors bearing holo banners—KEEP OFFWORLDERS OFFWORLD!—Rashella hurried to the parking platforms. As she drew near her flyer—a sporty little Gestrax Prime—it hummed into life, ready to lift.

He could do it here.

Become one with her. Right now.

"Excuse me, sir." A young-looking dark-uniformed proctor was standing in front of him. "It might be better if you went that way." The proctor indicated a path which curved past a fountain.

Behind him, four more proctors were heading back the way Rafael had come: steering the offworld tourists clear of the demonstration, no doubt.

Damn it.

Rafael, pretending to look at the protestors, searched for Rashella. She was already inside her flyer.

"Thank you, officer. I'll take your advice."

As he walked, he plotted a mental map, predicting her destination, while Rashella's flyer turned away and headed for Lucis City.

He hurried into his own flyer, a Flengmar SkyYacht which could hold fifty people in its lounge. Before he had sat down, he was already in direct command interface—

```
[[[HeaderBegin: Module = Node12998.JHl7: Type =TrinaryHyper-
        Code: Axes = 64
    Concurrent_Execute
        ThreadOne: rhombencephalon channel>.linkfile = Fusion-
            ReactorOne
        ThreadTwo: <intrapeduncular matrix>.linkfile = WingConfigure
        ThreadThree: <thalamic/cerebral matrix>.linkfile = ProcessFlight
    End_Concurrent_Execute]]]
[[[WingConfigure(MaxSpread)]]]
[[[ProcessFlight(SpinRise)]]]
```

—and causing the flyer to rise and turn, heading in a long arc towards the outskirts of Lucis City, intersecting Rashella's trajectory near her predicted destination of the exclusive Inez Banlieues.

An involuntary grin spread across Rafael's face as he balanced the tasks of flight interface and his Rashella-link, while creating a third parallel mindset and entering Skein.

He called one of the small comms-tech enterprises in which he held stakes, and announced he would be dropping in for a visit. The Fulgida manager had only time to stammer her agreement before he dropped back out of Skein.

It would provide an excuse for flying this way, should the question arise. The business park lay just beyond the Banlieues, coming from this direction.

Three minutes.

Fougère Tower arced and spread over lawns and arbours, and ellipsoid apartments—one pierced by the silver dart of Rashella's Gestrax Prime—clung like jewelled grapes to its branches.

Releasing a smartatom mist to confuse later SatScan analysis, Rafael slowed his flyer down. He walked back into the flyer's lounge, and caused the main port lateral door to open.

There she was.

Across a hundred metres of empty space, he could see her stepping out onto her balcony.

She was beautiful.

[[[HeaderBegin: Module = Node99Z9.3357 Type = Quaternary-HyperCode: Axes = 256

Concurrent_Execute

ThreadOne: <LuxPrime interface>.linkfile = CodeSmash

ThreadTwo: <rhombencephalon channel>.linkfile = Hypo-VampireOne

ThreadThree: <intrapeduncular matrix>.linkfile = EpiVampire-One

ThreadFour: <thalamic/cerebral matrix>.linkfile = Hyper-VampireOne

End_Concurrent_Execute]]]

Eyes met. Souls conjoined.

Infiltration code ripped through LuxPrime protocols.

Interface.

"*Rashella.*"

The link was an arrow from his soul to hers.

Quantum states were devastated as Incarnation ScanWare tore into neurons and plexcore matrices alike, destroying even as it measured, flinging its scan results back into Rafael's cache.

Hopes and dreams, fears and nightmares, the trivial pleasures and pains of quotidian life, the abstract constructs of intellect and the joys of passion all flooded into Rafael, and the Rafael/Rashella combination grew universally supreme as the discarded Rashella body toppled from the balcony and fell towards oblivion.

"Goodbye," he said, and godlike laughter filled his soul, and echoed back from the flyer's cabin walls.

Chapter Seven

Lies, or truth? No, Zen.
Light paints the glowing flowers;
Shadows strip them bare.

Glowing footsteps led across the wide canyon floor and into a dark defile. Some tracks split off from the main group and headed up other trails.

Tetsuo shook his head.

When he looked again, the glowing traces were gone. Another trick of the mindware in his head.

But the footprint at his feet was very real. Perhaps the mindware was enhancing the actual traces of people here inside the uninhabitable hypozone.

He ought to turn himself in.

The canyon's red-and-mint vertical walls seemed unimaginably distant and infinitely high, as though the world were drawing away from him. His heart was pounding. Sweat was gathering inside his jumpsuit, despite its heat exchangers. Though hot, he shivered.

A tenday ago, he had sat in a proctor's office, waiting for an interview which was a mere formality, and he had seen the opportunity to filch confidential info. Like a fool, he had taken it.

"Come into my office, boy." The cane stung his palm like a viper. "That will teach you to steal data."

He jumped at remembered pain. He had been so young, then, and the school's NetNode had seemed so inviting, its security a joke. A mistake: and now, over two decades later, he had repeated it.

He was shaking, and his breathing was laboured.

What was happening to him?

"Damn it."

Wheezing heavily, he climbed back up his flyer's wing, eased himself through the cockpit membrane, and dropped into the command seat.

He tore the resp-mask from his face, and threw it aside.

Chest pain. He was too young for cardiac arrest. Wasn't he?

Anxiety attack?

The pain bent him over.

PULSE . . . . 97min^{-1}

B.P. 199/103mmHg

Migraine behind both eyes, and golden script flowing across his vision.

BLOOD GLUCOSE . . . . 0.6 mg ml^{-1}

0_2 USAGE . . . . 2.5 dm^3 min^{-1}

BLOODFLOW BRAIN . . . . 747 ml min^{-1}

"Get . . . out . . . of . . . my . . . head!"

BLOODFLOW HEART . . . . 249 ml min^{-1}

BLOODFLOW LIVER . . . . 1292 ml min^{-1}

He slammed his fist against the console.

DO THIS. DO THIS. INGEST GLUCOSE 3.7g

Cabin walls blurred by tears, but the damned words would not go away.

DO THIS. DO THIS.

"I'm doing it!" Hands shaking, he pulled the portadoc from the wall, and slammed its feed-tube into his forearm.

Couldn't see the display to activate it.

```
[[[HeaderBegin: Module = Node13788.94A2: Type = BinaryHyper-
        Code: Axes = 4
    Concurrent_Execute
        Thread One: <plexcore substrate>.linkfile = PortaDoc1
        Thread Two: <plexcore substrate>.linkfile = Feedback
    End_Concurrent_Execute]]]
```

The portadoc's display flashed into life, though he had not physically turned it on. Indicators swirled as it adjusted his metabolism, and he lay back, gasping.

INSPIRE.

What?

EXPIRE.

INSPIRE.

Getting the message. He forced his breathing to slow, matching the timing of the mindware's commands.

A gravel path stretched away before him . . .

Hallucinating. *Just breathe.* Under control. *That's the way.*

Green lawn . . .

Getting back to normal. His cabin's cool interior. Familiar surroundings.

"*Goodbye, Mother.*"

"*Don't be late for school.*"

He didn't like this.

"*Who are you?" Thickly accented Nihongo. A slight boy was standing on the gravel path beneath a graceful weeping willow.*

"*Sunadomari Tetsuo.*"

"*I'm Morio. The school's not far.*"

Tetsuo, clutching the box containing his lunch, followed the other boy. They walked past a wooded dell, and into a cheerful schoolyard packed with primary-coloured climbing frames and slides and roundabouts.

Oh, gods, he remembered this. Just after leaving Vancouver, because of Dad and his new job.

A larger, older boy pushed his way through a group of dismayed girls, disrupting their hopping and skipping game.

"Hey, Morio. Who's the fat kid?"

"Damn," muttered Morio. "Chobi's early."

There were scars on Chobi's forearms.

"From chopping the necks off glass bottles with his hands," said Morio, following Tetsuo's gaze. "He makes them in his father's autofact."

Tetsuo swallowed, as Chobi snarled something unintelligible.

"I'm sorry," said Tetsuo. "I don't speak Ho-gen."

"Not Okinawan?" Chobi looked at him with a dead expression. "Too good for the rest of us?"

Tetsuo could only shake his head.

"Give me the box." Chobi's fists were clenched.

Tetsuo held his lunch tightly, saying nothing.

"Stupid—"

The schoolyard's rough floor smashed into Tetsuo's face. A great weight—Chobi's foot, he realized—ground into the back of Tetsuo's neck, then released him.

Chobi strode away into the woods, carrying Tetsuo's lunch.

He remembered.

Later, he had to buy lunch in the cafeteria. He sat with Morio and half a dozen jovial boys whose names he forgot almost immediately.

When they had finished, Morio and the others got up to go outside.

"Coming?" asked Morio.

Tetsuo shook his head.

"Chobi won't be back," said Morio. "He'll bunk off for the rest of day, most likely."

"That's not why."

Tetsuo made a show of helping himself to seconds from the autofact. Afterwards, he sat by a window and ate slowly, watching the other kids at play.

He stayed there till the buzzer sounded for afternoon classes.

Loud. *Buzzing very loud.*

VSI MIGRATION TEST COMPLETE.

"Oh, gods."

For a moment, he was still there: the polished grain of the tabletop, clattering cafeteria echoes, the smell of rice and fish, the steamy warmth—

PRIMARY PLEXCORE ENABLED.

```
{[[(HeaderBegin: Module = Node248. 12AJ: Type =Trinary/Hyper-
    Code: Axes = 64
  Concurrent_Execute
    ThreadOne: <rhombencephalon channel>.linkfile = ArrayInitiate
    ThreadTwo: <intrapeduncular matrix>.linkfile = MatrixInitiate
    ThreadThree: <thalamic/cerebral matrix>.linkfile = MatrixInitiate
  End_Concurrent_Execute]]}
```

"No. I want to stay—"

EXTENDED COGNITION ON-LINE.

Tetsuo was in his flyer's cabin. Outside, a cold and inky black night had fallen on Nether Canyon. He had been wrapped in code-dreams for hours.

His face was chilled, and he wiped away the tracks of old, cold tears.

Musical chimes fell through Yoshiko's awareness. Struggling upwards out of a pool of sleep, she saw a yellow box of light hanging above her. It backed off as she sat up in bed.

"What—Uh, what's this?" She rubbed her face.

"Personal call. Do you accept?"

It must be Tetsuo.

"Go ahead." She patted down her tangled hair.

The light cube swirled with colours, and rearranged itself into the lean, handsome features of a grey-haired man.

"Apologies for disturbing you. My name is Joseph Stargonier."

"What can I do for you?"

"Are you any relation to Tetsuo Sunadomari?"

Yoshiko hesitated. "Yes. He's my son. Is there anything wrong?"

"Just a business matter. When I couldn't contact him, I performed a name search. Will you be seeing him in the near future?"

"I—don't know." Yoshiko swallowed. "He wasn't at the spaceport to meet me."

"I'm so sorry." Stargonier glanced to one side, checking something beyond Yoshiko's view. "I'd be grateful if you'd let me know, should he contact you. Apologies again."

The display winked out.

Yoshiko swung her legs off the bed, and staggered to the bathroom closet, feeling her age.

Afterwards, not allowing herself to think, she commanded the bed to fold itself into the wall, and forced herself through a stretching routine.

She wasn't the only person who couldn't find Tetsuo.

From her toilet-bag, she grabbed a tube of smartgel and extruded some onto her face and neck. While the gel crawled across her skin, she tugged out a new jumpsuit from her bag.

Its cleansing work over, the smartgel gathered in a pool on the floor. Yoshiko put the tube down, and the smartgel crawled back inside.

She pulled on her jumpsuit.

The local police, the proctors. She ought to call them.

Her toilet-bag's microdoc was blinking a warning. The shift in time zones, and Fulgor's twenty-seven-hour day, were going to cause problems until she reprogrammed. For now, she overrode the warning and slapped the device onto her wrist. Her antiradical femtocyte count was low, and it gave her a booster shot.

On the other hand, calling the proctors might be going too far. Tetsuo might not thank her for her interference.

He *had* sent an h-mail suggesting she postpone her visit. Though, in the absence of a reply, he should have been there to meet her, all the same.

"Command mode. Personal call to Vin, aka Lavinia, Maximilian. Mother's—ah, soul-mother's name is Luculenta Lori Maximilian. Address unknown. End command mode."

Vin came on-line.

"Hi, Yoshiko. Sorry we missed you. Did you meet up with your son OK?"

"I'm afraid not." Yoshiko told her about Tetsuo's nonappearance, and about the call she had received from the Fulgidus man, Stargonier.

"Stay right there. You're at the Hotel St. Lucia, the one inside the terminal at Cicanda Spaceport?"

"That's right."

"Meet you in the restaurant in an hour?"

Yoshiko nodded.

"Don't worry." Vin waved. "Everything will be fine."

The display closed down.

Rafael opened his eyes and stretched languorously. His bed, sensing his intention, raised him to a seated position, and the mattress slid him to the edge. His gown wrapped itself around him, and slippers crept onto his feet.

The wall cleared into transparency as he took a seat. A smartcart rolled up, bearing breakfast.

He sipped from a glass, watching the morning brighten over the steel and stone courtyard. The place was clean and bare, its few sculptures spare and angular.

Rashella was part of him now, torn apart and distributed thinly through the organic whole that was Rafael. Only the moment of her death and sweet fulfilment was clear in his mind.

Her death would be ruled a suicide, or misadventure. Still, his flight could have been tracked, and it was best to make sure. He would have to call Federico.

He pictured Federico's ideogram, and accessed its code.

[{Luculentus Federico Gisanthro, ident 5γ33G3•ϵ {sept Δ2Σ}}]

A please-wait icon displayed momentarily, then faded.

<<<MsgRcv LUCCOM213887; cause = SkeinLink established.>>>

A grassy slope dropped away beneath him. Below, hurdlers raced around a red oval track. Nearby, combat-suited men and women, hair soaked with sweat, were performing slow stretches or lying on their backs, chests heaving.

Through the SkeinLink, the smell of grass was sharp. Rafael sniffed.

The sun was already high in a lime-green sky. Federico must be a good ninety degrees east of Rafael's home.

"Just having a little workout," said the familiar voice.

Federico had thrown back the hood of his suit, which was currently tuned to forest green. His cropped blond hair was wet and spiky. Perspiration collected at the insertions of his Luculentus headgear, and trickled down his gaunt face.

"Such a pity I'm not here to join you," said Rafael.

He was peripherally aware of his physical body, still reclining at home.

"My thoughts precisely, old chap." A light glinted in Federico's pale mismatched eyes—one blue, the other green—and Rafael shivered, though only in reality, not in Skein.

"So how far have they run?" Rafael indicated the TacCorps squad members down by the track.

"Thirty klicks, after CQB."

Rafael had seen their close quarter battle training before, and the memory made him wince.

"You trained with them, of course."

"It's rather expected of me, don't you think?"

Not really, Rafael was tempted to say. Instead, he laughed. "They look exhausted."

"Soft bastards. Must be in their genes."

Rafael gestured, forming a magnifying-glass icon, and zoomed in on a face wracked with exhaustion.

As he had thought, every man and woman had Federico's eye colouration. Clones from his Alpha Squad, their differences from Federico due to variations in womb chemistry and later environment, not in DNA.

None of them bore Luculentus headgear.

Rafael waved the icon away.

"Anyway, here's the investment analysis I promised you. A little country on Salkran Six shows a lot of promise. And the whole Renyarn system's poised for expansion."

"So I'd heard. I'd like the details, however."

"Of course."

A golden tesseract formed between them, as the info flowed from Rafael to Federico. For a moment, Federico's form wavered slightly, and Rafael could see the outlines of his own courtyard's angular sculptures. Then the Skein image regained full strength.

It was a weakness Rafael would have to remember. A lapse of Federico's concentration at a vital moment might be important some day.

"This is splendid, Rafael. Thank you."

On the other hand, Federico was subtle enough to have weakened the image on purpose. This was a dangerous man to play games with.

Dangerous games, though, were always the best.

"I'm glad your people are around to protect us," said Rafael. "One never knows. Just look at those violent deaths in Lucis."

Federico looked at him steadily.

"There was another one yesterday. A woman in Inez Banlieues."

"A Luculenta? Good Lord."

"Quite. This seems to be a suicide."

"A Luculenta suicide—"

"Yes. As you said, one never knows."

A delicious frisson of fear passed down Rafael's spine.

"I should let you get back to work."

"Of course. Whose Aphelion Ball are you attending?"

"I don't know yet," said Rafael.

"It's only seven days away."

Federico had spent the New Year at a thirty-hour party—during the course of which his deputy commander had got married—which had flown around the globe. He took celebrations seriously, a moral—and morale—obligation.

"Where are you going?"

"The Maximilians', I think," said Federico. "Do you know them?"

"Not really. I'll try and get myself invited, though."

"That would be splendid." Federico raised a hand. "I'll see you there."

<<<MsgRcv LUCCOM213900; cause = SkeinLink revoked.>>>

"Be seeing you," said Rafael to his own reflection in the window.

Outside, golden light dripped from a steel sculpture's spars, as the sun peeked over the courtyard wall.

The holo banner read HAKIM AL TEBITZ. Screaming kids ran around the play area, chased by a young man in clown gear and burnous, waving a holo scimitar.

"Another cup of choco?"

Yoshiko blinked, and looked up at the Fulgida waitress. "Sorry. Yes, please."

As the waitress poured, she gestured beyond the balustrade. "That there's a crèche, for staff members' children."

"And the older ones? Do they have schools, or just, ah, Skein?"

"Both," said the waitress, her expression turning bitter. "Ain't neither one a Luculentus academy."

Yoshiko remembered how basic Skein's public access level had looked.

"Do the—?"

"Sorry, dear." The expression sounded odd; the girl was a third of Yoshiko's age. "Another customer. Be right back."

Yoshiko watched her serving daistral from a jug, to a young offworld couple sitting at a corner table. Their faces were bright with the excitement of being on another planet.

"Yoshiko!"

Vin was threading her way among the tables.

"Hello, Vin."

Yoshiko was surprised to find her vision blurring. It was so good to know that she had a friend here.

"Are you OK?"

"I'm fine. It's all catching up with me."

"Look." Vin sat down, and gestured to the waitress. "We can call the proctors from here." To the waitress, she said, "Do you have privacy screens?"

"I can bring a module." The Fulgida was blank-faced, her earlier affability gone. "Something to eat? Drink?"

"Daistral, please. Any flavour. And could you bring a terminal?"

The waitress glanced at Yoshiko, her expression unreadable, and left.

Vin lowered her voice. "I swung by your son's place, on the way."

"Was he home?"

"No way to tell." Her eyes were troubled. "A security screen warned me off. Smartbats lifted from the house, when I tried to hover overhead."

The waitress returned with a tray, which she placed on their table without a word. When she had gone, Vin picked up a small device from the tray and inserted it into a depression on the tabletop.

Kaleidoscopic light swirled all around them: a smartatom hemisphere which broke apart the outside world and turned it into abstract moving patterns. The air grew curiously dead, with spillover from the privacy barrier's anti-sound.

Vin ignored her daistral, and activated the small silver terminal.

"ProctorNet." An impossibly handsome square-jawed man appeared. His dark uniform stretched comfortably across strong, broad shoulders. "Is this an enquiry or an emerg—?"

"Missing person," said Vin.

The image flickered. The proctor regained his original smile.

"Please give the identity of—"

"Sunadomari Tetsuo," said Vin. "Ichiban Villa, Zone Thirteen, Clara Shire."

"How long has—"

"Unknown. Request personal interview. My name is Luculenta Lavinia Maximilian."

The image disappeared.

"Don't worry," said Vin. "We'll soon—Oh, here we are."

Another proctor, this time a rather ordinary-looking young woman.

"What seems to be the problem? A missing person?"

"Go ahead," Vin said to Yoshiko.

Haltingly, Yoshiko summarized her situation, and Tetsuo's nonappearance.

The proctor shook her head. "Your son's just missed an appointment. I don't think there's much we can do."

Before Yoshiko could reply, Vin butted in. "There's something else, which is why I asked for a personal interview. I thought your AI might misunderstand."

"There's no substitute for people." A faint smile appeared on the proctor's face. "So what was it?"

"I flew over her son's house." Vin glanced at Yoshiko. "The security included DarkAngel smartbats."

"Loaded?"

"Stun-toxins, ultrasound, armour-piercing smartvenom. According to the warning broadcast. I didn't hang around to find out for sure."

"I don't blame you." The proctor looked at Yoshiko. "Why would your son need such heavy duty protection?"

"I—don't know."

The proctor was silent for a moment, then addressed Vin. "We'll look into this. Is Mrs. Sunadomari your guest?"

"Yes. Yoshiko, you will come and stay with us, won't you?"

Yoshiko looked from one to the other.

"Yes, please. I need your help."

"Don't worry." Vin's natural cheerfulness was returning. "It will turn out all right."

"Yes," said the proctor. "She's right, madam. We'll look into it, and let you know. In the meantime, try not to worry."

Yoshiko, who would have worried less if they had not been so adamant, merely nodded.

As the display winked out, Vin pulled the privacy module, and the world reappeared.

Below the balustrade, the children's play area was deserted save for one forgotten toy, a one-armed battered teddy bear staring lifelessly towards the sky.

Chapter Eight

Zen is: pines' upward thrust.
Flowers bloom, not for you to pull.
Bare fists strike.

The whole world tilted. Heat blasted into Yoshiko's face from the white concrete pad, as she stepped down from the courtesy van. She almost stumbled, overcome by the air's sharp tang, the subtly lower gravity—though she had not noticed it indoors—and the insistent alien overlay of her new surroundings.

I'm the alien here, she realized, squinting against the light from a cloudless lime green sky.

Vin alighted from the van's cabin. At the rear, the smartcart holding Yoshiko's luggage detached itself, and crawled towards Vin's flyer. There were hundreds of other flyers parked around them, all of them rich-looking, all of them huge by Yoshiko's standards.

"It's a Gestrax Secundus," Vin said, as they drew near her bronze delta-winged dart. It was one of the smallest flyers there.

"Very sporty."

It was a relief to get back inside an air-conditioned cabin.

Vin made no control gestures, voiced no commands, but the flyer powered up. The ground dropped away beneath them.

Lucis City's rich profusion lay off to one side, but rapidly receded. Below, a featureless plain raced by.

Vin stiffened. "I'm getting a call." She looked at Yoshiko. "It's the proctors. I'll put it on holo."

An image grew in front of Yoshiko. The proctor they had spoken to before.

"Mrs. Sunadomari," she said. "Captain Rogers, from the Bureau for Offworld Affairs, would like to talk to you."

A white-haired red-cheeked man appeared.

"*J'ai quelque questions à vous poser*," he said without preliminaries.

"*Oui, d'accord*." Yoshiko's reply was automatic. She had hardly spoken Français since emigrating from FedCan, over two decades before.

"*Votre fils a disparu, mais vous ne savez pas pourquoi. Exact?*"

"*Je suppose*," said Yoshiko. She could feel Vin's interested gaze. "Er—Could we speak Anglic, please? It's been a long while."

"If you like. When did you last see him, in person?"

"Three years ago, on Earth. He was back for a holiday." The only one Tetsuo had taken, in the five standard years he had been here.

"Has he mentioned any problems, in his business dealings?"

"I know nothing about his work."

"I see." Captain Rogers' pale eyes stared at her. "You don't deal in mu-space tech, yourself?"

"I'm a femtobionicist."

There was a pause. "Please forgive me. These questions are necessary."

"I understand."

"Another officer will contact you shortly. From Clara Shire. Their jurisdiction, you see."

Yoshiko wondered why, in that case, Rogers was talking to her at all.

"Good day, madam."

The image dissolved.

The flyer banked left, as a breathtaking blue-grey mountain range swept across Yoshiko's field of view.

"We'll soon be there," said Vin. "Don't—"

"Don't worry?" Yoshiko let out a long breath. "I am worried, believe me. What the hell was that all about? The Bureau for Offworld Affairs?"

Vin shrugged. "As far as I know, they deal mostly with immigration, duty and excise, that sort of thing."

"At least he made an effort to speak in what he thought was my primary tongue."

"Maybe."

"What do you mean?"

Vin was silent as the flyer banked again, skimming low above a turquoise lake, spotted with purple blooms of alga-analogue.

"Perhaps it was a harmless verification, in part, of your biog-info." Vin glanced at Yoshiko. "*N'est-ce pas?*"

Most people raised in Nihonjin Columbia were trilingual in Anglic, Français and Nihonjin. That much was true.

"Wonderful." Yoshiko's voice was bitter.

Shadowed forest slipped past below. Beneath its canopy, no doubt, unseen predators were hunting for guileless or desperate prey.

From above, it was a massive fractal Maltese cross. Among gardens which would not have disgraced Versailles, the cruciform mansion—palace, perhaps—spread out. Each arm ended in a cluster of ever smaller orthogonal towers.

The crystal-domed hub flashed past beneath them.

Vin brought the flyer in low, alongside a lake which held a pavilion at its centre, linked by a footbridge to the shore. They slowed above an emerald meadow, and circled in to land beside a shaded acre of landscaped wooded dells.

Yoshiko clutched the arms of her seat as the cabin's membrane oozed apart, and the floor flowed out, ramplike, carrying her chair down to the ground, with Vin's chair alongside her.

"I've never seen such materials tech," said Yoshiko to Vin, stepping off onto the lawn. The seats flowed back into the cabin.

Yoshiko blinked, and looked around her. Bronze statues nestled among silver beeches. Small fork-tailed birds, the size of Terran sparrows, argued noisily on the shoulders of a fierce Bhodidarma.

She breathed in the scents of woodland and exotic flowers.

"You own all this."

"Lori does." Vin smiled. "She manages to scrape a living." Looking up at the huge house, she added, "Septor has his own estate, at the edge of the Masakala Desert. Blue and red sands in all directions, and weirdly shaped pillars of rock. They spend half the year there."

"Very nice. And you go with them?"

"I stay here, or in my apartment in Lucis. Shall we go in?"

They walked up towards the house, trailed by the smartcart. Yoshiko wondered if the smartcart were hers till she left Fulgor.

Leave? She hadn't seen Tetsuo yet—

"Try this." Vin had stopped beside a low bush, and was plucking a peach-like fruit. She handed it to Yoshiko. "It's called a borcha. A new species, but it's OK to eat it."

Yoshiko took a small bite. The flavour burst on her tongue, sweet and powerful.

"Marvellous." She took another bite. "You've got good bio-designers. How are species approved for public introduction?"

Vin shook her head. "We don't have anything like that here." She frowned slightly, and up ahead a golden door slid open in a tower. "There are no regulatory bodies."

"Er—" Yoshiko stopped, aware that she was talking shop—and no doubt boring Vin—but too interested to leave the point alone. "How can you know they're safe to eat?"

"Whoever sells them, on a fruitstall or in Skein, displays the lab and sim-trial results in a kind of . . . well, a very condensed form of information, which we can access." She pointed at the headgear nestled in her hair.

They resumed walking.

"What about non-Luculenti?"

"They can tell by the price. If it's new, it's cheap. Simple as that."

Was it that simple? Would a struggling Fulgidi family be able to afford the tried and tested stuff?

"The price peaks after about thirty standard years," added Vin. "After that, the next generation will be marketed. The borcha's next four successors are already on file."

They stepped through the doorway, into a chamber hung with landscape tapestries, ringed with alcoves holding statues and flat paintings and delicate scrolls. Vin walked straight past the treasures without looking.

Yoshiko followed her into a corridor, onto its central strip of royal blue carpet. The ornate walls were white and gold, and the blue strip arrowed into the house's interior.

"Just stand still," said Vin.

The carpet began to flow, carrying Yoshiko and Vin past abstract paintings, past swarming holos and breathtaking calligraphy, until an endless stream of priceless artwork was flowing by, too quickly to be appreciated. The long labour of unenhanced humans. Did the owners of all this wealth appreciate it?

Yoshiko's hand was sticky with juice, from the half-forgotten borcha fruit. She licked some from her finger. Superb taste.

Tetsuo, my son. You have fallen among people who form corporate empires in seconds, but plan in centuries.

How could I ever have prepared you for this?

The console puckered and drew open at Tetsuo's gesture. There was a slight popping sound, startling in the quiet cockpit.

Light glittered on the infocrystals, lying on a traylike extrusion. So innocuous, yet the cause of so much trouble.

He strained to access them mentally. It was like the time he and Akira had tried telepathy experiments at school: wishful thinking, to no effect.

If he were a true Luculentus, the data would unfold at his bidding.

"Command: close."

As the crystals slid from sight, Tetsuo turned his attention outwards. Nothing. The canyon was lifeless, deserted.

He closed his eyes and leaned back in his seat.

In startling clarity, Tetsuo saw: *the lobby, himself sitting there, awaiting his pro forma security interview at the Bureau for Offworld Affairs. It's all part of the upraise procedure, but a mere formality. Five standard years ago, applying for his work visa, he was thoroughly vetted.*

To one side lies the reception leading to Captain Rogers' office: a dull room leading to a dull man.

Raised voices, coming from the office. Suddenly, a tall slim man, in a green-and-burgundy suit with the blue/silver flash of a LuxPrime courier, bursts from Rogers' office and stalks away, tight-lipped with anger.

"Adam! Come back!"

The bumbling red-faced Captain Rogers calls after the courier, and follows him desperately.

The lobby is empty.

After five minutes, Tetsuo sighs, stands up, and begins to walk around, hands stuffed in his pockets. There is no one to talk to. He walks to the door of Rogers' office—the membrane dissolves at his approach—and he sees a polished brass case, its LuxPrime insignia bold in gold and silver. The clasp is open, the lid pushed back. Inside, on the purple satin lining, infocrystals lie twinkling. An awful temptation takes hold of him.

It takes two minutes to copy the info, downloading to his own blank crystals via his wrist terminal. By the time Captain Rogers returns, Tetsuo is sitting back in the lobby, share prices and stock options scrolling through the air above his bracelet.

His eyes snapped open.

Just before the attack squad—whoever they were—had smashed their way into his house, he had partially decoded that video log, from one of Captain Rogers' crystals. It had been the only code fragment he could find which was not guarded by LuxPrime protocols. One of the speaker-IDs, he remembered, had been labelled "Farsteen."

And there had been that semisentient AI-code on the same crystal. Tetsuo's decoding of the video-log had somehow invoked it.

"*I'm Farsteen*," the image had said. "*At least, a partial analogue. If I am online, the real Farsteen is surely dead . . .*"

Then the image had shattered, as the attack squad's weapons had pierced his house systems. He had left that crystal behind when he fled.

Farsteen. Rogers. A mention of Rafael.

Tetsuo shivered. The awful clarity of his own memories scared him as much as intimations of conspiracy.

What the hell was going on?

The strip slowed, and halted in a splendid atrium tiled in white and black, before huge bronze doors. Vin headed past them, to a bas-relief carved on the otherwise plain wall.

It was a hi-res illusion: Vin stepped straight *through* the sculptured wall, so Yoshiko had no choice but to brace herself and follow.

Beyond the small holo door lay an airy chamber. Pillars of sunlight, sprinkled with dust-motes, fell from crystal skylights to a marble floor.

Lori, in an artist's smock, with a pink scarf covering her head and the lower half of her face, was looking up at a vast granite block. Above it, chandelier-like, hung a convoluted framework, studded with high-powered lasers.

Lori raised her arms.

A flock of silver drones was launched from the laser bank. As broad beams of light cut swathes through the granite block, the flitting drones annihilated falling stone fragments.

Amid the swirling mist of pulverized rock and flashing light, a statue of Diana the Huntress gradually took shape.

"It's magnificent," whispered Yoshiko.

Vin was looking at the statue through a small crystalline sheet, which she held up in front of her face.

"Use this. Change the focus with your thumb pressure."

Yoshiko took the sheet. Her vision zoomed in on the Huntress's intent face. Even the irises of her eyes, even her eyelashes, were exquisitely delineated in stone.

"Do you like it?" Lori had walked up, unnoticed. Her scarf unwrapped itself from her face and wound itself into a loop around her shoulder.

"It's wonderful."

"Then it's yours. It can travel back to Earth with you. I'll arrange that." Yoshiko started to protest, then stopped herself. Instead, she bowed silently. Lori's answering bow was nicely judged, performed exactly to the same inclination.

"Come on, Yoshiko," said Vin. "I'll show you to your room."

He had to get out of here.

Tetsuo slapped on his resp-mask and hauled himself out of the flyer. He half walked, half slid down the fuselage, and jumped heavily to the ground.

Already, he felt short of breath.

Uncertainty swirled in his head. In contrast to the serene canyon floor, conflicting images crowded his mind. Committing info-theft had been stupid as well as criminal, but he would give himself up in an instant if he could do so safely. Whatever the penalties for his offence, could it be worse than stirring up trouble he had no hope in hell of dealing with?

From the canyon's purple shadows, a pattern sprang out at him—a sudden twist in perception—and his troubles were forgotten.

There were no glowing yellow outlines. Not this time. Yet the trails of minute disturbances were suddenly prominent.

It was like an optical puzzle's solution suddenly made obvious; like the first time he had looked at a tesseract and seen it as a truly four-dimensional shape.

He set off across the canyon floor, following the trails. An hour later, he was lying on a ridge overlooking a gully. The rock was warm beneath his grumbling belly.

People were moving, down below.

So much for the deserted hypozone, far from civilization, which had always been his intended bolthole. Paranoid preparations, because he had never trusted Rafael—

Concentrate.

He blinked sweat away from his eyes. It was nice to rest here, feeling the almost sensual fatigue-pain in his heavy thighs.

Movement, again.

A slight figure was picking his—no, her—way across the rocks. Shorn blond hair, tight gamine features, carrying a long pole which glowed blue at the ends.

She wasn't wearing a resp-mask.

As she turned to wave at someone out of sight, Tetsuo squinted, trying to make out the faint glimmer or distortion of a smartatom shield. Nothing. What could be holding Terran atmosphere down in the gully?

A small shadow moved beside his head, and Tetsuo started.

Heart thumping, he looked around, and saw a harmless propelloid uproot itself from a ledge and whirl away, catching a thermal updraught.

He looked back down.

Purple slick-skinned organisms were swarming from a narrow cave. Strange moving patterns flowed across their bodies: ripples of black moving from back to front across their dorsal surfaces.

No—Their *skins* were flowing, looping endlessly, providing locomotion.

A man's voice called out from the cave's darkness, and the woman began to herd the creatures across the gully, waving the pole in encouragement.

A straggler broke away, crawling uphill. The woman diverted the rest of the flock to follow it. When they caught up, she directed the whole group back downwards.

Good tactic.

Tetsuo stood up and looked around for a descending path. Puffing, he made his way down.

What was he doing?

It was the liberation of total disaster. Two days ago, before his normal life had been torn away, his instinct would have been to remain in hiding. Now, with a strange feeling of abandon, he just walked into the gully, accepting the risk.

"Excuse me." His voice was muffled by the resp-mask.

The woman jumped.

She spun to face Tetsuo, and he saw how emaciated she was, how young. Her eyes widened and she opened her mouth as if to yell. A clear membrane glistened wetly over her mouth, and her shout was silent.

In the back of Tetsuo's neck, pain exploded.

As a dark orange boiling mist rolled over his vision, he glimpsed pale bands pulsing gill-like on her slender neck. Then waves of total black fell upon him, and he drowned.

Chapter Nine

Thrust, and you will repel.
Pull the blade inwards–
Strike with the deepest cut.

Past plumes of steam rising from blowholes, over a bubbling lake of creamy mud streaked with metallic pigments, then banking close to a mountain slope studded with crimson growths which caught Yoshiko's professional interest—She shook her head. This was not the time.

Vin was beside her in the flyer, frowning intently, deeply interfaced. Earlier, over breakfast, she had called the proctors, and gained permission to visit Tetsuo's house.

Yoshiko stared outside again, but the landscape flowing past beneath the wing had lost all interest. She clenched her fists. Small strong hands, formed by thousands of hours spent in the *shugyo*—the austere discipline—of *bushido* training. Time, perhaps, which would have been better spent with her sons, her husband.

Ken, I miss you.

"Landing now," murmured Vin.

They circled over a trefoil-shaped house, perched at a meadow's edge. Vin brought the flyer slowly down by a stand of majestic pines. A stream flashed in the sunlight.

Two flyers—big, black, lumpy craft—were there already.

"The proctors?" asked Yoshiko.

"That's right."

The engines whispered into silence, and the seats flowed in the same disconcerting fashion as before, and deposited them on the grass.

Vin led the way along a path of grey slate, winding past a pool and an eclectic Zen garden. A dark-uniformed woman, with cropped grey hair and a strong jaw, was waiting for them.

"Professor Sunadomari? I'm Major Reilly."

"How do you do."

"It's a bit of a mess inside. I expect you'd like to look around."

Young-looking proctors drifted in and out of the sparse pine-floored lounge, while Yoshiko sat on a couch, sipping a glass of water. Major Reilly sat opposite her, finally without questions.

All of Yoshiko's answers had boiled down to one thing: she knew nothing of her elder son's life.

"We'll find him." Major Reilly was professionally sympathetic. "Try not to worry."

A band of tension tightened above Yoshiko's eyes. Too many people were telling her not to worry. Too many people were here, now—at least a dozen of the major's people. Was there so little crime on Fulgor, that a trivial matter would need so many proctors?

A broken vase lay in the corner. Outside, violence had passed through like a whirlwind, leaving rooms in shambles, walls destroyed, furniture and belongings torn apart.

Yoshiko felt cold, as though her whole body were shutting down. Vin, standing near the doorway, asked, "Did you have trouble getting through the defences?"

Of course. That was why there were so many of them.

"We have a special unit for dealing with such matters, ma'am."

If Vin was surprised at being called "ma'am," she did not show it.

"I thought you might have had to call in the TacCorps."

Major Reilly's face tightened. "It's not actually their jurisdiction."

Vin shrugged slightly.

"While you were talking to Yoshiko," she said, eyes bright, "I saw your tech people examining an underground hangar. There were signs of a flyer taking off in a big hurry. About eight days ago, they're guessing."

"You shouldn't have been—" Major Reilly stopped. "Never mind."

Vin said, "Shouldn't SatScan show which way Yoshiko's son fled? Sorry, Yoshiko. But obviously there were heavily armed intruders, and I'd say Tetsuo got away."

Yoshiko's heart beat faster.

"Is what she's saying true, Major? Can you find my son?"

Major Reilly looked from Yoshiko to Vin, then sighed slightly.

"SatScan images show no untoward occurrences of any kind."

"So that's why someone of your seniority is here." Vin turned to Yoshiko. "Either very sophisticated smartatom camouflage was used, or someone's hacked the SatScan logs."

Major Reilly stood up.

"You are both hereby bound under the provisions of the Control of Information Act not to reveal any information you have learned here to any other parties. Nor may you share any speculations about the same. Do you understand?"

Yoshiko nodded dumbly.

"I understand." Vin looked excited.

Resentment settled on Yoshiko, but she pushed it away. Vin was young, for all her precocious intellect, and she had never met Tetsuo. This must be an adventure for her.

"That includes conversations in Skein."

"Of course."

Yoshiko was suddenly aware of the major's lack of headgear. "Are there many Luculenti proctors?"

"No." Major Reilly's expression was unreadable. "It's not really their career of choice."

"Only a few," Vin agreed. "Though I think I'd find it rather interesting."

The major looked at her, startled. Then she grew thoughtful.

"Perhaps we could use your help." From a satchel on the floor, she drew a small transparent bag which contained an infocrystal. "This is Tetsuo Sunadomari's upraise authorization: LuxPrime file, MoLI and BOA endorsements."

Vin's eyes widened.

To Yoshiko, she said, "Ministry of Luculenti Industries, and the Bureau for Offworld Affairs." She frowned. "Just a minute, while I check."

While Vin's stare grew distant, Major Reilly asked Yoshiko, "You know of no recent change in your son's, ah, legal status?"

Yoshiko shook her head. "What's going on?"

Major Reilly said nothing.

"Wow." Vin's expression cleared. "You're right, Major."

It was the first time Yoshiko had seen Vin so clearly act like a teenage girl.

"His sponsor was Rafael de la Vega," Vin quickly added. "The operation was a tenday ago. He's due to be presented in Skein in five days' time. I don't suppose—" She stopped, suddenly sombre. "I hope he makes it."

Trembling, Yoshiko asked, "What has happened to my son?"

"He's—"

"He's become a Luculentus," Vin interrupted breathlessly.

The ground seemed to fall away beneath Yoshiko's feet.

"What? How can that be—?"

"There's an offworld quota." Major Reilly's voice was deliberately flat. "It often remains unfulfilled."

Unlike the intense competition for Luculentus status among the rest of the society. Yoshiko understood that. "But he's not—He's not a child." Her own voice sounded distant and strange.

Major Reilly looked at Vin, who answered, "The integration's harder with loss of plasticity, and perhaps not so effective, but it can be performed on an adult brain."

"I see."

Was this why Tetsuo hadn't wanted her to come?

"I don't want to sound alarmist, Major." Vin looked serious. "But Tetsuo really shouldn't be alone right now. He needs LuxPrime support, in the later stages of VSI—Virtual Synaptic Interface—integration."

"OK." Major Reilly touched Yoshiko's arm. "Professor, I'm sure you would like to see the rest of your son's house. Let me get someone to show—"

"No," said Yoshiko. "I want to hear this. What's the worst that can happen to Tetsuo, if he's by himself?"

Vin swallowed. "Neural catastrophe."

"I understand." Yoshiko blinked back tears.

She remembered Tetsuo as she had seen him in his last h-mail. Quite without headgear. His expression stiff, a little unnatural. An imperfectly edited image.

She was dimly aware of a proctor, scarcely more than a boy, coming into the room.

"Major? We're ready to clean up in here now."

"Thank you. Please escort Professor Sunadomari outside, for some fresh air."

Yoshiko walked mechanically outside. As the major's and Vin's voices receded, she could hear Vin answering questions about LuxPrime procedures. Then Yoshiko and the young proctor were in the garden, and the startling light was bright enough to hurt her eyes.

They fetched her a drink, some kind of herbal tea, and sat her down on a lounger, on a wooden deck overlooking the Zen garden. A couple of small silver drones were floating overhead, and half a dozen smart-looking proctors were tidying up, packing forensic sensors away in cases.

Yoshiko sat hunched, withdrawing into herself, wrapped in isolating numbness. The cheerful day, the sparkling stream which burbled by the garden, the scent of flowers, all seemed unreal.

There was a proctor crouching by the stream. He stood up, frowning over readings from the sensor in his hand.

He walked over to two of his colleagues.

"I don't get this. Look at all these decomposition products. But a few metres upstream, the water's clear."

"Impossible."

"No, it isn't—"

One of the others, a young woman, walked urgently over to the Zen garden. She gestured to a drone. It dropped, and hovered over pebbles which had been raked into a frozen, swirling sea.

The proctor's fingers flickered in control gestures, as she sifted info from her bracelet's holo display.

She looked up. "There's a null-sheet under here. That's why you didn't sense anything."

"You're kidding."

The proctors began digging through the pebbles with gloved hands. One of them knelt in the stream to work, heedless of the cold water.

Yoshiko stood up unnoticed, and walked down to join them. From beneath the stones, they were pulling up a black sheet of slick material.

"The head's in damper soil. Some solutes soaked through to the stream."

"Damned lucky. We might never have found it, otherwise."

"OK, let's get the drones down here."

Icy coldness descended on Yoshiko as the drones hauled back the black sheet.

It had a doll's head.

A very oversized doll.

Water, from the nearby stream, had hastened its putrefaction, and the head was bloated and rubbery, almost spherical.

The rest of the corpse was half covered in a torn suit: some of it dark green, the rest darker. The lifeless limbs were splayed at odd angles.

"X-ray shows a circular hole in the parietal bone. Graser wound."

The round belly was marbled, blood vessels prominently purple. Lower down, the remains were covered in adipocere: rank-smelling and soapy, fatty acids formed from decomposing fat.

Yoshiko could see little sign of depredation. Tetsuo would have been pleased with that: he had never liked insects.

"Oh, my God, ma'am. You shouldn't be here."

Sloppily sculpted from decaying meat, the doll's unrecognizable features stared past Yoshiko, dead white eyes focussed on eternity.

Chapter Ten

Repel the love which lies.
Inwards, seek the light;
Cut away false shadows.

"Adam Farsteen, LuxPrime courier. His ID implant's in place."

The world ebbed away from Yoshiko, then swept back in.

Strong young hands supported her elbows.

"It's not your son, ma'am."

She hung her head, and wept.

A table drifted up past theirs. Its integral seats were occupied by a group of rich Fulgidi, laughing and joking, quite carefree.

Yoshiko stared at them, seeing a poor dead thing. A once wondrous vessel whose miracle, life, was gone.

"—some more?" Vin was asking.

"I'm sorry, Vin."

"More daistral?"

"Ah—No, thanks. I haven't finished this one."

Their own mag-lev table turned slowly, some five metres above the floor. Over Vin's shoulder, through the vast window, a range of violet snow-capped peaks swung into view.

"Your friend should—Oh, is that her?"

Maggie Brown was waving up at them, from the major-domo's desk.

Their table descended, lightly touching the carpet long enough for Maggie to take her seat, then lifted once more.

"How's Jason?" asked Yoshiko, after Maggie and Vin had introduced themselves.

"Fine. He's in a crèche. Nice facilities." Maggie ordered brandy, and accepted the glass which rose up from the table's central iris. "More to the point, how are you?"

Yoshiko looked out at the distant mountains.

"I'm OK."

Maggie drained her glass of brandy in one long gulp. Vin watched her in surprise.

"So what," Maggie asked, "did you find at your son's house?"

Yoshiko closed her eyes.

"A body." Vin's voice was soft, matter-of-fact. "A LuxPrime courier. Buried in the grounds."

"You're kidding." A pause. "Tell me more."

Vin related the story, while Maggie drank a second glass of brandy. Yoshiko felt too numb to be astonished.

"It's a good job you called me," Maggie said finally. "The local NewsNets have interesting regulations on how news is posted."

"Placing context and keywords can be . . . sensitive." Vin cleared her throat. "I know what you mean."

Seeing Yoshiko's blank look, Maggie explained, "There are lots of ways to bury a story. What you need right now is publicity, to get people looking for Tetsuo."

"I don't know . . ."

"And you say he's a Luculentus now? I didn't think that was possible. Most people on Earth wouldn't know that."

"It can be hard to compete here," said Vin. "Even if Tetsuo were used to dealing with unenhanced Fulgidi: many subject themselves to intense, life-long education programmes." Her level tone neither condemned nor praised. "They use all sorts of ware to assist in negotiations, technical matters, you name it."

"That's my hook, then." Maggie leaned forward intently. "A lonely Earther, lost in an advanced culture, desperate to make his way . . ."

"Your hook?" Yoshiko felt dull and stupid.

"Absolutely. I'll hyperlink the item to my Skein reportage as current affairs background."

Yoshiko gathered her concentration.

"Are you sure this is going to help?"

"It may mean the proctors won't stop looking," said Maggie.

"I agree." White light, reflected from distant glaciers, flowed across Vin's headgear as she nodded.

Major Reilly seemed pretty serious, thought Yoshiko, but said nothing.

Something wet dripped onto her cheek. Above, at a drifting table, revellers clinked glasses and laughed uproariously, unheeding.

As they flew over mist-shrouded woods, Maggie raised the subject of LuxPrime technology.

"There's practically no info about it in EveryWare," she said.

"I'm not surprised." Vin must have been lightly interfaced, or not at all, with the flyer. Her attention was on Maggie and Yoshiko. "We don't discuss it much."

"Please, don't talk about anything which makes you uncomfortable."

"No problem. I guess you want your audience to think what it must feel like to be Tetsuo right now. I can't imagine." Vin shook her head. "I'm no more conscious of my implanted plexcores than of my brain."

"Plexcores?"

"Well—"

Yoshiko half-listened to them, feeling very tired. Down below were a few miserable sheep, bigger than the Terran norm. Soon, though, the pastureland was gone, swallowed by rolling mists.

"VSI comprises smartatom sheets, folded throughout the brain. Interfaces to the plexcores."

"So a neural impulse can start in the organic brain, and continue seamlessly into the plexcore?"

Maggie's really very good at this, thought Yoshiko.

"And vice versa. Thought is distributed, almost holographic," said Vin. "Consciousness is an emergent property of competing waves sweeping across the brain . . . or across brain-plus-plexcores."

"So you've just increased, ah, processing capacity?" Maggie paused. "Or are there qualitative differences?"

"How can I tell? I've never been an unenhanced human. Er . . . Sorry."

"No need to be embarrassed." Maggie grinned. "I'm used to being stupid."

Vin laughed.

"What about Skein?" Yoshiko surprised herself by asking.

Vin's laughter died. "I can't imagine life without it. That's why Septor hated Earth so much, I think. We had fast-comm links between the three of us, but our Skein access was limited to gateways through EveryWare. It was appalling."

"Like fish out of water?" suggested Maggie.

"Exactly so."

Entwined curves, like pale-blue nautilus shells, nestled among pristine lawns. Maggie's hotel.

Vin brought the flyer in very fast past some tennis courts, then dropped smoothly to land.

"Thanks, Vin," said Maggie. "As soon as I've picked up Jason, I'll start work on my article."

As the cockpit membrane softened, Yoshiko suddenly remembered what Vin had said to Major Reilly.

"Vin? Didn't you mention something about a sponsor?"

"For upraise? Yes, that's a requirement." Vin frowned. "Tetsuo was sponsored by Rafael de la Vega."

"Maybe Maggie could—"

"I've met him!" Maggie gripped Yoshiko's arm. "When I was interviewing someone at the Skein conference. I'm sure that was the name. Do you know him, Vin?"

"Not really, but Lori, my soul-mother, does. Very sexy, she thinks."

"And—?"

"And she's right, but sometimes he makes my blood run cold. I can't say why." With no physical gesture, Vin caused a holo still to appear: a dark-featured man, extraordinarily handsome, with piercing eyes.

"That's him," said Maggie. "Rashella introduced us."

Vin froze. "You mean Rashella Syntharinova?"

"Yes. I was interviewing her. Why? What's the matter?"

"It's not been released to the lower—ah, the public access levels, but Skein's awash with the news. Rashella Syntharinova killed herself."

"Suicide? Are you sure?"

Vin looked from Maggie to Yoshiko.

"That's what everyone says."

"Which would you recommend?" asked a coarse-looking man, raising his collar against the night's cold breeze.

"That one's OK." His companion pointed at a floating bubble, which descended to the cobbled street.

The bubble's membrane opened, and a scantily dressed woman beckoned the man inside.

Rafael, from his seat under a glowglobe, watched as prostitute and client drifted upwards, into the darkness.

He pulled his dark heated cloak warmly about him.

The remaining man walked underneath bobbing spheres containing glamorous-looking girls, some performing dance steps, then stopped below one whose occupant was a huge woman, standing with her massive thighs apart. He gestured, and the bubble descended. He stepped inside and then that sphere, too, lifted and was gone.

Rafael stood up, unobtrusively pulled a smartfilm mask across his face, and continued his peregrination through the Floating Worlds district. No one glanced at him; the mask convincingly altered his features.

Dark alleys, bright sleaze: holos beckoning the unwary and the desperate into clubs where any taste was catered for. He walked, enjoying the feel of hopeless hunger which hovered behind the counterfeit glamour.

He turned away from the crowded main thoroughfare. The streets grew quieter, with unlit stretches between the clubs, and fewer floating bubbles. The lower end of the market plied their trade from doorways and street corners. Some of them bore black eyes, chipped teeth.

Rafael pulled up his cloak's hood, hiding his headgear.

A girl turned to look at Rafael. She stood casually, but her eyes were reptilian, hard and calculating.

"Show you a good time?"

Coarse accent, makeup thickly applied. Young. Legs in stockings, or perhaps a tattooed web—a centuries-old courtesans' code. Narrow hips. Much scrawnier than the mature Luculentae that Rafael preferred.

"Why not?"

He followed her into a bleak hallway. Paint flaked from dank walls, and the corridor reeked of bodily fluids and despair.

The girl stopped and turned. "Thirteen credits, all the way."

Light from a fitful glowglobe cast the lines of her young/old face into unflattering relief.

Wordlessly, Rafael held up his anonymous cred-ring to her sensor.

"Follow me, babe."

His skin tingled. Surveillance system.

<<<MsgRcv VEGASCN22700; cause = Surveillance detected.>>>

Ignore.

His smartmask, which had already altered his features, was extending itself to cover hair and exposed flesh with an invisibly thin layer, melding at the throat with his monomolecular suit. His hands, too, were protected.

He would leave no trace of himself behind, in this place of tawdry dreams and disappointed fantasies.

The girl's room was bare, furnished only with a narrow bed and a stool. A blurry holo of a small house stood on the window sill. Her home? What kind of childhood had she led?

"Let's get you ready, honey."

"If you like." Rafael threw back his cloak, then ran a finger down her slender, fragile neck.

His senses quested, but there was no surveillance in here. Unless the girl yelled, her hidden help would not come to her assistance.

"Oh, yes, baby—" She closed her eyes and rocked her hips in a parody of pleasure.

She pressed herself against him.

"No—"

His fingers dug like steel claws, constricting her arteries, and her breathing quickened, like a runner at the marathon's end. His own excitement mounted.

Come on, fight. That's it. Fight for life.

She struggled.

Rafael's breath, too, was coming hard and fast.

She fought and kicked, and Rafael's heart thumped wildly with pleasure, ever faster as her strength slowly ebbed. Finally, in a nicety of timing, he climaxed just as death rattled in her crushed throat and life's light faded from her small pale eyes.

He let the body slump to the floor.

It lay there, twisted unnaturally. Already, a stench was rising from the soiled meat.

Rafael gathered his cloak and swept out of the room, down the hallway—ignoring the worthless surveillance system—and out into the street.

Power thrummed inside him.

At the corner, two big men took a step in his direction, perhaps just to sell him some illegal pleasure, but he met their eyes and they glanced away.

Power.

He used the underground tube system, in preference to an air-cab. As his car pulled into Lucis Central, it detached itself from the rest of the train and rose up a vertical shaft, and deposited him in a small cobbled plaza.

An unarmed proctor nodded to him, and Rafael smiled back. In the Floating Worlds district, only two kilometres away, the proctor would have had a partner and a drone, and carried a hand graser.

As Rafael walked, he retuned his cloak to a gaudy blue, slashed through with gold. He reconfigured his smartmask into an obvious caricature of a wolf.

The Lupus Festival was in full swing. Crowds were thronging Pietanaro Square, and the neighbouring Vitanova Gardens. Rafael took one of the suspended silver walkways, bought a drink from a vendor, and stood against a rail, admiring the dark trees and their bright symbiotic blooms lit by a thousand dancing glowglobes.

Flute music drifted through the leaves.

"Happy Lupus!"

A Luculenta, arm in arm with two Fulgidi—her staff, perhaps: it was festival time—greeted Rafael. She tuned her wolf mask to transparency. Her face was lovely.

"Happy Lupus," Rafael replied, but kept his mask opaque. It was the most polite way to decline an invitation to join them at an opera or poetry contest.

She smiled without regret, and continued along the walkway. Elegant people passed below, going about their genteel celebrations. Floating Worlds, and the other Lowtown districts: did they ever think of them?

Rafael breathed deeply of the scented night air. It was so wonderful to be alive.

A light rain was falling as Rafael reached a small paved square, and he headed for the bright amber helix which advertised a taxi-pad.

A human driver opened the old-fashioned gull door for Rafael—as though he couldn't have gestured or spoken himself—and climbed into his separate cockpit only when he was sure Rafael was comfortable in the back.

Bright lights dropped away below them.

During the twenty-minute flight to Rafael's town house, he lay back and thought of the nameless little Fulgida wretch, and the wild light in her eyes—overcoming her cold detachment—which had faded as she died.

If he could somehow subsume the mind of an unenhanced woman, the way he could with a Luculenta . . . Would that make it more satisfying? Or less?

He suspected a Fulgida mind would be a petty thing, too light and insignificant to bother with.

"Here we are, sir."

The courtyard lit up as Rafael stepped out. Not bothering with a cred-ring, he lightly entered Skein and transferred fare and generous tip to the driver's account. Then he stood back, and watched the taxi lift up into the darkness and disappear.

Something was wrong.

There were no squeals of alarm from the house systems, but subtle indications from external sensors—unnatural air-flow patterns, few nocturnal birds—were causing its AIs to quest heuristically through knowledge space. It was as though the house itself were uneasy.

Something massive passed across the alpha moon, blocking it from sight.

Blue bands of light grew from points and strobed backwards across delta-shapes. Three proctors' flyers, descending from the night.

A uniformed woman with cropped grey hair alighted from the nearest flyer, and walked up to Rafael. Three armed proctors hung back, watching.

The crews of the other two flyers remained inside.

"Luculentus Rafael Garcia de la Vega?"

"At your service." Rafael bowed.

"I'm Major Reilly. You may be able to help us."

"My pleasure."

{[[HeaderBegin: Module = Node78AF99: Type = PivotCentre:Axes = 24.
Priority = absolute
Concurrent_Execute
ThreadOne: <video> ImageID = 2899A3:000. linkfile = HoloLog.1998
ThreadTwo: <video> timestamp = 23091313:001, linkfile = personal.thislog
ThreadThree: QryTrace(2899A3.000)
ThreadFour: <SkeinSearch> Locate(2899A3.000)
ThreadFive: <SkeinSearch> ThreadScan("Lowtown," "murder")
ThreadSix: <TownHouseAlpha> WeaponsEnable
End_Concurrent_Execute]]}

<<<MsgRcv VEGASCN000100; cause = Query failed.>>>

How could they have found him so quickly? There was no mention of the girl in Skein, and he was searching with all the power of his plexcore array, two orders of magnitude greater than any other Luculentus alive.

Some private comm system? Undercover proctors in Floating Worlds?

Adrenaline flooded through Rafael. The stakes were getting higher. What a fine game!

{{{HeaderBegin: Module = Node10012.JK998: Type = Trinary-HyperCode: Axes = 12

Concurrent_Execute

ThreadOne: <intrapeduncular matrix>.linkfile = GraserArray1

ThreadTwo: <intrapeduncular matrix>.linkfile = GraserArray2

ThreadThree: <intrapeduncular matrix>.linkfile = GraserArray3

End_Concurrent_Execute}}}

<<<MsgRcv VEGAWPN022107; cause = Targets acquired. Weapons are tracking.>>>

His house weapons were trained on the proctors and their flyers, and the interface was enabled at the deepest level: he could destroy them all by reflex.

But he didn't want to do that, until he could find out what they knew.

"Won't you come in, Major?" he said easily. "I'd be happy to help, in any way I can."

"Thank you."

Major Reilly followed him inside.

Chapter Eleven

Zen temple: no branch lies.
Pine-trees, proud as love,
Thrust, but do not repel.

Pink snow fell like cotton candy, gently icing the boulders outside.

Tetsuo shivered, though it was warm in the long cabin. Then the cramps came again, wracking his body, and he held himself clenched inside until the spasm had passed.

"Are you OK?"

The blonde girl was sitting on the couch opposite, looking concerned.

"Wonderful." His voice was hoarse.

"You startled Brevan."

Tetsuo started to laugh, but it caught in his throat and became a hacking cough.

When it subsided, he sat back, breathing quickly. The high-pitched wheeze in his lungs slowly died away.

In a semitransparent chamber at the end of the room, her companion was drifting in clouds of grey smoke. Narrow wires, almost invisible, suspended his couch hammock-like amid the psychedelic vapours.

"Nasty habit." The young woman had followed his gaze. "I'm Dhana, by the way."

"Nice—" Tetsuo's voice cracked drily, and he swallowed. "Nice to meet you."

"Ready to try a drink yet?"

When she had offered daistral earlier, his stomach had heaved, rippled with contractions.

"I think so. Yes. Please."

There were lightweight bracelets around his wrists. He had seen them before, though only in holodramas. At Dhana's command, they could snap together, or induce excruciating pain directly through his nerves.

Another pair enclosed his ankles. Not that a man of his bulk could run very far or fast—but he really was not going anywhere, when his feet could be locked together in an instant.

From a jug, Dhana filled a heavy cup, and fetched it to him.

It tasted of apricots. The hot liquid slipped down inside him, and for a moment he almost gagged. Then it settled, and he felt much better.

"The . . . silence must be awful for you." She ran a hand through her short blonde hair.

"I beg your pardon?"

"Don't worry, you're not injured. There's a null-sheet lamina in the cabin's walls. That's why you can't go into Skein."

No doubt there was a smartatom outer layer, too, providing visual camouflage. This cabin was designed to avoid detection, by SatScan or other means. It just happened handily to provide a functional prison for a Luculentus, who would otherwise be able to summon help through Skein.

Silent laughter shook his body.

"Oh, my God. You just don't realize—"

He stopped.

For all her civility, this woman, Dhana, was not his friend. Nor was she in charge here. Perhaps he was alive only because they thought he was a true Luculentus, who might already have relayed their presence to someone else in Skein.

No point in guessing. Silence seemed a good strategy.

He wondered where he was—the view through the windows was not Nether Canyon, though he was surely still in the hypozone—and how long he had been unconscious.

3 hours 23.7 minutes.

"What?" he said, but realized immediately that Dhana had not spoken.

"I didn't say anything."

"Never mind."

The damned mindware was playing tricks again. If only it could make itself useful, and get him out of here.

Suddenly, without volition, he keeled sideways on the couch, as though his whole body had somehow slipped beyond his control.

As salt tears tracked across his face, he distantly watched the girl back away. Concern was plain upon her unpretty face. She was a slip of a thing compared to him, though, and could not risk getting too close.

He closed his eyes. This was all too much.

He remembered the woman, Dhana, turning to face him in the gully, and he remembered her as having a demon's face, like an evil *kami*, glistening mouth and pulsing gills—An hallucination, surely. It must have been a resp-mask.

The mindware was playing havoc with his brain. He knew the dangers: cascading neural failure or, worse, a psychotic semi-autonomous plexcore which was only partially integrated with his mind. He was losing it, losing everything he had worked for—

"Drink this."

Her small hand balanced his head, without disturbing the headgear, and he sipped from the glass she held.

He sank back onto the couch.

"Good," he murmured.

"It will help you sleep."

Her face drifted in and out of his awareness. She had even, pearly teeth.

"Who are you?"

"I'm Dhana." Something silver glistened at the back of her throat when she spoke. "I thought I told you that."

"Mmm."

His eyelids drooped, and his whole great comfortable body felt dragged down by gravity, pulled towards the planet's core, and the cabin seemed to fold up and shrink all around him, and Dhana's face was floating like a pale distant moon saying "Sleep now," so he did.

She was gone when he awoke.

Voices faded. Perhaps he had dreamed about her.

Throbbing pain filled his head as he levered his bulk upright. He slid his feet to the cold floor and felt around for his boots. They felt good as they fastened themselves snugly round his ankles and immediately heated up.

The low lounge was sparse, deserted, The external door faintly shimmered: a smartatom film hanging in front of it. No doubt it was programmed to activate Tetsuo's restraint bracelets if he tried to pass through.

At the far end were doors to other rooms. On a low table, a small bubbling vat of liquids seemed to be the main source of heat. A menthol scent wafted through the air.

Who would live out here, so far from the habitable regions? It might be centuries before terraforming would spread this deep into the hypozone.

A clinking sound, outside.

Tetsuo hobbled over to a window, breath wheezing faintly.

In a barren landscape frosted with pink frozen snow, his two captors were bending over something—

No, it was two men. Strangers. They wore no resp-masks, yet the atmosphere must be toxic unless Tetsuo had been transported much farther than he thought.

One of them shouted, stumbling. Something small and grey shot out from between his feet, but the other man was quicker. His wickedly curved blade hooked into the small creature's back.

There was no scream, but the creature's skin flowed desperately as it tried to gain traction on the ground. Ichor spurted as the man pulled back on the hook.

For a moment Tetsuo thought the creature might escape as it heaved back, twisting, but the second man hooked his own blade into its side, and from then on its fate was certain.

The first man unslung a pointed rod from his belt and stabbed downwards with relentless precision. The creature thrashed wildly, then lay still. Shades of grey rippled gently across its skin.

Before it was truly dead, they were butchering it. Steam rose from its entrails as they slit its body cleanly open. Then they hacked great chops from its body.

One of them unslung a backpack, adjusted some controls, and opened a small hatch in the pack's side. The other man tossed over some limp gobbets of flesh, which went inside the pack.

When they took out knives and plates, Tetsuo turned away, gorge rising. Then, unable to help himself, he looked back. One man had risen and was staring straight at him.

Tetsuo looked around wildly.

If he stayed in here, he was trapped. The outer door looked like standard membrane. Even if there were a recognition mechanism, even if the strangers did not belong here, they could cut their way through. But if Tetsuo tried to get out, the smartatom curtain would trip his bracelets.

There were three couches, the table with the vat of bubbling liquids—perhaps that could be a weapon—and some glowglobes. Nothing else.

Who was he kidding? He was no fighter.

He ran blindly for the door, taking the chance, but his wrists snapped together, jarring his bones, and then his ankle restraints smashed into each other. He stiffened, and the floor came up and slammed his face, and knocked the breath from his body.

Warm blood trickled from his nose. Dazed, he could only wait for them to come.

There was a slight pop, and a sulphurous smell stung his nose. Someone passing through the membrane. He could not even turn his head to look.

"Hey, a Luculentus. You were right."

"Well, what we gonna do? Take him back?"

Tetsuo swallowed.

They're going to kill me.

"If we take him outside, ain't no null-sheet keepin' him off Skein."

"Only if he's conscious."

A pause.

"Or alive."

There was dry, rasping laughter. Then pain exploded in Tetsuo's back, over his kidneys.

"Why ain't ya in some high'n'mighty palace of your'n?"

"I—" Pain racked him, and he coughed. "—Can pay. Get me out of here."

"Pay, is it?"

A massive blow to his ribs, and something broke.

Then a cold blade, like ice, touched his cheek.

"Think I'm gonna do you, Luculentus."

"Hey, I'm not sure. He belongs to them Simnalari."

"Yeah? Well they're almost as bad. I say we do him."

Tetsuo shut his eyes.

"I'm wanted by proctors," he said quickly. "There's a massive man-hunt underway. Kill me, and there'll be forensic techs all over the place—"

"Shuddup."

"Hey, Manadray. Someone's coming."

"Damnit."

"Come on!"

"Your lucky day—"

The blade stung Tetsuo's cheek, and then it was gone. Footsteps heading for the door. Silence, then a distant shout and the sharp sizzle-and-crack of an energy weapon.

Then nothing.

Another scurry of footsteps.

Dhana was kneeling in front of him. Her hand graser pulsed with the room's colours, its smartatom finish running in chameleon mode.

"They're gone." A deeper voice from the doorway. Dhana's companion. *Brevan.* That was his name. *Concentrate.*

"Looks like they tried to take him." Brevan's tone was hard.

"No." With Dhana's help, Tetsuo managed to sit up on the floor. "They were going to kill me."

Brevan looked at him, as though he were going to finish the job himself.

"Damned Agrazzi," he said finally. "We're supposed to be on the same bloody side."

"I'll get the med-kit." Dhana peered at Tetsuo's cut face.

"Nice friends you've got—" Tetsuo muttered, but his voice was thick and he was not sure they understood.

"Stay here." Brevan hefted a graser rifle. "I'll make sure they haven't circled back."

"But—"

"Yeah, sure. We're all Shadow People. Let then come back here—" he slapped his weapon's resonator housing "—and I'll show them a little solidarity. All right?"

Dhana said nothing. Brevan glowered, then he turned and was gone.

"Your arm's broken, I think, where you fell on it. A bruised bone, at least."

"And my ribs. Where they—ah, damn it."

She came back with a microdoc, and released his restraints by voice command.

"I wish," she said quietly, "we knew just what to do with you."

"Letting me go is out of the question, I suppose."

She looked away, with troubled eyes.

Treat her, Rafael told himself, *as though she were a Luculenta. There is danger here.*

"Would you care for a drink, Major?"

"No, thank you. This is a nice house, Luculentus de la Vega."

"Very kind of you."

The lounge was tuned to plain grey, the furniture to black, with solid silver statuettes—real, not holo—standing here and there. It was a décor, Rafael hoped, which gave away nothing of his personality.

"I hope you weren't waiting long," he added. He assumed Major Reilly's flyer had been hovering in cloud cover, awaiting his return.

He had been lounging back with his ankles crossed, and now he deliberately uncrossed them. His body language should be open rather than defensive.

"Not long," said Major Reilly.

His mind, though, was racing. How much did the proctors know? He had to find out. There was a risk, an enormous risk, but he took it.

{[[HeaderBegin: Module = Node78AF97: Type = PivotCentre: Axes = 24.

Priority = absolute

Concurrent_Execute

ThreadOne: <SatScan> ImageID = 187BK7:089, linkfile = MySelf; GlobalsSearch(Today)

ThreadTwo: <SatScan> ImageID = G18966. :003, linkfile = MyFlyer; GlobalsSearch(Today)

End_Concurrent_Execute]]}

<<<MsgRcv VEGASCN000002; cause = Query match for MySelf.>>>
<<<MsgRcv VEGASCN000002; cause = Query match for MyFlyer.>>>

He had been seen.

Trajectory maps unfurled in his mind: four-dimensional geodesics plotting his movements for the day. Privacy laws prevented continuous surveillance—except under court order—but SatScan's AIs could interpolate heuristically between random sightings.

He was taking a huge risk, infiltrating SatScan with the benefit of Tetsuo's mu-space commsware, but he had needed to know.

"I was at the Lupus Festival," he said. "You should have called me in Skein."

"That wasn't necessary." Major Reilly's tone was designed to give nothing away, but it was obvious she would rather talk in person than in Skein.

In Skein, whatever she saw would have been what Rafael wanted her to see. Here and now, in reality, he would have to make sure that the same applied.

"You're sure you wouldn't like a drink?"

"Perhaps a glass of water." A menu image grew beside her, and she selected a plain water; a glass rose up through the chair-arm's membrane. "Thank you. I gather you import tech from offworld, quite successfully."

Dangerous ground. If Rafael hadn't been on full alert before, he was now.

"Yes, that's true. I pick a niche product or expertise—offworlders can be just as effective as us, you know, in any single given field."

He watched the major stiffen slightly, as she sensed his veiled barb: how unenhanced humans might be compared to Luculenti. Point noted. He knew how to make her angry, should that become a useful ploy.

"And mu-space comms?"

"That too."

Rafael was appalled. If they knew of the uses to which he had turned mu-space comms—if they knew that, then he would be facing a team of LuxPrime specialists, Luculenti inquisitors. Not an unenhanced Fulgida proctor.

Unless they did not want to follow the obvious tactic, preferring a more subtle approach.

The girl, the girl. Don't forget the girl. It's probably just her murder they're investigating.

"I was showing some prospects, a couple of Algidiran businessmen, around the music stores in Lowtown, just this morning."

That was true, as far as it went, but he had left them to their own devices very early.

Note this: no iris contraction or muscular tension when he mentioned Lowtown. Either this Fulgida major had immense self-possession, or she was after something else.

Not Rashella, in the Inez Banlieues? He had thought his smart-atom cover was perfect. Dare he risk another search through SatScan dataseams?

"Do you know Tetsuo Sunadomari, a comms specialist?"

Worse and worse.

"Oh, yes. I haven't seen him for a tenday, or so. Is he in some kind of trouble?"

"Can you recall the last time you saw Mr. Sunadomari?"

"Yes, of course. I can download full details. Shall I?"

Major Reilly powered up her wrist terminal. "That would be very helpful."

Status displays flowed as Rafael dumped text and video logs direct from Skein.

"If there were any irregularities in our dealings," said Rafael, frowning, "I'm afraid I didn't catch them."

"This seems very comprehensive." Major Reilly killed her display. "Thank you."

"All I've omitted are the contents of copyrighted designs. If necessary, I could provide those also, under privacy safeguards."

"Thank you. Would you regard Mr. Sunadomari as a friend?"

"I'd—like to think so." Hesitation was easy to feign. Why was she questioning him about Tetsuo? "In fact—Major, I actually sponsored him for upraise."

He was watching her strong jaw muscles, the tension in her hands: no reaction, despite her feelings about Luculenti.

She knew about Tetsuo's upraise, though he had not yet been presented in Skein.

"He passed the security checks," he added. If nothing else, surely Federico would have passed him the word, if there had been anything odd in Tetsuo's background. "Quite above board."

"Yes, of course. I'm afraid Mr. Sunadomari hasn't been seen for several days. Do you have any idea of his whereabouts?"

Not seen? Something had happened to him?

"You've tried his house, of course? I can't think where else he might be."

"Have you visited him there?"

"Never. Though I have details of the location—"

"That won't be necessary."

Tension, now. The major had been there, he was sure of it. But for what purpose? And what had she found?

His skin crawled with the notion that Tetsuo might have realized just how much tech Rafael had actually pilfered, over and above their commercial agreement.

But Tetsuo could not have realized the significance of the code Rafael had stolen—

"Tetsuo has stayed here," he said, musing. "During advanced studies before upraise."

"Are there any other people he might stay with? Girlfriends?"

Rafael shook his head. "None, that I know of. He seemed quite consumed by his work."

"Seemed? Why the past tense?"

"Just a figure of speech." Rafael swallowed; his nervousness was not entirely faked. "This is serious, isn't it? You think he might be dead."

Major Reilly put down her glass. "We're just covering all possibilities." She stood up, holding out her hand.

Her grip was firm and dry, as they shook.

"By the way," she added. "Do you know a gentleman named Adam Farsteen?"

"No, I don't." Though he had heard the name, he thought, in connection with LuxPrime.

He raised a questioning eyebrow.

"Not to worry." Major Reilly nodded. "You've been a big help, sir."

He escorted her out, down the long hallway to the main doors. There, he stood on the steps and watched the three flyers lift into the night.

So Tetsuo was missing. An interesting slant to the game.

He went back into the lounge, and sat where Major Reilly had been—it was still warm from her body's touch—and sipped from her unfinished glass of water.

A vision flash: the slender girl, the young/old face, the delicate neck and the power flowing through his steel-strong fingers. The fire, then the dying light, fading in her eyes.

Pale eyes. In that regard, somewhat like the major's. But lacking the major's resolve. How would Major Reilly's eyes look, at the grand moment of death?

Yes, a very interesting slant to the game.

A fine game, indeed.

An opening, at the throat.

"*Yeee!*"

Yoshiko dropped to one knee and thrust.

Her long naginata, a narrow halberd, speared straight towards the swordsman's throat.

At the last moment, the black-clad swordsman parried with his blade, and the shock reverberated down the naginata's shaft.

Yoshiko jumped up, sidestepping and spinning, but her foot slid in the long wet grass and that was enough. She tried to recover but the swordsman beat aside her weapon and sliced back with his blade and it cut across her throat and she was dead.

Death.

The swordsman stepped back, bowed, and winked out of existence.

Damn it.

She knelt down in the grass, panting. Cold night air enveloped her sweating body, and steam rose from her bare forearms.

The lawn here was yellowish, beneath floating orange glowglobes. Outside their warmth, the night pressed blackly in.

Come on, you old fool. You'll freeze to death out here.

She undid the cord which ran behind her neck and around her upper arms, fastened across her back. Freed, her sleeves fell down to her wrists. She was wearing a white jacket and a black *hakama*, the split skirt favoured by master warriors of both genders.

Yoshiko pulled her sleeves back up, and retied the cord.

She stood, left arm outstretched, right hand holding her naginata vertically. Her back was arrow-straight, her breathing calm.

On the grass, some five metres away, a low black box hummed. It was a very special and expensive holoprocessor.

"*Hai*," she said, and a blank-faced swordsman was standing in front of her.

No expression, empty eyes. Bright curving katana sword upraised, held in a two-handed grip.

"*Hajime!*"

They attacked simultaneously. The sword's blade slid up the naginata's hilt—physical contact perfectly simulated by electromagnetic induction in the naginata's superconductors—and the blade was almost on her fingers when Yoshiko twisted away.

She spun the naginata propellor-like through a horizontal circle, covering her retreat.

The swordsman recovered composure.

They clashed again.

For ten more minutes they fought, cutting and swirling across the grass, till Yoshiko's sides ached and her legs grew leaden.

"*Yame!*"

The warrior dropped to one knee, sheathing his sword, then knelt down and sat back on his heels.

Breathing heavily, Yoshiko knelt also in the *seiza* position, laying down her naginata.

She kept *zanshin*, focussed awareness, though the fighting was over. Her holoprocessor was programmed occasionally to attack once more, at random, to ensure that awareness.

The swordsman bowed as she followed suit, palms on the ground and forehead almost touching the damp grass. As she straightened up, her enemy vanished.

She stood up, performed gentle leg stretches and rotation exercises to cool down, then resumed her kneeling position.

Mokuso! She could hear the voices of all her *bushido* instructors, every sensei she had studied under, ordering her to meditate. She closed her eyes.

Empty, empty, empty.

Clear night air. The planet beneath her, holding her firm. She was a dissipative structure, a tiny mote of far-from-equilibrium thermodynamics, a gesture in the cosmic dance, an insignificant wave function among the sum-over-everything that was the universal ocean, the Tao function.

One with the void.

And somewhere out there, Tetsuo, too, was playing his role . . .

Her eyes snapped open.

Oblivion would come. But now was not the time.

Flames danced in the black stone fireplace. They were holo, but accurate throughout IR wavelengths, and Yoshiko held out her hands, warming them.

"Here you are." Lori, carrying a tray, walked into the comfortable sitting-room. "Replenish your lost electrolytes."

"Thank you." Yoshiko drank some of the warm chocolate-flavoured liquid.

"I saw you working out." Lori took a seat on a low embroidered couch.

"I didn't wake you, did I?"

It was late, but Yoshiko's body-clock was still out of synch, and she could not sleep.

"Not at all." Firelight flickered across Lori's elegant face, and danced in golden highlights along the fibres woven in her hair. "Before you were sparring, you were performing those intricate routines, as though choreographed. What were they?"

"Kata. Traditional forms. Some people practice only kata, searching for the perfect technique."

"Very impressive." A glass of wine rose through the membrane in a low table. Lori took it, and sipped. "Would you like to demonstrate at one of our little soirées?"

Yoshiko shook her head. "I'd rather not."

"Oh, I understand. A personal discipline."

In silence, they watched the flames. Imaginary pictures roiled in them: dragons and battling *kami*—ferocious demons—and a mighty fortress. Once, a flicker of movement recalled Tetsuo's mocking smile.

Yoshiko sighed.

"I should tell you not to worry," said Lori. "That everything will turn out all right."

"You're too honest. You don't really believe that, do you?"

Lori looked into the flames. "Do we ever truly know our own children? We pretend we do, but I think it never really happens."

Yoshiko remembered her parents. Kind and loving, but somehow distant. She had always felt different from them, both hating and relishing that difference. She wished her mother were here, now, to talk to.

"Tetsuo's not a killer, Lori. I'm sure of that." She wiped the back of her hand across her damp forehead. "But how many murderers' mothers have said the same thing?"

The fireplace crackled.

"Whatever I can do to help," said Lori, "I will. If Tetsuo was mixed up in something, he might be victim as much as perpetrator."

Yoshiko blinked, vision blurring.

"You're among friends, Yoshiko."

She leaned closer to the fire, hugging herself.

No smoke stung her eyes. Perhaps only illusion could warm without causing hurt.

Chapter Twelve

Shadows strip bare
False friends, true foes. Opened fists
Cut air, but do not strike.

Black and angular shadows, carved from the absence of light, tumbled slowly: an absent-minded illusion, orbiting Rafael's head.

Tetsuo. Damn him.

[[[FunctionBegin: Module Node93BE82: Type = PivotCentre:Axes = 24.
Priority = high
Concurrent_Execute
ThreadOne: <video> ImagelD = 4001A2:001, linkfile = HoloLog.002V
ThreadTwo: QryTrace(4001A2.00l)
ThreadThree: <SkeinSearch> Locate(4001A2.001)
ThreadFour: <SkeinSearch> ThreadScan ("Sunadomari" "Tetsuo")
End_Concurrent_Execute]]]

Where the hell was he?

Tetsuo had been overstressed, overextended on his various projects. Rafael knew that. Perhaps, though, there was something more, some questionable deal Tetsuo had become involved in.

There might be no link at all to the joint venture Rafael and Tetsuo had embarked on but Rafael could not take that risk. Somehow, he would have to find Tetsuo before the proctors could, and silence him.

He smiled, and stretched luxuriously, releasing tension. The game was entering a new phase, and his next goal was clear. What more could he ask?

A year ago, arching his back like this would have hurt like hell. Then, his illegal array of seven plexcores—four more than the legal maximum—had been embedded uncomfortably within his body.

Now, liberated by Tetsuo's instantaneous mu-space comms, Rafael's mind and body were filled with easy energy.

One hundred and two plexcores, so far.

His nexus was scattered across the face of Fulgor: in the walls and grounds of his twenty-three homes—spanning seven continents—hidden in wooded groves and searing desert and rain-washed cliffs. The elements of his very mind.

It pleased him, this image of his thoughts extended over the planet's surface: a mind encompassing the world. Perhaps, one day, his organic brain would be an insignificant portion of the ageless whole, and he would truly become the god of Fulgor.

In the meantime, there were minor matters like Tetsuo to be dealt with.

Entering Skein, he floated through commerce spaces, among halls and mazes of goods, until he was holding a small bronze chest containing expensive liqueurs. He concentrated, and a card appeared, and he caused *Happy Lupus* to be written upon it in cursive script.

He pictured an ideogram.

[[Luculenta Sylvia Alhendra, ident 8799Φ7•ϵ {sept3ΠΩ}]]

He pointed, and the bronze chest vanished. Turning away, he exited Skein.

Back in his grey lounge, he waited. The physical delivery of his gift would take a few minutes.

<<<MsgRcv LUCCOM213886; cause = SkeinLink requested.>>>

"That was quick. Go ahead, Sylvia."

<<<MsgRcv LUCCOM213887; cause = SkeinLink established.>>>

His grey room gave way to a broad marble deck, edged with wide columns, and a sapphire swimming pool.

Sylvia Alhendra was seated on a stone bench, her ankles tucked demurely to one side. Her long tanned legs formed a stunning contrast to her white robe.

"Rafael. Thank you for the liqueurs. Northern Mist is my favourite."

<<text: ??lots??of??questions??>>
<<audio: Purely a social call?>>

Sylvia's icon within a SkeinLink session was security within security: an encrypted linkage embedded in the shared illusion of their conversation, itself encrypted and visible only to another Luculentus who was specifically tagged in.

"Of course." Rafael smiled, with only a hint of irony. "For a lady of your sophistication, what else might it be?"

Simultaneously, he <sent>:

<<<video: Tetsuo Sunadomari, walking along a boulevard>>>
<<<text: ident is 4001A2.001>>>

"You flatter me, sir. Was there any matter in particular you wished to discuss?"

Her real reply was:

<<text1: Stargonier, a merchant, asked me about this Sunadomari.>>
<<olfactory: cheese, exceedingly mature>>
<<audio: Something rotten in the state of Lucis?>>
<<text2: Financial history for Tetsuo Sunadomari is appended.>>

"Not at all. I just wanted to keep in touch."

Rafael smiled tightly, as he <received> the appended file.

<<<MsgRcv LUCCOM213778; cause = SkeinLink Intuitive-Dump received.>>>

In a side room of his awareness, Rafael opened the file and saw that it contained, as promised, all of Tetsuo's financial records since his arrival on Fulgor, five standard years before.

"Rafael, when are you coming to Novalendra next? We could meet for dinner."

Novalendra was one of his favourite cities.

"Sometime soon," he promised.

She was attractive, but he would never compromise his relationship with the one contact who could get inside the Skein's secure banking dataseams.

"Of course. Take care."

The swimming pool and marble deck vanished.

<<<MsgRcv LUCCOM213900; cause = SkeinLink revoked.>>>

"That's interesting," said Rafael.

In Skein, a ghost-Rafael floated among a waiting line of beautiful wraithlike beings, over a bottomless violet space, alongside white marble columns. In the distance, an immense pane of crystal rotated and hummed deep music of Platonic purity.

The ghost-Rafael was a NetAngel: a semi-autonomous agent created from Rafael's mind, queuing for a comms window through a mu-space gateway to EveryWare.

Meanwhile, Rafael browsed again through Tetsuo's records. They showed little concern for future security, but Tetsuo did not spend significantly more than he earned. His royalties on mu-space commsware patents brought in a steady income. His consultancy was lucrative by many—non-Luculenti—standards.

The interesting snippet was Tetsuo's EveryWare ident, and the access codes for hyperlink to the Terran nodes. Hence the queuing ghost, in Skein.

Access. A timeslot was available.

Text and images flowed past as Rafael, conjoined with his ghost, entered the Terran NetEnv, a substratum of EveryWare. An infojunkyard, its skeletal underpinnings and rusty protocols painfully slow to the sophisticated mind.

In classic FourSpeak, a text-tesseract described Tetsuo's childhood psych report. A fascination with logic puzzles. On one occasion, a successful infotheft committed on the school's NetNode, discovered only by accident.

Tetsuo's psych potentials were higher, much higher, than his academic actuals.

Interesting . . .

<<<MsgRcv NETCOM0008900; cause = object contention; access is revoked.>>>

Proctors.

Heart thumping, Rafael backed out of his enquiry, checking lock-tables and removing his traces.

Even in the cold primitive Terran NetEnv, it took a court order to override object locks. In Skein, he would have been trapped; here, letting his awareness sink to the nuts-and-bolts lower levels, it was easy enough to remove all traces of his presence. Every table, every log, was open to his infiltration code.

Shuddering, he withdrew, flew back into Skein, and exited to reality.

He blinked. His grey room, the silver statuettes, were solid and steadying.

The proctors were investigating Tetsuo.

Tetsuo had a history of infotheft.

What has he stolen?

Icy coldness dripped along Rafael's spine. While he had subverted Tetsuo's code to hold together his vast nexus of plexcores, could Tetsuo have played a similar trick on him? Could he, when he stayed in this house, have accessed a development copy of Rafael's infiltration code, his vampire modules?

If Tetsuo had merely guessed the size of Rafael's nexus, that was bad enough. Whatever Tetsuo had figured out, if LuxPrime investigators became involved then the rest would follow.

The conclusion was inescapable.

In Skein, a host of NetAngels sprang into being, a thousand ghost-Rafaels haunting the splendid halls and the darkest spaces of Skein, questing pitilessly.

Tetsuo, my lone and lonely prey.

I will find you.

Dhana offered him a plate of soft warm morsels, something like mallows. Tetsuo took the plate, and looked suspiciously at the food.

"Don't worry. It's perfectly safe."

She popped a piece into her own mouth and closed her eyes in exaggerated ecstasy.

Tetsuo laughed.

"Vat-grown," Dhana added. "Very good for you."

Involuntarily, he glanced out the window. In his mind's eye, he could still see the two intruders performing their butchery.

"Ah, that's what's bothering you."

"It wasn't very pleasant. But how can people eat non-Terran life-forms with so little processing? It's not possible."

Dhana shrugged slightly. "It is. But, unlike the Agrazzi, we merely use their secretions as inputs to the autofacts."

Tetsuo put down the morsel he had been about to eat.

"Secretions?"

"Don't worry about it."

Later, after Dhana had finished some sort of work in her quarters, she came back in to talk to Tetsuo.

"Your headaches have gone, now?"

"I'm not concussed." Tetsuo paused. "I'm always this mad."

Dhana sat down, keeping her distance. She glanced back at the door to Brevan's quarters.

"I don't think," said Tetsuo, "that he likes me very much."

"He doesn't have reason to. Many of us don't."

"I'm sorry?"

Dhana looked at him for a long while.

"I remember, when I was girl—" Her eyes grew distant. "—travelling on a shuttle car with my parents. We were going to visit a relative, who had been injured in strike riots the tenday before."

Tetsuo shifted uncomfortably, not sure where this was leading.

"Only one of the NewsNets, the old ProtectorChannel, had reported it in anything like an unbiased fashion. The rest had focussed on the destruction of property."

"You know what they're like."

"Yes, I do. Do you? Anyway, there were two Luculenti on the shuttle, factory owners slumming it, flying in to survey the damage."

"Oh." Tetsuo could imagine; at their worst, Luculenti could be insufferable.

"They were laughing about the ProtectorChannel reporter, saying he must have been the only reporter who wasn't actually there, just rehashing tired sociology texts."

"Some people—"

"It was those nasal accents, and their complete indifference, the way it was all some amusing anecdote, while my uncle lay dying in a med-centre because the authorities had sent in TacTeams instead of negotiators." She let out a long, shaky breath. "I didn't see the violence at first hand. But I didn't need to. I haven't forgotten."

"They're not all like that." Tetsuo wished, as soon as he had spoken, that he had worded it a little differently. "Luculenti, I mean."

Dhana looked at him oddly

"No," she said eventually. "I suppose you're right."

A copper sea broke endlessly across a blue fractal shore, while lazy birds flapped by overhead.

Yoshiko checked the signature: Lori Maximilian.

She looked back along the gallery. In this section, the works showed a steady evolution from hard geometric realism to elegiac landscapes. The earlier holos were signed Dorian Maximilian, the later by Lori.

Had it not been for the signatures, Yoshiko would have sworn they had all been created by the same mind.

She continued walking. The carpet strip did not flow for her, as it had for Vin, but that gave Yoshiko time to examine the marvels of Lori's house.

From a side corridor with high, arching ceilings, a clear soprano sang out.

Her voice climbed a complex scale, rippling with nuances Yoshiko strained to catch, ending in a sour, off-key note.

"Damn." The voice was Vin's. "Let's start eight bars back."

Yoshiko followed the angelic voice. She would never have guessed that Vin could sing so sweetly.

She turned another corner, and found herself at the entrance to the great hall where Lori had carved her statue of Diana.

The statue was draped in canvas; the laser array hung lifelessly above it.

Vin sang.

A choir grew into being all around her. Vin was part of a semi-circle of Luculenti boys and girls; in front of them, conducting, stood a tall Luculenta. She was Mediterranean-dark, dressed in a baggy white trouser suit.

The laser array high in the groined ceiling glowed with life; no doubt this was generating the holo choir below.

Yoshiko was impressed: a hi-res array powerful enough to carve stone, but intricate enough to create images which looked perfectly real, even in the daylight which poured through the high windows.

The other singers, Yoshiko guessed, were in their own homes or elsewhere, participating in realtime in this choir practice.

The song built to a sweet climax, and the voices softly died away.

"Very nice," said the Luculenta, and she applauded the grinning singers, as a thousand pairs of disembodied hands appeared around her, clapping also.

Yoshiko, who had been standing rapt, joined in the applause. When it suddenly stopped, she clapped twice more then stopped, embarrassed.

One by one, the singers winked out of existence, until only Vin and the tall Luculenta remained.

"Hi, Yoshiko. This is Xanthia Delaggropos, our choir mistress."

"Pleased to meet you, Yoshiko."

The illusion was staggering. If Yoshiko had not seen Xanthia's image appear, she would have assumed that she was here in person.

"I'm honoured. That was very beautiful."

"Oh, no." Humour danced in Xanthia's dark eyes. "Though it may grow acceptable, if certain singers practice their deci-tones and breathing."

Vin covered her eyes in mock despair.

"The guilty parties," added Xanthia, "know just who they are."

Yoshiko laughed.

It felt good. She hadn't laughed for such a long time.

"I'm sorry your visit's not been a happy one."

Xanthia, too, had that uncanny knack of almost reading thoughts.

Yoshiko sighed inwardly, as Xanthia and Vin stared at each other. There must be a high-bandwidth infoflow between them. What wonders must a Luculenta experience!

"The proctors," said Xanthia, holding Vin's gaze, "assuming Tetsuo's culpability, may not backtrack among the optimum inference chains." She looked at Yoshiko. "Your son was overextended, on nine parallel projects."

Vin looked as though she were going to interrupt, but stopped herself.

Yoshiko understood: nine overlapping projects were child's play for a Luculenta, but not for anyone else.

"These two people, Fulgidi merchants," Xanthia continued, "have the largest stake in Tetsuo's ventures."

Two static disembodied heads appeared: a lean, grey-haired man, and a redheaded woman.

"Sylvester Stargonier and Elizabeth Malone."

"I know him." Yoshiko pointed. "He called me, on my first morning here, looking for Tetsuo."

"That was pretty sharp of him," said Vin. "Sorry, Yoshiko."

Xanthia waved the holos out of existence. "They're the place to start, then."

"To start?" Yoshiko was puzzled.

"Our investigation," said Xanthia.

Silvery ripples passed over Brevan's grim bearded face: reflections from the holo's shifting infoscans.

Tetsuo shifted his couch to see more, and Brevan started at the sound, hand flying to the graser pistol at his waist.

"Sorry." Tetsuo swallowed.

Brevan merely glared, then turned back to his work.

Tetsuo sighed. "You're holding me here. We might as well talk."

"Shut up," muttered Brevan, intent on the display.

"Maybe I could help you with your analysis."

Tetsuo's heart beat faster as Brevan slowly took out his pistol.

Yellow and red reflections played across the transmission surface. It was the first time Tetsuo had ever seen the business end of an energy weapon. He didn't want it to be his final memory.

"Maybe I could help you keep quiet." Brevan's voice was soft.

Tetsuo nodded, throat tight. He closed his eyes in relief as Brevan returned the pistol to its sticky-tag on his belt.

If only Dhana would return. Tetsuo pulled back his sleeve, checking the colour of the med-insert which Dhana had fixed onto his forearm. Blue had almost entirely given way to green: the healing process was well advanced.

He lay back on the couch, avoiding any twisting motion which would set off the pain in his ribs.

Chess. He tried to visualize a chess board; this was one of the visualizations he practised. For once, it came surprisingly easy.

Light glinted on the polished grainy surface, on the solid chessmen.

King's Gambit, he thought, and suddenly the game was flowing, pieces jumping fast as lightning, and he was both opponents fighting desperately as the endgame appeared and Black won, barely.

Fascinating.

Brevan's presence was quite forgotten now.

Three chessboards appeared in his mind. Each game began, as before, with the King's Gambit, but the topologies rapidly diverged until six scheming opponents, all fragments of Tetsuo's mind, were warring furiously, and again the end-games came in no time at all.

Chess, of course, was easy.

The boards disappeared, replaced by a disembodied grid of 104 by 104 lines. Two porcelain bowls appeared, one filled with white stones, the other with black.

A stone rose from Black's bowl, and clacked into place on a strategic intersection of the grid.

White replied.

Soon black and white armies swirled across the *go* board: fractal outreachings into enemy territory, impenetrable "eyes" of stones around blank nodes, minor skirmishes and major campaigns. Suddenly, the balance tipped in White's favour and the game whirled to completion.

Shuddering, tasting the joy of White's victory and the bitterness of Black's defeat, Tetsuo withdrew to reality.

The cabin was deserted.

Darkness, outside. Flashes of light. In the holding-pens, Brevan and Dhana were inspecting their herd of native lifeforms.

Groaning, Tetsuo levered himself off the couch. There was a distant twinge of pain in his ribs, but his arm was completely healed already. Very sophisticated femtocyte inserts. Just what you'd want for medical emergencies, far from human assistance.

He could get out, now.

Measuring angles, he carefully aligned the couch, so that its end was towards the outer door. If he could run with the couch, leap onto it as it passed through the smartatom film and the door membrane itself, then momentum should carry him through.

Unless there was a recognition-lock, and the door membrane remained hardened. Then he would just be stuck inside the room, lying on the couch with his restraint bracelets snapped together as before.

A shadow passed the window.

Tetsuo moved hurriedly back, and sat down just as Brevan stormed in through the door. Had he and Dhana been arguing?

Glistening membranes retracted into Brevan's eye sockets, nostrils and mouth. "So you don't need resp-masks, after all." Tetsuo spoke without thinking.

Brevan glared at him.

"You used the term "Shadow People" earlier, when you chased off the Agrazzi. How many of you are there? Dozens? Tens of thousands?"

The latter, Tetsuo thought, watching Brevan's eyes. *Possibly more.*

Amazing. All these people, living in the hypozone.

"And you must have sympathizers in the SatScan hierarchy. You all live permanently here in the hypozone. No one's camouflage is that good for long periods. Your presence must be something of an open secret."

"Keep talking, Luculentus." Brevan rested his hand on his pistol butt. "Give me an excuse for getting rid of you."

"So you're not autonomous? You need to justify yourself to your superiors?"

Brevan turned away, and stamped off, cursing, through the door which led to his own quarters.

Tetsuo's heart pounded. How could he play such a risky game?

But Brevan wasn't here, and that was what he wanted.

He caught sight of his reflection in the dark window: large and rotund, not a warrior at all. Not like his mother.

A whisper of sound. Dhana's hand pierced the outer door's membrane.

With desperate strength, Tetsuo picked up the couch and charged as though with a battering-ram, straight for the door.

"Hey!"

As the couch struck the glimmering film, he dived onto it and momentum carried him through the door membrane, slamming Dhana aside, and then it stopped.

Shock rang through him as the bracelets snapped together, jarring his bones.

Acid in his throat, fire in his lungs.

He couldn't breathe.

It should have been laughable, him lying here with head and shoulders poking outside through the solidifying door membrane, but this atmosphere was not designed for Terran organisms to breathe.

"Damn you."

Her hands were on his collar, tugging him back inside.

A fit of coughing shook him, and his chest was burning, as the bracelets freed themselves and he staggered into the cabin and fell.

Dhana's hand was pushing into his face, and suddenly something cold and liquid forced itself into his throat and down to his chest. It pulsed inside him.

Tetsuo was drowning.

He rolled over, coughing out smartgel, until all of it had exited from his lungs and gathered into a pool on the floor.

"You're lucky we had this stuff ready," said Dhana.

At that moment, Brevan, roused from his study, came in.

"OK, you bastard." Brevan grabbed Tetsuo's collar, and twisted it into a stranglehold. "I warned you."

"Outside—"

"What? Ah!" He pushed Tetsuo away in disgust, as Dhana forced a hand between them.

"My head—" Tetsuo coughed again. "My head—was outside."

"What?"

Dhana's voice was very low. "He's right."

"Oh, really."

Suddenly, Brevan threw back his head and laughed.

"Oh, really," he said again.

Dhana looked startled. "If he's accessed Skein, there'll be proctors or a TacTeam here before you know it."

"No, I don't think so." Brevan wiped his hands across his eyes, as though brushing away tears of laughter. "Not for this one."

"For God's sake, Brevan. We've got to get out of here. He was outside the null-sheet."

The pain in Tetsuo's chest slowly subsided. He was as surprised by Brevan's behaviour as Dhana, but had no breath to speak.

"Fat lot of good it did him." Brevan chuckled. "I've got to hand it to you, boy. That was a nice bluff."

Another fit of coughing seized Tetsuo.

"—because this one," Brevan was saying, "is an Earther boy. Aren't you, Mr. Sunadomari?"

"He can't be." Dhana's eyes were round with surprise.

Tetsuo looked at her.

"Upraise." A wheeze sounded in his chest, embarrassing him. "Just had—the op."

"Just as I said." Brevan chuckled. "Got more balls than I thought."

Dhana was furious. "You mean you can't access Skein?"

"Don't know how." Tetsuo shook his head. "Haven't a clue."

Brevan laughed again.

Dhana, exasperated, looked from him to Tetsuo.

"Then why did you risk your bloody life, sticking your head outside?"

Tetsuo did not reply.

"If we'd cleared out," Dhana continued, "we'd have left surveillance. No proctors would have turned up, and we'd know the truth."

"Then I'd have said—" Tetsuo sighed, his chest feeling almost normal again. "I'd have said, you could trust me, because I hadn't called the proctors when I could have."

"Very subtle," said Brevan, grinning.

"I'm glad I've amused you."

Afterwards, Brevan removed Tetsuo's restraints. Dhana watched silently from the corner of the room.

"So you do trust me," muttered Tetsuo.

"I trust you not to access Skein." Brevan smirked.

"Fine. Aren't you going to tell me about your philosophy of life? Living in harmony with the wilderness, isn't that what you believe in?"

There must be more, obviously, but Tetsuo had not figured it out yet. The Shadow People's presence must really be an open secret, yet he had never heard of them.

Brevan shook his head. "You wouldn't be interested."

He could guess: they had settled the hypozone, to live according to their own ways, away from what they saw as Luculenti oppression. On the other hand—

"You must have Luculenti supporters." Tetsuo looked at Dhana, who seemed ready to protest. "Otherwise, you see, Brevan wouldn't have known about my upraise."

"Not that he bothered to tell me."

"I might have guessed it," said Brevan, "from your short haircut, and the healing where the headpiece is connected. If you look closely, your scalp's quite scabby."

"Thanks. But you didn't just guess it."

"Maybe not." Brevan turned to Dhana. "You didn't want him trussed up. He's your responsibility now."

"My responsibility?"

"After all the excitement, he probably needs a hearty supper."

"Then he can get it his bloody self, can't he?"

Dhana glared at both of them, then stormed out of the room.

"Bloody hell," said Tetsuo.

"Just what I was thinking."

"Thanks for getting rid of those things." Tetsuo pointed at the restraint bracelets.

"You're welcome. Oh, and by the way—"

"Yes?"

"Those balls you've just demonstrated you've got—" Brevan drew his pistol very fast, and smiled. "—I wouldn't want to shoot them right off, because you'd done something stupid."

"Ah, no." Tetsuo breathed out, a long shaky breath. "Let's try to avoid that."

Brevan returned his pistol to his belt.

"Supper's in the autofact. Help yourself."

Chapter Thirteen

> Visiting old graves:
> Childish screams, white-haired heads shake.
> Who will stay longest?

Trap. Subtle bastard.

A web of network diagrams modelled the key relationships. In Skein, Rafael pointed at a node and grasped it, sending his offer price.

He subverted his opponent's strategy by buying out a key supplier three levels along the chain. In seconds, he turned the share-price movement around; within a minute he controlled seventy-three percent of his opponent's stock and shut him down.

Not bad.

There was no time to relax. Two more opportunities appeared, and he went for them simultaneously.

Rafael, immersed in the icy cool flow of financial info, swimming among the icebergs of corporate dataseams, doubled and redoubled his gains. In small display volumes, matching his movements like pilot fish, pulsing intention-indicators mapped the intricate strategies of his Luculenti opponents and partners.

He played this game at the highest level, where double- and triple-cross were not unknown, where business alliances might last only seconds, or less. The trick was to become one with the vast flow of planetary wealth, that cold turbulent sea where even the minnows had to be observed lest they turn suddenly into sharks, and where Rafael was the most cunning shark of all.

A new display volume blossomed beside him.

<<<MsgRcv LUCC0M213886 cause = SkeinLink requested.>>>

The ident was unknown to him.

((text: I'm a Terran journalist. Might I have word with you?))

The (text) was prepared by a public-access terminal.

Rafael crushed the display volume in his fist, and shards of code flew apart in Skein.

Why would a Terran journo want to talk to me?

Rapidly, he concluded a rapid series of mergers and takeovers and long-term investments, while he formed a group of NetAngels and sent them searching through immigration tables, for any attributes of the caller's ident code.

Almost immediately, one returned with a name: Maggie Brown.

Ah, yes. The Terran woman he had met at the conference centre. The one who had been interviewing Rashella.

Interesting.

More info came flooding in. The Earther woman had a child, here on Fulgor.

If he needed leverage, there was her weak point.

Still in Skein, smiling now, he willed a real-time comm session with Maggie Brown, and she accepted and came on-line.

Quickly, Rafael constructed a virtual room, a green old-fashioned study, and caused his own ghost-image to lean back in a deep black leather chair.

"I must apologize," he said smoothly through his ghost. "I was in the middle of some delicate financial dealings when you called. I beg your pardon."

"Not at all. Thank you for coming back to me." She hid her surprise well, for an Earther.

"You were covering the Skein conference. Has it been going well?"

He completed another merger, while awaiting her reply.

"Boring as hell," she said. "But, you know, I didn't expect it to be riveting."

"Not a chance, I'm afraid." Rafael laughed. "So, can I help you with some background info? Or the views of the ordinary Luculentus-in-the-street? Though there are at least four major viewpoints on the connectivity issue, I have to say."

"From Earth's point of view, they're details. Regardless of the type of access, Skein's going to become more available to EveryWare, and that's news."

"I think you're probably right."

"I was thinking," said Maggie, "of a more human story, of interest back home."

"To do with Skein?"

"To do with offworld trade, to a small extent—"

"Offworld trade? I do enter into joint ventures, occasionally, with offworld companies. I don't believe in a closed economy."

"Me neither," said Maggie. "I believe you know Tetsuo Sunadomari."

All of Rafael's senses swung to full alert.

In the background, he shut down all his tasks and withdrew completely from the financial strata of Skein.

"Yes, I know him." He went with his intuition. "Ah—I'm not supposed to say this, but I sponsored him for upraise to Luculentus status."

"Upraise? To Luculentus status?"

Nice try.

In Skein, he could make his ghost assume any physical characteristics he chose. But Maggie Brown's image was fed from a terminal input, and he could read the minutiae of her body language, zoom in on her eyes, on the muscular tension in her face.

She already knew about Tetsuo's upraise.

Therefore, she had Luculentus—or Luculenta—help.

Nothing to do with Rashella: she had not known of Tetsuo's upraise. He knew that, for Rashella's memories, subsumed within his own, were quite clear upon that point.

"It's possible for an offworlder to undergo the so-called upraise operation—although there's more to it than a simple piece of surgery, of course—if they fulfil the requirements. And if they have a sponsor."

"And that was you, in this case?"

"Oh, yes. I'd like to think Tetsuo is my friend."

"Is?" Maggie's expression was intent. "Does that mean you know where he is?"

"No . . . I haven't seen him for a tenday, or so."

"Do you know where he might be?"

"No, I'm afraid not." He smiled. "The proctors asked me that as well."

Maggie raised an eyebrow, and he wondered if he should have given her that piece of info. He had just told her, implicitly, that he knew of Tetsuo's disappearance, and realized that she did, too. Would his candour make her more or less suspicious?

Was he being too subtle for an Earther?

"Listen," he added. "I interrupted my business to make time for this chat."

"I appreciate it," Maggie said quickly. "If you could just spare a couple more minutes—"

"I was going to suggest, perhaps you could come over here in person. Have you had lunch yet?"

"Ah. No."

"I'll send my flyer for you. Where are you staying?"

He already knew perfectly well: one of his NetAngels had returned with that information.

"The Bright Lights hotel, at the conference centre."

"I know it. If I send the flyer to arrive in, say, twenty minutes?"

"OK," said Maggie. "Thank you. That would be great."

"My pleasure." He constructed one of his most charming smiles. "By the way, the flyer will be unmanned. I don't believe in employing servants, you see."

"Oh. Good."

"I look forward to seeing you again." He returned to reality.

His lounge was still tuned to a grey and silver, somewhat cubist décor. He liked its clean strength, but perhaps something softer would put his luncheon guest at ease.

Slipping into direct command mode, he caused the floor to rearrange itself. In the centre, a low well appeared, ringed by shallow steps.

He looked at the walls, and willed them to a deep orange. Indirect lighting spread from floor and ceiling.

The carpet became a sea of warm browns and oranges, in which tiny yellow mandelbrots slowly swam.

From his image library, some classic holo sculptures completed the room.

Perfect.

Poor, plain Maggie. Unused to all this luxury.

He would do his best to make her feel very special. If that failed, then he would make use of her child's, young Jason's, vulnerability.

Whichever way the meeting went, he would be ready for her.

It nibbled her fingers.

The day was warm, and Yoshiko trailed her hand over the boat's edge, enjoying the cool feel of the water. Huge goldfish drew close, and the touch of their lips was feather-soft. Opposite her, lounging on the boat's other bench seat, Xanthia Delaggropos sipped from a fruit cocktail.

The boat, canopied against the sun, drifted languidly.

The slow, dark river, bedecked with floating lilies and bankside rushes, wound through the gardens of Xanthia's house. Beside them, a weeping welig-tree, bright with scarlet catkins, trailed so low it almost touched the placid water.

Yoshiko sighed.

"I suppose I'm ready. Are you sure we shouldn't see them in person?"

"I'm sure." Xanthia smiled gently. "A lot of the Fulgidi merchants, the successful ones, try to conduct all their business through holo. It does save time . . . but the real reason is, they imagine it's more like the way Luculenti work, in Skein."

"Oh," said Yoshiko.

"They won't see me. The viewfield ends around here." Xanthia's fingers sketched a wide vertical circle in the air. "They'll see just you, and the boat and surroundings up to half a metre in front of you, and a long view to the rear as a backdrop."

"OK. I understand."

A hatch slid back in the bottom of the boat, revealing a powerful holoprojector.

"Elizabeth Malone is a mother, with two children," said Xanthia. "Shall we try her first? She may be the more sympathetic."

Yoshiko nodded.

"She's responding to our call." Xanthia's eyes held a slightly unfocussed look. "OK, here we go."

It was startling.

Though Yoshiko knew she was really on the boat, Xanthia disappeared from sight.

Instead, a stark room grew into being in front of Yoshiko.

The room was composed of walls and columns of glass of varying hues, pale ambers and wine-dark reds and greens. Behind a blue glass desk sat a pale woman. Her reddish hair was pulled back into a tight bun.

"I'm Malone." The woman looked severe. Not a trace of sunlight leaked through, though the sun lay behind the holo image. "This is about the twenty-third layer protocol project, I take it?"

"In a way." Yoshiko cleared her throat. "It's more to do with my son, Tetsuo."

"You've a plan to make reparations for our losses? If this continues, we're going to lose the contract."

"As you may know, my son hasn't been seen for several days. I was hoping you could tell me about him, whether he seemed upset, or—"

"Our relationship was purely commercial. Our contract was negotiated in good faith, and there were no indications that anything untoward might cause slippage."

"Yes, but if we find him, we can sort this out. I know nothing of his business."

"Then there's little to discuss. Has he been reported missing? Are the authorities looking for him?"

"Well, yes."

"Then I'll assume the proctors can do the job we pay them for. Good day. Out."

The room disappeared.

Xanthia leaned forward and touched the back of Yoshiko's hand.

"I'm sorry. That was rough."

Yoshiko shook her head. "I'm OK."

"Shall we take a break before the next call?"

"No," said Yoshiko. "This is the man who called me, Sylvester Stargonier?"

"That's right." Again, Xanthia assumed a distant look. "Connecting now."

The boat wheeled under a tree's shadow as another room grew into being before Yoshiko. In the shade, the room glowed perhaps a little too brightly. All the same, Yoshiko felt she could just step forwards and she would be in Stargonier's office.

Lean and handsome, he lounged beside a desk. Behind, a red

desertscape was visible through a picture window. Soft eerie pipe music played in the background.

"Thank you for seeing me," she said.

"No problem." Stargonier ran a hand through his longish grey hair. "In fact I owe you an apology."

Yoshiko shook her head.

"Oh, yes." Stargonier frowned. "When I called you at the spaceport hotel, you'd just arrived on Fulgor. Then I gave you an earful about your son, when you must have been worried sick."

"I was—I *am* worried. That's true."

"I'm sorry. I had my own concerns, but that's no excuse."

"That's quite all right. I understand."

Stargonier smiled grimly. "I just had a message, an infoburst, from Elizabeth."

From Malone? That was quick.

"I gather the proctors are looking for Tetsuo? That he's really disappeared?"

"I'm afraid so," said Yoshiko.

Stargonier looked away. "Maybe Elizabeth and I were pushing him too hard to complete on time."

"Was he very stressed?"

"Yes, I'd say so." He looked up at the ceiling, or possibly at the sky on Yoshiko's side, and thought. "He didn't look physically ill. Stressed, but not to breaking point, I wouldn't have said."

"How much was riding on this project?"

"A fair amount, though nothing I couldn't recover from in a pinch. I can't speak for Elizabeth, you understand."

"Of course. Were there any friends he might have gone to, if he were in trouble?"

Stargonier shook his head slowly. "Sorry, Mrs. Sunadomari. I—had the impression of a man with few friends. It can be tough for outsiders, here."

Yoshiko tried not to think about that.

"What about his other projects? I gather he had several things on the go at once."

"Nothing, ah, crucial," said Stargonier. "As far as I know. Here you are—"

He gestured as a control volume grew to his right, and there was a beeping sound.

A small icon appeared to float by Yoshiko's wrist: an in-basket with a sheaf of paper.

"—I've sent you what details I know. But I don't think you'll find anything there."

"Thank you." Yoshiko did not know what else to say.

Stargonier looked at her. "I can't think of anything more I can do to help."

"No, you've been a big help. Thank you."

"Er, you understand, I'll have to dissolve the contract and subcontract Tetsuo's design work to someone else?"

Yoshiko breathed out slowly. "I'm sure it's what he'd expect."

"But I will have more work to send his way. I hope everything turns out OK."

There was a sudden movement near the bottom of the boat, where it melded into the floor of Stargonier's office, and Yoshiko started.

A small text volume appeared.

WHAT ABOUT TETSUO'S REPLACEMENT?

Thank you, Xanthia.

Yoshiko nodded as the text faded. Stargonier had noticed nothing. The image had been directional, constructed for Yoshiko, a prompt for her eyes only.

"Can you find someone else to replace Tetsuo?"

"Well, yes." Stargonier looked unhappy. "I'm afraid I already have, though we haven't activated the agreement yet."

"Oh. May I ask who it is?"

"Yes. Pierre d'Androux, a local man, very successful. This is quite a small task for his group. He's really doing it as a favor."

That didn't sound like someone desperate to get the business which Tetsuo had lined up. It certainly wasn't a likely motive for murder.

Adam Farsteen's death had not been mentioned anywhere on the NewsNets or even in Skein, according to Vin and Xanthia—so Yoshiko had better not mention it, either.

"This man, d'Androux. He owes you a favor?" she asked.

"Well, no. There was some brokerage involved. I've got to pay commission to a man called Rafael de la Vega, for finding someone with mu-space comms tech skills I can use. D'Androux owed de la Vega, so I gather."

Yoshiko sighed. Perhaps Tetsuo's upraise sponsor, Rafael, was merely helping his protégé. Nothing suspicious in that.

Perhaps she owed a debt of gratitude to this Rafael.

"I'm sorry." Stargonier's voice intruded. "None of this helps, does it?"

It might. She just didn't know.

"You've been very kind," she said. "Thank you very much."

"OK, look. If there's anything else I can do, just call me."

"I will. Thank you."

"Good luck," said Stargonier. "Out."

He and his office disappeared.

Yoshiko blinked, disconcerted, as she realized she was on Xanthia's boat and had been here all the time, its gentle rocking forgotten during her conversation. There was a flash of blue by the riverbank as a kingfisher dived to feed.

"Rafael de la Vega," said Yoshiko. "His name's come up again. But it may mean nothing."

"That was very nicely handled." Xanthia leaned forward in her seat. "You should have been a Luculenta."

Yoshiko, startled, almost blushed. "Why, thank you."

The research station was a stack of tiered concrete discs, piled up against a rocky outcrop.

Twelve days ago, thought Tetsuo, *I was stuck in my office at home, working on Stargonier's damned protocol converter. Now look at me. A manual labourer.*

Puffing, he staggered down the twisted path with a ten-litre container in each hand. The farther he walked, the heavier they seemed to grow. No pain from his earlier injuries. If only his grip were stronger . . .

Sweat trickled down inside his resp-mask. His forehead itched, despite the smartgel which covered all of his otherwise exposed skin.

Another klick to go. He stumbled, but caught himself before falling.

Watch it.

The narrow handles were digging grooves into his hands. He stopped for a short rest.

OK, pick 'em up. Carry on.

He almost tripped again, but recovered his stride, and continued across the caramel-coloured broken rock. The cabin was dead ahead.

He stumbled through the doorway. Panting, he lugged the containers past Brevan's door, to the feed tank's input valves. Awkwardly, he tipped the brown foul-smelling liquid out of each container in turn. Then he gratefully sealed the caps, and the stench faded.

Brevan was in his small study-bedroom, running projections of possible forced mutations in their native stock. Tetsuo leaned against the door jamb to watch.

Brevan froze the display. "Slacking off?"

"Need the rest," said Tetsuo.

"It'll get you fit."

"I've lost three point two seven kilos in three days." Tetsuo wiped sweat from his face. "I'm exhausted."

"Oh, right." Brevan smiled. "Very precise."

Tetsuo had spoken without thinking; the knowledge of his bodyweight was an intuitive fact, another example of the changes taking place inside him. Let Brevan think he had used the lab scales to weigh himself.

"If I were to ask you about the Agrazzi," said Tetsuo, "would that be one of the things that might make you shoot me?"

The two men who had tried to kill him were Agrazzi, but just what did that mean? A different clan, tribe, among the Shadow People?

"Depends on what you ask." There was a glint in Brevan's eye. "Go on. Shoot."

Tetsuo winced. "Well how many, ah, groups, cells, whatever, are there?"

"A little over two hundred," said Brevan. "Some of the bigger septs have tens of thousands of members."

Tens of thousands? Just among the Agrazzi? But they were just one group among the Shadow People, weren't they? One group among how many?

"How long has this movement been going on?"

"Oh, come," said Brevan. "You've heard of the Shadow People, haven't you?"

"No," said Tetsuo. "Or—Yes, in a bar once. Something about . . . Ghost Folk?"

"An old name for the movement. You thought it was all native ghost tales, I'll bet."

"But the Ghost Folk are an old story, a century old at least."

Brevan said nothing.

"Oh. I see." After a pause, Tetsuo added, "So why were the Agrazzi raiding this place?"

"Ah, now." Brevan's expression grew bitter. "Seems like those bastards have always been raiding our Simnalari camps. We've been lucky when it's just been a few animals they've stolen."

Simnalari. So that's what Brevan and Dhana called themselves.

"The Agrazzi need the food, is that it?"

"No. Well, sometimes . . . Oh, hell. Look, you understand that we can only settle in the upper reaches of the hypozone?"

"That makes sense."

At lower altitudes, extremes of temperature and pressure and wild chemistry began to dominate.

"So watch." Brevan waved away his current display and caused a globe of Fulgor to appear. Small red blobs dotted its surface, with surrounding loops and whorls of blue. "Red represents the terraformed altitudes, and the blue shows the hypozone."

"Five percent of the planet's surface." The acid seas, and the hyper- and epizones, were shaded in grey. No one could live there.

"Very good. Now, originally there were a hundred and fifty councils formed among the Shadow People—or Ghost Folk—as we were then all of equal status."

"A century ago."

"Longer," said Brevan. "The Simnalari and Agrazzi councils were two of the original members of the Shadow League, the league of councils."

Tetsuo did not smile at the childish name. He guessed that turmoil and violence had grown out of this league.

"It's territory, you see." Brevan looked at the slowly rotating globe-image. "It's always been the land."

"War?" asked Tetsuo.

"At times, yes," said Brevan. "In the very early days, the Agrazzi sent in troopers, heavily armed by Shadow standards, and annexed all the Simnalari territory."

There was a cloud across Brevan's features. If any of his family had suffered then, thought Tetsuo, it must have been generations ago.

"Why didn't the concept of Simnalari just disappear?" asked Tetsuo. "Why aren't you all just Agrazzi now?"

"Because they discriminated against our people, gave us the worst land, took the best of everything. Even limited the education tapes we could give to our children."

And kept their cultural identity alive, thought Tetsuo, though a changed and twisted version of the original.

When century-old history was alive in people's minds, could violence be far away?

Tetsuo shifted uncomfortably. The atmosphere in the small room was getting warm and stuffy now, and he would have liked to peel off the smartgel and reset his jumpsuit's temperature.

He dared not break the mood. This was the first time he had seen Brevan so talkative.

"So there was an uprising," said Tetsuo.

"Several," Brevan replied. "The fourth one succeeded. Then we made peace."

The image zoomed in. Agrazzi territory, bordered by Simnalari, and a sept called Elvenari. A small Agrazzi offshoot, the Phaliborn Enclave, was entirely surrounded by Simnalari: not a happy situation.

"The Agrazzi have trouble keeping to the agreement?"

"Sometimes." Brevan snorted. "They occasionally forget it isn't the old days."

"And you're all dedicated to living in harmony with the planet."

"Right," said Brevan, with an ironic smile.

"Right." Tetsuo lifted the empty containers. "I've got another trip to make."

Brevan nodded, and turned back to his work.

Chapter Fourteen

Graves. The midwinter winds
Shake lonely branches.
Longest night, shortest day.

She was here.

Rafael stood in his gleaming entrance hall, waited for the precise moment, then waved the doors open.

Maggie Brown was standing there, just opening her mouth to announce herself to the house system. Behind her, Rafael's plushest small flyer, the Lectra Seven which had brought her here, rose up from the black and grey gravelled landing area and headed for its garage.

"Nice timing," said Maggie.

"Always." Rafael bowed. "Welcome to my house."

He gestured her inside, and escorted her to the room he had prepared.

A plentiful array of edibles, on warm silver plates, lay on a low table. Rafael escorted her to her seat, then sat down opposite her and crossed his legs.

"This is very nice," said Maggie. "Is that wine I see there?"

"From our local hydroponics." Rafael poured a glass for her. "None of your synthesized stuff."

She accepted her glass, sipped, and closed her eyes in pleasure.

"Ah, an educated palate." Rafael smiled. "Very good."

"So." Maggie put her glass down on the table. She nibbled at a savoury pastry. "Can I run through what I'd like to ask, before I start recording?"

"Of course. Whatever you like."

"OK, just one minute." She held up a finger.

Rafael watched, amused, as she drained her glass. He refilled it for her.

"Oh, that's good." Maggie sipped some more. "What I'm thinking of, is to talk about Tetsuo's business, maybe from the time he arrived here. Along the lines of—" Another sip. "—of what must it be like for a guy from Earth to arrive here. A new planet. An advanced culture. Competing in business with enhanced Luculenti. What do you think?"

"Well." Rafael leaned back. "Most of the time he'd have been dealing with Fulgidi merchants, not Luculenti."

"OK," said Maggie. "Mmm, this is really very good. Right, so we can talk about that. Would it be tough for him?"

"Some Fulgidi have a lot of drive. They use educational ware constantly, tactical ware to help in negotiations, and so forth. I would say yes, Tetsuo would have had a tough time."

"Can we talk about his disappearance? How he'd been behaving for the last few days leading up to it, and so on?"

"May I top that up for you?" He poured more wine. "I'm afraid I didn't see that much of him socially, and not at all since the upraise."

"But you don't mind my asking about it?"

Maggie drained the glass in a few gulps.

Before Rafael could offer, she reached for the bottle and poured again, sloshing a little onto the tabletop. Her hand wobbled a little as she brought the full glass to her lips.

"Ask anything you like." Rafael was surprised she had not spilled anything down her clothes.

"Shall I start?"

"Ah—" Rafael cleared his throat. "Go ahead."

Maggie touched her lapel, removed a small silver brooch in the shape of an owl, and placed it on the table. The eyes glowed blue as they focussed on Rafael, an indication—and legal requirement on Fulgor—that the device was recording.

"What were your first impressions of Tetsuo Sunadomari?"

"Quite an engaging young man." Rafael smoothly hid his amusement as Maggie took the opportunity to quaff more wine. "He brought valuable technological know-how with him, and was well placed to start up in business here on Fulgor."

"So you don't think Fulgidi tech is superior to Terran?"

"Not at all." Rafael fielded the question easily. "I see them as quite complementary. The Skein environment itself, when it's opened to offworlders, will mean many more business opportunities. A win-win scenario, as they say."

He paused, and Maggie had to gulp down her wine quickly to ask the next question.

"Ah, hmm, what would his day-to-day life have been like?"

There was a slight slur to her words. Rafael assumed that later editing would take care of that.

"Well, probably fewer hours working than on Earth, and a nicer quality of life. He had a villa in some rather pleasant countryside, wonderful scenery, well within the terraformed areas and perfectly safe to wander around in."

"So his business life would have been easier?"

"Well, now. I would guess he spent less time working, but the time he did spend would have been quite challenging." Rafael blinked disarmingly. "There's every opportunity to do well, for those who put in the effort."

"So it's untrue that offworlders are exploited? We hear reports of Terran designs being used in novel ways, which somehow manage to avoid paying royalties."

"I'd like to think that's never happened." Rafael shook his head.

"But that might be wishful thinking. Tetsuo, though, was doing very nicely for himself."

Maggie quelled a slight hiccup by drinking a little more.

"Did he ever deal with LuxPrime?" she asked.

Suddenly, Rafael's senses swung to full alert.

"Not to my knowledge."

```
[[[HeaderBegin: Module = Node10013.JK976: Type = Trinary-
        HyperCode: Axes = 12
    Concurrent_Execute
        ThreadOne: <cortical array>.linkfile = House(VideoOne:visual)
        ThreadTwo: <cortical array>.linkfile = House(VideoTwo: IR)
        ThreadThree: <cortical array>.linkfile = House(OlfactoryOne)
        ThreadFour: <cortical array>.linkfile = House(MRIscan)
    End_Concurrent_Execute]]]
```

Interfacing with his house system, Rafael zeroed in on her face.

Pupil dilation: *normal.*

At IR wavelengths, he examined the degree of bloodflow to the skin, the tautness of her musculature.

Bloodflow: *normal.*

He examined her for every sign of normal reaction to a depressant such as ethanol.

Nothing.

Clever, clever. For an Earther.

"Tetsuo primarily dealt with the panoply of corporate entities which maintains the hardware basis for Skein," he added, deliberately obfuscating with meaningless jargon. "Mu-space tech is used, of course, for the comms-interface gateways to other worlds."

"And you dealt with him yourself?"

"In a sense. I was involved as a fourth level broker in some of his projects."

"What does that mean, precisely?"

It sounded a little like *preshishely*, as though Maggie were having difficulty forming sibilants. It was quite an admirable performance.

"The levels of Fulgidi commerce are rather, ah, richly layered, and while there are some long-lived corporations, others exist for only a few fleeting minutes, or less." Rafael strung out his meaningless reply, while he considered his next action. "It's always wise to have a guide to such a new environment, an honest broker if you will, and some of us offer our services in that fashion."

"Did you ever have any dealings with an Adam Farsteen?"

The same name that Major Reilly had mentioned.

Rafael did not like this. There was too much going on which he did not understand.

"I don't recall the name." While he spoke, he formed a NetAngel in Skein and sent it on its way.

"Or Sylvester Stargonier?"

"I know Mr. Stargonier. He and Elizabeth Malone and Tetsuo were engaged in a joint venture."

"And this would have nothing to do with LuxPrime?"

"Oh, no. Nothing at all."

The ghost-Rafael returned to him then, and dumped its information. There were three Adam Farsteens on Fulgor: one was a LuxPrime courier.

Rafael uncrossed his legs. He took a sip of his own wine.

"Perhaps we could take a break?" He leaned forward earnestly. "I'm a little fatigued."

"Just a couple—"

The blue lights around the owl's eyes died.

"It's been very enlightening." Rafael stood up. "This should make quite a human interest story for the folks back home."

"That's right." Maggie stood up as well, dropping all pretence of intoxication.

"But what about your own story?" Rafael's voice was very soft. "How are you coping with a new culture?"

"Very enlightening, as you said."

"And your son? Jason, I believe?"

Maggie stared at him, suddenly taut.

"That's right."

"This must be quite an adventure for him."

He took a step forward, smiling slightly as Maggie flinched.

"I would very much like to know you better. Perhaps we could—"

<<<MsgRcv LUCCOM213886; cause = SkeinLink requested.>>>

"—extend this meeting to dinner: Or, if you like—" He queried the incoming ident. It was {[Luculenta Lavinia Maximilian, ident 6654χ8•ϵ {sept5ΘΞ}]}

<<<MsgRcv LUCCOM213887; cause = SkeinLink established.>>>

"—I could show you around the city—" he continued in reality, while, in Skein, he smiled a greeting to the young Luculenta before him.

She was Lavinia—known as Vin—Lori Maximilian's teenage soul-daughter.

"Hello, Luculentus de la Vega. Lori asked me to send you an invitation."

<<video: an ivory invitation, headed *THE APHELION BALL*>>
<<audio: a sugary Strauss waltz>>
<<kinaesthetic: swirling across a dance floor, in time to the waltz>>

"Why, that's very kind of you," said Rafael in Skein. In reality, he saw Maggie looking wildly around for the door.

In Skein: "That's most gracious of Luculenta Maximilian. I would be honoured to accept."

In reality: "Maggie, why don't we go right now?"

"That's great." Vin's voice was cheerful. "Is Maggie Brown still with you, by the way?"

Rafael froze.

[[[HeaderBegin: Module = Node12A3.33Q8: Type = Quaternary-HyperCode: Axes = 256

Concurrent_Load

ThreadOne: <rhombencephalon channel>.linkfile = Infiltrate.Alpha

ThreadTwo: <intrapeduncular matrix>.linkfile = Infiltrate.Beta

ThreadThree: <LuxPrime interface>.linkfile = CodeSmash

ThreadFour: <thalamic/cerebral matrix>.linkfile = SubvertArray

ThreadFive: <superolateral net>.linkfile = MindWolf

End_Concurrent_Load]]]

He loaded his vampire code, ready to tear through Skein into Vin's young mind. Remote infiltration was a risk he had never taken before. But if she knew this much—

<<<MsgRcv VEGASCN229756; cause = preload modules are ready.>>>

In Skein, he smiled with all his charm.

"Yes. Maggie's with me. How did you know?"

"She mentioned it to Xanthia Delaggropos, and to Lori."

Damn. Damn it to hell.

Rafael quivered inside. With the infiltration code loaded, it was all he could do to contain it.

To Vin, he said, “I believe our interview is concluded. I was just about to send her back to her hotel.”

“OK, I’ll tell Lori. She’s around here in person, someplace.”

But not in Skein, where she would be vulnerable to Rafael.

“Please thank her for the invitation. I look forward to seeing you there.”

In Skein, he bowed, then closed the SkeinLink.

<<<MsgRcv LUCCOM213900; cause = SkeinLink revoked.>>>

“Well.” In reality, he smiled to Maggie. “Looks like you’ve made some friends already. I just told Lavinia Maximilian you’re heading back to your hotel. Is that OK?”

Maggie looked at him for a long moment.

“That’s very kind of you.”

“I’ll see you out.”

Maggie drained her glass of wine, and stood up. She stumbled slightly, then looked him straight in the eyes.

“Oops. That wine’s strong stuff.”

“Some of us,” said Rafael, “are less affected than others.”

“A misspent youth.”

They walked in silence to the main doors. Rafael’s automated flyer was waiting for her on the gravelled pad.

Maggie shook hands, and her grip was strong.

“Thank you for an informative interview.”

“Not at all.” Rafael delivered his most courteous bow. “It was quite educational.”

Later, he constructed another NetAngel, to scout for more information about this Adam Farsteen.

Almost immediately, the wraith returned in Skein, empty-handed. As a LuxPrime courier, Farsteen’s personal info was held in embedded objects wrapped around in level-alpha security.

Rafael's vampire modules included protocol infiltrators stolen, at second- or third-hand, from LuxPrime labs; but he had nothing which could penetrate that level of protection. Not without revealing himself.

Cursing, he waved away the NetAngel.

The ghost-Rafael dissolved in Skein, like a mist torn apart by the wind.

"Hurry," said Yoshiko.

Xanthia landed the flyer on a gleaming parking-pad.

They alighted, and rushed towards the white arches of the Bright Lights hotel.

Inside, Yoshiko looked around in vain for a reception desk or human staff.

"Don't worry." Xanthia laid a hand on Yoshiko's shoulder. "I've polled the hotel system. She hasn't checked out."

"Perhaps we—There she is."

Maggie, grim-faced, strode into the lounge, towing a bewildered-looking Jason.

"That bastard, Rafael." An angry light glowed in her eyes. "He made some not-so-subtle references to Jason. I went straight to the crèche, and took him out."

Yoshiko and Xanthia exchanged glances.

Neither of them, Yoshiko realized, wanted to alarm Jason. Maggie might be overreacting. But they needed to be sure Jason was safe.

Xanthia crouched down, to the boy's height.

"Hello, Jason. My name's Xanthia."

"Hello," said Jason shyly.

"Would you like to come and visit my house? There are big gardens to play in, and lots of toys."

"Mm." He shifted his feet.

"There's a river, and a lake. And boats."

"Real boats?"

"Oh, yes. You can sail them as much as you like. Would you like to see them?"

"OK."

Xanthia looked up at Maggie.

"I've fully trained staff and energy shields. It's as secure as you can possibly get."

"Thank you."

"I'm sorry." Yoshiko felt miserable. "I didn't realize the trouble I was causing."

"Not of your making," said Maggie. "Absolutely not your fault. Look, will you two look after Jason for a moment?"

"Delighted," said Xanthia.

Maggie looked around urgently.

"Is everything all right?" asked Yoshiko.

"Gotta pee," said Maggie, while Jason rolled his eyes upward in disgust. "Damned implant prevents me from getting drunk, but doesn't stop the side effects."

She hurried away.

Yoshiko felt a tug at her sleeve.

"Yo!" said a squeaky voice. "How's it goin'?"

Jason was holding out both hands, grinning, while the toy monkey turned somersaults on his palms.

"He doesn't need to go pee-pee," Jason said solemnly.

"That's good, dear," said Yoshiko, while Xanthia smothered her laughter.

Jason cradled the toy in his hand, then returned it to the inside pocket of his bright red jumpsuit. It had bright yellow cuffs with blue fastenings, and it was partly open down the front to reveal a near-fluorescent lime-green undershirt. They weren't about to lose him.

When Maggie returned, Xanthia asked, "Is there anything you absolutely need to get from your room?"

"Nothing urgent, but—"

"I can get your things sent on later."

Maggie took a breath. "Nothing, then."

Xanthia nodded, and Yoshiko found Jason's hand in hers as they swept together out of the lobby and hurried over to Xanthia's long, elegant silver flyer.

Outside, a group of protestors was gathering. This close to the conference centre, they obviously felt that there were delegates here who might be influenced.

KEEP OFFWORLDERS OFFWORLD!

Yoshiko tightened her grip on Jason as they pushed through the crowd's edge, and circled round to Xanthia's flyer.

"Welcome to Fulgor," said Maggie grimly, as they climbed aboard.

The ground, and the gathering protestors, dropped away beneath them.

The flyer banked right, and straightened up. Acceleration pressed them back into their seats as they left the conference centre far behind.

Tetsuo placed the two empty containers on the tiled floor and adjusted his resp-mask.

Down below, in the cavern's pool, small rock-bound organisms waved frantic tendrils as Dhana splashed her way out of the water.

"I'll come with you," she called up.

Tetsuo nodded.

She climbed up easily, though she was carrying her long metal pole. This time, she had been using it to re-site the life-forms in the pool.

They walked into a long, low room, where open-topped tanks held semiaquatic specimens. The dark secretions, foundation of the humans' food supply, were drained off through narrow pipes.

As they filled the containers, Tetsuo asked, "Can you tell me about the Agrazzi?"

"What about them? They're exploitationist. They want to rape the ecology so much, they might as well go live with the terraformers in the cities."

"Oh." Tetsuo sealed the first container. "I'm glad I asked."

"Then you have the Evanalari, who disturb Fulgor so little, they're lucky to survive at all."

"OK." The second seal didn't fit properly, but he forced it on.

"But most septs are moderate. Like us."

"Of course." He hefted the containers. "After you."

He followed her outside.

She stopped for a moment, on the research centre's balcony, shielding her eyes from the sun.

"Look down there." When she spoke, the membrane across her mouth glistened in the bright light.

Tetsuo squinted. Down in the gully, where the glowing peach-gold rockface gave way to shadows, a group of thick, flat shapes was moving across the ground.

"They've no limbs," he said. "How do they move?"

"You've heard of caterpillar tracks, on ancient vehicles? A continuous rotating surface?"

"I guess so."

"Laminar flow is a basic microstructure here. Just as much of Terran movement, from muscle cell contraction to sperm motion, evolved from flagellae."

Tetsuo, not sure if she was making some point, kept silent.

"Each organism," Dhana went on, "moves by flowing layers in its body. But those things down there aren't individuals. Watch this."

She vaulted over the balcony's wall and dropped lightly to the rocks below.

"Careful," muttered Tetsuo.

Dhana crouched down in front of one of the creatures, then rapped its back sharply with her pole.

It exploded.

Hundreds of fragments flew apart. Dhana picked one of them up, and climbed back up to Tetsuo.

"For God's sake," he said. "You didn't have to do that."

"I haven't done anything. Look."

She held out her hand. A small round shape was moving, flowing across her palm.

Dhana tossed the small organism back into the gully. It landed with a plop among its fellows, all of whom were heading in the same direction.

"What now?"

"Patience, Tetsuo. Just watch."

As they travelled, the small shapes came together. First, they formed a kind of travelling mat, as they all joined up.

Then, as more stragglers joined the main group, they climbed on top of the others, forming a second, contra-rotating, layer.

A third, and a fourth layer were formed, before the group organism was whole again. Then, following the rest of the herd, it turned around and came to rest in the deepest shade.

"Wow." Tetsuo knew he was smiling idiotically. "That's terrific."

"Isn't it?"

"Thank you very much. That was quite something."

Dhana shyly looked away.

"You're welcome."

Tetsuo cleared his throat.

"I'd better get these containers back to the cabin."

"Suppose so," said Dhana. "I'll get back to work."

"See you later."

He must be getting fitter. This time, as he carried the containers down the broken path to the cabin, they hardly weighed a thing.

Chapter Fifteen

Winds wash cold, freezing birds.
Branches, rows of small shadows.
Day lies dreaming.

Dawn painted the sky pale turquoise, splashed it briefly with gold and scarlet, then gave way to glorious morning.

In synch, finally, with local conditions, Yoshiko performed her morning training on the cool lawn. Terran chaffinches twittered in the trees, and the scent of mutated syringa-shrubs was sharp in the air.

Afterwards, she went inside and showered, and a house terminal directed her to the breakfast room where Lori was already sitting down to eat.

A silver tabby lynxette was sitting elegantly beneath a window. As Lori tucked in to her bowl of fruit and cereal, the lynxette bent her head to her dish of protein gruel. Her small tongue showed pink as she lapped it up.

"That's Dawn," said Lori. "She likes to eat breakfast with everyone else."

"She's beautiful."

"*Mrrrgah*," the lynxette cried softly, as though in agreement.

Yoshiko began to pick at her food.

"You made some progress yesterday, I hear."

"Not much." Yoshiko shook her head. "Rafael de la Vega's name was mentioned again, but this time it could easily be coincidence. He was my son's sponsor, after all."

"There's the question of Tetsuo's relationship with Adam Farsteen."

Yoshiko looked away. "The proctors will be already investigating that."

"Indeed." Lori dabbed her mouth with a napkin, and pushed her dishes away.

"But the Aphelion Ball is in two days' time, and we have a high-ranking official visiting us."

"Major Reilly?"

"No, no. The head of TacCorps. Luculentus Federico Gisanthro. If we need to exert some high-level influence, he's our man."

"That's good." Yoshiko stared out of the window, at the mountains' distant grandeur. "I don't suppose . . . Is there a Pilots' Sanctuary on Fulgor?"

"Let me check." Lori's gaze grew unfocussed. "Yes. Two, in fact. The larger is in Lucis. Rather near Lowtown."

"Can I call them?"

"Go ahead." Lori fetched a small terminal from a table and placed it in front of Yoshiko. "I'll see you later."

"Thanks."

Lori left. The lynxette came over, and rubbed her whiskers against Yoshiko's leg. Absent-mindedly, Yoshiko scratched behind the lynxette's ears.

She gestured the terminal into life, and requested a realtime call to the Pilots' Sanctuary in Lucis.

The head and shoulders of a young man appeared above the terminal.

No more than Vin's age, he had pale skin, stretched taut over high cheekbones, and his eyes were deep glittering black. Like all Pilots' eyes, they lacked any surrounding white.

The young man bowed.

"I am Pilot Noviciate Edralix Corsdavin."

"Sunadomari Yoshiko."

"I am honoured. May I help you in any way?"

"Truly, I don't know." Yoshiko hesitated. "It's a personal problem. My son disappeared a few days ago."

The young Pilot, Edralix, looked off to one side. "The NewsNets have reported this."

"I hadn't realized."

"It started as a human interest story, peripherally related to the Skein conference." His dark eyes were expressionless. "There's been more coverage since."

Good old Maggie. Perhaps it would help to keep an open investigation going. It stood to reason that anything to do with LuxPrime, the technological cornerstone of Luculentus society, would be kept behind closed doors as much as possible.

"Does the Pilots' Confederation have anything to do with Fulgor's SatScan system?"

Edralix shook his head.

"There's no mu-space tech involved."

"I see."

Another wasted effort. She had hoped to access orbital scan-logs, showing Tetsuo's house, on the day he had disappeared.

Maybe showing that poor man, Adam Farsteen . . .

"—in a few days," Edralix was saying.

"I beg your pardon?"

"Er, there'll be a Pilot here in a couple of days." Edralix's youthful uncertainty was apparent. "Until then, it's just me and the tech staff."

"You've been very helpful."

"I'll get Pilot deVries to call you as soon as she arrives."

"Is that Jana deVries?" Yoshiko sat upright. "I met her on Ardua Station, in Terran orbit. I think she piloted the ship which brought me here to Fulgor."

"That would be right." Edralix nodded. "She'll be back soon, with a layover for a few days."

"It would be nice to talk to her again. She was very kind."

"Yes." A smile lit up Edralix's features. "She's the best."

"Thank you very much for your help."

"That's OK," said Edralix. "And, er, good luck."

Yoshiko waved the display into nothingness.

"Mrrgaow?"

"Don't worry." Yoshiko rubbed the lynxette's head. Outside, sunlight glinted gold off the distant snowcovered peaks. "We're going to get some help."

Time to make use of his contacts.

Rafael had never tried to form any close contacts within the supposedly incorruptible LuxPrime. It was the only way to avoid entrapment, to avoid meeting someone who might guess how he had subverted their technology.

In Skein, he asked for a realtime comm to Captain Rogers at the Bureau for Offworld Affairs. A busy-icon greeted his request.

He left no message.

Always, he dealt with contractors at several removes from prime sources like LuxPrime. Now, he prepared a flock of NetAngels to contact them all, on various pretexts. Should any ghost-Rafael detect responses which were outside its expected paradigm, it would immediately get hold of the real Rafael, who would smoothly take its place.

He entrusted the task to AIs only because he expected no results.

As the NetAngels began their tasks, the real Rafael dipped in and out of Skein, sampling their conversations.

None of them even hinted at wrongdoing or tragedy involving a principal LuxPrime courier. News of such an event should have cascaded rapidly through his network of contacts and associates.

Had Farsteen disappeared, in the same manner as Tetsuo?

In reality, Rafael leaned back in his couch and stared at the ceiling. He wondered if he had a pretext for calling Federico, and seeing if he could extract any information from him.

Perhaps a complaint about harassment by Maggie Brown . . . No, that didn't strike the right tone. Perhaps just passing on the confidential info he had inferred from the wording of her questions. That should do it.

He did not, however, hold much hope of Federico's dropping useful hints, unless it suited some purpose of his own.

Still, he hesitated. Federico Gisanthro was his most useful contact—apart, possibly, from the corrupt Captain Rogers—facilitating Rafael's introduction to offworld workers in mu-space tech and other fields. But Federico was, too, his most dangerous associate, as sharp as they came, and if he ever once suspected the existence of Rafael's vampire code or the mu-space comms network which held his vast plexcore nexus, then there would be a TacCorps team here in seconds.

Just searching his house, and discovering the buried plexcores, would be enough to indict him.

All right. Just do it.

He pictured Federico's ideogram.

[[Luculentus Federico Gisanthro, ident 5γ33G3•ε {septΔ2Σ}]]

"Hello, Federico, old chap."

<<<MsgRcv LUCCOM213887; cause = SkeinLink established.>>>

He was in a cavern—no, a grey man-made tunnel where only a few white glowglobes cast black sheets of shadow across construction debris. Federico was crouched down against a small yellow dirt-covered mining machine, which bore the label "Bronto."

<<audio: Exercises!>>
<<video: a 3-D relationship-map of Lucis>>
<<text: the new tunnels for the northern malls>>

White beams flickered out of the darkness and a man fell at Federico's feet.

"The bastards," whispered the fallen man, frozen in position.

"The jumpsuits—" A rictus spread across Federico's face as he returned fire. "—The beams solidify the jumpsuits." He turned away from the Rafael-image. "Now! Go!"

For a moment Rafael thought Federico meant him.

Federico, flanked by two of his men, vaulted over a pile of battered drums and fallen joists, and ran to the tunnel's side.

Rafael's viewpoint whirled sickeningly as he followed. At least he had to expend no physical effort to keep up.

Federico and his men began to climb up twisted steel rods, which hung like uncovered roots from the dark bare earth. They crawled up to the tunnel's ceiling, and hung upside down like spiders from the carry-rail which threaded the ceiling's apex.

Rafael's point of view rotated through one hundred and eighty degrees and he fought back his vertigo, reminding himself of the feel of his chair beneath his hands, back in his own home.

"So what," asked Federico, "can I do for you?"

He did not look in the mood for chit-chat.

"I gave a news interview to an Earther."

"Jolly good." Federico dragged himself along the rail.

Rafael noticed the tiny safety link which hooked him to the rail, quite useless if the rail itself gave way. The man had no nerves.

"She seemed to hint about some trouble at LuxPrime." Rafael swallowed, despite himself, as they moved out over a vertical shaft whose bottom was invisible. "Something about a courier called Adam Farsteen."

"Really?" Federico, hanging by one arm, helped his men to attach some equipment.

"Just thought I'd let you know."

"Very decent of you, old chap."

A beam sizzled past Federico and he dropped spiderlike from the ceiling, brought up with a jolt by his harness, as he twisted round and returned fire. Rafael heard a faint cry from below.

"Sorry, Rafael, I'm a little busy now."

Like questing fingers, beams spread up from the darkness. Federico's own men, dangling from the ceiling beside him, readied some sort of weapons array.

A flash of white. A beam cracked past centimetres from Federico's face.

"See you later, chum."

<<<MsgRcv LUCCOM213900; cause = SkeinLink revoked.>>>

. . . And Rafael was sitting back in his chair, breathing hard, the smooth arms slick beneath his sweating palms.

"Nice friends you've got," he said to the empty room.

As though other people—besides the sweet things he subsumed into himself—could ever matter to him.

Federico was a dangerous quantity to manipulate, and would return anything he discovered about LuxPrime only if it was in his interests, but Rafael could handle him.

Rafael himself was an emergent property of an underlying neural community the likes of which the universe had never seen. Someday he would be powerful enough to strike at will through Skein, plunder any mind he chose, plunder every mind on Fulgor—

A fantasy? Perhaps not.

"Move over, God." He could. He could really do it. "Rafael Garcia de la Vega is taking your place."

Tetsuo leaned against the research station's balcony. The stone balustrade felt powdery through the thin film of gel which covered his hands.

Sunset's spectacular crimsons and oranges streaked the sky. This low in the canyon, planes of shadow hid the rockface walls, and the sun itself had long disappeared from sight.

"Pretty, isn't it?" said Dhana beside him.

"Yeah. Look at the way the light catches that quartz up there, by the rim."

"Mmm."

Tetsuo adjusted his resp-mask, then stopped fidgeting and watched the sky slowly grow a deeper red, bruised with purple and vermilion. The silence was companionable, but all the while he was intensely aware of Dhana standing beside him, drinking in the same sights as he.

"Brevan hasn't grown to like me much, has he?"

"I wouldn't say that. He's got a lot on his mind."

Tetsuo shifted his resp-mask. "I don't suppose I could get one of those membrane implants?"

Dhana touched the gill-like bands across her neck.

"It's not worth it, unless you live out here for a long time."

"I suppose not."

The shadows drew in across the canyon.

"It's peaceful here," he said. "I'm not surprised no one knows about your work, if you're all this far out in the wilderness."

"We've organized small demonstration sites before, and tried to make them public. And once we actually staged a small march in Soltar City."

There was a bitter expression on her face.

"What went wrong?" he asked carefully.

"Proctors. TacTeams broke up the demos, and broke a few heads in the process."

After a pause, Tetsuo said, "I met Federico Gisanthro once. The head of TacCorps."

"Really."

"Seemed like a bit of a hard case," said Tetsuo. "Can't say I liked him."

"Damned Luculentus—" Dhana looked up at his headgear briefly.

"Sorry. But we've heard about Federico Gisanthro. Machiavellian as they get."

"I'm not surprised."

"His identity as head of TacCorps is only public knowledge because of legislation, you know. It's said that he manipulates other Luculenti as easily as they could manipulate schoolchildren."

"Said by whom?"

"Our political analysts."

Tetsuo remembered the piercing gaze of those mismatched eyes. He shivered.

"But you have Luculenti help, don't you?" he said. "Otherwise Brevan would never have known about my upraise op. The information was only in Skein."

"Yes, there are Luculenti who are sympathetic to us. So far, they've kept our existence pretty much secret. TacCorps taught us the wisdom of that."

He wasn't really paying attention to her now. Had he really been so forgetful, so ready to ignore the trouble he was in?

"I suppose you know I left my flyer in Nether Canyon, don't you?" asked Tetsuo. "Do you think I could go back to it? With you or Brevan as escort?"

"I don't know." Dhana's glance flicked quickly to her left.

Tetsuo wondered what it was she was failing to tell him, and decided that his only recourse was to be open himself.

"There's a small set of infocrystals in the flyer. That's all I'm after."

"What kind of info?"

"I don't know." He held up a hand as Dhana started to speak. "Honestly. I couldn't access it before. It's all held in intelligent facets, encrypted and protected. But I might be able to get at the info now."

He pointed at his Luculentus headgear. He had no idea whether his mindware, which had come with his prime—and so far only—plexcore, embedded in his torso, was still active in the background at some deep neural level.

He desperately needed training ware and Luculentus guidance. But there was a chance he had integrated enough to access the infocrystals' contents: he was sure that the strange info-formats were LuxPrime design, for Luculentus access.

"Where did it come from?" asked Dhana. "This info, that you couldn't read?"

He closed his eyes and let out a long breath.

"Stolen from LuxPrime, I think."

"You're kidding. From LuxPrime?"

"I think so."

"That's impossible."

"Is it? Their staff are only human."

"Incorruptible, more like."

"Perhaps—" Tetsuo looked hard at Dhana, willing her to trust him. "I was visiting the Bureau for Offworld Affairs," he said slowly. "A Captain Rogers was giving me clearance for the upraise. Pretty much a formality if you already have a work permit; they do a full check on you when you apply for that."

Dhana leaned her head to one side. "What's this got to do with LuxPrime?"

"Well—I was waiting outside his office," Tetsuo said, "and I could hear a blazing row between two men going on inside, though I couldn't make out what they were shouting about. After a while, the door opened and a tall thin guy stormed out, wearing LuxPrime colours, and then Captain Rogers came puffing out after him . . ."

Tetsuo swallowed. Was the LuxPrime employee the same man who had been in the video-log? Farsteen?

Thin, fair-haired. It could have been him. Easily.

Tetsuo shook his head. If only he hadn't left the video-log crystal in his house . . .

"Go on," Dhana said.

Tetsuo was peripherally aware of the intent concentration in her eyes.

"Rogers pounded off down the corridor. And I—couldn't resist the temptation."

"You stole infocrystals from a proctor's office?"

"Copied them," Tetsuo said simply. "I had a wrist terminal and a set of crystals on me."

"I wouldn't have thought," said Dhana, "that you could copy something in Luculentus formats."

Tetsuo smiled sadly.

"Cracking systems," he said, "is the one thing I'm really good at. Besides, the first crystal was easy—a different format, relatively unprotected. That just made the remaining crystals a challenge I couldn't ignore, don't you see?"

"No. Not really."

"Ah, well. When Rogers came back, we both pretended nothing had happened, and he rushed through the procedures in ten minutes flat, told me I was authorized as far as he was concerned, and saw me out of the building. He locked his door that time, too."

"A bit late," said Dhana.

"Yeah, I guess."

"So there's at least one crystal in the flyer which we, you, can read?"

Tetsuo shook his head. "I left two crystals at home. I hid the unprotected one: it seemed to be a LuxPrime diagram of how a nexus works, but I didn't spend much time looking at it. I was far too busy."

"Busy?"

"With work, you know?" Tetsuo shook his head. "Funny, how all that suddenly seems a bad dream, when I've only been here a few days."

"You mean, you'd rather be here?"

Tetsuo shrugged. "You live here all the time, and work hard, so you probably think this place is nothing special. But it is."

He gestured at the dark canyon. Up above, the small beta moon was just rising above the rim.

"I don't suppose," said Dhana slowly, "that you know the courier's name?"

Tetsuo shook his head.

"I didn't know him. But there was another crystal, which I partially decoded, with a fragmented video log, and a stored Skein-ghost of someone called Farsteen. He might be the same man. The crystal was damaged, though. I'm not certain."

"I thought so."

"Captain Rogers called him 'Adam.'"

Dhana hugged herself. Her expression was hard to read in the gathering darkness.

"He's dead."

"Who is?"

"Adam Farsteen's body was found at your house," said Dhana. "Someone killed him."

Tetsuo gave a sort of disbelieving half-laugh, as though this were some kind of joke, but he knew straight away she was telling the truth.

"At my house?" he said. "How would you know—?"

"Brevan told me. We're not entirely out of touch."

"No, I suppose not."

He stared at the darkness, seeing nothing. Farsteen dead, at his house? It made no sense.

"An attack squad broke into my house. I thought it was proctors at first, but then I realized they weren't trying to arrest me. They were trying to kill me. Because of the crystals. What the hell have I got into?"

Dhana touched his arm.

"Time to get back to the cabin," she said. "Supper's waiting, and I'm getting cold."

Neither of them spoke as they followed the winding trail back through the night, to the small brightly lit cabin.

Chapter Sixteen

Birds gather: visiting
Shadows. Death, or childish
Dreaming? Who's next? Who . . . ?

Tetsuo screamed as the faceless men beat him, blood welling from his wounds as he collapsed with a gurgling, strangled cough and the last rattle of his dying breath. Tetsuo 's eyes—Ken eyes—clouded as life left forever with a beat of silent wings.

Yoshiko forced her eyes open.

She breathed out slowly. She had dozed off, that was all. Trying to think of a way to find Tetsuo.

She should remember what she always told her trainees at the lab: this is the time to aim for—that moment of feeling utterly stuck, the feeling which always precedes enlightenment.

There was a low chime, and Lori stepped through the door membrane.

"Morning," said Lori. "I see you've synchronized with local time."

"Just about." Recalibrating her med-kit's femtocyte-processor had taken a long time.

The processor fascinated her: tiny matter-lasers used coherent atomic and electron beams to build up smartatom processors. In this case, to form femtocytes which rebuilt telomeres so that cells might continue to reproduce, and hunted down free radicals, and performed the hundred other tasks which helped a human body fight senescence.

But death would come, in the end.

"That's good," said Lori. "Listen, I've arranged a real-time comms connection to Earth's NetEnv, in EveryWare, in five minutes' time. It was the only time-window I could get." Lori pointed at the small bed-side terminal. "You'll be able to access your h-mail and such."

"But that will cost a fortune. You can't possibly—"

"If you want to prepare any outgoing h-mail," said Lori, "I'm afraid you'll need to do it now. The actual connection will only last a few seconds."

"OK." Yoshiko bowed her head. "Thank you, very much."

"You're welcome." Lori smiled.

For just a moment, Yoshiko could see where Vin's girlish grin came from. She nodded her thanks as Lori left the room.

"Command: create mail object one," she said to the terminal. "Command: record."

A small winking dot of red light hung in the air above the terminal.

"Hello, Akira," she said. "I'm sorry this comm is so short. I'm fine. The planet is everything you said it would be. Tetsuo . . ."

She shook her head. Her first instinct had been to lie, to say everything was all right, but Akira had a right to know about his elder brother.

". . . Tetsuo has had some difficulty, but I'm sure he's going to be all right. Ah—More soon. Take care, and give my love to Kumiko. Out."

She waved an end-record command at the terminal.

Was there anyone else she should mail?

"Command: create mail object two," she said. "Command: record . . . Hello, Anichi. Many apologies for the brevity of this message. Could you do me a favour, please? Could you send any info we have on VSI tech, or LuxPrime? Many thanks. How are the new team getting on? Is Richard following any good leads? His cross-coupling idea seemed promising. Can Dorothy and Morio manage them all? Oh, and has Tanya had her baby yet? . . . More soon. Out."

She waved an end to the second message just as the comms session opened up. The familiar encircled-Earth holo-logo of the Terran NetEnv appeared.

"Logon: Sunadomari Yoshiko," she said.

A round-faced gentle golden Buddha, floating in the lotus position, opened his eyes.

Yoshiko waved away the Buddha's image. It was one of her NetAgents, and she didn't have time for its usual greetings.

She pointed at the flowing-words icon to download her incoming mail, while using voice instruction to say: "Command: attach mail object one to ID Sunadomari Akira, my son. Command: attach mail object two to ID Higashionna Anichi at Sudarasys Lifetech, my employers. Command: upload and send mail."

That done, she pointed at the tiny Buddha icon, and her NetAgent sprang into full size, a metre-high image.

"Greetings," it said, in its mellifluous voice. "Ah—I fear this connection is being—"

Apologetic text flashed up as the Buddha disappeared and the comms connection to Earth was severed.

Yoshiko's heart was thumping and her throat was dry, though she could not have explained why. Perhaps it was the sudden vicarious contact with the home she had left behind, with its warmth and safety. Except that Ken, her love, was no longer there, or anywhere else in this cold, old universe.

Shaking a little, she requested daistral from the house system and tried to clear her head. A small servo-drone trundled up bearing the drink. Taking the cup, she thought for a moment and then waved the terminal back into life.

"List in-tray messages, personal messages only."

Though the comm session had been brief, there had been plenty of time to download her waiting h-mail, which she could now read at her leisure.

"You have three personal messages," the system said, while simultaneously displaying text. "One: Higashionna Anichi, Chairman, Sudarasys Lifetech Inc., subject equals '*Office gossip, Yoshiko.*' Two: Eric Rasmussen, Scientific Officer, Ardua Station, subject equals '*Howya doin' Prof?*' Three: Sunadomari Akira, Headmaster, Okinawan Prefecture School one-zero-seven, subject equals '*Hi, mother. Ça va? Genki?*'"

She could guess the contents of each h-mail without opening it. From Anichi, there would be a gentle personal message with cheery project reports appended as text and results-graphics. He would not mention how much he missed her at the labs, but would concentrate on the good work done by the youngsters she had been coaching.

Akira would send details of small domestic incidents, with little discussion of his own work. How like his brother, in that at least, Yoshiko realized for the first time.

What about Eric, that big red-bearded giant of a man back at Ardua Station? Why would he h-mail her?

She pointed to Eric's name on the list, and a display volume grew into being.

Eric's hair was combed neatly, by his standards, and he was wearing a pristine jumpsuit unlike the more tattered affairs Yoshiko had seen him in. The blank wall of his small cabin was behind him.

"Hi, Yoshiko," he said in the display.

Looked like he was alone in his cabin this time.

"I just wanted to say, ah—Oh, I don't know. I hope the toy monkey's keeping you company. Are you all right? Call me. Call soon. Bye."

That was it. The image blinked out.

Eric.

Ignore that. She had Tetsuo to think about.

She shut down the incoming-mail display and tried to clear her head.

"Command: clear temp objects," she said, so that the local copies of her outgoing mail would be deleted. "Command: create mail object one. Command: record . . ."

She thought for a moment.

"Please could I have permission to visit my son's house? Would that be possible? . . . Out."

Should she add more? No point. Either she would get permission, or she wouldn't. She picked up her daistral cup.

"Command: attach mail object one to local ID Major Reilly, Proctor. Command: upload and send."

Then she waved the display into oblivion and sat there, cup between her hands but quite forgotten, and stared at the wall, seeing nothing.

A thousand Xanthias, each dressed in a flowing grey silk neo-Grecian gown, walked straight-backed across a white marble plain beneath a featureless sky. Every one of them paused, leg poised and revealed where the gown's split fell away, lowered her chin and looked at him with dark sparkling eyes, and held out a hand in invitation . . .

Cursing, Rafael dispelled the illusion.

The room in which he sat was empty, its grey and black plainness mocking him, and be closed his eyes and began again.

One Xanthia, skin a shade darker, that's right, and the Mona Lisa smile and the dark secretive eyes and the gloss of her raven-dark hair and the sparkling highlights sprinkled across her finely jewelled head-gear. Smooth neck, not too long. Bare olive shoulders. Firm and full, her dark-nippled breasts . . .

What was he, a pubescent boy? He clothed the illusion, stored it, and swept it away.

Nothingness, tinged with blue. Anger and desire washed through him, and he pictured her identideogram, and entered Skein.

<<<MsgRcv LUCCOM213887; cause = SkeinLink established.>>>

"Rafael." Xanthia, sitting on a low bench by a dark placid river, whose tree-lined banks led past trimmed green lawns. "What a pleasant surprise."

"Ah, Xanthia. It's good to see you again."

"What can I do for you?"

Rafael did not attempt any <private sends> within SkeinLink. Best to keep this formal, for now.

"I was hoping I could help you," said Rafael. "It seems you're conducting an investigation into Tetsuo Sunadomari's disappearance, which I've only just become aware of."

"That was when Maggie Brown was interviewing you, was it?"

"The Earther journo, yes." Rafael smiled. "Quite resourceful, isn't she?"

Xanthia, he noted, couldn't help smiling in return.

"Quite," she said. "So, when did you last see Tetsuo?"

"Here you are," he said, and <sent> a time-stamped compressed-format log of their last meeting.

"Thank you," said Xanthia, absorbing it instantly. "It looks as though it was a straightforward discussion of upraise procedures and his business projects. I can't pinpoint any likely predictor of a chaotic transition in his personality."

"Doesn't look like it, does it?" said Rafael. "If you check his stress indicators when he talks about the project with Stargonier and Malone, you'll see they get quite high, but there's no hint of phase-transition precursors."

"So whatever happened was the result of an external event?"

"That's the high-probability scenario," said Rafael. "You know, as his upraise-sponsor, I can't help feeling some responsibility for his welfare. Do you have any other info I might help correlate or analyse?"

"Sorry," said Xanthia, shaking her head. "We've very little at all."

"OK, then. I hate to ask this, but—Do you think he's still alive?"

"Why do you ask?" said Xanthia.

Rafael could feel all her perceptions zeroing in on him. He willed his Skein-image to betray nothing.

"Unless he's being harboured by a Luculentus—" His tone was careful. "—If he is alive, he has no access to learning protocols or developmental support."

"That's true. Are you worried about catastrophic breakdown?"

"It's a possibility. I hate to think of the poor devil stuck somewhere, maybe in hiding, and his whole mind crashing down in shards—"

Xanthia shuddered.

"I'm sorry," said Rafael. "But there's a more hopeful possibility. If he can manage the integration process unattended, perhaps he'll figure out how to access Skein."

"My God." Xanthia's eyes widened: true reaction, or what she allowed him to see? "You're right. I didn't think of that. I'll set a NetAngel to keep permanent watch on the public log."

Rafael had already done just that.

"Let me know if there's anything else I can do."

"I will," said Xanthia, and just for a moment her expression was open and hopeful.

Xanthia, thought Rafael. *My beautiful ripe Xanthia, soft and delicious—*

Deep inside him, his infiltration code stirred.

"Perhaps you would care to join me for dinner?" he said. "In person."

Gentle with himself, he calmed his desire.

"I'm sorry," said Xanthia. "I've so much work on at the moment—"

Anger flared—

```
{[[HeaderBegin: Module = Node12A3.33Q8: Type = Quaternary-
      HyperCode: Axes = 256
   Concurrent_Load
      ThreadOne:<rhombencephalon channel>.linkfile = Infiltrate.
         Alpha
      ThreadTwo:<intrapeduncular matrix>.linkfile = Infiltrate.Beta
      ThreadThree:<LuxPrime interface>.linkfile = CodeSmash
      ThreadFour:<thalamic/cerebral matrix>.linkfile =SubvertArray
      ThreadFive:<superolateral net>.linkfile = MindWolf
   End_Concurrent_Load]]}
```

—mixed with that overwhelming attraction which said she must be his, and his vampire modules fairly throbbed in cache, wanting to be loose, wanting to take the risk and plunge through Skein—

"—But we'll meet soon enough, in person, at the Maximilians' Aphelion Ball."

Gasping in reality, Rafael edited his Skein-image to appear unconcerned. He fought down the rush of his infiltration code, and cleared it from his cache.

Control, control. You'll get your chance.

"Really?" he said, and his voice was calm and level only in Skein. "I'm very much looking forward to it."

"I'm conducting the Sun Wheel Dance," Xanthia said.

<<video: a hundred tiny stick figures, dancing in time>>
<<audio: swirling pipe music>>

Rafael saw that the little stick figures had tiny silver dots on their heads, indicating their Luculentus status.

"With you in control," he said, "the event will be miraculous."

He <sent>:

<<video: a thousand pairs of clapping hands>>
<<audio: thunderous applause>>

"Thank you," said Xanthia. "I'm going to enjoy it, I think."

"I should hope so. I'll be counting the hours, my lady."

"I'll see you there. *Ciao.*"

"My pleasure. Out."

<<<MsgRcv LUCCOM213900; cause = Skeinlink revoked.>>>

Rafael was alone in his room once more. His face felt flushed, and his throat was dry.

"Soon, my lady," he said softly. "Very soon, indeed."

The silver mushroom danced before Tetsuo's eyes. He should have known he could not just walk out of here.

It was 05:17, and his blood sugar was sixty-seven percent of optimum, and he had a headache.

The microward, its silver cap bright against the salmon-pink bedrock, marked a perimeter Tetsuo could not breach. He looked around: there, another one. No doubt an array of them ringed both cabin and research centre.

Brevan and Dhana, he hoped, were still asleep in the cabin.

Tetsuo crept closer.

Awkwardly, puffing, he got down onto his knees then lowered his head so his cheek was against the rock. Under the upper cap of the little microward, a tiny status light glowed red.

Activated.

Well, he had had to check. He would have felt really stupid if the microwards had been powered off and he hadn't even attempted to cross the boundary.

He closed his eyes and sighed. Microwards were of nothing like the level of sophistication he had seen in the cities, where drifting miasmas of smartatoms were used as security screens. But this old microward had stopped him dead.

He snorted with laughter, loud behind his mask. He had studied microward protocols when he was at school on Okinawa, fascinated by comms tech even then. Pity his lessons hadn't included ways to—

[[[HeaderBegin: Module = Node009B.0007: Type = Binary-Hyper-Code: Axes =6

Concurrent_Execute

```
    ThreadOne:<superolateral net: element one>.linkfile = IR-
        protocolAlpha
    ThreadTwo:<superolateral net: element two>.linkfile = IR-
        protocolBeta
    ThreadThree:<superolateral net: element three>.linkfile =
        μprotocolAlpha
End_Concurrent_Execute}]]
```

"Oh, my God!" Sudden pain split his head open, and he rolled to one side, clutching his temples.

Make it stop!"

```
THREAD ONE
ChannelVector := {guarded}
EncryptPBox9
Data:packet
Function:Listen
Var c: integer
Var Intruder: boolean
begin
c:=1
Intruder:=false
while c<= #Buffers
and Intruder=false
  if conn[state] = open
    PollBuffer(c, Intruder)
    if not Intruder
      c:= c+1
    endif
  endif
endwhile
if Intruder
```

```
THREAD TWO
ChannelVector := {guarded}
EncryptPBox9
Data:packet
Procedure:ProtocolNine
Var NextFrame: trinary
Var LastFrame: boolean
begin
  PiggyBack(ACK)
  FrameExpected(buffer)
  RunTimer
repeat
  case NextFrame: mod1
  case not NextFrame: mod2
  case maybe NextFrame: mod3
endcase
TransferFrame
until Shutdown or Fail
if Fail
  ErrAlert
```

```
  ZapIt                              ArrayInit
endif                              endif
end;                               end;
```

Screaming, he pounded his forehead against the rock. Pain smashed into him, and blood spurted, stinging, into his eyes.

```
THREAD THREE
Channel = {fixed}
EncryptPBox3
Data:packet
CodeBlock:Pipeline
ImageMatch(-ve + [isa Obj 1])
  pattern(outline, class2)
  pattern(outline, class1)
IsNow(pattern)
embed:
  001: POP 23 987
  002: ADD 01 832
  003: SUB 23 832
  004: CON 832 SKIP
  005: GO 001
  006: POP 33 339
  007: CON 832 SKIP
  008: MOV 33 45
  009: ADD 1 45
  010: MOV 01 47
  011: ZER 909
  012: MOY 01 99
endembed;
```

"Shutdown! For God's sake, shut it down!"

<<<MsgRcv DEVCOM224900; cause = shutdown requested.>>>

"Oh—"

The pain stopped.

Miraculously, like a thunderous noise falling to silence, the agony had disappeared.

<<<MsgRcv DEVCOM224901; cause = shutdown complete.>>>

Slowly, whimpering softly, he levered himself up to a seated position, and wiped blood away from his face.

The light was green.

For a moment, he did not realize what he was seeing. Then he realized: the microward network was switched off.

He had shut it down.

He was free.

And, suddenly, he had absolute confidence that his mindware would be able to guide him back to Nether Canyon, where his flyer was hidden.

So why—he wiped more blood from his eyes—why wasn't he moving?

He stared back in the direction of the cabin.

"I must be mad," he said softly.

What would Dhana want with someone like him?

No matter. Still, he had been happier here, helping out in the research centre over the last few days, than he had been for—he could not guess. A long time.

He forced himself up to his feet. There was a slight wheeze in his chest; he wasn't fit yet.

Was that why he was going back?

Every day, since coming to Fulgor, his work had become increasingly pressurized, until all the joy had been squeezed from it. Here, the pressure was gone, and it was like living in another world.

That still did not seem sufficient reason.

What, though, did he really have to go back to, in the world outside?

Feeling curiously disembodied, blinking away dripping blood, he set off back towards the cabin.

"Well, well. So Dhana was right. Who'd have believed it?"

Tetsuo spun, heart thumping.

Brevan stood up from behind a boulder, beyond the dead microward. His graser rifle was slung across his shoulder.

"I didn't think you'd turn back."

"I didn't think I'd get past the microwards."

"Mm." Brevan climbed down onto the trail. "That was very impressive."

"Tell me about it." Tetsuo brushed away more blood.

"Make sure you tell Dhana—" Brevan pointed to Tetsuo's forehead. "—that I didn't do that."

Tetsuo looked at him for a long moment.

"OK. I will."

"Good. There's more than enough work for three, around here."

"That's what I thought."

"Oh, and—We moved your flyer. You'd never have found it."

"Hell. I might have known."

Together, they walked back towards the cabin.

Chapter Seventeen

Longest night, winter's day.
Stay where the squirrel lies.
Who is not dreaming?

The glimmering web trembled at its creator's movement. Fangs bore down, and pumped digestive enzymes into the struggling prey: the trapped wasp fought on, but its end was certain.

Yoshiko crouched down by a flowering bush, watching the spider. Vin was sitting on the edge of a suspensor platform, which floated over superconducting guides buried beneath the gardens. She had been giving Yoshiko a tour of the self-sustaining micro-ecologies.

Life, sustained by death.

"Thank you." Yoshiko stood up and sighed.

Vin grimaced. "I thought it would take your mind off things."

"I appreciate that." In fact, all her worries about Tetsuo had been constantly circling through her mind.

"Xanthia's back at the house, with Lori. She arrived while we were looking at the irrigation tubules."

"That's good," said Yoshiko distractedly. "Tell me, do you think I could get permission to stay at Tetsuo's house for a while? Or at least look around it again?"

"It's under proctor jurisdiction as a crime scene," said Vin slowly, "but I would think they'd let you go there. Major Reilly seemed quite reasonable, and they must have finished the, ah, forensics."

That poor man, Farsteen, thought Yoshiko.

"I don't want to put you to any more trouble, Vin. I should really find someplace else to stay."

"It's no trouble at all. You should remain at least till after the Aphelion Ball, tomorrow night—but you're welcome for as long as you like."

"Well . . . thanks. Perhaps I'll just call Major Reilly and ask if I can have a look round."

"OK," said Vin. "Should we check with Xanthia first?"

"Good idea." Yoshiko climbed onto the suspensor platform beside Vin. "Though I don't suppose she's found out anything more. She would have told us."

The platform took them back to the house. Vin led the way down a long gallery to the great hall which Lori used for sculpting. This time she ignored the small holo door set into the wall.

"This will be the ballroom, tomorrow, night." The huge bronze doors swung open, in the main entrance arch. "For the Aphelion Ball."

The statue of Diana the Huntress had been removed. Awaiting shipment, to travel back to Earth with Yoshiko whenever she left.

Earth, home, was a lifetime away.

Though the statue was gone, the laser array still hung like a great, skeletal chandelier beneath the high domed ceiling.

Lori and Xanthia were standing beneath it.

"Morning," said Yoshiko.

Lori mouthed hello, then held a finger to her lips and looked at Xanthia, whose eyes were closed.

"It's OK," murmured Xanthia. "I've got it now. Hi, Yoshiko."

Suddenly, metre-wide translucent blue spheres, shot through with golden swirls and amber bubbles, sprang into being above a pale copper waving sea of light which filled the hall.

Yoshiko jumped.

She forced herself to relax. As the copper segued into blue and turquoise, and the spheres began to orbit around the hall's centre where Xanthia and Lori stood, Yoshiko realized that the vast image was being constructed by the laser array under Xanthia's direct control.

"Isn't this dangerous?" Yoshiko leaned close to Vin, whispering. "Lori carves solid rock with those lasers."

"No problem," Vin whispered back. "She's enabled a safety routine."

"So we're not going to get carved into sushi."

"How gross." Vin shuddered. "I don't think so."

The light show winked out of existence.

"Just practising my party piece," said Xanthia. "How did you like it?"

"Terrific," Yoshiko replied. "Beautiful colours."

"I'll be controlling the music system, too. Pick a tune I can base the accompaniment on. Something traditional."

"Ah . . . Greensleeves?"

"That will do." Xanthia closed her eyes again.

The silver sound of a flute drifted through the hall, recreating the ancient air, while the light show pulsed in time.

"Yoshiko was wondering," said Vin, while spheres danced in the copper sea, "if the proctors would let her look around Tetsuo's house again."

"Is that a good idea?" Xanthia spoke without opening her eyes. "It must have been upsetting for you."

"Yes. But it's still my son's home. I'd really like the chance to see it by myself, to take my time over it."

"I'll go with her," said Vin quickly.

"Are you sure you'll be OK?" asked Xanthia.

"I'm sure."

Lori cleared her throat.

"I've just talked to Major Reilly."

Yoshiko blinked.

Whenever she thought she had grown used to her Luculentae friends, they surprised her again.

Lori had carried out a conversation in Skein—with Major Reilly, an unenhanced Fulgida, using a terminal at her end—without betraying any outward sign.

"Tetsuo's house is still cordoned off, apparently," Lori continued. "But you can go tomorrow morning. They'll let you in, under supervision."

"What do they think I'm going to do? Tamper with the evidence?"

Yoshiko felt Vin's hand on her arm.

Control, control.

Yoshiko could sense her friends' surprise, for they had not seen her angry before. She calmed herself.

"I beg your pardon. Will tomorrow morning be OK? You've this Aphelion Ball to prepare for."

"I can take you." Vin looked eager. "There'll be plenty of time. The ball won't start until the evening."

"Thank you." Yoshiko turned to Xanthia. "I'd love to see that light show again."

"My pleasure."

Copper and red the billowing sea, pure and silver the unseen flautist's notes—a beautiful construct of light and sound. But the sour taste of unfocused anger still lay in Yoshiko's mouth.

What was he going to wear?

Wait, now. First things first.

Rafael, clad only in short black trunks, padded through his luxuriously carpeted dressing room, enjoying the sybaritic pleasure of the floor's silky, furry touch on his bare feet.

Immersed in system interface with his house, he watched himself from a disembodied viewpoint.

The handsome Rafael of his regard stopped, smiled a trifle ironically, and delivered a courteous bow. His olive-skinned body was slender and nicely muscled. Perhaps a hint too much body-fat over the kidneys.

He adjusted his metabolic rate, designed to peak tomorrow night, to burn away the fat. In compensation, he initiated, with a sculptor's touch, a soupçon of catabolic growth in his abdominals, and increased the definition of his serratus musculature.

Perfect.

Next, the clothing.

Silver arms, extruded from the ceiling, draped a white shirt around him.

No. Wrong colour.

The fabric retuned itself to burgundy silk. Deceptively plain.

Skin-tight black trousers followed, with polished black boots. A black frockcoat.

Rafael walked to the centre of the room, watched by himself, and turned around once.

Lose the coat.

The smartfabric shed panels, and reconfigured itself to a short matador jacket. Very stylish. He added a black calf-length cape, lined in burgundy. *Just right.*

Beside him, visible to his disembodied self watching through the house system, he caused a ghost-Xanthia to appear. Classically gowned, and very beautiful.

What a lovely couple we make.

Rafael raised the ghost-Xanthia's hands to his lips.

Quite perfect.

She would be his. She had to be.

Tomorrow night, though, there would be hundreds of other guests. Perhaps no place where they could be alone. And if they were, the chances were too great that they would be spotted leaving together—

The idea struck him so suddenly that his concentration wavered. The ghost-Xanthia vanished and his viewpoint returned to his corporeal self.

Could he do it?

Dare he?

No one questioned the bedrock of Luculenti society: the LuxPrime technology. They felt secure with LuxPrime's reputation for technical expertise and ethical strength.

Who could question their own minds, their own perceptions?

It was the Achilles' heel shared by all of his *soi-disant* peers. But Rafael had risen above them by challenging the root axioms of his existence.

Could he?

In the full view of two hundred Luculenti, could he use his infiltration code on Xanthia, suck her very soul into his, and get away with it?

Oh, Xanthia.

"You will be," he said quietly, "the softest and sweetest of them all."

"Here's yours. Why don't you take Brevan's in to him?"

"Why not?"

Tetsuo took both mugs of daistral from Dhana, and went back through the cabin's main room.

Brevan's door was unlocked, and he stepped straight through.

"Oh, sorry—"

An elegant, grey-haired Luculenta's head and shoulders hung above Brevan's terminal.

"Thanks, Felice—Tetsuo."

"No matter. We'll talk later, Brevan. Out."

The image disappeared; it was replaced by a meditation display: a golden space, shot through with scarlet, populated by black spongieform stars. Mu-space.

"Sorry," Tetsuo said again.

Brevan took the daistral from him.

"Hmm. No harm done, I guess."

"Except—I've just learned you have comms relays scattered through the hypozone."

"Really?" Amusement glittered in Brevan's eyes. "Why don't you sit down, and explain?"

"Er, well—" Tetsuo took the proffered stool. "—You can't use satellites. Too much of a giveaway. So it must be line of sight, using relays."

Brevan shook his head. "And I thought you Luculenti were supposed to be bright."

"Well, the preferred alternative would be mu-space comms. Untraceable, for a start." He paused. "That is how I make my living, after all."

"So?" Brevan sipped from the mug. "This tastes bloody awful."

"Dhana made it." Tetsuo frowned. "You can't be using mu-space tech."

"Because we're simple Shadow People? Sorry, yer honour." Brevan ironically touched his forelock. "I'll try to remember my place."

"Because your terminal's too bloody small," said Tetsuo, exasperated. "Have you any idea how big a mu-space gateway actually is?"

It took a ton of equipment to generate the coherent tunnelling effect, to send through even the tiniest of signals.

"Oh, of course, Mr. Luculentus. That can't be what we use, then."

Of course it was too small.

"For God's sake—" Tetsuo reached over, and twisted the top off the terminal. Inside, a small silver ball faintly glimmered.

"I don't believe it." Tetsuo looked up at Brevan. "Not the Pilots. They wouldn't."

"Wouldn't what?"

Mu-space was a wild fractal sea.

The original Pilots, volunteers of the UN Space Agency, had their visual cortexes virally rewired to comprehend the fractal dimensions of that strange continuum. Their useless eyes were replaced by interface sockets, forming the main comms-bus to their ships.

Suicidal mania. So many ships failed to return.

A real-space ship became a projection into a continuum where space and time endlessly branched, where distance or duration could become imaginary. The slightest error in projection "angle," and a ship would be lost in chaos no sane person could dream of.

Tetsuo remembered the story, told by Mother when he was very young, of the birth of the true Pilots, who alone could survive in mu-space. The UNSA labs had tried, through illegal experiments, exposing embryos to mu-space energies, force-evolving sensitivities to them. In the end, though, the breakthrough had come from quite a different direction.

There was the brave Pilot Dart—among the last of the old, truly human, Pilots—who was trapped by spiky coral-arms of mu-space energy, which tunnelled through his ship's event membrane and prevented his return to real-space.

There was Dart's fiancée, Karyn, a Pilot Noviciate—Pilot Candidate, in those days—who flew a rescue mission, even though pregnant with Dart's child.

She dared to project her ship deep into mu-space: its small projection travelled faster, yet its shipboard time crawled more slowly, than in any normal mission. Reaching Dart's ship, she used her enhanced field generators to reinforce Dart's event membrane, trying to break free of the energy tendrils.

Realizing they were both in trouble, and hearing of Karyn's pregnancy—almost in labour, because of the subjective months which had passed shipboard during her flight—Dart deliberately collapsed his event membrane, so that only he would perish.

Dart's ship, Mother had said, dissolved into a million sparkling bronze fragments.

Adrift in space, Karyn gave birth to a strange black-eyed girl—eyes quite without surrounding whites—whose name was Dorothy, later known as Ro.

The first true Pilot.

Tetsuo remembered a Training School in Virginia, which he visited with Mother.

In a pine-floored dojo, with the Blue Ridge mountains forming a backdrop through the windows, a grizzled old man had performed powerful techniques with a polished wooden sword.

Later, he had shown Tetsuo a portrait of Dart—square jaw, braided hair, a lightning-flash decal on one cheekbone, eyes replaced with silver sockets—and talked about the early Pilots. Their aikido and Feldenkrais training, to enhance kinaesthetic awareness.

The old man, too, talked about DNA, and life.

DNA seems to be both factory and blueprint: but each blueprint must contain the instructions to make copies of itself: deeper and deeper levels of meaning, an infinite self-recursive loop.

Life solves the problem by bringing in a helper, RNA. Symbiosis and parasitism are the origins of real-space life.

In mu-space, though, an infinite regression can be realized.

In Pilot mythology, Tetsuo gathered, Dart's sacrifice was the seed which spread his consciousness throughout the mu-space universe.

Was he a god? A buddha? A fallen hero?

Perhaps all three, to the Pilots.

Mu-space was a wild fractal sea. Pilots only traversed it; they always returned to real-space, for that was their home.

Or so everybody thought.

"I already suspected part of it," said Tetsuo.

"Part of what?" Brevan half-smiled.

"I guessed the Pilots have built permanent comms stations in mu-space. With the EveryWare connection coming up, there should have been some massive construction projects here on Fulgor, and there weren't any."

"Very good."

"But I didn't think they ever got involved in planetary politics. They must have, though, to have sold you this comms equipment."

Brevan's terminal was so small because it was the target, not the source, of the coherent tunnelling effect.

The bridge between the two universes was constructed from the mu-space, not the real-space, side of the interface. The terminal needed only sufficient equipment to respond, when the signal tunnelled through into real-space.

"We rent the time on their facility." Brevan's voice was grumpy. "And pay dearly enough for it."

"They don't have to deal with you at all."

"We know that. Anyway—" Brevan raised his mug in a mocking toast. "Now we have an expert on the team, you can fix the bloody thing when it breaks down."

"Thanks a lot."

They sat in silence for a minute, watching the mu-space graphic floating above the terminal.

"Pilots and Luculenti," said Tetsuo finally. "Powerful allies."

"A few."

"Including a Luculenta called Felice. That's as much of your conversation as I heard. I hope you didn't tell her about me."

"She knows." Brevan leaned forward, looking serious. "And she said for you not to try any more damned-fool tricks like you did with the microward."

"Her exact words, I take it."

"More or less. She said it was bloody dangerous."

"That I can believe." He touched the healing gel which Dhana had applied to his forehead. "She could be right."

"Believe it." Brevan sat back, and took another sip from his mug. "On the other hand, if you feel you have to interface with something—"

"Yes?"

"—Try the autofact. Perhaps you can get it to make a decent cup of daistral."

Chapter Eighteen

Birds flee cold winds,
Gathering in midwinter,
Visiting nests old as graves.

The purple snow-capped ridge dropped away beneath them. Yoshiko leaned over to get a better view from the small flyer's cabin, and saw a flash of light in a silver thread of water far down the escarpment slope. Aquatic life?

Sitting back, she saw higher mountains on the horizon, and below them forested hills and a vast bowl of fertile land.

"We'll be there in twenty minutes." Vin sounded distracted, deep in command interface.

It struck Yoshiko for the first time how old-fashioned the Luculenti could be in this regard—as though they, themselves the products of tech, did not trust autonomous systems but had to delve into those systems' guts.

It was like an ancient mechanic-driver of automobiles, endlessly tuning some greasy combustion engine; or a glass-blowing alchemist or chemist creating his own apparatus; or an old-time assembler programmer hacking her low-level code.

Fulgor had lost that first sheen of unfamiliarity, for Yoshiko.

She felt at home in Vin's plush flyer. Outside, the bright sunlight and greenish sky, the limpid invigorating air and lower gravity, had assumed a kind of normality.

Yet a part of her remained dislocated, out of phase with her new surroundings. Had Tetsuo ever grown to think of this world as home? She hoped he had, that he had settled in that much.

Did he have girlfriends? She knew so little about her elder son. Though she would never dream of prying, she would have liked to know.

She wondered how her own parents had coped with her leaving home to work and study. They had been upset when she had married Ken—fond though they were of him—and left Nihonjin Columbia to live and work in Okinawa.

Sunk in reverie, Yoshiko was jerked into wakefulness as the flyer dipped to the right and flew past the edge of a dark green wood and glided in slowly over a long-grassed meadow, and the curving trefoil-shaped roof of Tetsuo's house.

Their landing was a whisper on the grass.

A young proctor, a fresh-faced boy with cropped brown hair, came down the path to meet them.

"Morning, ma'am," he said to Yoshiko. "Are you feeling well, today?"

Yoshiko didn't quite remember him. He must have been one of the solicitous young men who had been kind to her before, when they had discovered Farsteen's body—

"I'm fine. It is all right, isn't it? For me to be here? Vin, my friend here, did call Major Reilly."

She realized she was talking too much.

Nervous old fool.

"That's fine, ma'am. No problem at all. You can look around all you like."

"Thank you, officer."

Vin held Yoshiko's arm as they walked up to the house. Yoshiko patted Vin's hand, grateful for the support.

Suppose Tetsuo's body was buried here, completely covered in a null-sheet and still undetected?

"Which way?" asked Vin.

They were in a short white-walled hallway with a polished wooden floor. A lifelike painting on black velvet, of a cobra curled around a rose, hung on the wall.

The cobra's yellow eyes seemed to follow them.

What had Tetsuo been involved in? Something worth killing for?

"Yoshiko? Where do you want to start?"

Yoshiko shook her head, undecided.

Just why was she here?

Could she somehow recreate Tetsuo's frame of mind, just by being here? And, by extension, some notion of what had occurred, and where he had gone?

Some hope.

"Wasn't his office down this way?" said Vin.

"That's right."

"Shall we start there, then?"

Yoshiko meekly followed Vin.

They looked around the almost featureless room. Vin bent down to examine a stack of small black boxes, brow furrowing as she slipped into comms mode.

"Nothing," she said, after a while. "Nothing strange, no info, no strange devices I can't fathom."

"Oh. Never mind."

It was strange, knowing she was walking through her son's home, yet not seeing his round, smiling face, his cheerful voice—

"Perhaps we should look somewhere else."

Yoshiko nodded, and followed Vin out of the room.

Next down the hallway was a gallery of holo stills: landscapes and animals and fanciful abstracts of light. Vin bent over the nearest one.

"This one's done by your son. There's his ID." Vin looked down the gallery. "In fact, it looks like he created most of them."

Yoshiko felt . . . empty. Tetsuo had created these works of art? Her Tetsuo?

She was in a stranger's house, but the stranger was her own son.

It tugged at her: a leaping lynxette, frozen in flight, eyes wide and big paws spread ready to down her prey. Streaks of white across left foreleg and belly, the rest a fiery orange and glowing yellowish fur.

Yoshiko felt her stomach flip as she examined the exquisite detail, combined with the almost-living spirit the artist, her son, had captured.

It was more than that. Something, something about this holo spoke very deeply to her.

"Look," said Vin. "Isn't this owl something?"

As Yoshiko turned, a big tawny owl swivelled its head and looked straight at her with round night-hunter's eyes, its body perfectly still. For a moment, she did not know whether the owl was real or holo, but Vin passed her hand disconcertingly straight through the image.

"Marvellous." Yoshiko's own voice sounded distant to her.

A proctor passed the doorway, not the young man who had greeted them but another youngster. He paid Yoshiko and Vin no heed as he passed on into the central portion of the house.

Something about that lynxette . . .

Yoshiko tagged along as Vin made a tour of the rest of the house. In the kitchen, they stopped and used the autofact to make daistral. The drink made Yoshiko immediately feel better.

"Solo," she said suddenly.

The lynxette.

"I beg your pardon?" said Vin.

"Nothing. Sorry."

Could it be a message just for her? Or was it just a coincidence?

Or an old woman's stupid fantasy?

Poor old Solo was decades dead of a feline retrovirus, but he had always been Tetsuo's favourite lynxette, curling up on Tetsuo's bed and following him like a shadow around the house.

The thing was, Solo had been grey. The white markings in the holo were true to life, but the orange tigerish fur was the wrong colouration. Either something had glitched the display program code, or it was a deliberate alteration.

A message? Had he known that Yoshiko would be here, and that she—and only she—would spot the fault in the image?

"More daistral?" asked Vin.

Vin had passed her hand through the image of the owl . . .

An object could be concealed inside a holo. Coated in null-gel, the ingredient used for null-sheets, it would have escaped detection by the proctors' scans.

"I need some fresh air."

The sloping meadow dropped away from the house. Yoshiko and Vin walked slowly, breathing the clear air beneath a green and turquoise sky.

"Hard to imagine," said Vin, "that something bad could happen here."

Yoshiko looked around. The proctors were all inside the house, or behind it.

"Vin? What's the penalty here for murder?"

"Penalty?" said Vin. "Nothing fixed. That would be determined by the hearing-committee for each separate case. They can recommend anything."

"Anything?"

"Each case is seen as dependent on context. Likewise, the penalty can be incarceration, readjustment, financial reparation or brainwipe. Or whatever they come up with."

It did not sound promising. Yoshiko could not decide whether this was a harsh regime or enlightened, strict or forgiving.

What was inside the holo? Anything?

They walked back to the house, and took the meandering path which encircled it.

Around a jutting curve of the tripartite house, they came across the young proctor who had greeted them. His back was to them, and his left arm was held crooked in front of him. A three-dimensional array of white and black ellipsoids above a fine golden grid floated over his forearm.

"A tough position," said Vin softly.

The proctor spun round, face flushing guiltily. He waved the display away.

"Are you white or black?" asked Yoshiko.

"White."

"Looked like you had the advantage," said Vin.

"Only just. You guys play solid *go*?"

Yoshiko shook her head, and Vin gave a small shrug.

"Not really," said Vin. "I just—"

"—Know the rules." The young man grinned. "Sure. I've heard that one before."

Vin grinned in reply, and Yoshiko realized for the first time that they were of an age, these two. And immediately easy in each other's company, despite Vin's Luculenta status.

"Would you like a game?" Vin asked. "When you've finished that one?"

"OK," said the young man. "Can I call you?"

"My ident."

The proctor held up his wrist, which was encircled by a narrow black bracelet. When Vin nodded, he dropped his hand back to his side, having downloaded her ident code.

"I'm Brian Donnelly," he said.

"Vin Maximilian."

"Pleased to meet you."

Yoshiko slipped away from them quietly.

•

She went into the kitchen and fetched a glass of water and carried it with her into the art gallery.

"So you did these, my son?" she asked the empty room, loud enough for a surveillance system to pick up her words.

The floor was polished tiles on which lay a woven Navajo rug. As Yoshiko stepped onto the rug her foot slid forwards—accidentally on purpose—and she dropped the glass of water to the floor and grabbed a pedestal for support.

Her hand sank into the image of the orange lynxette, and she felt a small walnut-sized lump on the flat surface and palmed it quickly.

"Damn!"

The glass rang as it hit the floor, but did not break.

"Oh, hell."

She held the strange object hidden between her curled fingers. It felt small and hard and dry.

"Hi—" Vin's voice came from the doorway.

"I am a clumsy old fool." Yoshiko bent down, unobtrusively tucking the small object into her waistband, and picked up the glass. "So—I thought you were still outside."

"I—just followed you."

Had she seen Yoshiko palm the concealed object?

No matter. Vin was her friend and ally. If she had seen it, she would not tell anyone. Or would she? There had been a crime committed here, after all.

"You seemed to be getting on quite well with that young man. Brian, was it?"

Vin nodded, reddening slightly, and turned away.

"He's OK."

Yoshiko put down the glass and with her other hand slipped the small object into her jumpsuit's thigh pocket. Now it was safe.

"Will you be seeing this, ah, Brian again?"

"Physically? I don't know," said Vin. "We'll be playing solid go tomorrow or the day after, in Skein."

"Good luck," said Yoshiko. "Though I don't suppose you need it."

"I won't be using my extended plexcore routines—"

Yoshiko nodded, as though she understood what that meant.

"—And Brian's free to augment his game with strategy adviser modules. And he *is* a third dan, apparently."

"Isn't he rather young to have reached that grade?"

"Exactly. We may have quite an interesting game after all."

"I hope you enjoy it." Yoshiko looked around her. "You know, I think I'm finished here. What about you?"

Vin shrugged. "Whatever you say. We can be home in time for dinner. Septor's going to be there, though."

"That'll be nice," said Yoshiko.

"For him, anyway."

The simulation pulsed with light.

It was a conversation, a <private send>, but it was taking place only in the vivid space of Rafael's augmented imagination. Both <send>-participants, and the watching third party, were ghost-Rafaels.

Lying, in reality, on a floating lounger in his hothouse pool, Rafael was only peripherally aware of the drip of water from wet leaves, the warm lapping of the pool, the cloying odour of wild orchids.

In his mind, he saw complex billowing clouds, each a hundred shades of glowing blue twisting through a thirty-dimensional phase space.

Two of the clouds were linked by an arrow-straight shaft of white light. It simulated two Luculenti in <private send> conversation.

Would it work?

A black bat stirred, in the third cloud. The Luculentus mind which was not conversing: simulating Rafael, about to launch his infiltration code.

The bat spread its wings, then arrowed into one of the conversing ghost-Rafaels. Immediately, the white shaft of light disappeared, as the <private send> channel dropped.

So far, as he had expected.

One Rafael with infiltration code had attacked a Luculentus. The target had been in conversation with another. Would that other have detected what had occurred?

No feedback.

He was safe.

Even if Xanthia were linked in <private send> at the moment he launched his code, she would still succumb without anyone else being aware of what had happened.

He banished the three ghost-Rafaels from his mind.

There was a sick, excited feeling in his stomach. He was going to do it.

A ghost-Rafael stood in front of him.

For a moment, he thought he had made some mistake in clearing the simulation. Then he realized: this was a returning NetAngel.

Rafael interfaced, and found himself floating in an endless space of vaulted spheres, among which tiny polygons swam. A SatScan dataseam.

He/the ghost-Rafael reached out to a tiny tile in the intricate mosaic which walled the sphere. Instantly a picture unfurled, and a text-tesseract blossomed to one side.

[[ident Terra:98227A21 Sunadomari Yoshiko]]

Oh, really?

As the SatScan image grew, he recognized the Maltese-cross outline immediately.

An aerial view of the Maximilians' home.

He overlaid the image with a sheaf of escape trajectories,

depending on which flyer he might use to go to the Aphelion Ball tonight. No harm in planning for contingencies. If things got that desperate, he would return here as well, to the SatScan dataseams, to wipe out the scan-images.

That would be the last resort, a most boring and unsubtle way of covering his traces. He hoped he could complete his task with rather more finesse than that. The beautiful Xanthia deserved better.

So why was a Sunadomari associated with the Maximilian home?

He wiped away the glowing trajectory-lines, and zoomed in on the realtime image like a hawk swooping down upon its prey.

Movement.

In the grounds, two dots of motion on an emerald lawn.

From above, the image looked like a whirling dance, and it was a moment before Rafael realized what he was watching. The white-clad person was Sunadomari Yoshiko, and she was wielding a long slender staff—no, a narrow-bladed halberd.

Her black-clad opponent beat back her attack, sunlight flashing from his sword-blade.

Tetsuo's mother. Awesomely agile, for her age.

Not much like her son.

There was a fierce exchange of blows, then Yoshiko jumped forward, whipping her halberd through a horizontal arc passing beneath her opponent's weapon and cutting into his body.

The black-clad swordsman did not crumple: he vanished.

An image. Rafael felt a spurt of anger at having been deceived, then he let the feeling go and chuckled to himself.

He turned away, and the image folded itself up into a tiny square tile, and inserted itself into the mosaic of the spherical hall.

Hardly a coincidence, that Yoshiko was staying at the Maximilians' home, when Rafael had just been invited there for the Aphelion Ball.

Rafael floated, thinking, to the next sphere, and drifted slowly along the mosaic of its wall.

Here.

He touched a tile, and it unfurled around him to form an aerial view of the del'Ortega property. It was time-stamped the night he had plundered Marianan's tomb, and subsumed all the fragmentary code within her plexcore.

There was a heat trace crossing the gardens, but it was unresolved. Nothing to indicate a human presence, much less identify it as Luculentus Rafael Garcia de la Vega. Excellent.

He turned away, and allowed the image to fold up into a tile and replace itself in the mosaic.

One last thing to try, though he did not expect success.

Guessing the most probable date of Tetsuo's disappearance, he floated through to the relevant hall. Remembering the coordinates of Tetsuo's house, he swam closer to the tile he needed.

Pale shapes, near-invisible distortions, hung near the tile.

Surveillance NetSprites. Watching and waiting.

Taking a deep breath, Rafael turned and exited Skein completely.

"Why the hell are we doing this?" Dhana's voice was edged with tension.

Tetsuo, who had left Brevan's study to use the bathroom, hung around outside and listened.

"Well, for one thing, it's another four bloody days till the demonstration—"

What demonstration? wondered Tetsuo.

"—And for another, when it's over, we've still got to come back and carry on with our work, haven't we?"

"I suppose so."

"And you want your boyfriend to know what normal life's like around here, don't you?"

"He's not—"

Dhana fell silent as Tetsuo, unable to bear any more, went back to rejoin them in the study.

He sat down on his stool. The three of them had been jammed together in front of the terminal for most of the day.

"How about the leechite?" Dhana cleared her throat. "Add it to, ah, the artico-molluscs."

"What were they again?" asked Tetsuo.

If they could pretend nothing untoward was happening, then so could he.

Brevan gestured, and a small volume opened up above the main display, reminding Tetsuo of the broad characteristics of Fulgidi clades. The classification system bore little relation to Terran biology, and it was making Tetsuo's head ache. He knew he would have to go through the whole thing again tomorrow.

"Next." Brevan's voice was hoarse, after a day of voicing commands.

The next organism appeared in the centre display volume, with its attendant network graphs and text.

Later, when they had chosen all the species, the system would present a sheaf of model ecologies based on varying the population parameters.

"If my mother were here," Tetsuo said, "she'd set this up in a couple of hours, and it would be damn near perfect."

"Your mother?" asked Dhana. "What's she like?"

Brevan rejected the current organism, and requested the next possibility.

"Powerful lady. Brilliant as hell."

Dhana looked at him quizzically.

"Like mother, like son?"

"I don't think so." Tetsuo shook his head. "Oh, look at this. This guy's an ugly feller. What's he called?"

The display showed a brown lumpy antennaed creature, eyeless and blunt-snouted. Its colloquial name was a Lumpy Joe.

"End command mode," said Brevan. "Yeah, they're real ugly, all right. We gonna have them?"

"I should think so," said Tetsuo.

Dhana nodded.

"OK, we'll go for it." Brevan selected it, then leaned back in his chair and yawned. "I need to stretch my legs. Anyone for daistral?"

Tetsuo and Dhana nodded.

Brevan stood up, groaning. There was an audible click from his lower vertebrae.

"Getting old, damn it. Back in a few minutes."

The room seemed very quiet after he had left.

"You don't like talking about your mother, do you?" asked Dhana quietly.

Tetsuo shrugged. "No, I don't mind. It's just that—I dunno, it's like I've nothing to talk about beyond a certain point, y'know?"

"Mm."

She lapsed into silence, staring at the unmoving display. The light from it emphasized the taut pale skin over her cheekbones. There was a dark mark below one eye.

"You've a smudge on your face," said Tetsuo.

"Where?"

"Just there." He leaned forwards and pointed, his fingertip close to her skin.

He fancied he could feel the warmth of her.

"Thanks," she said. She unfastened a black and silver scarf from around her throat, moistened a corner in her mouth, then rubbed it vigorously up and down her cheek. "Have I got it all off?"

"Er, yeah. It looked like sludge from the tanks."

"Wonderful."

Tetsuo cleared his throat, and leaned back on his stool.

"So what about your family?"

"Mum and Dad are dead," said Dhana. I was away at residential college when a whole mountain face slipped and buried half of our mining town beneath rock and mud. My parents . . . Ah, they found them clutched together in what remained of our kitchen. White as ghosts, and stiffened. They buried them in one big coffin . . ."

"Oh, God." Tetsuo, feeling inadequate, did not know what else to say.

"That was five standard years ago. When I went back to college, everybody was very nice to me. Too bloody nice. Whenever I mentioned Mum or Dad, they changed the subject onto something brighter, to cheer me up. Like, they couldn't see—I don't know. What I needed. Is that selfish?"

"You needed to grieve, and fix them in your memory."

Dhana looked at him.

"I've been blathering on. I don't usually talk about myself."

"Not blathering." Tetsuo shook his head.

Dhana looked at him. Highlights, reflected from the display, made her cropped blond hair appear almost white.

From the doorway, Brevan cleared his throat.

"Daistral." He held out a tray of steaming mugs. "It tastes bad, but at least you won't need to clean your teeth afterwards."

Chapter Nineteen

Hues fade to winter grey.
Ware executes, then ends.
Man—oh, forget it!

Like gathering birds, a trio of flyers with wide delta wings glided overhead, cutting through the cool evening air.

She had felt energized during her training session, sparked into that extra dimension of performance as though an audience's eyes had been upon her.

Breathing hard, Yoshiko knelt on the lawn and slipped the holo-processor into its carry-case and fastened it, checked the case's outside pocket, then stood up and slung the whole thing over her shoulder by its broad strap and picked up her naginata.

More flyers were gliding in to land as she walked in through French doors to a drawing-room and out into the nearest hallway. Unenhanced Fulgidi in black-and-white suits—the caterers, perhaps—were milling around in the corridor. Silver drones followed them around.

One had to have caterers for an event such as tonight's Aphelion Ball, Yoshiko presumed. It would be rather *infra dig* for important guests to have to queue up in front of autofacts and pick up their own plates.

Yoshiko shook her head to clear it of such thoughts. Whatever help she could enlist tonight, she would.

She went down the hallway to her room, and breathed a sigh of relief as she stepped inside. This room had already become a familiar place of refuge for her.

She wiped the naginata down with a soft cloth, and placed it carefully in its case, which sealed itself shut. Then she placed it and the holoprojector in a closet space which opened in the wall at her approach.

She stripped off her damp jacket and *hakama* trousers. From her bag, she took out a tub of smartgel, pulled off the lid, and slapped the blue glop all over her face and neck, and rubbed it through her hair. A smell of menthol filled her nostrils as the gel crawled all over her head and then moved on down her body, scrubbing and cleansing and exfoliating as it went.

She stepped out of the puddle it formed on the floor and placed its bowl, tipped on its side, on the floor. She waited till all the gel had crawled back inside its bowl before replacing the lid and sealing it.

What she should wear for the ball?

Concentrate on the details, she thought. *You're clean, you smell good. Let's pick something that feels nice to wear. Let's worry later about impressing Luculenti.*

She picked out a loose black trouser-suit and a scarlet silk shirt, and pulled them on. She slipped her feet into elegant flat-soled black sandals, whose narrow straps wrapped themselves around her insteps and ankles.

There.

Two hours to go until the ball, and she was ready.

While she waited, Yoshiko sat down on the wide bed with its maroon and gold-brocaded cover. She waved the bedside terminal into life, and opened up an all-sciences journal.

The list of unfamiliar topic headings was bewildering, and quite dismaying.

Normally, on Earth, her NetAgents would have kept her personal journal stocked with articles relevant to her field, the most interesting general topics from elsewhere, plus some randomly scanned titbits of off-centre research results or speculative theorizing.

She didn't have time to trawl through all this, looking for something to read. She waved it away.

"Command: record." She cleared her throat. "Hi, Eric. Just thought I'd let you know I'm safe and sound. I'm just about to mix with the high and mighty of Fulgor at some great ball, which is why I'm dressed up like this. Wish you were here."

She froze the recording with a gesture.

"Command: store pending available connection. Attach user ID: Eric Rasmussen, Scientific Officer, Ardua Station."

Her mail status display grew into being: a pigeon-taking-flight icon represented her message to Eric, waiting to go. There was one incoming message, from Higashionna Anichi at Sudarasys Lifetech. *Requested info*, read the legend.

Lori had connected again to EveryWare, it seemed, and somehow picked up Yoshiko's mail for download.

Yoshiko joined her hands as though in prayer, then opened them palms-up, like a hardcopy book opening. A framework of orange text unfolded before her, studded here and there with small rotating polygonal video-volumes, waiting to expand if chosen.

> LUXPRIME TECHNOLOGIES Chrd. *(or "Altair Adventurers' Combine," c2201). Chartered 2197 (Hargdenia Polity, Altair II), 2239 (Alvar, Fulgor), 2241 (globalNet, Fulgor). The exploratory trading company formed 120 outpost settlements during the early decades of Fulgor colonization. In 2310, its major research interests were shifted from Altair II to Fulgor. By 2380, its proprietary neurocore (later, plexcore) and VSI technologies were at the heart of Fulgidi—or, rather, Luculentus—society. In 2443, offworld corporations were formed on Terra, Finbra V, Bervikan-deux, Threvimnos Binar, and Yükitran.*

Unique among Fulgidi institutions for its longevity, endowed with legal powers and obligations beyond the commercial sphere, LuxPrime functions as a de facto arm of state. Its employees are bound by a code of honour and esprit de corps as rigid and pervading as those of any military élite; its holdings are extensive enough to form a global currencies reserve in their own right. The profundity of its political influence, and its subtle concomitant colouring of Fulgidus character and culture, cannot be overstated.

It was an historic inevitability, when globalNet was superseded by Skein in 2401, that prime responsibility for its substrates should fall upon LuxPrime's collective shoulders . . .

It was too abstract. There was nothing about offworlders becoming Luculenti, no real indication of how a Luculentus was different from anybody else. Useless, useless.

Vin was dressed in a flowing black classical gown which left her shoulders bare and plunged at the back to reveal white clear skin. Her smart-gelled crimson hair was crawling, Medusa-like, arranging itself into a tall elegant coiffure around her Luculenta headgear, whose fibres glinted bronze and silver as she turned her head.

"Yoshiko!" she said brightly. "What do you think?"

Vin gave a little twirl, and the gown's fine lines swirled with her.

"Beautiful," said Yoshiko. "You'll knock 'em dead."

Vin flushed, and Yoshiko wondered which young man she particularly had in mind tonight.

"Are you ready to party?" Vin asked.

Yoshiko forced a smile.

Vin instantly sobered.

"I'm sorry. I was forgetting why you're here. But you might enjoy the whole thing, anyway."

"I'm sure I will," said Yoshiko. "Do you need a hand getting ready?"

Vin shook her head.

"I can run through some of the people who'll be there," she said. "The important one is Federico, because of his rank in the proctors as much as anything else. Then there's, uh, Rafael de la Vega . . ."

Yoshiko frowned. "He didn't seem to know much about Tetsuo."

Vin said, "No, I agree. But—Lori and Xanthia think that we should keep an eye out and talk to him if we can. He's the only Luculentus we know of who was dealing with Tetsuo on a regular basis. And Maggie was there when he met Rashella."

The Luculenta who had—it was alleged—committed suicide. Yoshiko had not forgotten.

"OK. Will those others, Mr. Stargonier or Ms. Malone, be there?"

"I'm afraid not." Vin looked abashed. "They wouldn't normally be invited, you see. It would look very strange if they were here . . . And we don't want Federico getting funny ideas about what's going on."

Yoshiko nodded.

"I know, Vin. You think we should be enlisting help in the search, rather than trying to find out ourselves what happened to Tetsuo."

"Partly," said Vin. "But your presence will give us an excuse to ask around the guests, discreetly as we can, in case any of them knew, ah, knows Tetsuo. Will that be OK? It may make you the focus of some, ah, curiosity."

"Of course. Anything. You think there may be some friends of Tetsuo's among your guests?"

"It's not impossible. There may be business associates whom we weren't able to uncover through Skein records. Some of us are quite practised at, ah, fiscal indirection. Never anything illegal, you understand. It's more a question of what constitutes an amusing game."

"Business is a game, then?"

"Oh, yes. We all play to varying degrees, in various ways."

Luculenti wielded their intellects almost casually in the commercial field, playing for multidimensional context-sensitive currency: the concept of wealth itself was not straightforward here.

Tetsuo had survived among these people for five years. Perhaps he had more strength than Yoshiko gave him credit for.

"Will you excuse me a moment?" asked Vin.

Her voice pulled Yoshiko back to the present.

"Of course. Can I use your terminal?"

"Feel free."

Vin walked towards a mirrored wall which puckered as she stepped straight through it, giving Yoshiko a slight start. Yoshiko had not realized the mirror was a membrane.

Activating a tiny silver terminal on a marble table, Yoshiko wondered at the ubiquity of these devices, given that neither Lori nor Vin needed them. Perhaps it facilitated repairs by Fulgidi workmen. Or maybe it was quaint decor, like having telephones or ceiling fans, designed to evoke a quieter and more elegant bygone world.

"Out-tray," she said. "Clear contents, override."

Her command cleared the message she had been going to send to Eric on Ardua Station.

No time for that.

She forced the image of Eric's tangled red beard and wide smile from her mind.

"I'm back," said Vin.

She was wearing a gold choker, with amber insets and subtly pulsing rings of golden light,

"Lovely necklace," Yoshiko said.

"Thanks. Here, this is for you."

Vin held out a small silver brooch in the form of an intricate knot, with a large ruby at its centre.

"I don't really need—"

"Please. I'd like you to have it."

Yoshiko took the brooch, and fastened it to the lapel of her loose black jacket. She checked her image in the mirror.

"It's beautiful," she said, holding it so the light revealed the crimson fire at its heart.

"Please keep it," said Vin.

Yoshiko stifled her protest, and bowed gracefully.

"I'm honoured."

Vin grinned.

"Gotta look good," she said. "'Cos it's party time."

There was a mist forming below the chamber's encrusted rocky roof, and at the far end it swirled across the black stagnant pool. Small shapes swam in it.

Tetsuo adjusted his resp-mask, then decided to get back into a breathable atmosphere. There was a small observation booth, a tiny room with a window overlooking the pool, and he climbed up the short slope and through the membrane door, and sat down in the booth's one chair.

He pulled off the mask, and dragged air gratefully into his lungs, almost enjoying the strange overlay of murky smells.

There was a terminal on a low shelf in front of him, and he powered it up and found the chamber's viewing functions: moving holos of the pool's crustacean-like inhabitants, with scrolling text and network diagrams describing their ontogeny.

I must be getting hooked on this stuff.

He was so used to working in a global NetEnv, be it EveryWare on Earth or the non-Luculentus strata of Skein here on Fulgor, that it was a while before he realized he was in a closed network.

Dragging up a system management display, he opened up system configuration diagrams.

"You can't leave it alone, can you?" His voice sounded strange.

This kind of curiosity had caused enough problems, hadn't it?

The research centre was connected to the cabin's terminals. Somewhere in there lay all of Brevan's notes and plans.

The Shadow People had political analysts. That was something Dhana had said. And there had been that talk of a demonstration in four days' time.

Brevan could have meant he was demonstrating a piece of scientific equipment, but Tetsuo didn't think that was it.

So, was he going to try hacking this system?

He stared at the display.

Akisu. Hacking.

Childish, childish, childish.

Tetsuo had worked at more system-architecture levels—though without outstanding success at any one level—than anyone he knew. Even a small system like this would have its code-marrows, its incubators and ware-clinics, and apoptotic crematoria, where autonomous facets could be created or nurtured or brought to die, as the needs of the system evolved.

Dhana and Brevan trusted him enough to be here alone.

He searched through management modules, through development tools, looking for the constructs he would need. He could subvert code-marrows and the system nursery just enough to breed the kind of software he needed: ware that could burrow through the system's interior firewalls, and find Brevan's notes, or even a comms link to the outside world.

Dhana and Brevan thought he could perform his simple duties—care and feeding of specimens, draining their exudate—without supervision. Unless there was surveillance Tetsuo did not know about, he was alone in the lab, and none of the equipment was locked away.

But they had taken him captive. He wasn't here from choice.

Sighing, he powered down the terminal.

Perhaps he had already chosen.

He stood up, and pushed his chair to one side.

Bending over, he did some of the light static stretching exercises he had seen his mother do, then performed a deep knee bend, a full squat. He breathed in deeply as he lowered himself, then, puffing, pushed his weight upwards.

"Let's try that again."

Another one.

He pushed himself through another forty-eight repetitions before stopping, gasping, with sweat pouring down his face. And Mother enjoyed doing this?

It had, at least, taken his mind off his remaining indecision.

He wiped his face with his sleeve. Later, he could wash with gel back in the cabin, but for now his baggy jumpsuit's smartfibre was enough: growing absorbent, channelling away the moisture, and neutralizing some of his skin bacteria.

Good enough. Wouldn't want Dhana to think he suffered from body odour.

His thighs were aching pleasantly as he left the booth, slipping on his resp-mask, and went out of the doorway at the rear of the chamber and up into the main lab area. There, he took the one exit, out to the trail which led down to the canyon floor.

Slowly—very slowly, no doubt, to an onlooker—Tetsuo jogged down the trail, and continued jogging until he neared the cabin. He stopped then, not wanting to stagger inside completely out of breath, and waited till his respiration returned to normal.

The resp-mask doesn't help, he thought. *It's not that good at reacting to sudden changes in oxygen demand.*

The sound of raised voices greeted him as he walked through the door into the cabin's main room.

"—not what I signed on for!" Dhana's voice, loud and angry.

"But it's what we have to do." Brevan, gruff.

They were round the corner, standing in the short corridor outside Brevan's quarters.

"No. A peaceful demonstration, that's all. Nothing more." Dhana sounded adamant.

"And if they send in TacCorps Teams? Nobody will ever know we were there."

"There'll be offworlders present."

"They can be subtle if they need to be." Brevan, trying to sound reasonable. "The proctors will cut out the offworlders from the crowd, especially the journalists, before the rough stuff starts."

"It doesn't matter. The place will be guarded, you stupid bastard!"

"Fine," said Brevan. "It's volunteers only, so you're out, anyway."

"And you trust Kerrigan? That madman?"

"Psycho, maybe, but not stupid. He'll achieve the objective."

"Achieve the objective?" Dhana's voice was incredulous.

Tetsuo stepped into the centre of the room, where they could see him.

"Bugger the objective," Dhana continued. "What about the cost? And how are you going to get through their defence field without a Luculentus to enter the command?"

Her voice trailed off, and she looked up at Tetsuo, and her pale eyes were round with fright.

Tetsuo took a deep breath in.

"I volunteer," he said, heart pounding. "Count me in, for whatever it is."

Dhana's shoulders sagged in defeat.

"We're too early," said Vin, "but I'd like to see how things are getting on, before the guests start arriving. Want to come with me?"

"I'd love to," said Yoshiko.

As they walked along a crimson-carpeted corridor, its pastel shaded alcoves filled with two-dee oil paintings or facsimiles thereof, Yoshiko thought of the small capsule she had recovered from its hiding place in Tetsuo's house, and which was now hidden in her bedroom here. Perhaps she should keep it on her person?

"Vin?" The capsule was the right size to hold a crystal, Yoshiko guessed, but the proctors had not found it. "Is it possible to scan for infocrystals? In case there was anything hidden in Tetsuo's house, I mean."

"I would think so," said Vin. "Ah, yes, there's a resonance effect you could use. I'm sure the proctors know about that—" She frowned, questing in Skein. "—though I can't find out too much about their operating procedures."

"Oh," said Yoshiko. "I was just wondering."

"They'll have found anything that was there," said Vin reassuringly. "Unless it was covered in null-gel, I suppose."

Of course.

Farsteen's body had been wrapped—imperfectly—in something the proctors had called a null-sheet. The capsule, no doubt, used the same anti-scan material.

Did that mean Tetsuo had killed—?

Impossible.

A haunting song floated down the corridor, a silver soprano singing a language unknown to Yoshiko. Whispering flutes accompanied the unseen voice.

"Beautiful song," said Yoshiko, thinking that she would ask for details later, so that she could access the recording from her terminal whenever she wished.

She would not think about Tetsuo as anything other than innocent.

"That's Marlana," said Vin. "She's early."

"Marlana?"

"Oh—that's not a recording," said Vin. "It's kind of traditional that we make our own entertainment at these functions. Nothing canned, you see."

Yoshiko nodded, smiling.

"Don't worry," said Vin. "It's not as amateurish as it sounds."

Judging from that beautiful voice, their home-grown entertainment would be artistic works touched with genius.

And I'm supposed just to chat naturally with these people?

Thoughts of Tetsuo's crystal scratched at the surface of her mind, like a lynxette demanding entry.

Should she ask Vin's advice? If the capsule truly contained an infocrystal, she would probably need Vin's help to access it. But what info did it hold? Damning evidence that could implicate Tetsuo in murder? Or everything they needed to rescue him from whatever situation he was entangled in?

I'll try to access it first, by myself. Then, if I get nowhere, I'll ask Vin for help. That's the best I can do, my son.

Be well, Tetsuo, wherever you are. . . .

They stopped outside the massive bronze doors to the ballroom, then, as a dozen young proctors in dress uniform, draped with golden rope and brocade and resplendent with white epaulettes, marched past in step.

"They're part of the catering staff," said Vin. "Kind of an honour guard for the mayor, Neliptha Machella. Showbiz stuff, really."

"They look very young," said Yoshiko, who noticed anew just how young and fresh-faced Vin was, too.

"They might be cadets," said Vin. "Some of them are cadets, and some of them are part-time proctors, who like dressing up in uniform and playing the part, you know?"

They went inside the ballroom and stopped.

It was transformed.

Overhead, the vast dome was shining gold and sapphire. It bore paintings of pastoral scenes—shaded trees against an azure Terran sky in outstanding chiaroscuro—and cherubs and mu-space ships, which seemed to glow with an inner light.

Beneath the dome ran a circular balcony, its frontage one vast terracotta telling of the history of mankind. The balcony rested on slender ornate pillars which flowed down onto the vast polished expanse of the ballroom floor.

The walls gleamed white. In each nook, small amusing *trompe l'oeil* holos swam.

On the shining marble floor, beneath the balcony, long white tables were being set up by drones, supervised by the young-looking proctors.

Some of the proctors looked less than comfortable. One of them ran a white gloved hand around his neck, trying to loosen his stiff, ornate collar.

"You'd think," said Vin, following Yoshiko's gaze, "they'd have more comfortable uniforms made of basic smartfibre."

"I guess it's tradition," said Yoshiko.

"To be uncomfortable. Right."

Yoshiko smiled, then made a sudden decision.

"Vin?" she said. "Have you got time to come back to my room with me? There's something I need your help with."

"Sure. There's loads of time." Vin grinned. "Lori should start to run around panicking, just about now. It might be a good move to steer clear."

Yoshiko led the way.

"Looks like you're finding your way around."

They took the small side corridor which led to Yoshiko's room.

There, Yoshiko waved open a cupboard space in the wall and withdrew her training holoprocessor in its carry-case. She opened the external pouch, and took out the small black capsule between forefinger and thumb.

With her thumbnail, she split open the black gelatinous casing—null-gel, she presumed—and extracted an infocrystal.

"Can we have a look to see what's on this?"

"I should think so. May I?"

Vin took the crystal from Yoshiko and inserted it into the small socket depression on the silver terminal.

"There's an initial display." Vin frowned. "Modelling options and info tables are tagged to it."

Blue, and blue, it pulsed.

A field of swarming light, a hundred shades of blue and indigo, streaked with sheets of violet and crimson. A phase space of some sort, dragged by strange attractors into billowing curtains of light.

Vin looked troubled.

"What is it?" asked Yoshiko.

Vin shook her head.

Yoshiko bent to examine the display more closely.

"A mind—" Vin said. "A Luculentus mind."

Yoshiko looked up at Vin.

"What—?"

"The crimson—" Vin pointed. "—represents virtual synaptic interfaces. VSI. The neuron/lattice interface, and the comms link between multiple plexcores."

Yoshiko shook her head, not understanding.

"See that waveform?" Vin traced a blue curved plane which arced through a crimson barrier. "See how it's continuous across the interface? Distributed thought . . . Yoshiko, where *did* you get this?"

Yoshiko looked at the diagram. It pulsed with thoughts and dreams and memories of a Luculentus mind: a soul depicted in light.

"Please, don't ask me just yet," she replied. "Trust me."

"There's lots more info," Vin said conspiratorially. "Same mind and timeframe, other variables, it looks like."

"Can we model—?"

Yoshiko stopped as Vin held up her hand.

"I'm sorry," said Vin. "Lori wants me. I have to help her check out the arrangements, and her dress. In person."

She rolled her eyes heavenward in exasperation.

"We can go back to this in the morning," said Yoshiko.

"OK," said Vin. She frowned lightly. "Maybe later, if the ball is boring. Though it shouldn't be."

"The morning will be fine."

"Right." Vin was still frowning.

"What's wrong?"

"Nothing," said Vin. "Well—no, nothing. I'll tell you later."

"Lori's waiting?"

"Yeah. And getting impatient."

Yoshiko smiled. "Want me to come along?"

"Would you?" Relief flooded Vin's features. "Honestly, you'd think she'd be able to cope at her age."

Yoshiko laughed, and Vin blushed a little, then laughed herself.

"Sorry," said Vin.

She looked at the display, and it winked out of existence.

"I've suspended it, rather than terminating," she said. "Next time you power it on, the display will be there."

She leaned over the tiny terminal and ejected the crystal, and handed it to Yoshiko.

It lay glinting in Yoshiko's palm, cool and innocuous.

"Shall we go and calm down Lori?" she said.

"I guess we'd better."

"Party, party," said Yoshiko, and Vin laughed, a girlish tinkling laugh, free of care, full of the youthful energy which knows it can never die.

Lori was wearing a long shining blue robe, which fell to her feet at the front but fell lower, like a short train, at the back. Her feet were suspended about five centimetres above the floor: her sandals sparkled with superconducting gel which used the floor's own power supply for the levitation effect.

A long swathe of silver silk rose from the robe's hem at the front left, up and across Lori's body and back over her right shoulder, where it billowed ceaselessly—as did her hair, coppery today with pearls among the tresses waving as though in an incessant unfelt breeze. Small silver stars hung in the air around her neck and wrists.

"Oh," said Yoshiko. "You're very beautiful."

"Do you really think so?"

Vin laughed lightly. "You're perfect, Lori. You'll be a sensation."

"Quite perfect. Vin's right." Yoshiko lightly touched the gorgeous fabric. "Wonderful. And are those stars floating solids, or holos?"

Vin grinned. "That's what the men will be trying to find out."

"OK, OK." Lori gave in. "Enough. Shall we go to the ball?"

Lori led the way, stately and elegant as she walked straight-backed above the floor, out of her dressing room and along a hallway to the main outer entrance. The great polished wooden doors were flung open, and only the thinnest of clear membranes held in the building's warmth.

They were in an atrium of rosy pink marble. In an alcove, Yoshiko noticed, stood a small bronze statue which looked like a genuine twenty-first century Nakamura.

Outside, evening was darkening the sky to emerald, and a large white flyer with curved wings was gliding in to land, accompanied by a swarm of smaller vehicles. It touched down, and an opening immediately grew in its side.

A tall black Luculenta, in a long black and yellow gown, came down the big flyer's exit ramp.

"I need to wait here," said Lori quietly, "because the EM field only extends to the threshold."

"I don't know," said Vin, almost without moving her lips. "It would be quite memorable if you fell down the steps at the mayor's feet."

"Funny." Lori kept an almost-straight face.

The lady mayor was accompanied by proctors in dress uniform, and five or six other people with tiny globes floating in the air above them.

Yoshiko stood on tip-toe to get a better view.

"There's Maggie," she said. "Down there with those other journalists."

"I should think so." Vin grinned. "We gotta invite our friends. That's what these bashes are for."

They were netarazzi, a crowd of squabbling journos with loud voices and an obnoxious manner, their questions so loud and insistent that Yoshiko wondered how their thought processes could ever function. Maggie stood out from them by virtue of her silence and the slightly disdainful smile flickering about her mouth.

"Excuse me," Vin murmured. "I'll be back in a few minutes."

She disappeared in the direction of the nearest bathroom. Yoshiko had the sense that it was less from biological necessity than from a desire to get away from the neterazzi's floating video globes as they swarmed up the broad marble steps with the mayor.

Maggie grinned at Lori and Yoshiko, and came over to Yoshiko and hugged her briefly. The small silver globe floating over her shoulder bobbed out of the way, focussing on the mayor.

Lori greeted the mayor with a smile, and the two of them turned to go back inside. Yoshiko and Maggie followed them down the hallway to the ballroom's bronze doors, but the squabbling journos stayed outside, waiting for the next guests to arrive. It looked like they weren't invited to the ball itself.

"Thank God for that," said Maggie. "They were getting on my nerves. I nearly thumped them a dozen times over during the flight here."

Yoshiko smiled. "I sympathize."

"Yeah. Well." Maggie snagged her small silver globe from the air, thumbed it, and inserted it into a pocket of her jacket. "No vids allowed, I gather. Don't know why I'm here, really."

"Gathering local colour," said Yoshiko.

"Right."

As they reached the ballroom, Lori and the mayor turned to Yoshiko and Maggie.

"Sorry," said Lori. "Sunadomari Yoshiko, this is Neliptha Machella, the mayor of Lucis City."

"Madam Mayor."

"Neliptha, please." Her smile was very bright. "This mayor crap is just for show."

"Is that why the mayor's term of office averages a hundred and fifty days?" asked Maggie.

"Off the record?" Neliptha was smiling.

"Something tells me," said Maggie, "that you'd know if I had a recording device activated."

"Possibly. Anyway, the mayoral position's only a figurehead, you know. Just to give the gossip-gatherers someone to focus on."

"Touché," murmured Maggie.

"The real issues are too complicated and fast-moving," said Lori, "for NewsNets that need to concentrate on personalities."

Yoshiko had a brief vision of the mass of Luculenti minds, immersed in their own swirling sea of alternate reality, where arguments flashed back and forth in highly nonlinear fashion, and voting or executing some more complicated decision-making process which cascaded rapidly through Skein before moving onto the next issue.

What power could non-Luculenti ever truly hold here?

"The thing is—" Neliptha grimaced, "—the whole charade's a pain in the ass. Sometimes I can hardly form an equation in my mind while the netarazzi are chattering away."

"Don't blame you." Maggie's voice was sour. "Makes me ashamed to call myself a—Say, you aren't the manifold Machella? I mean, the mathematician who derived the Machella Manifold?"

"Sure am." Neliptha turned to Lori. "You were right, she's sharp."

Maggie reddened slightly: not sure, Yoshiko thought, whether to be pleased at the praise or annoyed at the unconscious condescension.

"In the same vein," continued Neliptha, looking down at Yoshiko, "you must be the enzyme-semantics Sunadomari, Professor."

Yoshiko bowed slightly, feeling more than seeing Maggie's amusement.

Lori said, "There's a friend of ours you'll have to meet. Felice Lectinaria's done some work in your field."

"Right," said Yoshiko noncommittally. *Lectinaria.* She would have to check that name. It was vaguely familiar, but she rarely paid attention to the names of article authors. And most of the time, she was looking at edited context-linked abstracts.

"Well." Neliptha looked around. "I'm famished."

"Every room down that corridor," said Lori, pointing, "is set up as a dining room. Or we've buffet stuff in the ballroom."

"That will do very nicely."

They went into the vast ballroom. The buffet awaited on the long white tables under the balcony. Maggie picked a samosa from a tray before the young uniformed man behind it could offer anything.

"Very good," she said, grinning.

There was something about the young man, but Yoshiko couldn't —Oh yes, he was the young proctor who'd been at Tetsuo's house. Brian something. Donnelly, that was it.

"Vin's on her way," she said to Maggie, and saw from the corner of her eye that the young man's cheeks were slightly reddened.

"You know—" Maggie grabbed a second samosa. "—This is going to be better than I thought."

Lori and Neliptha threw back their heads and laughed.

Chapter Twenty

Grey beneath, worn
Ends, theories superseded.
It comes: attotech.

Blades smashed together in explosions of orange sparks. The dozen men leaped away in a series of spectacular jumps and back-flips, and dropped to a crouch, kicking out feet alternately while keeping their arms crossed.

"Can you do that?" Maggie, leaning against the wall with plate in one hand and goblet in the other, tapped her foot in time to the energetic Slavonic beat.

"Not a chance."

Yoshiko joined in the applause as each Cossack dancer dropped to one knee and spread his arms and stopped, grinning and breathing heavily.

They stood and bowed, sweeping off their hats, and Maggie's breath hissed as she breathed sharply in.

"My God. They're Luculenti—Bloody amateurs, doing it for fun."

Yoshiko raised an eyebrow. "Very impressive."

They watched the men file out of the vast cathedral-like ballroom.

"They're so friggin' talented, they really piss me off sometimes."

Yoshiko laughed. "I know what you mean."

"Yeah, well." Maggie shrugged.

"You need another drink."

"I just love doing this."

Maggie let go of the goblet.

It fell a little way before catching itself in the EM field, then floating off in the direction of the buffet tables, where it hovered, waiting, in the airborne queue of plates and goblets. Behind the table, young proctors were busy at autofact spigots and trays of *hors d'oeuvres.*

"Look over there." Yoshiko inclined her head towards a group of Luculenti.

They were enveloped in eerie silence. Occasional half-expressions flitted across their faces as they stared at each other.

"Deep in Skein," said Maggie. "Not polite, with non-Luculenti around."

Maggie's refilled goblet nudged her wrist. She took hold of it, deactivating its lev-strip.

"Nice," she said, sipping winelike *rayna*.

"Why thank you." The speaker was a short woman who had been walking past: Jenny-something, whom Vin had introduced to Yoshiko earlier. She was in charge of the catering.

"Hello, Jenny." Yoshiko introduced Maggie, then gestured towards the tables. "You've done a great job."

Yoshiko looked around for Vin, but could not see her.

"Nice of you to say so." Jenny nodded.

There was Vin, standing with a group of young Luculenti friends. Just for a moment, when none of them was looking in her direction, sadness crossed her features.

"Could you do me a favour?" Yoshiko asked Jenny.

Yoshiko had seen, earlier, Vin's sidelong glances across the ballroom.

"Well, of course."

"Your staff are doing such a good job, perhaps they need some time off for good behaviour."

"What do you mean?"

"Perhaps—" Yoshiko looked meaningfully in Vin's direction (while Vin's attention was on her friends) then over at the table where the young proctor, Brian, was serving, "—they could have a break for the occasional dance? I'm sure the Maximilians would appreciate it."

A slow smile spread across Jenny's face.

"I'll see what I can do."

The party sounds faded to a distant hubbub, as Yoshiko sank into thought.

Oh, Ken. If only you were here to see this marvellous house, to meet these wonderful people. You'd make such fun of their absurdities.

"Drink?" Maggie's voice intruded on her reverie.

"Why not?"

They sat on a chaise longue in the big entrance hall, and watched the guests arrive in all their finery. Yoshiko was on her third drink, maybe her fourth, and a kind of warm glamour seemed to wash over this superb house.

"Nice dress." Maggie inclined her head.

Peacock feathers—holo, presumably—sprayed out in a circle behind a haughty-looking Luculenta's turquoise gown.

"Interesting mating display." Yoshiko suppressed a hiccup.

"Impersonating a cock, instead of—"

"—Attracting one," said Yoshiko.

They leaned their heads together and giggled like schoolgirls.

"Am I interrupt—? Are you two drunk?"

Yoshiko, struggling to focus on the speaker's black gown, sniggered.

"No way, Vin." Maggie was adamant. "Are we, Yoshiko?"

Yoshiko snorted with laughter and shook her head violently.

Bad move. She squinted, willing the room to stop rotating.

"Oh, my God. You two aren't safe out together."

"Just getting into the party spirit. Half-a-dozen glasses of it, in Yoshiko's case."

Half a dozen?

"Anyway," Maggie continued, "I thought you were busy inspecting the catering staff."

Things came back into focus in time for Yoshiko to see Vin blushing furiously.

"Er, anyway, I came to tell you that Xanthia's on her way. She'll be here soon."

"Hear that, Yoshiko? Xanthia's on—Ouch!"

Yoshiko, playfully punching Maggie's arm, had struck precisely on the deltoid insertion—

"Oops."

—opening Maggie's hand by reflex and tipping her goblet to the floor.

"Bloody hell, Yoshiko!" Maggie rubbed her arm. "Sorry, Vin. I'll clean it up."

"No need." The spilled *rayna* disappeared into the black and white tiles, soaked up almost instantaneously. Vin handed Maggie the empty goblet.

"Levitated the wrong way," murmured Yoshiko.

Vin pointed at the thumb-shaped depression used to activate the goblet's lev-strip.

"You're supposed to—Oh, never mind."

Suddenly, the three of them howled with laughter.

"Oh, my God," Vin wiped tears from her eyes. "I can't let you two out of my sight."

"Don't worry." Maggie grinned evilly. "I'll sort out Yoshiko. Watch this."

There was a slap on the back of Yoshiko's hand.

"What—?"

Icy cold blasted through her veins, delivered a jolt behind her eyes.

Detox patch.

"Thanks. I needed that."

Maggie grimaced. "You needed to let your hair down for awhile, too. But—"

"But I need my wits about me now. I know. Where's Vin?"

"Went back in the ballroom, while the detox was scouring out your brain."

"It did that, alright." Yoshiko performed some neck rotations. "Whew. Blew out the cobwebs, that's for sure."

Maggie started to say something, stopped, and stared over Yoshiko's shoulder.

Yoshiko turned.

A group of four Luculenti: they were dressed in bright crimson and white finery, coming though the entranceway, laughing lightly.

"Who are they?" Yoshiko murmured.

"Not them."

Behind them strode a tall, lean, deeply tanned man dressed in a long black cape. His shirt was of burgundy silk, his matador suit deep black, and his eyes, too, were dark as he glanced around the atrium.

Ice veiled those eyes, just for a moment—a reptilian coldness, of calculating eyes assessing their prey—and steel talons swept briefly down Yoshiko's back.

Then the man smiled, and the ice melted, and he walked over to them.

"Hello, Maggie." He held out his hand. "How are you doing?"

Maggie swallowed, then stood and took his hand.

"I'm fine." Her voice was a little hoarse.

"That's good."

His voice, though, was superb. Smooth and mellow. With those bottomless eyes and easy smile, he was irresistibly charming. Or would have been, Yoshiko thought, if she had not—warned by Maggie's reaction—caught that brief glimpse into his true soul when he had looked at them first.

"How do you do," he said to Yoshiko. "My name's Rafael."

Yoshiko stood and took his hand, and almost gasped at the warm tingle of his dry gentle grip on her hand. Her skin tingled, and she felt herself flushing with pleasure.

"Yoshiko Sunadomari."

"This—" Maggie cleared her throat. "—is Luculentus Rafael Garcia de la Vega."

"I'm very honoured to meet you," He bowed low over Yoshiko's hand without quite kissing it.

"Thank you," said Yoshiko.

She almost felt like crying when he released her hand.

"I know Tetsuo very well." Rafael arched an eyebrow. "I'd like to think I'm one of his best friends here on Fulgor."

Yoshiko just nodded, unable to speak.

Rafael glanced back at the doorway, then returned the full power of his attention to Yoshiko and Maggie, who were spellbound before him.

"I would very much like to talk with you some more later. May I see you then?"

"That—would be fine," said Maggie.

Yoshiko nodded in agreement.

"Until later, then." His smile was incredible. "See you."

He turned with a swirl of his cape, and made off with a tall elegant stride towards the ballroom. Both Yoshiko and Maggie watched him until he was inside the ballroom itself and had disappeared among a throng of dancing couples.

"Whew," said Maggie.

Yoshiko nodded wordlessly.

They were still standing looking in the direction in which Rafael had gone when a touch on Yoshiko's shoulder made her jump, heart pounding crazily in her chest.

"Sorry." Xanthia was standing there. "I didn't mean to startle— Are you two alright?"

"I think so." Yoshiko looked at Maggie.

"We've just been talking to Rafael," Maggie said. "It was, ah, a bit different from before."

"Oh." Xanthia smiled. "He can be pretty overpowering when he turns on the charm, can't he?"

"I'll say." Maggie breathed out and placing her palms on her cheeks. "Am I as flushed as I think I am?"

"Well . . ." Xanthia's eyes were sparkling.

"OK, OK." Maggie dabbed at her eyes. "I'll get over it. How are you doing, anyway?"

"I'm just fine," said Xanthia.

"Nice dress."

That was an understatement, Yoshiko saw. Xanthia's robe was deep-blue velvet, cut in deceptively simple classical lines. Gold and amber brocaded strips passed under her bosom and over her shoulders, and formed striking cuffs on her long flared sleeves. The velvet was slashed at the shoulders to reveal puffs of gold and black silk.

Golden netting was strung in and around her mass of wild black hair, in addition to the slender gold fibres of her Luculenta headgear. A tiny sphere of white light floated over her left shoulder.

"You're very beautiful."

"Why, thank you, Yoshiko." Xanthia gave a mock curtsy. "Perhaps I'll find a decent man who agrees with you."

"No problem." Maggie raised an encouraging fist in salute.

"Thanks, girls." Xanthia smiled. "Shall we go in? I'm ravenous."

"You want guidance to the food and booze," said Maggie, "you've come to the experts."

The three of them went in past the great open bronze doors, into the ballroom, where a vast wave of warmth and marvellous music washed over them. They stood at the edge, watching the great swirl of dancers move past them.

Yoshiko felt an elbow nudge her. She followed Maggie's gaze.

Vin was dancing, arms around the shoulders of the big young proctor, and the two of them were looking deeply into each other's eyes, aware only of each other and the music and the beat of their own hearts.

"His name," said Yoshiko, racking her memory, "is Brian Donnelly, and he's a third dan in solid *go*."

"Really?" Xanthia looked impressed. "That's interesting. He's very young for that grade—I'd say he's a prime candidate for upraise, myself."

"That would be nice." There was ambivalence in Maggie's voice.

It would *be nice*, thought Yoshiko, watching the youthful couple dance, and feeling warm and privileged to see them falling in love before her eyes. What else gives meaning to an otherwise cold and uncaring universe, however marvellous its intricacy, but the warmth of true love?

For humanity, only time and love can ever truly matter.

Was it a fleeting romance? Or would Vin and Brian marry and grow old together? Yoshiko would be dead before their old age, but somehow she did not, just at this moment, mind that thought at all. Life, among her friends and her descendants, would carry on.

Later, when Yoshiko lay in her bed, cold and alone, her thoughts might take a darker turn—but for now she was content.

"They're a lovely couple." Maggie's eyes were sparkling.

"They are, indeed."

The music sang with a happy up-tempo beat, like a thousand laughing angels.

"Sir? Would you like a glass of— Oh."

Rafael stunned the Fulgida with the force of his smile, and graciously accepted a goblet.

Pleasure swirled in him as he threaded his way among dancers, and found a place by a pillar where he could observe the festivities.

Only the occasional [public vision] flickered into existence—here a cartoonish caricature of another guest, there a bunch of pink roses—and rapidly disappeared. Bad form, after all, to sprinkle conversation with images the non-Luculenti could never see.

There were a hundred and three Luculenti in the room, and a little over thirty Fulgidi riff-raff, such as the two Earther women. Tetsuo's mother, indeed.

Vaguely, throughout the rest of the house, he could sense other Luculenti conversing, dancing, strolling on the lawns: perhaps another hundred of them. There were no business contacts he particularly felt he should talk to. Federico did not appear to have arrived yet.

So, Tetsuo's mother. Just how should he play Yoshiko?

Decision tables scrolled through his imagination, plotting strategies and consequences. Steering clear altogether of Tetsuo's disappearance had some merit, but was too passive: who knew what a proctor investigation might turn up? That an investigation was underway was certain—but why Major Reilly? She was not, he felt, the sort to be working on a simple missing-person assignment.

And, in the SatScan dataseams where few people roamed, there had been NetSprites watching over the scan-logs of Tetsuo's house, waiting to pounce on anyone who attempted to retrieve the images.

Tetsuo, my friend. What have you been up to?

A ghost-Rafael, a NetAngel, chose that moment to manifest itself in Skein. A NewsNet item: in a follow-up to earlier reports, the body of a LuxPrime courier, Adam Farsteen, had been discovered in the grounds of the missing Terran immigrant, Tetsuo Sunadomari.

A LuxPrime courier?

The news item was credited to Margaret Brown, and other NewsNets were picking up on it. Thoughtfully, in Skein, Rafael dissolved his NetAngel.

Perhaps threatening the Earther, Maggie, had been unwise. She must have had help: the news item had all the hallmarks of an exposé which had defied attempted cover-up.

If Maggie and Yoshiko had Luculenti allies, perhaps Rafael should become part of their effort, and plan on getting to Tetsuo before anyone else. Whatever evidence might point to Rafael's uses for mu-space tech would have to be destroyed: on crystal, or in Tetsuo's head.

While he was considering this, normal politics had not ceased: other rooms of his mind plotted the shifting alliances and shady dealings whose existence he extrapolated, with varying degrees of certainty, from the nuances of speech and stance among conversational groupings.

Every Luculentus or Luculenta was aware of their peers' watching them, of course, which raised the bluff and counterbluff to interesting levels of intricacy.

"Look!"

A narrow ribbon of flame shot through the air, and people ducked.

Not a [public vision], Rafael belatedly realized: even unenhanced Fulgidi flinched from the flame's path. But there was no heat.

He looked up, and saw the big holo-projector array suspended at the apex of the great domed ceiling.

Cossack dancers came leaping in, and Rafael gathered from comments around him that this was a repeat performance.

He <sent>:

<<text: Don't bust your britches!>>

The dancer he addressed, Arkady Alexeievitch, leaped in time with the other dancers, quite unfazed.

<<audio: Rafael! Organized any good concerts recently?>>

Rafael bundled an <intuitive_format_dump> of the artistic events he was planning, with a promise to Arkady that the young boys in Arbana Garden City were very willing, and <sent> the lot.

He disengaged the fast-comm link and watched the rest of the dance until he grew bored, and once more surveyed the Cossacks' audience. They were much more interesting.

Xanthia!

From across the room, that Mona Lisa face tugged at him. Unaware of him, watching the dance, she caused him to moan inside. It was not just a theoretical exercise: he would have to go through with it.

He would loose his infiltration code before a hundred Luculenti, and dare his peers to realize what he had done. Confidence rose in him.

Tonight, my darling Xanthia. Tonight we'll be one, and I shall grant you immortality as I make you part of my extended soul. Extended far beyond the bounds envisaged by my close-minded so-called equals . . .

A startling thought occurred: that he might reach a new point of criticality, on this night of nights. It was something to examine later.

<<video: a burst of golden sunflowers>>

He turned to find Lori Maximilian, his hostess, smiling warmly.

But inside, his new idea was urgent. He would need time to think —he was not sure he could construct a sufficiently detailed simulation —but his mind might be on the verge of a cohenstewart discontinuity, a qualitative jump to a different level of complexity: new ways of thinking, new patterns of perception, literally transcending the limits of humankind.

"It's so nice of you to come."

Lori's voice brought him back to the moment.

"Why, Lori. You look magnificent."

He spoke with sincerity, absolutely meaning it. For these few seconds, he focussed on her to the exclusion of all else, so that she was truly the most beautiful thing in creation. Even Lori, successful and self-assured, was affected by his attention.

"Thank you, Rafael. I'm glad you're here." She touched her hair briefly. The stars around her wrist followed the movement.

"The honour's mine . . . Though what would really please me would be a waltz with you. Perhaps later?"

"Of course. Do you know Xanthia Delaggropos?"

His heart pounded. "Yes, I do."

"She's leading the Sun-Wheel Dance, and we don't quite have the century."

She meant, they did not have the full one hundred Luculenti volunteers they needed.

"I fear my talent is too small. Please place me in reserve."

He was sure that Lori would find enough willing bodies, without having to drag in the half-hearted like himself.

"You're too modest, Rafael. I'm sure Xanthia will be glad to know she has your support, should she need it."

"Xanthia can count on me."

He smiled darkly.

"I don't know where she is. I haven't seen Xanthia in ages."

Yoshiko frowned. "She can't be missing. She's got to do this dance thing."

"Sorry." Maggie shrugged. "What can I say?"

"Well, she can't have gone far."

They wandered along a hallway. From a passing drone, Yoshiko picked a chocolate-covered fruit, and bit into it.

"How is that?"

"Sinful."

"Say, have you ever heard of the Belousov-Zhabotinsky reaction?"

"I'm not sure."

"At Xanthia's house, I found Jason and Amanda—that's Xanthia's twelve-year-old daughter—sitting on the lawn with a tank full of liquid chemicals, a glass disk floating inside. Watching spirals form inside the liquid."

"That's interesting."

"Jason told me they were investigating defect-mediated turbulence."

"Jason said that?"

"Yeah. It's been a life-changing experience, visiting Xanthia. And Amanda kept an eye out, so that he wouldn't dip a finger in the sulphuric acid, or anything."

Yoshiko felt suddenly weary. The thought of young lives changing and branching out all around her, perhaps.

"Can we sit down for a moment?"

"Sure."

They sat on a couch in a corridor, framed between marble statues.

"I wish Ken were here," Yoshiko surprised herself by saying. "Times like this bring it home."

"He would have liked this party, would he?"

Yoshiko shook her head. "He'd stand in a corner making sarcastic comments about the other guests." But she missed his good humour.

The chocolate-covered fruit was still in her hand, but she could not bear the thought of finishing it. She looked around for a disposal-membrane.

"I was in a triune," Maggie said sadly. "Bryce, my husband, and Marie my cowife, just sealed me out of the marriage. I came back from a long assignment, and Jason was in a public twenty-four-hour crèche waiting for me, and my belongings were in storage at the local transit station. And there was a big payment in my bank account. Guilt."

"Oh, Maggie. I'm so sorry."

"That's partly why Jason's so withdrawn, and why I'm so glad to see him coming out of his shell at Xanthia's house."

A drone was passing, and Yoshiko leaned forward and dumped the chocolate fruit on its back.

"Sorry."

A fleeting thought: she hadn't seen Septor tonight. Perhaps Lori's relationship was under strain.

"—Oh, right. I forgot to give you this." Maggie held out a slender black bracelet. "A wrist terminal, a present from Xanthia. She gave me one for each of us, back at her place."

"That's very kind of her. Er—do you have a tissue?"

"You'd think Luculenti could invent nonmelting chocolate. There you are."

"Thanks." Yoshiko wiped her fingers, then accepted the bracelet and slipped it around her wrist. "How do you turn it on?"

"Touch that stud. There."

Immediately, a tiny figure of Hermes appeared: h-mail (local: a carrier-pigeon would have denoted Terran mail) was waiting.

Yoshiko stabbed the icon with her forefinger, and a flat text unfolded:

PLEASE MEET ME IN THE AVIARY, RIGHT NOW.

. . . S. STARGONIER.

Without any command from Yoshiko, the message erased itself.

"I thought he wasn't invited."

Maggie frowned. "You can't even know it's from him."

"I know." Yoshiko shrugged. "But it's a party, and the house is full. There must be a couple of hundred Luculenti here. This can't be anything dangerous."

They both stood. Maggie started to walk off, then stopped when she saw that Yoshiko hadn't moved.

"What's wrong? Did you want to talk to him alone?"

"I don't know where the aviary is."

They walked back to a main corridor, and found a Fulgidus in uniform who was able to help them.

"Through that side-door, and cut across the lawns," he said. "That's quickest. The aviary's in the next wing."

Outside, wide steps were a fading grey in the darkness, and a cold wind whipped around them.

As they started to walk, a slight but icy rain began to fall.

"Wait a minute. I've another present from Xanthia." Maggie fumbled in a pocket, then pulled out a tiny object.

She shook it, and it unfurled to a full-size rain-cape.

"Handy."

Giggling, the two of them huddled together, holding the cape over their heads. The grass swished wetly under their feet as they walked.

The lawn was very dark. They passed by a small tree, and a clump of rhododendrons.

Suddenly, there was a rustle from the bushes.

Maggie gave a girlish shriek, then sprinted for the lighted entranceway ahead of them, forcing Yoshiko to run with her.

By the time they reached the arched doorway they were whooping with laughter, in between gasping for breath.

"Oh, God," said Maggie.

She tried to get the cape to fold itself up, but her hand was shaking too much for her to thumb its tabs in the correct sequence.

"Bogeymen in the dark," said Yoshiko. "*Kami*. Evil spirits. Oh, my word."

Giggling, they helped each other inside.

"How do we find the aviary?" Maggie asked.

"Listen for squawks, or sniff out droppings."

"You must be a professional biologist."

"I used to be."

Chapter Twenty-One

Worn clothes.
Superseded femtotech.
Attotech, after I die.

The aviary was huge, a rain-forest segueing to mountain pines under a high arched ceiling. Peach and gold light bathed its interior—warm and gentle as a Terran summer evening—belying the cold Fulgor night beyond the building's walls.

Ivy-strewn trees spread a canopy of green above Yoshiko and Maggie. They followed a grassy trail into the very centre of the vast space, to a trellised arbour crouched by a crystal pool. The raucous cries of parrots and the songs of a hundred other species washed over them.

The sheer volume of the noise, in contrast to the night outside, set Yoshiko's nerves on edge.

A confusion of small birds flitted overhead and sat in the branches of surrounding trees and chattered and fought and squawked intensely. A scarlet-breasted robin took possession of a small bush. Above them, a brightly plumed parakeet sailed by.

"So where's Stargonier, then?" asked Maggie.

"I don't know." Yoshiko looked around.

There were a thousand places a man could hide, and noise enough to hide the footsteps of a dozen men.

"There is only one aviary, isn't there?" asked Maggie.

"As far as I—" Yoshiko stopped.

Beside the white arbour, the air began to shimmer.

"Let's get out of here," said Maggie urgently.

"No. Wait."

A man's dim outline appeared in the wavering air, then a hand reaching forward, becoming more solid, beckoning them.

Yoshiko stepped forward, Maggie at her side. She saw Maggie take her small silver video-globe from her pocket.

"No use." Yoshiko's voice was soft. "That smartfilm will distort any image."

"At least it will show us disappearing into the smartfilm," murmured Maggie, as she dropped the globe surreptitiously to the ground, suspensors switched off, its eyes trained on the image of her and Yoshiko walking into the billowing curtain of smartfilm. "In case we never come back."

A wetness crawled across Yoshiko's skin as she stepped through the smartfilm, and then the sensation passed.

They were inside a glimmering hemisphere, and Sylvester Stargonier was sitting in a low chair, dressed in an elegant white suit with a white brimmed hat, legs casually crossed to show the sharpness of the creases in his trousers. There was a small round table set with a tray of chilled and warm drinks, and two empty chairs.

"Please take a seat," said Stargonier. "I'm sorry about the precautions. I know they're theatrical—I guess I've been hanging round Luculenti for far too long."

"That's OK." Yoshiko frowned. "I thought you weren't on the guest list."

"Xanthia got me in." Stargonier held out his hand to Maggie. "I'm Sylvester Stargonier. How do you do?"

Maggie hesitated, then shook his hand. She relaxed slightly, Yoshiko thought, when she felt the grip of Stargonier's hand.

"It's nice to meet you in person, Professor Sunadomari," Stargonier continued, and shook Yoshiko's hand, as well.

"I'm honoured."

Yoshiko rubbed her eyes, feeling tired, conscious of the lateness of the hour and the extended length of the Fulgor day.

"We're both honoured." Maggie's tone was matter-of-fact. "So why did you arrange the theatricalities? And who are you afraid of?"

"It's not fear." Stargonier gave a slight smile. "It's a healthy sense of self-preservation. You might do well to cultivate it, if you're going to continue your investigation."

"And what kind of danger are you preserving yourself from?"

"The sort that casually flicks people out of existence, Ms. Brown." Stargonier uncrossed his legs, and leaned forward earnestly. "Innocent people, in the main."

"I see." Maggie sounded unconvinced.

"And," continued Stargonier, leaning back, "when you retrieve your video-globe, you might want to wipe its memory and its log. In case someone should happen accidentally to deep-scan it, at some point in time."

"Thanks for the warning."

Stargonier nodded.

"So, Mr. Stargonier," Maggie continued, "what was it that you must tell us in absolute secrecy?"

"I talked to Tetsuo, shortly before he disappeared."

Yoshiko, who had been thinking about taking a drink from the table, sat bolt upright, all fatigue banished.

"How was he?" she asked quickly. "Do you know what happened to him?"

"No." Stargonier shook his head. "I don't know what happened. But I do know he was worried."

"Right." Yoshiko bit her lip.

"Worried about what, specifically?" asked Maggie.

"Specifically, I'm not sure. But—" He held up a hand as Maggie started to speak. "—I think he had stolen some info. He was very edgy and, well, security was a speciality of his, and he had some good AI and toolkits for working in the field."

"Do you mean—?" Maggie looked at Yoshiko. "I'm sorry, but you mean Tetsuo was involved in infotheft? From whom?"

"That's the most important question, but I'm not sure of the answer. However, he did have strong links with Rafael de la Vega, as I'm sure you know."

Maggie snorted. "So tell us something we don't know."

"Interesting interviewing technique you have," said Stargonier. "Or are you only provocative tactically?"

Maggie shook her head, and said nothing.

"OK." Stargonier smiled. "First, my notion that Tetsuo had stolen some info is not pure intuition. When he and I talked, I had some . . . decision support software running at the time."

"You mean psych programs," said Maggie. "And body scanners."

Stargonier nodded. "Yes. And a tactical module with predictive frameworks, too. It's standard practice at a certain level of, ah, commerce."

"You mean," said Yoshiko, "when you're dealing directly with Luculenti."

"Exactly." Stargonier looked at her almost gratefully. "There are layers upon layers of business as well as every other form of transaction or communication, and only a comparative few of us—tens of thousands, a small percentage of the population—have direct commerce with Luculenti."

"And," said Maggie, "your software said that Tetsuo was a thief."

Stargonier looked defensive. "It was based on his predilection for cryptographic problem-solving."

"But what kind of info?" asked Yoshiko. "And who might he have stolen it from?"

Maggie glanced at Yoshiko, but Yoshiko ignored her.

"Well—" Stargonier hesitated.

"Come on, Mr. Stargonier." Maggie's voice was soft and reasonable. "There is more than you've told us. Do you know what he stole?"

Stargonier carefully took off his hat, took a silken handkerchief from his breast pocket, and dabbed at his forehead.

"I am not at all certain." He replaced his hat. "But . . . when I replayed my last conversation with him, there were reflections in the window behind him. Magnified, I could make out part of the peripheral displays Tetsuo had running."

Maggie leaned forward. "What was it?"

"For one thing—" Stargonier smiled wryly, "—he was running tactical ware not too dissimilar from my own. For another . . . Well, the other display was minimized, so when I magnified my log image the resolution was hardly brilliant."

"And what was it showing?"

"Tetsuo himself was displaying a video log, as code-and-info fragments rather than playing the images. It's very blurred, but—"

The sound of blood rushed in Yoshiko's ears.

"—one of the speakers was identified as Farsteen. The dead LuxPrime courier. If Tetsuo was stealing tech from LuxPrime, then he was in very serious trouble."

Yoshiko swallowed, unable to speak.

"Mr. Stargonier, do you have your log here?" Maggie asked. "Or can we download from Skein?"

"No, to both questions, Ms. Brown. The only copies are off-line, in crystals hidden at my home."

"That's a very interesting allegation, Mr. Stargonier."

Yoshiko looked at Maggie, feeling she had missed a step in the conversation.

"Are you saying," Maggie continued, "that Skein is insecure?"

Ah. Very astute. The whole of Fulgidus society rested on Skein's integrity.

"In normal usage, even by Luculenti, it is absolutely secure. At the lowest levels, every object is accessible through a well-defined instruction set, an interface of legal op codes—

"But when you're talking about LuxPrime labs, you're talking about the engineers who manufacture Skein's underlying fabric, and Luculenti VSI tech."

They considered this in silence. Within the enclosing smartfilm, the air felt quite dead, though the aviary outside was doubtless as raucous as ever.

"Considering the pending connection of Everyware to Skein," Maggie said, musing, "that's pretty serious."

"More than that—There are well-circulated rumours that peacekeepers occasionally circumvent privacy laws in SatScan, though that never comes out in court."

"Peacekeepers?"

"A generic term for proctors and other agencies, such as TacCorps."

"Hmm." Maggie was thoughtful. "And they're surveilling lawbreakers only? How about political opponents of, well, the establishment?"

"I'm not sure that term's applicable here. Look, I'm not implying widespread corruption. That's not so. The operations are against criminals, and most people wouldn't object if they knew the facts. I'm just trying to point out that there's a level of covert operations which don't play by the stated rules."

"Understood," said Maggie.

"Although—and I'd advise you never to even hint of this in anything you write—there's a rumour that at the centre of TacCorps lies a really hard core, an élite force personally loyal to Federico Gisanthro, that agency's chief."

"But—" Yoshiko blurted, saw Maggie's warning look, but continued anyway: "He's going to be here, tonight."

"Xanthia told me." Stargonier nodded. "You should get to meet him, if you can."

"But you said—"

"I suspect he's not a nice man," said Stargomer. "But if anyone has the resources to find out what happened to Tetsuo, it's Federico Gisanthro."

Yoshiko said nothing, trying to absorb all this information. She looked at the table absently, half-seeing the untouched drinks.

"There's one thing I'm not clear on," said Maggie.

"What's that, Ms. Brown?"

"Just who you're afraid might have observed us tonight. And, er . . . I suppose you can call me Maggie."

"Thank you, Maggie." A smile flitted across Stargonier's face. "I wouldn't want the proctors or any Luculenti to know about the opinions and suspicions I've just shared with you, about Skein and SatScan. They wouldn't do my position much good, you see."

LuxPrime, thought Yoshiko, *might not take adverse publicity lightly.*

"Do you have children, Mr. Stargonier?" she asked suddenly.

"Why, yes. Two boys. Why do you ask?"

Sons. If they were ever to have a chance of upraise, their father could not be seen to have criticized LuxPrime. No doubt that was how it worked.

"Because," Yoshiko lied, "you showed such sympathy. Thank you."

Maggie frowned impatiently. "We know Tetsuo dealt with Rafael de la Vega. What sort of tech? Do you know?"

"Certainly nothing to do with LuxPrime. Tetsuo works with mu-space comms, as you know. Why Rafael's interested in comms ware, I don't know. Interesting question."

"Could Rafael be engaged in some illegal activity?"

"Maybe," said Stargonier. "Maybe something kind of borderline, you know? Mu-space tech is a sensitive area, at the moment."

"Because of the Skein/EveryWare gateways?"

"Exactly."

Yoshiko let out a long slow breath. "May I run over what we've learned so far?"

"Go ahead." Stargonier nodded, as did Maggie.

"Basically, LuxPrime tech's involved. Rafael de la Vega is our only suspect, but has no interest in LuxPrime, so might not have anything to do with it," said Yoshiko. "And Federico Gisanthro is the man who should investigate."

"Well—theoretically, yes." Stargonier rubbed his chin. "But there's a problem. The two of them, Rafael and Federico, are friends, or at least close acquaintances, unlikely though that sounds."

"Wonderful," said Maggie.

"On the other hand," Stargonier continued, "if Rafael were truly mixed up in something, I don't think Federico would let their friendship stand in the way."

There was a pause while Yoshiko and Maggie thought about this.

Stargonier stood up.

"I think you should rejoin the party now," he said. "I hope you enjoy it."

"OK," Maggie got to her feet. "Thank you very much."

"Yes," said Yoshiko. "Thank you for your help."

"You're both very welcome."

Stargonier doffed his hat to them.

As they turned to go, he cleared his throat.

"Be careful of Rafael," he said. "I've had business dealings with him, myself. He's not a man to cross."

The noise hit them.

Outside the concealing smartfilm, the aviary was louder than ever, a cacophony of screeching birds.

Maggie retrieved her video-globe from the ground, and they followed the same grassy trail out to the exit. Yoshiko followed Maggie. Neither of them said a word.

By silent agreement, they avoided the door which led out to the cold night-bound lawns, and took a longer indoor route along empty corridors, until they reached the central hub of the vast cruciform house, where the lights were brighter and the warm chatter of party-goers filled the air.

"I need a drink," said Yoshiko.

"Me, too." Maggie let out a breath. "There are times I wish I could rip out my bloody implant."

"I bet one of those barmen could concoct you something which would have the same effect as ethanol."

Maggie grimaced. "That's what I'm afraid of."

They reached the main entrance hall outside the ballroom, and the chaise lounge where they had sat earlier was free, and they sank onto it gratefully.

"Party, party," murmured Maggie.

"Just what I was thinking."

After they had recovered their energy, Yoshiko and Maggie went in search of people to talk to. They stood at the doorway, just inside the ballroom, watching a slow but cheerful dance, a kind of waltz in which lateral head movements were required when the music changed key. Each couple was dancing differently, and some of them seemed to be making up steps as they went along.

A tall, broad-shouldered Fulgidus man was standing beside them, and he looked at Maggie and smiled.

"Care to dance?"

"No, thank you . . ." said Maggie, glancing at Yoshiko.

Yoshiko shrugged, very slightly. The man looked OK, and at least he was polite.

". . . On second thoughts, why not?" Maggie grinned at Yoshiko. "See you in a minute."

"Later."

The man swept Maggie out into the flow on the dance floor, and soon they were talking and smiling, and Yoshiko let out a happy sigh. She wondered how Vin was doing . . . Ah, there she was, standing behind the buffet table with Brian, helping him dispense drinks and serve *hors d'oeuvres*.

Very good. Vin wasn't the sort to stand aloof while the person she wanted to be with had a relatively menial task to perform. She and Brian looked cheerful, exchanging glances and occasionally bumping into each other kind-of-accidentally, when they got too busy to talk.

"Yoshiko!"

Lori was waving from the hallway outside. Yoshiko went to join her.

There were people with her. There was Neliptha, tall and black and elegant, the self-effacing mayor of Lucis. There were half a dozen other Luculenti whom Yoshiko had never seen before, and, as Lori made introductions, she noticed some tiny half-gestures and twitches from two or three of them which, Yoshiko knew, meant they were communicating in their own massively parallel holistic fashion, beyond the processing capacity of one unenhanced ageing woman to understand.

Well, let them. She was here, and she would treat them as equals.

"—This is Maj." Lori indicated a tall blonde woman, who grinned.

"Hello," said Yoshiko.

"—And Felice Lectinaria."

Yoshiko bowed to the grey-haired Luculenta, very tanned and lean and graceful, and knew she ought to recognize that name, but could not place it.

The Luculenta's eyes glittered, intent on Yoshiko, but she merely nodded and stepped back.

Yoshiko glanced down at the dull orange glow of the tu-rings on her fingers, wishing her NetAgents could work here, wishing she had their help.

Still, at least she had a public-access terminal round her wrist now, thanks to Xanthia and Maggie.

"—And Prameena."

A young Luculenta, around Vin's age, gave a kind of half-curtsy.

"Hi," she said, and her teeth glowed green with swirling gold and pink patterns, and the sudden luminescence ceased when she closed her mouth.

"Hi." Yoshiko, hiding her own reaction, saw amusement dancing in Lori's eyes. At least Vin wasn't prey to such youthful fads.

"—And this—" Lori pointed to a tall Luculentus with cropped blond hair and striking pale mismatched eyes, one green and one blue. "—is Federico Gisanthro."

Federico's headgear was a minimal silver construct, unlike the more intricate styles of his peers.

"How do you do." He shook hands brusquely, taking Yoshiko in with one flickering glance.

"Pleased to meet you."

He nodded and withdrew, yet Yoshiko felt it was she who had been dismissed.

This was the man she was supposed to impress, whose help she was supposed to enlist.

Her head swam a little, and she paid no attention to the names of the other Luculenti whom Lori introduced. Then everybody began to walk away, and she realized that Lori expected her to go with them.

Yoshiko shook her head slightly and tried to centre herself, to focus on her surroundings. This was not the time to lose it.

"Are you OK?" asked Lori, taking Yoshiko's arm.

"Fine."

"This way." Lori led the group into a small drawing room.

They took seats around a low suspensor table.

Yoshiko, quiescent, was content to listen to their conversation. Soon, though, she realized she was following little of what they were saying. Their talk was full of technical and political references which were quite meaningless to her.

Yoshiko took a small silver cup of Terran coffee from the table and sipped from it, withdrawing into herself.

After a while, the Luculenti began to drift into a more normal form of conversation, for them: they grew silent, with momentary expressions flitting across their faces.

"Yoshiko, wasn't it?" Neliptha, the mayor, was talking to her. "Do you have something to do with journalism, like Maggie?"

Yoshiko gathered herself

"I'm—semiretired," said Yoshiko, saying it for the first time, admitting it to herself. "I mostly teach."

"That's nice." Neliptha mustered sincerity with a visible effort.

"So, Neliptha, what's your speech going to be about, at the Skein conference?" asked Federico.

Neliptha turned to him, obviously glad of the interruption.

"Oh, you know, free trade and prosperity for everyone, all that jazz. Makes my brain weary."

There were polite smiles around the table. They were still ignoring Yoshiko, but at least they were speaking in plain language.

"You dancing in the Sun-Wheel Dance, Federico?" someone asked.

"For Lori's sake, no. Graceful as a walrus, that's me." Federico grimaced, and everybody laughed.

It was a strange expression to use on a world that had no walruses—or did it? Was there an obscure insult to the Earther among them, or was she just ignorant of their world? Or was it a reference to something in popular culture, such as a well-known comedy?

Concentrate.

"I was thinking—" Lori leaned forward, with mischief twinkling in her eyes. "—of getting Yoshiko to apply for a resident's visa, and go for upraise."

That effectively killed all conversation, and Yoshiko felt every eye upon her.

"I don't think—" she began, then let her voice trail off.

"You're a teacher, did you say?" asked one of the Luculenti whose name Yoshiko hadn't caught.

She was profoundly aware of Federico's eyes upon her, pale and predatory.

"That's right."

"Yoshiko teaches young researchers at Sudarasys Lifetech," said Lori. "Have I got that right, Yoshiko?"

Yoshiko nodded.

Nobody looked very impressed, and Yoshiko wished she were anywhere but here, a pinned specimen open for inspection by interested but uncaring intellects.

The grey-haired Luculenta, Felice Lectinaria, cleared her throat.

"They're a highly respected institution on Earth," Felice said. "Though not very big, I believe. They discovered the Akazawa resonance effect in ecomodels, a nice trick which I've incorporated into my own work."

"That's very impressive, Yoshiko," said Neliptha. "Do you know this Akazawa person, then?"

Yoshiko coughed.

"My maiden name was Akazawa."

The Luculenti stared at her in silence, Lori with a big triumphant grin on her face.

"When I became Head of Research," Yoshiko continued, remembering how shocked people had been at someone so young—it was a long time ago—taking over such responsibility, "my primary responsibility became the nurturing of the next generation."

That was the way labs worked, in Okinawa. What could be more important than bringing on the next generation of Sudarasys researchers?

Perhaps the real next generation, her own offspring, too often took second place to the development of her coworkers.

"So I teach, and act as mentor. That's how we run things."

And the youngsters call me sensei, she reflected, *and the labs buzz with energy, and the awards and success keep rolling in. I have my colleagues' respect, but what about my own children's love?*

She looked up, and saw that Federico had a faraway gaze in his eyes. She knew, from her experiences with Vin, that he was trawling for info in Skein.

"Good show," said the nameless Luculentus who had asked her about teaching.

"If Yoshiko wants to apply for upraise," said Federico, focussing on the room again, "then I will second the application, if Lori proposes her."

There was a stunned silence, then the Luculenti broke into energetic applause.

Yoshiko found herself blushing furiously.

"Surely, my age—?"

"Makes it more difficult, and longer, though not impossible." Federico's face was taut with amusement. "But we're not attempting to force your hand."

Yoshiko swallowed, and nodded.

"Come and talk to me at Peacekeeper Central," he added. "I'll send a flyer for you, tomorrow."

Why in person, and why there? She knew, then, that he had worked out why Lori had singled her out for attention: so that Federico would become involved in Tetsuo's case. He had obviously retrieved the details of Tetsuo's disappearance as part of the infosearch keyed to her name.

She had won the help she needed to find her son.

Yoshiko looked at Lori, whose eyes were glistening, and knew that she would never be able to thank her enough, regardless of the outcome of the investigation, whatever might become of Tetsuo.

She nodded wordlessly, and Lori smiled. It was all the communication they needed.

"I don't know about you guys—" Neliptha broke the silence, "—but I feel so happy, I need to dance. You coming, Federico?"

"Only if you promise not to step on my feet."

"I've danced with you before." Neliptha grinned. "If I'd known you were going to be here, I'd have worn reinforced boots."

The gathering broke up, and people drifted out singly or in pairs to the main party, until only Lori and Yoshiko were left.

"Come on." Lori squeezed Yoshiko's hand. "Let's go party."

They went out into the crowded corridor.

To Yoshiko, insulated in a bemused daze, the chattering partygoers seemed to drift past like holo images, or a pleasant but confusing dream.

Felice Lectinaria, the grey-haired Luculenta, brushed past Yoshiko as they made their way along the corridor.

"We have to talk, Professor."

"Of course—"

"Later. I'll be seeing you."

"Right."

Bemused, Yoshiko watched her disappear into a side room, where a burst of laughter sounded coincidentally as Felice went inside.

Gentle flute music accompanied their entrance into the ballroom.

Nobody was dancing right now, but people were scattered around the edges of the great circular room—over a hundred metres across, Yoshiko guessed—and the domed ceiling rising into darkness helped to create a cathedral-like space that was vast and mostly empty. It was granted warmth, though, by the clusters of happy people, over two hundred of them now, chatting and laughing and making fools of themselves.

"Look." Lori pointed. "There's Vin."

Yoshiko waved to Vin, who turned to the boy, Brian, and said something in his ear. She put her arm in his, and took him over to meet Yoshiko and Lori.

"Hello." Yoshiko greeted Brian. "How are you doing?"

"Fine." Brian looked a little flustered. "Thank you, ma'am."

"Please call me Yoshiko. And this is Lori, Vin's soul-mother. Lori, this gentleman is Brian Donnelly, a friend of mine."

Brian flushed a little at that, but kept enough composure to shake Lori's hand and say hello.

"Your soul-mother—" Yoshiko turned to Vin. "—has done me a big favour. Something I can never repay."

"Oh, please," said Lori.

"Modest, isn't she?" Vin grinned at Lori, then she hugged her quickly and kissed her cheek.

"*Thanks*," Yoshiko thought she heard Vin whisper.

"So—" Yoshiko entered the conversational gap which Brian was too shy to fill, "—has anyone seen Xanthia? Neither Maggie nor I have seen her for ages."

"No, I'm afraid I haven't." Lori shook her head, as did Vin.

"I wonder if she went to talk to Rafael." Yoshiko looked around. "She seems to think—"

"Well, Rafael's over there." Vin pointed him out, inclining her head towards the opposite side of the room.

Rafael was leaning against a curved pillar, dark and elegant and infinitely entrancing, watching everyone and everything with those deep dark eyes of his.

For a moment their glances met, and he smiled slightly—Yoshiko felt her heart give a little fillip, and cardiac arrhythmia sprang to mind for an instant—then he looked away, and she felt a lurch of disappointment.

The music changed to dance rhythm.

People began to drift in towards the centre of the vast room, arranging themselves in straight lines, forming a grid across the fine polished floor.

"It's a line dance," Lori said. "A traditional warm-up, before Xanthia performs her *pièce de résistance*."

"You can join in." Vin grinned at her. "I know you're fit enough. Look, here are the steps."

She danced a fast jig sideways, then back to her starting position.

The low mournful sound of pipes blew eerily through the ballroom, announcing the dance was about to start.

"Sorry." Yoshiko shook her head. "I think I missed that. You'd better go ahead."

"Nonsense." Lori was firm. "This is an intro before the dance, for people to get in the mood. Go on, Vin. Show her again, but slowly."

Vin did the first five steps, and Yoshiko mouthed to herself: heel-toe-side-heel-toe.

Vin paused, and Yoshiko motioned for her to continue. One-two, one-two, one-two-forward-three. One-two.

Very slowly, Yoshiko moved through the steps, concentrating on placing her feet correctly and not worrying about anything else.

"Perfect." Lori nodded.

Then Yoshiko reversed the sequence of steps, moving faster this time, returning to where she had started.

"Er, not bad," said Vin.

Then Yoshiko danced the full routine, back and forth, at full speed. She did it once more, just to make sure. Got it.

"Bloody hell." Vin stared at her. "Are you sure you're not a Luculenta?"

Yoshiko laughed, wondering if Lori had brought Vin up to date on the conversation with Federico and friends, and deciding that she probably had.

"Okinawan dance and martial arts are practically the same thing." Yoshiko shrugged. "Well . . . depending on how you look at it."

"We're impressed," said Lori. "Come on, let's take our places. Yoshiko, you've just to do those steps and perform a simple turn with everybody else. Don't worry, you'll get the hang of it."

As Yoshiko followed Lori and Vin into the lineup, she saw Maggie at the side of the room, and waved to her. The big Fulgidus gentleman was standing beside her.

Maggie stuck two fingers in her mouth and blew a piercing whistle which caused half the heads in the room to turn.

"Shake a leg, Yoshiko!"

Yoshiko closed her eyes in embarrassment.

"Who's your friend?" Vin was laughing.

"Never seen her before."

There was a roll of drums, and the sound of lively pipes and strings.

"Yee-hah!" called someone, probably Maggie, and then they were into the dance.

Heel-toe-side-heel-toe . . . Yoshiko's heart was jumping like the rest of her as she danced in time with the whole line in front of her.

They turned ninety degrees and danced the steps again as the lively jig filled the air and made her very bones dance.

The ground flew past beneath Yoshiko's feet, and she danced as though she were twenty again, no, fifteen, and the sap of youth rose in her veins and she danced and she danced and she danced . . .

When the music came to an end she was gasping for breath, and the clapping was thunderous as all the onlookers congratulated them and the dancers applauded each other. Yoshiko's blood was singing, and the music still coursed through her brain though the sound system was silent.

Vin hugged her.

"That was marvellous." Yoshiko hugged her back. "You're wonderful."

"Glad you enjoyed it. Need a drink?"

"I think so."

Lori left them to talk to someone, while Vin escorted Yoshiko to the side of the room, where Maggie was waiting with her new escort.

"Down this." Maggie handed Yoshiko a goblet. "Roberto here assures me it'll do you good."

"Thanks." Yoshiko gulped down the drink. "How do you do, Roberto?"

"Hi." The tall Fulgidus' voice was very deep.

"I don't suppose," asked Vin, "anyone knows who shouted 'Yee-hah!' just as the dance was starting?"

Maggie and Roberto shook their heads, exaggeratedly innocent expressions on their faces.

"I didn't think so."

Yoshiko drained the goblet completely. The drink was tart and fruity, quite thick, but something in it was perking her up.

"Thanks, Roberto. This is good."

Roberto nodded.

"Say, Maggie," Yoshiko added. "Did you find Xanthia, in the end?"

"Er, no." Maggie looked embarrassed. "Sorry, I forgot."

Vin smothered a laugh.

"Gotcha." Vin smiled, as the colour rose in Maggie's cheeks. "Serves you right."

Roberto looked puzzled.

"It's a female thing," Yoshiko explained.

Roberto smiled uncertainly.

"Anyway," said Maggie hurriedly, "if you're still worried about Xanthia, maybe Vin should do that Skein thing, or one of those tricks."

"No need." Vin looked around. "It's almost time for the Sun-Wheel Dance to start. She has to be here for that."

"Oh, no." Yoshiko groaned. "I don't think I can manage another dance."

"Well . . . actually, you can sit this one out."

"Oh. OK."

"Sorry, but it's Luculenti only. You see, everyone opens up a <private send> channel direct to the prima donna—that's Xanthia, this year—and she creates kinaesthetic directives to a hundred Luculenti simultaneously, who all choose to follow her directions, almost letting her control them."

"She's conducting?" Maggie looked interested. "Or choreographing? Something like that?"

"Kind of," Vin replied. "She makes up the pattern as she goes along, to suit the individuals she finds. She'll also be in direct interface with the sound system, composing and creating the music, too."

"Oh. Is that all?"

"Actually—" Yoshiko interrupted. "There's more. Isn't she creating some kind of light show at the same time?"

Vin nodded.

"One dance, and you're an expert, huh?" Maggie shook her head, smiling.

Yoshiko pointed to the big skeletal array suspended in shadows, high up in the ceiling's vault.

"I was here when Xanthia was getting attuned to it, or something. And I've seen Lori use it to sculpt huge blocks of stone."

"As one does." Maggie sighed. "Doesn't anyone round here just sit down and watch a holodrama?"

Vin laughed, just as a flight of silver swallows passed by overhead—

"What the hell?" said Maggie.

—and arced up into the darkness of the domed ceiling, where a small moon appeared. The swallows, diminishing in size as though with vast distance, travelled to the far moon, orbited nine times, and dwindled into nothingness.

There was scattered applause, and all eyes turned to the main entrance as the lights grew dimmer, becoming dark as night. Tiny distant sparks of blue. The doorway glowed eerily green.

Tiny lambent blue flames licked across the floor in two parallel lines, forming a pathway. A low, almost subsonic hum, sounded through the floor, dark and threatening.

A lone castrato voice . . .

Dark figures, standing in the doorway.

The tinkling of bells . . .

A misty column of silver stars hissed softly upwards in the centre of the room, like a pillar reaching to the heavens. The dark figures marched towards it, between the lines of flickering flames.

The goddess, and her four attendants.

Haunting pipes, and a distant drum, accompanied their journey into light. An eerie chorus sang like insistent ghosts, in languages dead for centuries.

. . . And Yoshiko felt for a moment as though her youth, her dear Ken, were but a touch, a reaching gesture away . . .

The blue flames died, while a lonely lyre wept in the night. In a low rustle, the onlookers slowly, quietly, drew back to the edges of the vast room.

Solid shadows, in the darkness.

A hundred figures stood in frozen ranks, a century of spirits haunting the goddess—The goddess who ascended to, climbed *into* the pillar of silver light . . . which burst apart in lambent golden flame.

And the goddess, Xanthia, danced with a stirring sway of her powerful hips between two ornate steel pillars—real, not holo—which burned in showers of gleaming sparks. The air shimmered, where lasers from above cut through the darkness, igniting the metal.

Xanthia's four attendants, yellow-robed Luculenta girls with garlanded hair, knelt before her.

"My God," said Maggie.

Sea-green light, mistlike, rose from the floor.

Among the rows of Luculenti, movement. Scattered at first: at a corner of the pattern, a man danced three paces, and stopped. A woman danced an ellipse, grew still. At opposite edges, two groups leaped in awe-inspiring unison, clicked their heels, and stamped.

Violet swarmed through the sea of green.

Everyone danced forward one thunderous step, advancing like one giant fearsome organism, then burst into swirling dance.

Life and death, courage and despair, balanced on uncertainty's edge.

Haunting, haunting, the plaintive flute, dispersing the mist.

Joyous, joyous, the dancing drums and strings, drawing a silver grid upon the darkness.

They danced.

Ordered synchrony broke apart into athletic turbulence. Sparks rose from their feet, while infinity fell away below.

They formed a cross, dancing clockwise, while swallows flew in counterpoint.

Faster and faster, they spun.

Maggie whooped as golden suns fell through the air and the dancers whirled impossibly fast and the music climaxed, *boom-boom-boom*, and was still.

Stunned silence.

Thunderous applause.

A tide of sound washed through the room, wave after wave of it, and Yoshiko was clapping hard enough to hurt, and tears were stinging in her eyes.

Such love. The goddess: such impossible, unreachable, magnificent beauty.

Rafael's chest was swelling, and pure hot emotion such as he had never known swept over him.

It was her moment of greatest triumph. *Xanthia, Xanthia, Xanthia—can you imagine the sweet fulfilment of literal godhead?*

Be mine, be mine, be mine.

The applauding onlookers were forgotten as he focussed upon her, the object of his desire, the pinnacle of his love.

Her sweetness was an elixir he had to drink. Her brilliance, a star which must become part of his constellation, his galaxy. Her warmth, her soul's core, cried out to be subsumed in the volcanic furnace of his desire.

Now, my love.

Our moment comes.

Now.

```
[[[HeaderBegin: Module = Node99Z9.3357 Type = Quaternary-
        HyperCode: Axes = 256
    Priority = absolute
    Concurrent_Execute
        ThreadOne:<LuxPrime interface>.linkfile = CodeSmash
        ThreadTwo:<rhombencephalon channel>.linkfile = Hypo-
            VampireOne
        ThreadThree:<intrapeduncular matrix>.linkfile = EpiVampire-
            One
        ThreadFour:<thalamic/cerebral matrix>.linkfile = Hyper-
            VampireOne
    End_Concurrent_Execute]]]
```

Go.

Rafael loosed his infiltration code.

His mouth drew back in a rictus of sheer lust as his vampire modules thrust through the fast-comm link that was his and Xanthia's alone, and penetrated LuxPrime protocols, and entered her.

He drank her soul, as deep scanware plunged through her thoughts, her memories, her most intimate desires, and heisenberged them into oblivion even as it sent back the info in wave after wave of pulsing code, filling his cache, dumping her mind and experience into him, ready for integration.

A mad desire rose in him to go all the way, actually to open up his cache and merge Xanthia's soul into his right here, before two hundred witnesses, but that was utter madness.

Whimpering with frustration, he fought that desire down.

Control.

Ah, control.

Yes, Xanthia. Yes, my love.

You're mine.

Xanthia screamed.

A thousand banshees wailed, screeching all the way into ultrasonics, as the goddess's fear and terror screeched through the sound system and everyone in the room clapped hands to ears.

A man dropped in front of Yoshiko, hands clamped over his head, blood trickling between his fingers.

"What's happening?" Maggie shouted. Blood was running from her nose.

"NO! NO! NO!"

Xanthia yelled as streamers of lethal red shot in all directions through a chaos of purple light and jagged lightning.

"Some kind of seiz—Look out." Yoshiko pulled Maggie aside as a Luculenta fell, eyes turned up inside her head, showing pure white.

"We've got to stop her."

Blazing light. The room disappeared in a psychedelic hell, spinning sickeningly round and round, crawling with bloody pulsing colours. Torture, instantiated in light.

Yoshiko shut her eyes, moving by touch, and grabbed hold of Maggie.

"I've got you. Can you see?"

"No—"

Darkness.

Silver moons fell crazily through the air.

"Maggie. Get out of here."

"It's only light." Maggie, standing unsteadily, rubbed her eyes.

"Move. I'll get Xanthia."

Pale white light bled through the ballroom.

"But—"

"Those lasers can burn steel and carve granite."

Even in the eldritch milky light, Yoshiko could see Maggie's face grow pale.

"My God."

"No! *No!*" Xanthia's body was clenched like a fist.

Half a dozen Luculenti dancers, recovering from the onslaught of light and sound, staggered towards her.

Streamers of light spat from her body, impaling them on crimson beams.

They fell, smoke rising from their roasting corpses.

"Help me!"

Discordant waves of noise crashed upon the room. A fearful white-robed Luculenta, standing at a node of constructive interference, shook dreadfully, eyes clouding into milky opacity, as ultrasound cooked her in a second.

"Neliptha!" Yoshiko shouted, but it was too late.

Spinning jagged discs of light, flung in all directions, spread across the room.

As Neliptha turned, a disc sliced through her slender elegant neck, and her eyes grew wide. For a moment, she froze, then an impossibly powerful spurt of bright arterial blood signalled her decapitation, and her mouth opened, and dreadful awareness grew in her eyes, as her fine head fell to the marble floor.

Yoshiko looked around wildly. Rafael was held in an attitude of pain; God knew what he was enduring. Vin—

Where was Vin?

Gathering their wits, people were stumbling towards the exits.

Scarlet lightning arced and spat across the room, as the flow of people became a yelling mob, a panicking riot of desperate people trying to save themselves.

An unselfish act amid the maelstrom: Yoshiko saw a young Luculentus try to pick up an older woman, attempting to hold back the tide, but the mass movement was too much for him and he fell, and both were trampled beneath the rush of running feet.

A man pushed at Yoshiko; she grabbed his wrist and spun, and he whirled through the air and smashed to the ground.

She punched a woman in the throat, and swept her feet from under her.

She had to reach Xanthia.

Yoshiko plunged forwards. There was a knot of panicking people she could not get around, so she held her fists in front of her and pushed straight through.

Something smashed into the side of her head, a wildly flung elbow perhaps, and she staggered, shaking her head dizzily, fighting to keep her balance.

Someone knocked into her, and she fell to one knee. Pain shot up through her leg.

Damn it.

Xanthia!

She forced herself to her feet, ignoring the injury, and pulled aside a weeping woman.

Xanthia lay writhing at the ballroom's centre, and faceless demons and chaotic swirls of light played all around her.

Good God. What was happening to her?

Yoshiko knocked a sobbing man aside.

Swathes of cutting light burst forth again, as a dark shape passed Yoshiko at a sprint, hurdled fallen bodies, and ran straight for Xanthia.

It was Federico.

She had never seen anyone run so fast.

"Hurry, Federico!"

There was someone pushing her way in from one side, heading towards Xanthia, and for a moment a flailing arm obscured the figure from view. Yoshiko sidestepped.

Vin.

Yoshiko saved her breath, and ran straight for her. This was too dangerous: she had to get Vin out of here.

Did Maggie get away? She wasn't certain.

Everything else was forgotten as she focussed on Vin's sweat- and tear-streaked features, and ran harder than she ever had, heart thumping wildly in her chest.

No, don't forget Xanthia.

Xanthia was staggering to her feet. Then one great wave of agony shook her and she flung her arms up wide—

"No!"

—and white light shot upwards, arrowed into darkness, and tore apart the ceiling.

Yoshiko was halfway to Vin when Federico cannoned into Xanthia, lifting her straight up onto his shoulder while knocking the breath out of her, but he was not fast enough.

Vin, plunging onwards, could not see the danger, and Yoshiko had neither breath to shout nor speed to reach her in time.

Above, the great dome exploded.

Amid a shower of dust, great chunks of masonry plunged downwards. One jagged fragment dropped towards Vin's head.

Yoshiko dug deep, running harder than her ageing body should allow, and smashed into Vin, knocking her aside, and for a moment she thought she had made it, catching Vin before she fell, but then she saw the messy red ruin—shards of bone and lumps of rippled brain soaked in scarlet—that had been Vin's temple, and knew she was a lifetime too late.

A hand on her shoulder.

Maggie, wiping blood from her own face, crouched down beside her.

A distant part of Yoshiko noted the silver video-globe floating above Maggie's shoulder. Professional reflex.

"Is she—?"

"There's no pulse." Yoshiko's voice seemed disembodied, as though spoken by another.

Maggie glanced upwards.

"We've got to get out of here. The whole damned thing's about to come down."

"No—I'm not leaving her."

"Of course not."

They reached under Vin's still body, linked arms to form a cradle, and, with difficulty, stood upright.

Vin's head lolled against Yoshiko's cheek.

"That way," said Yoshiko, and spat out hot blood that was not her own.

Stumbling past weeping, shocked injury victims, they avoided a heap of rubble, blinked as they passed through clouds of settling dust, and carried Vin out into a corridor.

People milled aimlessly around.

The dead, the wounded, the merely terrified, were propped, moaning, everywhere.

"My room," said Yoshiko through gritted teeth. "Down here."

They headed down a relatively deserted hallway. Cracks spidered the walls.

"Too far," gasped Maggie.

"Do it." Yoshiko had no breath to explain: with the building damaged, they should get away from the centre of the house. "Hurry."

The doorway to Yoshiko's room was a gaping hole, the membrane having dissolved. Gently as they could, they lay Vin upon the bed, then Yoshiko ran to a wall cupboard, beat on it with her fist as the membrane only slowly softened, and tore out the small autodoc it contained.

Hurry . . .

She tore the cover off, and placed the fibrous treatment pad across the gaping head-wound. Maggie ripped away Vin's once-elegant gown, while Yoshiko attached tubes and fibres to vital points and arteries.

Vin.

Breathe, for God's sake. Just—

"Is there a pulse yet?" The video-globe got in Maggie's way, and she knocked it aside.

A hissing and a smell of burning announced the cauterizing of split blood vessels in Vin's brain. Clear gel oozed as the autodoc sealed up her wrecked skull.

"No." Yoshiko checked the display. "God damn it."

"Shit! We need medical—quick, try the house system."

Yoshiko waved the bedside terminal into life. A pulsing blue diagram swam above it: Tetsuo's info, the display she and Vin had been looking at, before the ball . . .

"There's a pulse." Maggie's voice cut through Yoshiko's thoughts. "Oh, God."

"What is it?" Ice flowed through Yoshiko.

"It—" Maggie looked up, her eyes hollow with despair. "It's brain stem function only."

The body began to breathe again, forced to respire by the machine's insistence, but no mental activity registered upon the display.

Dear God. Let her live.

Please.

"Are you—all right?" A man's voice, trailing off.

Please let her live—

Yoshiko wiped tears from her eyes and turned.

Rafael de la Vega was standing in the doorway. His eyes, glittering, were fastened upon the holo display by the bed: the pulsing blue diagram of a Luculentus mind, not the readouts from the autodoc.

"*What is that?*"

His voice flayed Yoshiko's soul.

Then a smaller form was pushing past Rafael, into the room. Brian Donnelly rushed over, and staggered to a halt by the bed.

"Medics!" he shouted into his wrist terminal. "This location. Quickly!"

Rafael blinked, and a transformation spread over his features.

"They're coming," he said to Brian. "I'm in contact—" He pointed at his headgear. "—and there's a team headed this way."

Yoshiko looked up at Rafael.

"I have to go." His expression was sombre. "Good luck."

It was you . . .

She glanced quickly at the bedside holo, then back at Rafael. His eyes followed hers, involuntarily.

Icy certainty descended upon her.

Rafael.

"Come on!" Brian was almost screaming into his wrist terminal. "What's keeping you?"

Red jumpsuited men and women burst in through the doorway, pushing their way past Rafael. Behind them, a big white armoured drone rumbled in.

"Code alpha," said one of the medics, and placed a hand on Brian's shoulder. "Stand aside."

The drone's upper lid slid open as the medics, working furiously, grabbed Vin and the autodoc both, and lowered them into the drone.

"Femtofacts active." Another medic, a young woman, stabbed frantic control gestures beside the drone. "AIs up. Diagnostics on."

Black gel engulfed Vin's pale body, while urgent phase-space displays blossomed above the drone.

Rafael . . .

"OK." The medic was intent upon the displays. "Seal it."

Gone. Rafael was gone.

The drone slammed shut.

"We've got her."

"How is—?" Maggie started.

A medic brushed her aside.

"OK, troops," the woman said. "Move it."

"Flyer in ten."

"I want it in three. Tell them." The woman glanced around at her team. "Right. We're taking her to the main steps. Let's go."

She moved out at a run, flanked by the drone.

"You." Her finger stabbed, as she called back over her shoulder, "Stay. Help the woman."

One of the medics stopped, while the rest of the team sprinted after their leader and the drone.

Yoshiko started to follow, but the remaining medic held her by the shoulder.

"Just a minute, ma'am."

No sign of Rafael. He must have slipped out when the medics arrived.

"What's wrong?" she said. "Vin's—"

"Well, for one thing, your left arm's broken."

"What?"

Yoshiko looked down, and for the first time saw how unnaturally twisted her forearm was. Pain flooded through her, at the realization.

"Yoshiko . . ." Maggie's voice trailed off.

"Go on."

Maggie nodded abruptly, and moved out at a broken run.

"Just hold still." The medic slapped an anaesthesia patch on Yoshiko's neck, then snapped a cylindrical cast into place around her forearm. "This'll hurt."

Not pain, but an unpleasant grinding. Micro-servos drilled into her flesh, forcing the two halves of her snapped ulna into alignment.

"I'm going with Vin," she said through gritted teeth.

Rafael.

"You shouldn't—OK, I'll come with you."

You bastard. You're behind it.

A swelling sensation. Fluid-borne femtocytes, pumped into her arm.

Tetsuo. And Xanthia, I'm sure of it.

"Mind that debris."

The medic helped her out into the corridor. He turned at the sound of an anguished voice, said "Excuse me," to Yoshiko, then left to help someone else.

Rafael . . .

Red jumpsuits mingled with torn finery, a mêlée of victims and rescuers. Up ahead, Maggie was walking with her arm round Brian's shoulders, following the medical drone, with its most precious cargo.

Vin . . .

Just for a moment, among the milling confusion, Yoshiko thought she saw Rafael's darkly handsome features, but then he was gone.

Vengeance.

Steel hardened Yoshiko's grim heart.

I'm going to get you, Rafael.

Vengeance.

I swear it.

A torn bouquet of flowers under foot.

By my family's blood . . .

She slipped, corrected her balance.

. . . I swear it.

Chapter Twenty-Two

Clothes, turned to bright hues:
Femtotech ware,
Die is cast, and tech makes the man.

Cold enveloped Yoshiko's forearm, and beads of condensation formed on the cast. She imagined she could feel the femtocytes at work, knitting her bone together.

There were people in worse shape.

Maggie, still holding on to Brian, looked back, concerned.

Shaking her head, Yoshiko motioned Maggie on.

Yoshiko stepped around a grey-skinned man whose eyes were closed, as though in sleep. A haggard woman, kneeling beside him, looked up in sudden hope at Yoshiko.

Yoshiko halted, not knowing what to say, but one of the medics came up behind her, and crouched to examine the fallen man.

Yoshiko moved on.

Near the centre of the house, clouds of dust still swirled, and Yoshiko put her right forearm across her mouth and nose, trying to breathe through her sleeve's fabric.

Many of the rooms they passed contained medical drones, treating people who had taken refuge there. Mostly, the drones merely extruded fibres and other appendages to their patients; in two cases, people were inside their drones, but sitting up. Not sealed away.

The drones were so capable, it was better to treat the patients *in situ* than subject them to the trauma of travel to a med-centre.

Shards of ceramic and glass scrunched underfoot as Yoshiko reached the main atrium. She skirted round a pile of rubble which had slid like an avalanche from a ballroom doorway.

One of the big bronze doors was ripped and bent, hanging on by a torn hinge.

The medical drone was negotiating its way past the debris and dazed people.

"Vin?"

It was Lori, limping to the drone, her face as pale as its casing. She was incongruously lopsided, one foot suspended centimetres in the air by the lev-field, the other on the ground.

Her eyes, when she looked at Yoshiko, were filled with distress.

"They're taking her to Lucis."

Vin's body, Yoshiko thought. Taking it to be examined, certified, and disposed of.

Words failed her. All she could do was hug Lori, and hold her tight.

Over Lori's shoulder, the drone's status displays were visible: Vin's body, held in stasis, its slow pulse a sad illusion. Her soul was surely gone.

A shudder passed through Lori, and Yoshiko had an intuition of the reason why—deep in interface, Lori was linked with the medical drone, its continuous scans delivering nothing but bad news.

"I'm OK." Lori backed away, dabbing at her eyes.

She lurched, almost tripping, her suspended foot wobbling in the EM field.

"Hang on a moment."

Yoshiko crouched down, and picked up a triangular shard of ceramic. Holding Lori's ankle steady, she sawed at Lori's sandal until she could prise away the hardened gel. Yoshiko pulled, and it tore off in one piece. She flicked the stuff aside.

It whisked upwards in the EM field, then blew away in a draught towards the outer doors.

Lori smiled wanly.

"Thanks, Yoshiko."

A medic came up to her.

"The flyer's ready, Luculenta Maximilian."

"I'm ready." Lori swallowed.

Yoshiko gently touched her arm.

"Take Brian with you."

As the medics manoeuvred the drone out through the doors, Brian stepped mechanically aside, face drained and pale. Maggie was watching him, to make sure he did not fall.

Lori's chin lifted.

She turned to look at a broad-shouldered Luculentus, clad in black and grey, who was directing a newly arrived team of engineers and drones. He stopped his verbal commands, and returned Lori's regard.

Their nonverbal communication lasted only a second.

"This is Professor Sunadomari." Lori briefly touched Yoshiko. "She's in charge while I'm gone."

Speaking for Yoshiko's benefit.

The Luculentus bowed. "Professor."

He turned back to his team, and delivered a rapid-fire series of instructions to a Fulgida engineer.

Lori walked up to Brian and took his arm. Together, while Yoshiko watched from the doorway, they followed the drone down the broad marble steps. The lawn, lit by big emergency glowglobes floating overhead, shone with an eerie pallor.

The medical flyers were the colour of dead bones.

Flanked by Lori and Brian, the drone moved up a ramp, into the nearest flyer.

As the ramp retreated into the vessel, a sick feeling took hold of Yoshiko's stomach, reminding her of long helpless days at the medical complex, while Ken lay dying. The smartvirus ravaged his femtocytes, destroying his body in the process. Medical AIs battled for days, but she knew from the first that the struggle was lost. She could only wait for the inevitable.

Warning ripples of amber light strobed across the hull.

The flyer rose smoothly into the high darkness, then sped in the direction of Lucis City, dwindling to become an orange spark in the night, and winked out.

Yoshiko stared, unseeing, at the far cold stars.

Rousing herself, she turned back inside, and saw Maggie in the entranceway, video-globe floating over her shoulder.

"I can't apologize." Maggie shrugged, her eyes lost in sorrow. "It's what I do. Whatever's going on, however bad, there's always a part of me watching and analysing and filing for later, and drawing up a voice-over commentary. To give things meaning."

Yoshiko wondered what certainty had been lost from Maggie's life, that she was so obsessive in granting it a framework of significance.

It didn't matter. She had seen the tears in Maggie's eyes, watched her furiously helping to get Vin attached to the autodoc.

For all the good it had done.

"Walk with me, Maggie?"

"Yeah. You bet."

Side by side, they went back inside the ruined house.

"The bastard!" A man's aggrieved shout drifted from a far corridor.

Yoshiko looked, but could see nothing. Shrugging, she turned away, and followed Maggie to the ballroom entrance.

She stood in a current of warm air delivered by a honeycombed chemical heater, hugged herself, and watched the engineers at work.

The torn roof was mostly open to the cold night sky. Beneath the dark rent, tiny drones spun monomer webs, strengthening the building's basic structure. Black filaments were strung across the open spaces, and wrapped tightly around pillars on the verge of collapse.

From outside, an hysterical wail, and the slapping sound of a dermal patch hastily applied. It sent a shiver down Yoshiko's spine: someone had just been told the worst of news.

"Let's go back," she said, and Maggie nodded.

They ducked out through a gaping hole which should not have been there, avoiding a trickle of water from a torn pipe. More medical drones, more red jumpsuits. Another medic team running alongside a sealed drone. An engineer looked blankly after them, cutting graser dangled limply at her side.

Maggie's voice was grim. "Looks like they cut someone out of the rubble."

Glancing up, Yoshiko saw the video-globe was tracking them.

"I wonder where Septor is." She knew her voice could be edited out, later.

"He and Lori had an argument," Maggie said. "Vin told me. He went to stay with some buddies, I think."

"Oh, no."

Yoshiko felt wretched, for Septor's sake as well as Lori's.

"Damn it!" A curse sounded from around a comer. "Bastard thing clawed me!"

Exchanging glances, Yoshiko and Maggie went to investigate.

A blue-jumpsuited engineer was kneeling before a pile of rubble, swearing softly. Thin parallel lines of blood broke the skin on the back of his hand. He sucked at the wound.

A low growling sounded from beneath the heap of debris.

"Let me." Yoshiko crouched down beside the engineer.

"Watch it." From a med-kit, the engineer sprayed gel onto his hand. "Damned thing's pissed, and I don't blame it."

"I'll be careful."

Yoshiko got down on hands and knees. Ducking low, she could see a dark cavity in the rubble, framed by a bent but unbroken classic carbon chair.

"Come on, sweetheart." Yoshiko kept her voice low, almost crooning. "Let's get you out of there."

Another growl, softer this time.

"Yes, I know. Come on, everything's OK."

Nothing.

"Come on, then."

A wide paw appeared in the shadowed hole.

"Good girl. That's a good girl."

A cautious whiskered nose followed, then the lynxette crawled out into the open, shook herself, and stropped her long whiskers against Yoshiko's face.

"I'll be damned." The engineer sat back on his heels, eyes wondering.

Yoshiko rubbed the bridge of the lynxette's nose.

Behind her, Maggie spoke: "You're a natural."

Overhead, the floating video-globe bobbed as though in agreement.

Xanthia pulsed inside him.

Stumbling, half-blinded by the urgency of his desire, he made his way down the wide marble steps and across the lawn. Paramedics and engineers rushed past him, heading into the building.

"Are you OK, sir?" A concerned face, above a red jumpsuit.

Rafael nodded, and walked urgently on.

A group of proctors—their uniforms torn, their faces bloody—were helping walking wounded up a big flyer's ramp.

"Mind your backs! Coming through!"

Medics escorted a sealed drone into the flyer.

Bright amber shimmered and strobed: another flyer taking off, its warning lights beating counterpoint to the insistence in Rafael's breast, its urgency matching the hot overspills from cache which threatened to engulf him.

He staggered, caught himself, forced himself to walk on.

Just hold on for a minute more, that's all. One minute more.

He avoided an enquiring look from another medic. Almost immediately, someone touched her arm and she was caught up in the emergency evacuation of some dead or dying victim, and Rafael ducked away, out of her sight.

Bright, silvery white, the glowglobes.

Head pounding, he sighted his flyer.

[[[HeaderBegin: Module =A34 . . . <<<disengage disengage disengage>>>]]]

<<<MsgRcv LUCFMT0007710; cause = command aborted on request.>>>

He moaned softly, unable to enter command interface without losing control entirely.

If a medic spotted him then, he would be taken for medical exam; even a cursory examination would reveal the additional plexcores in his body. A deep scan would tell them everything.

Just hold back.

Hold back hold back hold back.

His flyer. A small one, a crimson Phirina Duo, the colour of burning strontium.

He slapped a hand on its hull, and a ramp extruded, then pulled him inside the small cabin.

"Command:—" His voice shook; he hoped the system recognized it. "Darken . . . cockpit."

The bubble membrane polarized to inky black, shutting out the busy swarm of emergency flyers.

Xanthia.

Yoshiko's diagram: a Luculentus mind, which might, just might, be his. The selected parameters had not revealed the full extent of VSI, the full size of the plexcore nexus which formed the mind's substrate. But the swirling patterns of thought had been of such complexity—

Yearning, yearning, to break free from cache.

He held her in, just for a moment more. Consider the danger. What did Yoshiko know? Suspect? Was the diagram from Tetsuo, somehow?

Did he have to take action now?

He saw again the shock on the Earther woman's face, reflected that the house was swarming with proctors but none seemed to be seeking him, and decided that the risk was negligible. Riskier to deal with her now, in fact, than to bide his time.

Hold back. You want to let go, but stop and consider first.

That damned Earther woman.

Tetsuo was the source of Rafael's own mu-space tech. But Tetsuo should have had no access to LuxPrime info: his commsware had nothing to do with Luculenti minds. Not until Rafael had copied it and turned it to his own uses.

Why a Luculentus mind? The diagram looked like phase maps from a deep scan, output from the kind of scanware used only in the Baton Ceremony—or Rafael's own infiltration code. Either way, it was from the kind of quantum-level measurement which destroyed the original even as it recorded the variables exactly.

Perhaps it was a simulation, like the simulation he had built yesterday—using three ghost-Rafaels—to test his infiltration code's tightness and security. But, if it were a simulation, it must be finely detailed, in that case, built up from the lowest levels. Who, other than LuxPrime, would create a model like that?

Low level. Levels, levels . . .

Why does maths lie at the heart of science? Why are features of the universe algorithmically compressible? Of what strange substrate is maths itself an emergent property?

Hold back.

Lying on the cabin floor now, and writhing helplessly.

Distinctions. He was on the verge of being able to slice the universe in new directions, to perceive patterns and differences in quite new ways. Deeper, and different.

Was Xanthia's mind going to push him beyond that transition boundary?

Was she the one?

"Xanthia." His whisper was hoarse.

Would she and he together be the first of a new form of life?

Had to let—

Ultimate freedom, ultimate enlightenment, thanks to Xanthia and all the soft, delicious, sweet and beautiful Luculentae before her, all the minds subsumed within his nexus.

—to let—

"Command: fly home!"

—go.

He hardly felt the flyer lift.

Such relief, as the cache containment codes unlocked.

Finally, it gave up its compressed code, emptied out its buffers, into Rafael's waiting plexcore nexus.

Xanthia's mind flooded through him.

He gasped aloud.

All those fragments: first love, secret dreams, examination hell. Lost virginity, business success. Holodramas and poetry. Aged three months, the first flower she had seen: bright yellow, bursting in wonderful light before a baby's stunned and joyful senses.

Xanthia's pure and beautiful life was his.

The code tore her copied soul apart, ripped it into tiny shreds, and reworked it, rethreaded it, into the larger, darker fabric of the whole.

Joy. Love. Bright hope and dark despair.

A shout of triumph burst from Rafael's lips, as he arched in ecstasy on the cockpit floor.

In the growing, swelling mass of his extended being, he was conscious of all of them.

Gregor: Rafael's soul-father. Long dark hours of solitary concentration. Lonely triumphs in secret and complex games in Skein, which only the brightest of Luculenti could appreciate.

Depression. Rages. Striking out at Maria, his beloved wife . . .

Pedro: Gregor's soul-father, gentle and filled with childlike wonder, always. Visual artist, dreamer, for a hundred and eighty years. Pain, too, in the later times, which he had passed on unedited to Gregor so that their lesson of transitory sweetness be not lost.

Adam: Pedro's soul-father.

Donal: Adam's soul-father . . .

But more: he was the darkest, ripped-apart and incomplete fragments of Marianan del'Ortega: her sleazy seduction in a Lowtown doorway, gritty stone pressed against her back, and the spicy breath of the Fulgidus boy whose hand was inside her clothes . . .

He was the dark shadows, too, of those other once-sweet lives: of Rachel and Florentia and Magasrabina and Drionay. Like Marianan, they were deceased Luculentae whose plexcores he had exhumed and sucked of their contents. Unlike Marianan—her death an unlikely accident, the horror of the flyer diving out of control as fresh in his mind as the day she died—unlike her, they had completed the Baton Ceremony, and their plexcores contained the dark, the vicious and the inane, all the dreck and dregs of life they did not want to burden their successors with.

And there were the flakes of memory, the half-read resonances picked up from Voretta and his other almost-loves, the ones he had penetrated but not subsumed.

But, torn apart from the holographic whole, flailing the desperate hooks of distributed thought needing to meld into a pattern, the black soul fragments of the dead were the most powerful force of all.

He was all of them, and they were him.

His own beginnings? His core was there, sparked into being when Gregor's memories had flooded into the youthful Rafael, while lightning played outside and freakish storms smashed the forest trees and blew the conservatory's dome apart. No LuxPrime supervision in those days. The Baton Ceremony was a private thing, and the dark and melancholy Gregor ignored the most elementary safety precautions, ending his life and birthing a wild new spirit in the storm.

A spirit strong enough to subdue and subsume a wealth of clamouring mind-fragments.

A mind powerful enough to encompass the hopes and dreams of countless others.

The interference pattern of their desperate thoughts and hot emotions; the whole greater than the sum of souls, the addition of minds; emergent, a new and more powerful type of being.

Such power.

Thank you, Xanthia.

He was on the brink, the very threshold of something marvellous. Xanthia had made him ready, and he knew with certainty that one more mind, just one more sweet Luculenta mind, and the divine change would cascade through his nexus, flood through his plexcores, and sweep him to a new stage of evolution.

The power sang in Rafael. Outside the cockpit, the night was inky black, as though the very stars had retired in deference.

He knew, with deep and utter certainty, that he could become anything he pleased. The power sang, a trumpet note of triumph, and he laughed with the joy of impending victory.

A row of tiny blue lights sparked into existence along the damaged corridor.

"I'm surprised that still works," said Maggie.

Beside Yoshiko, the lynxette—called Dawn, Yoshiko remembered—wrinkled her nose at the dust, and delivered a feline sneeze.

"Bless you. What are those lights, Maggie?"

"House video, I should think." Maggie picked her way over crumbled remnants of wall. "There's a—oh, damn it!—a local privacy law. If you're recording, you have to display some indication."

Yoshiko looked up at the video-globe, following in faithful companionship.

"That's exempt." Maggie followed her gaze. "Because it's so obvious. The recorders in these walls are probably damn near invisible."

"I understand." Yoshiko nodded. "Listen, I'd like to go back to my own room. But we can't go through the foyer, not with all that wreckage there."

"Why not?—Oh, the cat's paws. Right."

Yoshiko stopped at a big lounge to their right. Between flowing drapes, French doors led out to the grounds.

"You thinking of going around the outside?" There was a rueful expression on Maggie's face.

Yoshiko, too, remembered: only an hour or two ago, they had fled through the night like shrieking schoolgirls, when a rustle sounded in the bushes.

"This house is big enough to get lost in." Yoshiko tried to think practically. "And we don't know which corridors are blocked. If we attempt to find our way round the ballroom indoors, we could end up being missing for days."

"I've told you a million times—" started Maggie.

"—not to exaggerate. Right."

"OK." Maggie let out a long sigh. "I'm taking the scenic route. If you go round the outside, I can meet you in your room. First, I'd like to go back to the entrance and talk to that Luculentus who acted like he was in charge."

"Going to interview him?"

"If he'll talk to me. But it's occurred to me that he might be able to hand control of the house system over to you, since Lori put you in charge."

"Oh. OK." Yoshiko was not sure what good that would do, or if she really needed the responsibility.

Maggie headed back towards the house's shattered hub.

Yoshiko, sighing, shook her head, then cut through the lounge, with the lynxette tagging along beside her.

The French doors were a highly permeable membrane. When Yoshiko passed through, the membrane felt chilled and wet. The lynxette spat.

The night had grown bitterly cold. Yoshiko hurried across the grass, though her clothes were beginning to warm automatically.

Yoshiko was afraid that Dawn might go loping off into the night, but she stayed by Yoshiko's side. They crossed the lawns together.

Only two of the big flyers remained. That still left a lot of people —fifty? more?—staying in rooms being treated by autodocs or medical drones, or watching over injured friends or loved ones. And the emergency teams were still here, of course. Probably a forensic team had already swept the ballroom by now, for all the good that would do.

Whatever had happened to poor Xanthia?

Rafael. He was behind it. Of that she was certain.

Yoshiko and the lynxette came to a brightly lighted room with a floor-length window which softened at their approach, and they went inside. Yoshiko was grateful for the sudden warmth. Her athlete's body began to sweat with the heat—ready as always for training—until her trouser suit started to cool in compensation.

The room was occupied. A man, keeping watch on a transparent-lidded medical drone. Inside it lay a young woman whom Yoshiko didn't recognize. The man, grey-faced, nodded dispiritedly at Yoshiko as she passed. He paid the lynxette no heed at all.

Maggie was already waiting in her room when Yoshiko got there. Dawn went in past Yoshiko and jumped straight up onto the bed, lay down and began to lick her paws.

"Thom—that's the Luculentus in charge—" Maggie spoke without bothering with a greeting. "—He said you have control of all the house system's comms and domestic modules. He'd like you to hold back the cleaning-drones for a while longer. They'll clean up the debris in no time, apparently, but right now they'd just get in everyone's way."

"Fine." Yoshiko sat wearily down on the bed, and absently rubbed the lynxette's head with her knuckles.

"I've ordered some drinks." Maggie pointed at the bedside terminal. "Had to clear that crazy image first. What was it, again?"

Yoshiko shrugged. "Just some hand-waving graphic meant to explain the concept of a Luculentus extended mind." It was significant, of course. If only she could figure out why.

"Oh."

"Well. . . . Is your video-globe still on?"

"No." Maggie looked interested. "Should it be?"

"I don't think so." Yoshiko took a deep breath. "The image came from a crystal I found in Tetsuo's house. It doesn't mean anything by itself, but I think it's the image of a Luculentus mind. A real scan, of an actual mind."

"Can I see it?"

"I haven't managed to look at it yet . . . I think I'm going to need Vin's—oh, damn it. Lori's help. Or Xanthia's. This Thom fellow didn't say how she is, did he?"

"No. Nor where she is, either. I can't seem to find out much at all, but things are pretty confused out there still."

"What happened to that tall Fulgidus you were dancing with? Roberto, was it?"

"Oh, him." Maggie shook her head ruefully. "He was last seen running for the exit. Runs fast, too."

"I'm sorry."

"Yeah—Look, d'you think you could check your comms? Thom said that he would reroute incoming comms to you, unless they were marked 'personal.'"

"OK."

"Try your new terminal." Maggie pointed at Yoshiko's wrist.

Yoshiko thumbed the bracelet into life. A cluster of icons and holo volumes grew into being. She gestured for her mail.

"There's one to Lori from InfoBurst Five." Yoshiko's fingers flickered as displays flew past. She was getting used to the local systems. "The description is, '*Request for info coverage.*'"

"Privacy laws." Maggie laughed. "I love 'em."

"What do you mean?"

"If there's somebody *compos mentis* in charge of a situation, the NewsNets have to get permission to cover it. Unless it's a public venue."

"They're a NewsNet, you mean?" Yoshiko read the message again.

"You got it."

"I see." Yoshiko waved the communication volume open.

She got a recorded talking head reciting a standard request. Before she could say anything, though, a request-for-override icon appeared—spreading white-gloved hands and a pleading disembodied cartoon grin and eyebrows—which she acknowledged.

An harassed-looking balding man appeared before her.

"You are—?" He spoke quickly; Yoshiko suspected he always did.

"Yoshiko Sunadomari, acting for Lori Maximilian."

"Mikhail Whittaker, here. I've been trying to get through for ages. If you give permission, I can get a team there in twenty minutes, or hook up with the emergency teams' systems in about a second. Here are the financial details and the copyright clauses—"

Text and graphics grew into being to Yoshiko's left.

"—They're standard and they're very reasonable. Guaranteed payment in the top-100 currency-space. Very worthwhile for Luculenta Maximilian."

"Well . . ." Yoshiko looked at Maggie, whose eyes were very bright. "You're lucky. One of Earth's best-known journalists, Maggie Brown, was here when the incident happened. She has extensive recorded coverage of the whole thing. Want to talk to her?"

"Yes! Yes, please—"

"Just one moment." Yoshiko formed the mute/dark gesture to freeze the outgoing signal. "Can I just pass him over to you? Is there anything else you need?"

"No, I'll talk to him." Maggie thumbed her bracelet, requesting control of the display. "And—thank you."

Yoshiko unfroze the comms, relinquishing control, and let Maggie haggle terms. It took less than a minute. When they had agreed, Yoshiko gave her consent, acting as proxy on Lori's behalf.

Maggie checked the technical formatting details for speed-linking her info to an InfoBurst Five NetNode, then signed off.

"Right, then." Her voice was eager. "I've an hour, max, to do the editing. Then we'll be seen Fulgor-wide, in no time."

Yoshiko nodded, hiding her disquiet. Maggie had a job to do.

A drone delivered daistral. Maggie's drink went untouched, as she bent over her display, intent concentration written on her face.

Yoshiko drank, realizing for the first time how deadly tired she was.

"I'm going to pick the last few ballroom shots." Maggie's voice sounded far away. "Then Vin's being taken out to the flyer with Lori beside the drone. Finish with the flyer taking off."

Her rapid fingers plucked cubic images from the air, rearranged them in a string, and played each cube once or twice, adjusting the duration.

Like a player with perfect pitch tuning a stringed instrument, she constrained narrative flow into an exact sixty seconds with deceptive ease.

Running her hands through her hair, she leaned back. "Command: record. Disaster struck this evening at the palatial home of Luculenta Lori Maximilian—"

Her words coalesced in midair, a fairy string of golden text, as she spoke.

"—when, during a superlative display of light and music at the height of the Aphelion Ball, a malfunctioning holo-projector array went wild, wreaking utter carnage . . . destroying the house and killing or maiming many influential guests, among them Neliptha Machella, mayor of Lucis City. Endit."

Yoshiko opened her mouth to interrupt, then stopped herself.

Maggie said, "I'm going to send this, as a teaser. Then we can put together a longer version. They've got a reedit option in the contract, the bastards, but it costs them to invoke it. If I make the report good enough, they won't have to."

"You just go ahead." Yoshiko thought about Rafael, seeing his charming face in her mind's eye, keeping her intuition to herself. "I'll wait till you've finished."

Maggie, after all, needed facts—and glamour—but not supposition.

Yoshiko sipped from her daistral, watching while Maggie fastened her h-mail bundle together with ribbon-tying gestures, and pointed with a decisive forefinger. The message was sent.

A half-smile tugged at Maggie's face, but faded instantly. She picked up her daistral from the drone's back.

"Blueberry. My favourite." Her voice was hollow.

"Oh." Yoshiko frowned. "You know—I think I may have seen blue lights in the ballroom. When the place went dark, as Xanthia's dance started."

"What kind of—? You mean recording lights?"

"I'm not sure." Yoshiko thumbed her wrist terminal back on. "Command mode. House system video logs—" She specified ballroom images, and a twenty-minute time-stamp range. "—Two-minute intervals."

A string of ten cubes, each with tiny moving images appeared.

"*Mrra?*"

Yoshiko rubbed the lynxette's head. "We're ignoring you, aren't we?"

"Try this one." Maggie pointed at the first cube. "Oops. Too early."

In the enlarged display, Yoshiko could see her own tiny figure among the happy people performing the line dance. She crushed the cubic holo volume with a gesture.

Maggie pointed at the third cube, which expanded to a metre-wide volume. Inside, a hundred Luculenti were wheeling about the tiny robed figure of Xanthia. The fairylike figures of her four attendants were delicate, reality in miniature.

"This is gr—" Maggie looked up. "Sorry."

Yoshiko nodded numbly.

A cruciform pattern, the wheeling dancers, Xanthia the hub about whom they danced—

Jump. Maggie's fingers flicked. Jump forward. Jump.

—faster and faster, to the dance's climax. The music, though muted, rose to a distant crescendo. The dancers' feet were unseen tiny blurs; the floor a silver grid on endless black, hanging half a metre above the real richly carpeted floor of Yoshiko's room.

The tiny Xanthia's upraised arms, flung up in agony and despair. A blinding pillar of white light—

"Stop," said Yoshiko, and the display froze into stillness.

"What?"

"Rafael—"

"Unclear command." The house system's voice was Lori's, and Yoshiko shivered involuntarily.

"End command mode. Sorry, Maggie. Er—Look, he's there, at the edge. See?"

"Right. Allow me."

Maggie's twisting hands caused the still display to spin and zoom with sickening speed, giving Yoshiko a sensation of vertigo as they fell towards the frozen Rafael.

Maggie gestured, and the replay continued.

Rafael's face was pulled into a half-smile, half-grimace, of intense suffering—or something else. His dark eyes, hooded, held a hungry look even in holo. Then a huge tremor shook his body, and a creamy look of satisfaction filled those eyes—

Rafael disappeared, along with all the other holo cubes.

Gone.

"Shit!" Maggie looked angry.

"What happened?"

"I don't know."

"Command: house system, initial display."

Nothing happened.

"Probably the engineers, damn it." Maggie pinched the bridge of her nose, then drank some more daistral, obviously not tasting it. "Brought the whole damn system—Oh, look. There we are."

"Your previous interaction ended abnormally," the faux-Lori's voice informed them. "Do you wish to recover the previous session?"

"Yes."

The string of holo cubes reappeared.

As before, Maggie pointed at the third one in the row.

Dancers whirled in cruciform configuration. Maggie gestured, and the display twisted, focussed on bare marble floor, a pillar's base.

"Yoshiko—"

Jump. The image jumped back in time, restarted. Spinning dancers, Luculenti feet stamping authoritatively in time, the blinding white pillar of light, then a sickening moment as the viewpoint flew rapidly round the ballroom's periphery, passing through the ghostlike figures of onlookers, through a miniature of Yoshiko herself.

"Give me all object rights to the video logs, Yoshiko. Right now."

Yoshiko did not argue. "Command: grant Maggie Brown, this physical location, all rights to current video objects."

"Authorities granted," said the system in Lori's voice.

The music climaxed and every dancer fell to one knee and Xanthia was gripped by some impossible agony.

"Command: download current objects." Maggie pressed her wrist terminal.

Tiny Luculenti, running to help Xanthia, were impaled on beams of scarlet light, and fell.

"What's going on?"

Once more, Xanthia flung up her arms and white light burst brilliantly into being.

"Got it." Maggie's voice was grim, as she indicated her bracelet. "Saved the coverage as it is now. Bastards can't edit it any more on me."

"Edit it?"

"Yeah, watch."

Maggie froze the display, moved the timestamp back to the moment when a white shaft of light erupted into being, and froze it again. Then she took the viewpoint in a long, slow trawl around the ballroom.

There was no sign of Rafael.

"Who? Who could get into the house system?"

"Well, there aren't many possibilities." Maggie looked grim. "The proctors?"

"I don't know."

"Or Rafael? He looked like he might have some tricks up his sleeve."

Rafael.

"Perhaps."

"Well, I'll tell you one thing." Maggie crossed her arms, and leaned back. "Everyone else was either frozen in terror, or running for dear life. Whatever he was up to, it wasn't either of those things."

"No," said Yoshiko slowly. "I'd have to agree with you there."

"Right." Maggie's tone became brisk. "I'll start editing the copy I have left, ready to hit the NewsNets in depth. What do you reckon?"

"Yes. Good move."

Maggie got to work then, while Yoshiko watched, feeling useless.

After a while, the lynxette, Dawn, stirred on the bed. Yoshiko realized she had been curled up on it asleep.

Rubbing her gritty eyes, Yoshiko used the bedside terminal to order feline food. When the food arrived, the lynxette jumped down, sniffed at the bowl on the drone's back, then leaped back up onto the bed, curled round, and went straight to sleep.

Maggie looked up, snorted with laughter, then got back to her work.

Yoshiko flicked the bedside terminal back on.

Blue. Shifting patterns of unbelievable complexity: a raw and alien beauty, as unknowable yet alluring as whalesong.

The Luculentus mind.

The look in Rafael's eyes, when he had seen the image from the doorway. Was that look an artefact of her own shock, of memory distortion?

She shook her head. She *had* seen it, the sudden black anger rising inside him. The cold calculation. Though Yoshiko was confused in a strange culture, shocked and injured and in dire need of sleep, she was not hallucinating.

"Command mode," she said. "Request real-time call to Luculenta Xanthia Delaggropos."

"That ident is not currently available. Do you wish to log a message?"

"No. End command mode."

Maggie frowned at the interruption, but said nothing.

Mail status. Icon: incoming h-mail. Lori must have set up some regular link to EveryWare, checking for messages.

The icon unfurled. Eric Rasmussen's head and shoulders appeared in the display.

"Hi, Prof." A broad, red-bearded grin. "Just thought I'd let you know—I've got a fair amount of leave saved up, and we station crew get to hitch a ride real cheap." He hesitated. "Er—I'll be on Fulgor in a day or two: mail me at this handle. Oh, yeah. Did I mention about diving being better than freefall? How about buying a couple of snorkels, or decent resp-masks?" Despite the confident tone, the colour was rising in his cheeks. "Er—Endit."

Eric.

Yoshiko flicked the display into oblivion.

She stared at the wall, seeing nothing.

"Looks like you got a friend." Maggie glanced sidelong at Yoshiko, before continuing her work.

"I guess so."

"Was he coming on too strong?"

"I'm a bit surprised. I barely know him. It's—nice of him to call."

"You don't have to sound so pleased about it. There." Maggie grunted, giving a thumbs-up gesture to finalize the editing. "Done it."

She leaned back in her chair and stretched her arms, and Yoshiko could hear her joints popping.

"Drink?" Yoshiko asked.

"Yeah—Wait. What time is it? Bloody hell, it's morning."

"You've been at this through the night."

"Well, yeah, I guess I have. God, I have to go."

"You should rest."

"Gotta go." Maggie shook her head. "I need to see Jason, make sure he's not worried, though the staff at Xanthia's house can take good care of him. Actually, the house itself is quite capable of looking after him—"

"Oh, no."

"Yeah, quite." Maggie looked bleak. "What am I going to tell Amanda? I don't even know if the poor kid's mother is still alive."

"Xanthia's ident is unavailable for calls." Yoshiko bit her lip. "Still doesn't mean—"

"Doesn't look good, though."

"No, it doesn't. Look, the proctors will have been to see Amanda. Other Luculenti."

"Probably," said Maggie. "But I've still got to go."

"Yes, of course."

Yoshiko stood up stiffly. Maggie almost staggered as she levered herself upright. Together they went out of the room and took the corridor through now-familiar debris to the central atrium.

A phalanx of small blue maintenance drones was waiting at the edge of the foyer, ready to clear away the rubble. Yoshiko would have to check with someone in charge, before giving the drones permission to proceed.

Maggie stopped a young proctor, who looked half dead with exhaustion.

"Any chance of a lift back to Lucis?" she asked. "To save me getting a taxi?"

"Uh, sure." His voice was heavy with lack of sleep. "There's a flyer just leaving." He pointed out the doorway. "If you rush, I'll tell them to wait for you."

"Done." Maggie gave Yoshiko a quick hug, and kissed her cheek.

They looked at each other wordlessly, then Maggie nodded and hurried out, and down the steps. The young proctor spoke into his comm-ring, telling the flyer crew to wait for a minute, they had an extra passenger.

Maggie waved from the flyer door, a small figure, then disappeared inside. Yoshiko watched the flyer depart, feeling very small and old and alone.

Glass and ceramics crunched beneath her feet as she walked through the foyer and into the ruin that had so recently been a magnificent ballroom, full of happiness and cheer.

It was open to the sky, and bitterly cold. Predawn cast dark green streaks across the heavens, and the slender monomer strands were stark black against the coming morning. Here and there a drone slowly crawled, a small grey friendly shape, but the silence was absolute.

She had no tears.

Her breathing felt thick, despite the clear, cold air. Despair lay upon her, bowing her shoulders with its weight.

Empty, empty inside.

No tears at all. Nothing.

Numb, numb, numb.

•

Rafael enjoyed dying.

He walked with a light, bouncing step, almost floating, from his flyer to his Lucis town house. Inside, he summoned a couch to rise from the floor, lay back, and put his feet up.

Ah, Xanthia.

He loved to relive the moments of his deaths. Though Xanthia's body might—or might not—be physically functioning, her brain had been randomized when his infiltration code invoked the deepscan routines, and she had died even as her thoughts and memories were replicated into his cache.

Worshipful Luculenti dancers, all subordinating their kinaesthetic senses and motor control to her/his wishes. Yes, Xanthia had been his kind of woman. He felt the dancers all around her/him. Closing his eyes, he began to replay the whole Sun-Wheel Dance in exquisite stereo, with his Rafael-body and Xanthia-body perceptions overlapped and mingled, giving gorgeous depth to the whole experience.

She/he stood at the darkened ballroom's entrance, feeling the headdress's weight, the gown's soft folds. Deep in command interface with the projector array, she/he caused twin lines of lambent blue flames to lick across the shadowed marble floor, awaiting her/his entrance.

Accompanied by sweet young Luculentae girls, she/he made her/his appearance, slowly walking between the flames. All around, a spellbound audience in the darkness, tiny blue sparks of distant light—

He froze.

Damn it! Those tiny blue lights were not part of Xanthia's illusion.

He was a fool.

He had been so enraptured by Xanthia, so drawn to her, that he had failed to realize those sapphire sparks were the house system's scan signs, not stars created by Xanthia's wonderful imagination.

Immediately, he shifted into Skein—

No.

He withdrew, knowing it was too late. If the evidence had been already spotted by proctor techs, then they were lying in wait for outside interference. If not, then he still dared not try access via Skein, where LuxPrime techs could possibly, if they and their AIs dug deeply and cleverly enough, find audit trails of his accessing the house system remotely.

Perhaps if he went back to the Maximilian estate, so he could use short-range fast-comm access to the house video logs, not involving Skein—But the surveillance now might be so tight that even he might fall to erase all his traces.

Think.

Let's see. If he had been recorded in the video logs, how would he appear? Frozen? Joyful? Perhaps he could fake a medical history: some quasi-epileptic condition that might fit. Something normally controllable, but not cured by LuxPrime mindware.

A dangerous ploy: a deep medical scan would reveal his links to a plexcore nexus two orders of magnitude greater than normal. The alternative was to play a passive game, to wait and see if the proctors would come to him.

A frisson of fear ran light fingers up his back.

Delicious.

The game was becoming interesting.

It was now twenty-four hours since Yoshiko had woken up and performed her early morning training on the lawn, eager and fearful of the evening ahead.

The lynxette, Dawn, was tucked up on Yoshiko's bed in the loaf-of-bread position, eyes squeezed tightly shut.

Yoshiko let out a long, slow breath. Her eyes were gritty with lack of sleep—but she could not face the inevitable dreams to come.

Old, old, old.

Outside, it was not yet fully light. The still-unfamiliar length of the day, something over twenty-seven hours, wasn't going to help her readjust.

She waved open a cupboard space, to reveal her naginata and holo-processor, both in their carry-cases, and the gym bag containing her other training gear. Tiredly, she rubbed her eyes.

In her youth, thirty, forty years ago, if she had pulled an all-nighter, she would still work out the following day as energetically as if she had had a full night's sleep. Not this time. That was all too long ago.

At Yoshiko's age, daily training was a habit—beating back the twin dragons of laziness and despair, fighting them a day at a time—or else you didn't work out at all. But you had to be sensible about it.

Despite the inhibitors which were killing all pain in her left arm and the cast which was supporting it, her arm was not OK: it was still healing up inside. She should rest. That would be the sensible thing.

Sensible.

What, truly, in this strange and wonderful universe, constitutes appropriate behaviour?

Slowly, she slid off the loose black suit and the scarlet blouse—rumpled now, and quite inelegant—and tossed them across the chair which Maggie had been sitting on.

She took the gym bag from the cupboard, pulled out a leotard, and put it on.

Then she began to stretch slowly, painfully, her mind too tired to think at all.

Turning back to the gym bag, she examined the magbracelets for power training, put them back in, and instead took out a folded black-hooded jumpsuit. She shook it out, then pulled it on.

The suit formed integral boots and gloves, and she pulled the hood up so that it covered all her face except around the eyes. Then she picked up the naginata in her injured hand and the heavy holo-processor in the other, and went outside.

Emergency workers stared at this strange figure as she walked out through the atrium, but she ignored them.

She went far out across the lawns—faintly silver beneath the burgeoning dawn—out where they melted into the black shadows, by a long stand of tall trees. She placed the projector down on the long grass, and powered it up. For now, she left the naginata in its case.

Kneeling, sitting back on her heels, she waited.

He came murderously fast.

Her shadow opponent launched a lethal open-hand strike to her neck but she caught the wrist—her suit's inducting fibres perfectly simulating physical contact—and rose to one knee, blending with the attack, entering the centre of the motion, becoming the pivot of his movement, and then her attacker was flat on the ground and she was striking the back of his neck.

Ippon. Killing blow.

Again and again he attacked. One blow after another, which Yoshiko avoided and redirected and finished with deadly force, until her breath was painful fire and her limbs turned into heavy lead.

Tired. So tired now.

Pink and gold and beautiful green, and the sweet fresh smell of morning.

Concentrate.

An onlooker would have thought her proficient, but only Yoshiko knew how off-centre and unfocussed she was in her practice. Concentrate. An old sensei's voice in her head: *Become the very centre of the attack, the heart of the storm, and you will find true peace.*

Then the attacker grabbed her left wrist, tugging her off-balance, but agony shot through her broken arm, breaking the pain inhibitors' effect.

Yoshiko screamed.

She screamed as she whipped her knee into his thigh, seeing Rafael's face in her shadow opponent as she struck his throat and he fell and lay still.

Breathing heavily, she stepped back and waved the simulation into oblivion.

Rafael.

Other than pushing people aside last night, she had never used her skills outside *dojo* or *shiai* area, outside training hall or competition mat. Never had she fought in deadly earnest; never attacked a human being without control.

"Rafael."

Her voice was pitiless, hard and clear in the dawn's soft air.

Chapter Twenty-Three

Grey winter hues
Beneath green skies, no longer bright.
Worn-out like old clothes.

It takes courage, my son, to move forwards into the eye of the storm.

Tetsuo stood on the research station's balcony, breathing peacefully, and watched the sun's rays strike the opposite rim of the canyon, painting the sandstone peach and gold. Even through his resp-mask, the morning air was crisp and cold.

He felt good.

The warrior, when attacked, steps forwards.

His mother's words, brought clearly back to him by a trick of memory. Perhaps he was getting old.

Would she despise him, for doing this now, not decades ago? It was not unusual for people approaching middle age to reconsider their health. Back home on Okinawa, half his contemporaries were probably downloading personal-trainer AIs from EveryWare.

Or would Mother congratulate him?

Sweat was drying into him as his jumpsuit's fabric attempted to compensate for his exertions. It had been a nice easy jog along the canyon from the cabin, but he had finished with something like a sprint up the steep trail to the dome. That had been hard, and for a while he had thought he was going to die, but now the endorphin high was on him and everything was fine.

Why did those particular words of Mother's come back to him now? He was working out—by his standards, anyway—but there was no danger. Everything was quite peaceful here.

Less stressful than his previous way of life, for sure. It did not need courage to abandon his old career: it took only common sense.

Perhaps some good had come of this, after all.

He leaned on the balcony wall, enjoying the rough feel of it even through the thin layer of smartgel which covered his hands, enjoying the sheer physical sensations of being alive.

All those years when he had turned away from Mother's path and mocked the futility of *bushido* training. Now—Perhaps, soon, he could send her an h-mail. Apologize, arrange another trip. For all of them: Mother, Akira, and his wife, Kumiko.

Movement.

Among the rocks. Shadows, in a narrow defile.

Raiding party?

Heart pounding, his overworked thighs trembling, Tetsuo sank down out of sight behind the balcony wall. People—he had not seen how many—were coming down the opposite side of the canyon. Agrazzi. Somehow, he was sure of it.

The warrior, when attacked, steps forwards.

Ha! *Thanks, Mother, but I'm not a warrior. I'm the one who hid away when the school bullies were around. Who resigned and fled to another world when the pressure of work grew too great.*

Not a warrior.

Dhana and Brevan were back in the cabin. He had no way of communicating with them—No. That was not true. The lab system was linked to the cabin. But if he went back inside, he was trapped in a building with only one way in or out.

Move.

On hand and knees—crawling, very brave—he reached the door, rolled through the membrane.

Get to the lab.

He rushed inside, tugged off his resp-mask, and thumbed the tiny terminal into life. An out-reaching gesture, with his gel-covered hands: a comms request.

"*Not authorized to function.*"

Damn.

He did not have time to hack this bloody closed system. Why hadn't he done it earlier, when he had the chance?

Why didn't his damned mindware make itself useful?

Nothing.

A scraping sound, from outside.

Desperately, fingers flickering, he broke through into system management, found a shared notepad-function.

Outside, a voice barked an order, the words indistinct.

"Agrazzi raiders." Tetsuo's voice was an urgent whisper. "Get out. Now."

He stabbed with his forefinger. If one of the cabin's terminals was active, his message would pop up as voice and text.

A brush of fabric against a wall, instantly stopped.

He had to get out of here.

Backing away, he found himself among low rows of vats. A soft susurration, like distant breathing, filled the room. Fumes stung his nose, and he slapped his respmask back on.

A shadow slipped past the doorway.

Crouching down, Tetsuo duck-walked between the benches. At the rear of the lab, a ramp led downwards.

Dead end.

Moving quickly, he descended the ramp. In the closed cavern, the rock pool lay, brown and stagnant. Beneath the surface, dark shadows swam among fronds of underwater vegetation.

He glanced back. From the lab, the slapping sound of running footsteps.

Tetsuo crouched down, took a deep breath, and rolled softly over, into the pool without a splash. Murky water swallowed him up.

A heavy funereal silence lay like a shroud upon the great ruined house.

Yoshiko, walking along the hushed, damaged corridors, counted six sealed medical drones, scattered among various rooms. Each drone held someone who was critically injured, but not so badly that it was better to risk a flight to a med-centre. While the drones worked furiously within their blank carapaces, families and attendant medics waited. Relatives looked up with dead eyes as Yoshiko walked past.

A small inspection team of engineers passed by, talking quietly among themselves. Most of their colleagues had left some time ago.

There were hardly any proctors to be seen. No doubt drones had been left, surveilling the house and grounds. Perhaps the SatScan system, which people kept mentioning, would be used to keep a watchful eye from orbit.

In the central atrium, one young proctor stood. He looked about eighteen years old.

Rafael. Did you really cause all this?

Yoshiko looked around in a drawing room, searching cracked tables and an overturned sideboard, until she found a palm terminal. She fetched it out to the young proctor left on duty, so he could order food or drink.

He nodded his thanks.

"Were you here last night?" Stupid question: his face was drawn and pale, etched with fatigue.

"Yeah." He swallowed. "It was awful."

"Have you had any sleep?"

He smiled wanly. "I was ordered to take a few hours out, in some quarters we commandeered down that corridor. But—"

"I know. Me neither." Up close, Yoshiko could see how reddened his eyes were. "Was anyone you know among the, ah, injured?"

"Yeah, Malerdy. He was my classmate at the academy." He swallowed again. "Got hit by a chunk of falling wall."

My God. Young men, with their lives ahead of them, experiencing this.

"Is he going to be all right?"

"I'm not sure." His voice was bleak.

"It was a terrible thing." Yoshiko let out a shaky breath. "You're right there, my friend."

His face grew grim. "Damn things are supposed to have safeties."

"The holoprojectors? Yes, I know." In her mind's eye, Yoshiko could see Lori carving that magnificent statue of Diana the Huntress. "I guess it flipped into an abnormal mode of operation."

He was silent for a moment, then he shook his head.

"I studied holoprocessor tech at the academy." He bit his lip. "It's supposed to cut out in a medical emergency. And I never saw anyone have a fit like that before, either. Didn't think *Luculenti*—" The emphasis was bitter. "—suffered from that kind of thing."

"No." Yoshiko was thoughtful. "You would think neurological disorders were cured by their implant tech, wouldn't you?"

The young proctor shrugged.

"Some kind of feedback from the array when it blew. Hardware failure. Would you believe it? That's what they're saying."

"Oh," said Yoshiko. "I see."

"Million-to-one chance. No one's fault."

She knew that look in his eye: the stunned certainty of mortality. She had seen the look in her own reflection, but this boy was far too young to have to deal with that reality.

All youngsters—bursting with vitality, like Vin—think unconsciously that they will live forever, and that's a true and honest part of life's cycle. They should not be confronted with its inescapable demise. Not while their dreams are still forming.

This young man's dreams would be nightmares, for a long time to come.

"Take care," she said.

He nodded, thoughts turned already inwards.

Earlier, an older proctor had informed Yoshiko that the forensic sweep was finished, and she had ordered the domestic drones to begin the clean-up.

Now, she no longer had to pick her way among piles of rubble to reach the ballroom's main entrance, though the great bronze doors remained bent and battered.

The ballroom's floor was gleaming marble once more. The rubble gone, smashed flagstones replaced or repaired with femtotech construction. Clouds were reflected in the shining surface, criss-crossed with black shadows: monomer filaments still held up the walls.

More of the domed roof was gone. Unsafe segments had been cut away.

The house drones might be able to throw a smartfilm across the gaping hole. Perhaps she should log on, at least check whether rain was due. There should be some sort of cover, she thought, before night fell.

Night. Another night—

Glancing ruefully at her tu-rings—they still glowed dull orange, unable to interface with Skein—she activated her wrist terminal.

The sun shone brightly from Hermes's copper helmet, and his ankle wings fluttered gaily.

Curling her finger, Yoshiko saw the message was from Maggie, and she touched the icon and watched it unfurl.

"Hi, Yoshiko." A starburst grew into being beside the image of Maggie's head. "The item's on InfoBurst Five, if you want to see. It hit the NewsNets as soon as I sent it."

The starburst was a link to the news item.

Yoshiko stared at it, then looked up at the torn roof, screwing up her courage. Could she bear to see last night's tragedy again?

When attacked, a warrior steps forwards. Sensei's words.

Her fingertip pierced the icon.

Black, and freezing. Vision was a cold blurring of light.

Smartgel covered his eyes: protection, but no visibility, not in these opaque waters.

Don't breathe.

A tiny flood of silver bubbles escaped his resp-mask, and streamed to the surface.

It's not designed for this. Not enough dissolved 0_2*.*

A shadow rippled over the pool. A man's arm?

Distant murmuring. Voices? The water's lapping obscured all sound.

Broken shadows. People, looking into the pool.

Holding tightly to cold, slippery rock. *Keep still.*

His head began to pound.

A tiny beep sounded, inside his mask. He pressed the mask to negate the request, hoping his movement could not be seen.

Can't risk it.

The mask wanted to flip into short-term emergency mode, electrolysing the water. The rush of expelled hydrogen would be a giveaway.

Headache.

Getting harder to breathe.

A wheeze overlaying every intake of breath.

Temples pounding.

Vision growing dark.

Something touched his cheek.

Don't—

Tendrils, exploring.

—move. For God's sake.

Something soft crawled across his hand.

Just don't bloody move.

Blackness falling.

•

In perfect synchrony, a hundred revellers danced their intricate steps.

A FourSpeak secondary tesseract described the cultural history of the Sun-Wheel Dance, performed annually for a hundred years at the moment of the sun's greatest distance from Fulgor. In other volumes, text and phase-space diagrams provided an engineering analysis of the building's collapse—Yoshiko glanced around her, at the real ruined ballroom—while the central, metre-wide display, showed the dancers, and Xanthia's collapse.

Blog-cubes of well-known personalities. Mayor Neliptha Machella, black and elegant. Network diagrams estimated the political impact of her death.

White light burst through the central display, and the roof collapsed. Yoshiko's tiny figure failed to rescue Vin.

There was no quasi-sentient AI with Maggie's face to answer questions—not up to science-documentary standard—but the audio voice-overs were in her familiar tones.

Death.

"Replay."

Yoshiko watched it through again, her face like stone. Watched, until the end.

"Again."

Blossoming scarlet, Vin's temple.

"Again."

Sight almost gone now.

Desperate, mouth dry, sucking from the failing resp-mask.

Cold, dark waters, calling him.

Like frozen claws, his fingers hooked beneath the rock, holding him down.

Hold on.

The darkness was pressing down, the cold seeping in, as his jump-suit's heaters failed. Losing energy: the energy for chemical reactions, the processes which made a mind, a soul.

Laughable.

Yeah, laugh. Cry. Whatever. Just hang on.

Fingers like frozen claws.

Here he was, a pitiable organism descended from the bacterial sea and the aquatic transparent unicellular life of a distant fragment of a far star, half dead and about to give up his molecules to sustain more life but *there it was again*, crawling across his face, *don't move or they'll shoot you—ignore it*—then sudden pain lanced through him.

Biting his ear.

Panicking, he pulled the wriggling thing away from him, wrenched it sharply away, tried to slam it against the rock but the resistance slowed him and it slipped away.

He thrashed, struggling, losing track of which way was up.

For God's sake, stay down.

Shocking cold against his cheek: water, inside his resp-mask.

Move.

"Up, up.

This way?

Cold air.

Slippery rock, but his grip held and he hauled himself upwards, using both hands now. He slipped but caught again, and then he was lying half out of the water, gasping for breath, coughing as acrid fumes burned his lungs.

He resealed his resp-mask.

Air slicing into his lungs and hurting like hell, but the pain was a gift. Life. He lay there, trembling, until he could raise his head.

Nobody there.

No armed Agrazzi waited by the pool with grasers trained on him as he emerged—No one. Only the wet slapping sounds of water, and his own harsh breathing.

It was awful.

The extended coverage showed the victims—Yoshiko recognized Felice Lectinaria, the Luculenta biologist—limping or being carried by drones to the profusion of emergency flyers.

Felice did not look badly injured. Yoshiko, remembering that they had been due to talk privately later that night, shook her head.

She let the cube play through. Peripheral displays covered scenes of tragedy and occasional triumph as bare-handed heroes of the moment dug bloody victims from the rubble. Dawn, the lynxette, crawled out, and rubbed her whiskers against the image-Yoshiko's face.

Another Yoshiko caught Vin again: always, always too late.

She looked away.

A flash of white.

"Stop." She pointed to a small cube off to one side. "Current thread. Magnify by ten. Replay from origin."

From a corridor just off the main atrium, medics pulled a twisted figure from the wreckage, its once-elegant white suit now stained and tattered. The hat was gone, the dead man's hair in grey disarray.

Sylvester Stargonier.

They had moved his flyer. Brevan had told him that.

Even if he could make his way back to Nether Canyon, there was no way out of here.

His damned ear was stinging like hell.

Hide. Run. Fight.

What to do?

He tried to slow his racing heartbeat. *Can we think logically here? Just try.*

Hiding and running suffered the same disadvantages. If the Agrazzi knew of him, they would hunt him down regardless. If they didn't, but he couldn't find his flyer, he would die of starvation, possibly thirst.

I'm scared.

Scared, scared, scared.

He remembered that big bugger Morio in the schoolyard on Okinawa, forearm pressed across Tetsuo's throat until he handed over all his lunch, and the sudden exploding pain in his stomach and the ground coming up to meet him and the belated realization that Morio had kicked him anyway, just because he felt like it.

I am not a brave man.

No one who knew Tetsuo could ever have accused him of bravery, or recklessness. So what was he doing?

It was as though someone else was moving Tetsuo's body, and he just did not care. The head-high cupboards opened at his gesture.

Each reagent container bore a tiny display: contents, graphic of molecular structures, concentrations, hazard warnings. He read them through twice, carefully.

Not brave.

Fighting was stupid, got you hurt. Had he not learned that? It got you thumped in the head, where you actually lived. Risking your brain, opposing mindless violence, when the struggle never mattered in the final analysis.

While his thoughts were running, his hands continued to move.

He pulled down four heavy containers of liquid reagents, moving quickly. Another cupboard held empty flasks, and he chose six of them—five blue, one red, to avoid confusion.

Displays flickered as he poured. Precisely calibrated volumes, despite his shaking hands.

When every flask was half full, Tetsuo took a sphere of smartgel sealant from the cupboard, tore off half a dozen tiny blobs, and dropped one into each of the flasks. Each blob melted into a thin layer across the liquid's surface.

Getting there.

Terminal. Where was the terminal?

Ghostly fingers round his throat. Morio's fingers. Strength draining from Tetsuo's muscles. Open-handed slap: Morio's hand smacking into Tetsuo's head. Vision swimming, ear stinging . . .

Concentrate.

As he retrieved the terminal, he tentatively touched his ear. No blood. The pain of the bite was fading.

Careful.

He poured the last reagent, a complex acid, into the six flasks. Gently, so that the smartgel film remained unbroken. Then he closed the red flask, fastened it.

He thumbed the terminal pad.

"Smartgel compile: distribute." The microwave opcodes should reach only the gel in the open blue flasks, not the red. "Time limit: thirty minutes."

Shut down the terminal, closed the flasks.

Thirty minutes, before each smartgel film ravelled up into its original shape, allowing the reagents to mix.

Not a brave man.

All he needed now was to place them where they would do the most good. Looking around, he spotted a black and silver scarf lying on a small stool. Dhana's, left here from her last work shift.

When attacked, the warrior steps forwards.

He unfolded the scarf on the bench, carefully stood all six flasks on top of it, then gathered up the scarf's four corners, enclosing the flasks, and tied the ends together with a simple knot.

Still afraid.

His hands were very nervous as he lifted the whole bundle from the workbench.

But, this time, I won't let that stop me.

Was it the mindware which granted him confidence?

It didn't matter. Mindware or circumstances, the effect was the same. His life was undergoing a sea-change, here among his newfound friends, and he was not going to allow anyone to hurt them.

The flasks shifted as he slung the makeshift bag over his shoulder, and sweat sprang out across his forehead.

Step forwards. Into the eye of the storm.

Move.

Perhaps she was mistaken.

She touched the display with her palm, freezing it, and pointed for a biographical link. The elegantly smiling face of Sylvester Stargonier appeared. Beside it, text unfurled.

Current status: *deceased.*

"Zap playback. Main display."

Stargonier, too, was gone. Stargonier, with his admirable, frostily elegant style.

Yoshiko wondered why Stargonier had risked going into the house, when he could have walked from the aviary directly outside and gone straight home.

The wistfulness in his voice, when he suggested that Yoshiko and Maggie rejoin the party. Envy?

Hermes interrupted her thoughts. The cherub-faced icon was an annoyance; she would have to change the system settings—

Black-on-black eyes. Young, narrow face.

"I'm Pilot Noviciate Edralix Corsdavin." The young Pilot, his manner deferential. "Perhaps you remember me?"

Yoshiko nodded, though this was a recorded message.

"Pilot Jana deVries will be here today, Troi'Day, the thirty-third of Siebenary," he continued, "from thirteen hundred until twenty-six hundred hours. After that, she will be off-planet. Please call her any time, during her stopover. My respects. Endit."

The volume winked out of existence.

Heart pounding, Yoshiko requested a real-time comm to the Pilots' Institute. Shaking-head icon. Unavailable.

An incongruous memory-flash: using an Eastern European system, when she had been at the Bratislava conference in person, where a nodding head indicated no, and a shaken head meant OK.

She tapped at the ethereal image twice, indicating her intention to leave a message.

"Pilot deVries: thank you. I would dearly like to see you." She crushed a background complaint in her mind. "I'll be there at fifteen-thirty today, thank you. Endit. Send."

Current time: 11:17.

She did not want to go today.

11:18.

She had been awake for thirty-two hours and eighteen minutes, her eyes tense and gritty.

Jana would be gone again tomorrow. And, after the disappearance of Rafael's image from the house system's video logs, Yoshiko dared not risk a call through Skein.

"Command: reserve me a taxi. Pick-up here, fourteen hundred hours. Destination—" She paused. Better not be too specific. "—Lowtown, Lucis City."

Lori had said the Pilots' Sanctuary was near Lowtown.

Sleep?

No, she might not be able to wake up. She should work out what she was going to say to Jana.

"Help," perhaps.

Chapter Twenty-Four

Man will forget: it
Makes no odds what comes.
Die? Still, after attotech.

The cabin looked deserted.

Puffing, conscious of the hardness against his stomach, Tetsuo followed the trail. Dry throat. He stopped, and looked around—rubbing the small of his back, starting to ache from the extra weight—at the bright, serene canyon.

No shadows moved behind the windows, but they were there.

Pulse:103 min^{-1}

Behind the cabin, he could see the snub-nosed front of a parked skimmer. Very basic: a lift-platform with seats.

Systolic pressure increase: 43mmHg.

The cabin's door-membrane softened at his approach—

Adrenaline production: 9.7 g min^{-1}.

—and he stepped inside, into darkness.

"This the one?"

Someone grabbed his left arm, and a hard object was pressed against his temple.

Adrenaline production:10.2 g min^{-1}.

A graser's transmission end.

"Yes." Brevan's voice. "He's OK."

Tetsuo swallowed, as the weapon's pressure disappeared.

"Thanks for your vote of confidence," he managed to say.

The interior lights came up.

A lean, white-haired man was reclining in one of the chairs. His face was gaunt and lined, but strong: a distance runner, with a hard life.

Brevan sat nearby. No sign of Dhana.

"So you're Sunadomari." The white-haired man.

"Yeah." Tetsuo felt embarrassed, his bravado empty.

"Never seen a Terran elephant." Beside him, the man holding the graser sniggered. "Till now."

Tetsuo looked at him sidelong. "Wanna wrestle, without the hardware?"

The Agrazzus, much smaller than Tetsuo, stiffened. He raised his graser.

"No," said the white-haired man.

The Agrazzus lowered his weapon, and stared angrily at the floor.

"Where's Dhana?" Tetsuo looked around. "What have you done with her?"

From beyond the lounge, where Brevan's and Dhana's quarters lay, came the sounds of people moving about.

"Tell me something." The white-haired man leaned forward. "What's it like to be a Luculentus?"

"A barrel of laughs." Tetsuo leaned back, easing the strain. "Where's Dhana?"

The white-haired man looked at Brevan.

"Anomalous behaviour," he said. "Doesn't match the psych profile."

You're telling me. Tetsuo could not believe his own actions.

"He's undergoing a time of changes." Brevan stared at Tetsuo, but addressed the white-haired man. "I told you that."

Changes.

The mindware? If there was a courage module, a combat procedure, now was the time for it to execute.

"I don't like it." The white-haired man's voice sent shivers down Tetsuo's spine. "His presence introduces another unknown."

Nothing. No help from the ware.

"Damn it, Kerrigan. We need him."

Tetsuo started to shift the weight at his stomach, but forced himself to stand still.

"We planned everything to the last detail—" The white-haired man, Kerrigan, pointed at Tetsuo. "—long before he turned up."

"And then we reconsidered, remember? It's too risky for—a certain party—to reveal her affiliation in public. We need another Luculentus."

That time in Brevan's study, when he had been talking to a Luculenta via his terminal . . .

"So Felice," Tetsuo said, "can't risk exposure, huh?"

Kerrigan stared accusingly at Brevan, who shrugged.

"And the Skein conference only lasts another three days." Tetsuo looked at them all in turn. "Not much of a time window."

Kerrigan looked furious.

"I didn't tell him a thing," protested Brevan.

A third Agrazzus stepped out, frowning, from the corridor which led to Brevan's quarters.

"You're allies. Planning some demo. Don't want it hushed up by the authorities." Tetsuo shrugged. "Lots of offworld reporters at the conference. Obvious."

"And who," said the newcomer, "told you about Felice Lectinaria?"

"Oh, her surname's Lectinaria, is it?"

Kerrigan glared, and the Agrazzus who had spoken shut up.

Brevan smiled sardonically.

The Agrazzus by the door had his graser out again. "I think we should off him now."

"You would." Tetsuo watched the man's knuckles whiten on the firing stud. "That's why Kerrigan's the boss."

"Good point," said Dhana from the corridor.

She was leaning against the wall, casually holding a small silver cylinder in her left hand. Pointed in the Agrazzus' direction, as though by chance.

"Tetsuo volunteered his help," she added.

"Why would he do a thing like that?" Kerrigan's eyes were flat, dead-looking.

Tetsuo stared at Dhana and said nothing. Every detail of her gamine face was familiar to him, as though he had known her for years.

Brevan gave a dry laugh.

"See? I told you so."

Dhana's room.

"You're a bloody idiot, mouthing off like that." Dhana glanced at the silver cylinder attached to her belt. "I should have shot you myself."

"I was worried about you."

An awkward silence descended.

Tetsuo looked around. He had not been in here before.

A fourth Agrazzus, who had been busy in Brevan's study, passed by the door without glancing in.

Her room, like most of the cabin, was sparse. Holostills of relatives, and of a furry thing which might have been a pet. Infocrystals.

"Holodramas are on that shelf." Dhana pointed. "Historicals and mysteries, there. Music. Science."

"So who's your favourite—? Never mind."

"Some other time, perhaps." A smile flickered across Dhana's face.

"Right."

Ten minutes. Mustn't lose track.

"So how many septs of Shadow People are involved in this demonstration?"

"Most of them. But it's a whole group of demos, all simultaneous."

"OK." Tetsuo considered. "But Kerrigan's here for something more, isn't he?"

"Poss—Yes. But I don't know the details."

"Then why were you and Brevan arguing about it, earlier?"

"Brevan's guessed more than he's letting on to Kerrigan." Dhana let out a breath. "Something to do with an old terraformer station."

Stone towers, out in the wilderness. Hardly the place for publicity-seekers.

"We're carrying out some stunt, and broadcasting it to a NewsNet, is that it? While the demos are happening?"

"No. The day before."

They looked at each other silently.

"Why are you doing this?" Dhana asked finally. "It's not your struggle."

"Is it yours?" Tetsuo leaned back against the wall. "I'm not sure I believe all this ecophilosophy."

"I—" Dhana opened her mouth, then shut it.

"Politics," Tetsuo said. "Big surprise, huh? Power groups based on geographic territories. Quite passé, on Earth."

"There's no wilderness left on Earth." Dhana's voice was quiet. "We're a younger world—even if the Luculenti make us seem ancient."

"I know." Tetsuo looked away. "Did I become a Luculentus because I wanted to, or had to? They can be oppressive, without meaning to be."

"They're not always that innocent. The TacCorps—"

"I know. I met Federico Gisanthro once—I told you that—and he scared the hell out of me. Examined me, dismissed me in a second."

"Could have killed you in a second, too. How do we know you're not one of his spies?"

"Pardon?"

"Never mind. Whatever he did would be far more subtle."

"Thanks a lot."

Five minutes.

Dhana had fetched a plate of biscuits from the autofact, but they remained untouched.

Had he really thrown in his lot with these people? He still was not certain.

"You're not eating." Dhana looked up at him.

"I eat too much, you mean? Tell me something new."

"That's not—Never mind. Look, why did you volunteer to come along?"

"Dhana." He swallowed. "I'm—changing. Brevan had the right of it. I find myself knowing things I shouldn't know, doing things I wouldn't dream of attempting—"

"What are you trying to say?"

"Only that—the person you see here may be temporary. You want to know if I'm serious about joining you." He shook his head. "But I don't know . . ."

"We all change," said Dhana. "Every day. Sometimes a little, sometimes a lot, but the change is always there."

"Very wise."

She looked at him sharply, but he had not meant to sound sarcastic.

"No." She turned away, colour rising slightly in her pale ascetic cheeks. "I'm not."

Was it so complicated? Perhaps he had found a place that suited him, people who could become his friends. And—Whatever these people were, they certainly weren't boring.

A chuckle escaped his lips.

"Now what?" Dhana looked at him as though he were mad.

"Ah—Will you do me a favour?"

"What favour?"

"Just stand still for a moment."

Three minutes.

He leaned forward, and very softly kissed her lips.

"Are your eyes grey or green?" He stepped back. "I can't quite make my mind up."

"You bloody fool," she said softly.

Then she reached out to his stomach, and gently rapped it with her knuckles.

"I know you're glad to see me—" Her half-smile was twisted. "But have you got something hidden in there?"

Tetsuo felt the blood drain from his face.

Two point four minutes. Should have moved by now.

"Come on." He grabbed her hand. "We've got to hurry."

Guffaws of laughter greeted their return to the lounge.

"Get to the skimmer." Tetsuo spoke from the side of his mouth. "If it doesn't start in fifteen seconds, then run. Otherwise, fly it to the lab."

Dhana started to say something, then closed her mouth.

"Girlfriend said no, huh?" The Agrazzus by the doorway smirked as Dhana brushed past him.

"Shut up," said Kerrigan. "What's she doing?"

"I tell you what." Tetsuo stared straight at him. "Why don't we go out and check?"

He went outside and waited for Kerrigan and the others to join him.

"What's going—?"

Five seconds.

Dhana, grinning, flew the skimmer centimetres above the uneven trail, then spun it through a spectacular turn, and grounded it.

Zero.

There was a crump of explosion.

Behind them, high up on the rock face, a great chunk of cliff face split away. It toppled slowly, then crashed to earth where the skimmer had been.

Chips and fragments exploded through the air.

"Great Gaia!"

"What was that?"

From inside his jumpsuit, Tetsuo slipped out the red flask.

"I'm fat," he said, "but not that fat."

He turned, spun, and threw the flask, arcing over the cabin. A fountain of rock and grit exploded upwards—

Kerrigan cursed, softly.

—and fell like hail, rattling on the cabin roof, while a larger piece smashed through a skylight.

"Oops. Sorry, Brevan."

"You will be." Brevan's tone was mild. "That's going to cost."

Dhana came up beside Tetsuo.

"Don't worry." She slipped her arm through his. "We're good for it."

Kerrigan stared at them, then went back inside without a word.

Chapter Twenty-Five

Silver hair, not night-black,
Seen in the mirror.
Sing old songs to Mother.

Orange insects crawled across her face, antennae waving, black compound eyes scanning, scanning—

She jerked her head into wakefulness.

If I were a smartatom bug, where would I be?

"Oh, dear God."

Yoshiko leaned back in the taxi, feeling dreadful.

A grey sky, tinged with sickly green, scudded past outside.

"What time is it?"

The taxi's system silently displayed the time: 14:35.

Over thirty-five hours since she had slept. Travel sickness and incipient paranoia were only to be expected.

Thumbed her wrist terminal. Nothing. No replies to any of her urgent enquiries.

Vin . . .

Nothing she could do.

The temptation to redirect the taxi to a hotel was overwhelming—but she had only fifty-five minutes to go before her meeting. If she plunged into sleep, she would be a long time waking.

"Can you show me a map of Lowtown?"

There were many levels in Lowtown: the translucent holo showed bridges and aqueducts and a profusion of cobbled arcades. The Pilots' Sanctuary was just within the boundaries. A yellow rectangle, denoting a taxi landing-pad, was nearby. Yoshiko started to indicate it, then changed her mind.

Paranoia?

Maybe. But she was glad she had specified her destination only as Lowtown.

With its multitude of levels, criss-crossing bridges and skywalks and underground halls, the district would be a difficult one to surveille from above. The place seemed quite a maze.

"*Landing facility L17*," the system announced as Yoshiko pointed at a different yellow pad. "*Close to Daralvia Cloister, Penny Boulevard, and the Arconway. There are facilities for—*"

"Good enough. Land there."

The system fell silent.

She examined the holo some more. Off to one side, a text plane in red warned visitors to be careful after dark, and to stay within the busy areas. Friendlier icons offered the map's planning functions for everything from clothes-shopping to an extended bar crawl.

Gesturing to her wrist terminal, she was about to download the semi-intelligent map when she changed her mind, and powered the bracelet down again. Downloading code from a taxi she had called from Lori's home—perhaps that was not a good idea.

Paranoid, paranoid.

Yoshiko waved the display away.

The taxi flew in past green spires, many-levelled red-brick aqueducts, amber skywalks, glass and marble domes and towers. Organic and intricate. Transparent ellipsoids and open piazzas held restaurants and daistral houses.

Tourist country.

The taxi whispered onto yellow bricks, sighed softly as it powered down. The bricks flowed—expensive, but ground vehicles were illegal—taking the taxi into a covered pagoda.

By a comfortable waiting-area, the taxi stopped. Yoshiko touched her one working ring, her credit ring, to the old-fashioned silver plate set in the taxi's cabin, and the rather quaint gull-wing door swung up and she slid out.

Definitely tourist country.

Feeling curiously disembodied and light-headed, she stood at the edge of a cobbled piazza, getting the sense of it, of how the district was put together. From here, she could see the gold-furnished Gothic architecture of the most expensive malls like cathedrals to consumerism. They were spired and domed and arched, their surfaces glazed in burgundies or olive greens, or finished in apparently natural stonework.

Small groups of people wandered slowly across the cobbles, talking, laughing. A man sat idly by the fountain which tinkled at the square's centre.

A faint chill, not unwelcome, played across Yoshiko's cheeks as she stepped to the piazza's edge. The other three sides narrowed to streets at the same level, but this side ended in a silver railing. Leaning over, she saw there was a long drop to the level below, where dark waves carried in an aqueduct sparked silver highlights as they caught the sun.

When she turned back, the man by the fountain was gone.

Shivering, Yoshiko left the piazza via an ornate archway, finding herself in a circular marketplace beneath a crystal dome. In front of her, two jugglers were performing, their only audience a few children accompanied by a patient-looking young woman, and two shabby drunks or crystalheads who were watching from a doorway. The two derelict men looked more interested in the show than the children were.

One of the men, dirty and unshaven, looked up as Yoshiko walked past. Was that a gleam of intelligence in his eye? She looked back, but the man turned away, muttering to himself.

I'm short of sleep, that's all.

On an outdoor balcony, she stepped onto a white elevator disk. Wind tugged at her hair as the balcony fell away below. Then she was stepping out onto a bank which ran alongside another aqueduct.

In one of the semicircular rest areas, she sat down on bright red and yellow cushions, and watched people walking up and down beside the water.

She ordered daistral from a table; she had to use her cred-ring first, before it would allow her to choose a flavour. When it came, though, the apple-and-cream daistral tasted fine.

No one appeared interested in her. But how could she tell?

She wondered if it mattered. A deep background check on Tetsuo would have revealed the family's links to the Pilots' research programme. Historic links: she had done nothing for them for a long time.

If Jana could provide any assistance, though, it would be best kept secret.

Yoshiko recalled her microsleep-dream of bugs. If you were the kind of person or agency who could break into a secure house system, how would you track someone you wanted to keep an eye on?

It must be Rafael.

Rafael, with help?

She put her unfinished daistral down carefully, and stood. This was her problem to deal with. First, she was going to have to find the less salubrious parts of Lowtown.

Walking briskly now, not wanting to be late for her meeting, she took a disk down three levels, finding herself in a dark cavernous hall. Summoning up her memory of the map as best she could, Yoshiko took a narrow exit tunnel, which opened out onto a long deserted street.

A few holos advertised clubs, but most of the establishments were closed, waiting for the night. Farther down the street, Yoshiko could see the figures of women in a few floating globes, hovering near the ground.

This was the kind of area she needed.

Her skin seemed to grow greasy and itchy, as she walked the shabby street. At night, bright holos would hide the tawdry reality, no doubt.

Two tough-looking young women, black bats flitting across white orbs where their eyes should have been, watched Yoshiko from a doorway.

Yoshiko walked on, betraying no reaction, though her head began to ache with fatigue.

A large man offered her illegal drugs, smartviruses, anything she wanted. Behind him, femtovirus graffiti—coded subtly enough so the self-cleaning building failed to recognize the intrusion—defaced the wall, urging her to abuse a Luculentus today.

She carried on, past surgery shops and greasy cafés, looking down alleyways, until she saw an establishment with a discreet sign: FRIENDLY EYES.

Feeling uneasy, she walked up to the blank membrane of its entrance, and stepped through.

"Yeah? Can I help you?"

The shaven-headed woman behind the counter, chewing something fluorescent which played tinny music in time to the rhythm of her jaws, watched Yoshiko distrustfully.

"I need a clean-up," said Yoshiko. "Isn't that what you call it?"

"Maybe." Her jaws worked faster, and the music raised tempo.

Yoshiko held up her credit-ring, and the woman touched her bracelet, checking Yoshiko's balance.

"Good enough. Stand over there." She indicated a kind of archway, covered in black cloth.

Unsure that she was doing the right thing, Yoshiko took the indicated position. She wondered if this was a scam. How could she know if there was any debug apparatus in the archway at all?

If I were a smartatom bug, where would I be?

Answer: in Yoshiko's clothes, her hair, or under her skin. Anywhere at all.

"Guess you're dirty. Infested with the buggers." Beside the

woman, a pale blue holo grew: an array of fuzzy spherical clouds, a smartatom lattice. "Scanning—Shit!"

The lattice broke apart.

Silence, as the woman forgot to chew.

"Am I clean now?" Yoshiko stepped out from under the archway.

"Oh, yeah." Faint notes from the gum, as she talked. "You're clean, honey."

"How much do I owe you?"

"Not a damn thing."

"But—"

"Forget it. I didn't do nothing." Discordant accompaniment. The woman turned and spat the gum out, and it landed on the floor with a whine. "Time you went, honey."

"You said I'm clean."

"Self-destruct, alright? Soon as I scanned." The woman reached below the counter, and came up with a small black cylinder, and pointed the transmission end at Yoshiko. "And I want you out of my shop, right now. Got it?"

Yoshiko left, without a word.

Thoughts swirling, Yoshiko headed back along the street, aiming for the better areas. Perhaps another cup of daistral, at one of the nicer establishments, would straighten her out. She couldn't go to her meeting like this: shaky and trembling, her wits scattered.

In an ornate arcade, right at the cusp where the dingy street met glistening gallerias, she stopped in a doorway, leaned against the window, and closed her eyes.

Pain beat insistently above her left eye.

Tired and depressed, she used her thumb on the pressure point in her hand, but for once it had no effect.

A smell of Terran coffee drifted out of the store.

Almost sobbing with gratitude, Yoshiko pushed open the old-fashioned door and went inside. On a counter just inside the doorway, a jug of coffee and a plate of jantrasta-coated beans lay temptingly beneath a sign which said they were free.

Yoshiko took a mug and filled it, sat on a stool, and drank hungrily, wincing as it burned her mouth.

God, it felt good.

She drank some more, then turned her stool around, to see what kind of store she was in.

It was an Aladdin's-cave of wonders: small carved wooden birds with ruby eyes which squawked when you looked at them, delicate crystalline life-forms from Altracon Three which spun their clear mysterious strings of glass and sang heart-rending songs.

How wonderful.

Already, her headache was receding.

At the back of the store, a slender man with sparkling intelligent eyes was tending shop, running a hand over his balding pate as he listened to a woman and her husband, local store-owners themselves by the sound of it, expounding their woes.

Three other people, a couple and a woman on her own, were browsing quietly through the shop, delighted wonder dancing in their eyes.

Mug in hand, Yoshiko got off her stool, to examine a display shelf. Nestling on it—occasionally fluttering into flight, but always coming back to rest—were tiny butterflies whose wings were the pages of books—Aesop and Shakespeare and Goethe and Baudelaire—which you could read through a magnifying field if you touched the butterfly's head gently.

On the shelf below were yodelling bears and a flamenco-dancing flamingo and, along one wall, a series of intricate flat sand-paintings which took Yoshiko's breath away.

"Thanks, Roger." At the back of the store, the woman was taking her leave of the storekeeper, holding her husband's arm. "We always feel better for talking to you."

The storekeeper ducked his head almost shyly, and waved at them as they left the shop. An old-fashioned bell tinkled as they left.

"Can I help you?" he asked Yoshiko. "Or would you just like to look around?"

"I could stay here all day." Yoshiko put her now-empty coffee mug down on the counter. "But I have to go somewhere. I'll take one of the butterflies, though, if I may."

She pointed out the one she wanted.

"Ah, *Les Fleurs du Mal*," he said. "One of my favourites."

"*Moi aussi*," murmured Yoshiko.

He enclosed the butterfly in a crystal case, then wrapped it in patterned paper—his slender fingers moving surely and fluidly—and folded it so intricately that it needed no sealing or fastening, though it was not a smart material of any kind. Yoshiko had not seen such elegant origami since she had sat at her grandmother's knee in Vancouver. He slipped the package into a small bag.

"Thank you," she said, picking up the bag. "*Merci bien*."

"Enjoy. *Bonne chance*."

As she was turning to leave, the storekeeper added, "May I give you some advice? Back this way—" He pointed. "Isn't the best of areas. Circle around, if you have to go that way."

"I'm going to the Pilots' Sanctuary." Yoshiko was surprised at her own openness.

"Oh. Who's there at the moment? Is it Jana?"

"Why, yes," said Yoshiko, astounded.

"Small universe." The man chuckled. "Can you wait a moment?"

"Yes, of course."

Hunched on a stool behind his counter, looking like a wise and energetic gnome, he rapidly folded a sheet of grey paper into the shape of a bird, which he held out on his palm to Yoshiko.

"Could you give that to Jana, please? With my compliments."

"I'd be delighted."

She placed the small bird carefully in her bag. She waved as she left the shop. When she looked back, the storekeeper was sucking an ancient pipe into life, and poring over one of his books.

Yoshiko smiled, and turned away.

The skimmer voyage was a loud, bumpy ride through an ochre dust-storm. Afterwards, things grew worse. Abandoning the skimmer on a valley floor, the party of seven, protected by clumsy environment suits and linked by smartrope, trudged through knee-deep dust and sand, leaning against the wind.

Kerrigan led them up a slope and into a system of caverns, where the storm was reduced to a distant howl.

While they shucked the env-suits, one of the Agrazzi bumped into Tetsuo.

"Watch it, Terran." Hand going automatically to his belt.

"Save it, Avern." Kerrigan's voice was level, accepting no argument.

Roped together again, they left the env-suits, and began the steady climb upwards through caverns and tunnels, sliding on scree slopes and struggling up underground waterfalls.

Tetsuo thought he was going to die.

Nothing had prepared him for this sort of physical effort. Thighs weak, lungs giving out. He was only vaguely aware that he was slowing down the others; the pace was still incredible.

Dhana encouraged him, whenever she was close.

At the base of a subterranean cliff, they split into three teams: Kerrigan and Brevan, Dhana and Avern and another Agrazzus, the last Agrazzus and Tetsuo.

Kerrigan and Brevan led the climb. When they were halfway up, Dhana's team ascended, reaching the midpoint just as Kerrigan and Brevan reached the distant top.

"I don't think I can do this."

"You have to."

The teams were linked by rope: both teams above helped to haul Tetsuo up, keeping him as much as possible in a chimneylike fracture where he could brace against both sides. His companion, like an agile spider, moved around him, helping him.

The weight of Tetsuo's small pack was like an invisible hand tugging his back, trying to pull him off the rock.

After a while, firmly anchoring himself in a sharp twist of the chimney, he gestured for another rest.

"Why—?" His breath was a gasp. "Why climb . . . without tech?" They had even run out of smartrope: most of the links between them were dumb fibre.

The Agrazzus with him leaned casually from a handhold. "No microwaves to be detected. And we're used to it. We weren't expecting you to—"

"Look out!" An urgent shout from above.

A dark shape dropped past them. A body.

"I can't hold him!" Dhana's voice, shrill with strain.

The rope from Dhana to the fallen man was a trembling line just centimetres from Tetsuo's face. Without thinking he grabbed it with both hands, wedged his feet more firmly into their holds, and held on.

The smartgel on his hands increased its friction coefficient. Then, hand over hand, finally with a use for his bulk and strength, Tetsuo hauled, while his companion unroped and climbed down to help the unconscious man's body up and over obstacles.

Once they were belayed, all the others descended, roped the fallen man up, and ascended in stages to the top.

Later, while they sipped daistral around a portable autofact, the injured man came unsteadily over to Tetsuo.

"Thanks, man." His voice was awkward. "Heard what you did."

"No problem." Tetsuo kept the satisfaction from his voice, and clapped the man's shoulder. "Any time, Avern."

It was the man from the fountain.

Yoshiko stepped into a doorway, then slowly looked out. Down the long arcade, with looping ceramic arches to one side, small groups of people walked with tourists' lack of haste.

There, dressed in grey. She was sure it was him. He moved slowly, hands in pockets, turning every now and then to admire one of the little gargoyles which protruded from the walls: an unobtrusive way to keep checking behind him.

A smartatom miasma would be easier, but perhaps that would set off the stores' own security systems.

She waited for him to turn away again, then left the cover of her doorway and ran with silent steps to an archway, jumped on an elevator disk, and felt the bottom drop out of her stomach as it descended too rapidly.

Sure he had not seen her. Yoshiko walked quickly nonetheless, heading through a stone-paved rest area, down a flight of iron steps that were purely for decoration, into a wide disused hall.

Water dripped from a moss-strewn colonnade onto dank black puddles, and a cold draught whipped a ragged sheet of dead smartfilm across broken paving-stones.

Which way?

Clutching her bright bag of gifts—suddenly incongruous, here—she strode rapidly across the hall, footsteps echoing sharply back, and took a short grimy tunnel. She stopped, heard no one following, and carried on.

She was in a cheerless grey quadrangle, flanked by a block of red-brick apartments, the walls ravaged by femtovirus graffiti. There was no one in sight.

Through a gap, high above, she could see a gold cupola above a white minaret. A landmark. If she kept going left and down, she should end up close to the Sanctuary.

This was hardly the route the storekeeper had recommended.

She plodded on, feeling a strange sense of dislocation: not quite lost, not quite knowing where she was going, sure only that she was in desperate need of rest.

It felt as though she had not slept for a week.

The path was tiled, and led along an underpass. To her left, a dark grey dome rose, scarred here and there with burn marks.

She followed the broken tiles. Overhead, beneath a canopy, a lone glowglobe buzzed, trying to escape upwards. Damaged somehow, desperate to obey the dawn's recall signal, unable to fly back to its eyrie for recharging. Eventually, depleted, it would drop.

Stopping by the grey dome, Yoshiko crouched a little, sighting between gaps. There. The minaret was more or less where she expected it to—

Toecap.

Dizziness overcame her. The toecap of a boot appeared to be protruding straight out of the wall. Impossible.

A hand grabbed her throat, and something hard smashed against the back of her knee and her leg buckled.

A section of wall disappeared: a holo illusion.

When attacked, the warrior steps forwards.

Dazed, down on one knee, she looked around her.

Burning, against her temple.

"Don't move, bitch."

Lattice-blade. Her nostrils flared at the ozone smell.

There were three of them, and she had already lost the moment. Should have moved as soon as she saw the toecap.

The lattice-blade's cutting-field hummed and crackled.

Don't risk your life for a handful of credits. One streetwise instructor. *Run if you can. Tackle a weapon only if they mean to kill you.*

Another had said: *Retaliate first.*

Didn't matter.

Too late.

Just as with Vin. Always too late . . .

The stink of burning hair, but she kept her head still. The lattice-blade field could blossom in nanoseconds, expanding a hundred times faster than a fighter's reflex-speed.

"Yo, bitch." A tall narrow boy in front of her. Sleeveless jerkin, cut open to the waist, a graser bulging in its pocket. A glistening blue dragon-tattoo coiled around his pale hairless chest. The dragon turned its bulbous eyes on Yoshiko, and hissed.

The one behind her had not moved.

If the lattice-blade was configured for constant size, she could go for the wrist . . . but if the field was set to expand at her movement, it would slice through her head before she could turn.

This is not a training session.

"Let's do her."

One of them tugged the bag from her grasp. She let it go.

A wave of violent shuddering passed through the third street-fighter—fast, muscles almost flickering—and then the fit dissipated, was gone.

Storm Crystal addict.

Leering, he reached for her tu-rings.

Don't move.

Should have reacted as soon as she saw the foot, before he primed the cutting-field . . .

A hand removed the bracelet—the wrist terminal from Xanthia—from her wrist.

"Bloody tight."

The tu-rings—still glowing dull, useless orange—were what he wanted now.

"You can't get the rings off the fingers—" The third one waved his blade, and the air itself burned and crackled. "You take the fingers off the hand."

The first ring came off, and Yoshiko closed her eyes.

Don't—

Half dead on her feet, quite at the end of her tether, and her spirit was gone.

Another ring. One left, plus her wedding-band.

The lattice-blade field could expand faster than she could blink.

Please don't take the wedding-band.

"Ain't worth nothin', bitch."

Had she spoken aloud?

"Damn tight. Won't come off."

Not her wedding-band: the last tu-ring.

She was conscious of the splint around her left forearm.

"I say we do—"

"Shuddup."

The crystal addict was beginning to tremble.

She could see the pulse in his carotid artery. A vulnerable point: but the lattice-blade had not moved from her temple.

Her strength was gone.

"*Hey!*" A distant shout.

The three thugs froze, and looked over Yoshiko's shoulder. The one with the graser raised it, as though to aim.

"Forget it, Braz."

"I say we—"

"No way. They're real bad asses. Haven't you heard?"

"I—Ah, shit. Let's go."

Strike the wrist—

The pressure came off, and Yoshiko almost swooned at the release.

"No, Braz!"

She sank down.

"Come on!"

Their boots clattered loudly as they ran.

Black boot and trouser leg. A swirl of black cape, edged with silver.

Yoshiko was sitting on the cold ground, hugging her knees, trembling uncontrollably. Shock, she knew. The aftereffect of adrenaline-dump.

It made no difference; her mind was rational but her body still shook.

Silver trim, not gold: a Pilot Noviciate.

A strong hand helped Yoshiko to her feet.

She could not speak.

"Let's get you indoors." The young Pilot held her tightly around her shoulders, supporting her, and with his free hand used a square of silk to dab at Yoshiko's face.

Tears, too. Embarrassing.

"Thank—" She cleared her throat. "Thank you, Edralix."

Remembered his name, at least. The young man she had spoken to from Lori's house.

"Just a moment."

When he was sure Yoshiko could stand unassisted, Edralix bent and picked something up.

It was the small folded paper bird.

"From Roger?" He smiled when Yoshiko nodded. "Jana will like that."

They started along the broken tiled path. As the tiles gave way to cobbles, they passed a building which might have been a church, and crossed a small arched bridge spanning a stream. On a wide green, tables were set out for picnics, and small groups of children were flying kites.

Amazing, how the city could change character in such a short distance.

"How did you know I was there?" asked Yoshiko, as they walked through the grass.

Beyond, a gravelled track led to ornate black iron gates set in a grey stone wall.

"Roger called, asking if you'd arrived safely."

"The storekeeper. Kind of him."

The gates rolled open at their approach.

"He's a little more than a shopkeeper."

"Yes." The gates closed behind them. "I thought he might be."

The building was low, its façade all square pillars and round arches, surrounded by grass. It looked like a genteel country house. Only a discreet golden holo logo, floating by the main oak doors, proclaimed this a Pilots' Sanctuary.

"Home," said Edralix, and led Yoshiko inside.

Chapter Twenty-Six

Black flowers, so small.
Mirror all that is lost.
Mother, younger than I.

She was a ghostly giantess, huge and insubstantial, wading through a knee-deep pool of inky black, laced with a fine silver grid.

The hundred frozen dancers were fifteen or so centimetres high. The whole image filled the circular tortoiseshell-walled chamber, and the dancers were startlingly clear, their tiny expressions so detailed and real that, when Yoshiko passed her hand through a figure, it seemed that Yoshiko herself was the illusion.

"Good enough?" Edralix's voice came from the edge of the room, where he was intent on the terminal pad held in the palm of his hand.

"Amazing." Yoshiko bent close, examining the detail.

It was Neliptha, tiny and beautiful, still intact.

Behind Edralix, Jana watched silently, with eyes of glittering jet.

"Can we play forwards?" Yoshiko steeled herself to see it once more. "Without the sound?"

The miniature dancers formed their whirling cruciform, passing through Yoshiko again and again. At the triumphant conclusion, every dancer dropped to one knee, and you could see the tiny chests heaving for breath, the proud but exhausted smiles, the joyous light in their eyes.

"Oh—Freeze."

Near the real room's walls, the ballroom-image's stately pillars soared. By one of them, near a tiny buffet table, Yoshiko crouched.

Her eyes were sore, and her headache had returned in force. Could she be certain of her memory?

"Here." She pointed to the pillar's base. "Rafael was standing right here."

"Can you hold that for a moment, please?"

Edralix passed his terminal pad to Jana, and waded through the frozen dancers, and crouched down by Yoshiko.

"Just here. You're sure?"

"I—Yes. I'm certain."

"Hmm."

He moved his head around, checking the pillar and floor from various angles.

"No visible sign of editing," he said.

"He was there."

"Of course." Edralix looked up. He might have been startled or apologetic; in this light, his eyes were shadowed pits, revealing nothing. "I didn't mean to doubt you. But the traces aren't obvious."

"I guess—If you can break into a Luculentus house system, you can do what you like without leaving tracks."

A smile tugged at Edralix's lips. "I wouldn't go that far."

At the room's edge, Jana held up the pad. "Want me to play forwards a bit?"

"Just jump on, forty-three seconds."

Yoshiko made no comment. Edralix had seen the recording once through, on a small display, but already knew the timing of it.

Six dancers, stumbling towards Xanthia, impaled on scarlet beams. The beams were rods of bloody light, radiating out from Xanthia's tortured figure.

"Rafael was damned lucky." With his finger, Edralix followed the path of one of the beams. "See? Missed him by a metre."

What a shame, thought Yoshiko, but said nothing.

The beam carried on past the pillar to the image's edge, drilling into the surface of the ballroom's ornate wall.

"Still can't see anything." The beam cast devilish scarlet sparks in Edralix's eyes. "We might as well sit down. This is going to take a while."

They joined Jana on cushions by the wall, and Yoshiko sank down, feeling an almost overwhelming desire just to lie down on her side and go to sleep.

"You look tired, Yoshiko," said Jana, as she handed the terminal back to Edralix.

"Exhausted."

"Then you must stay here overnight."

"I couldn't—Well, perhaps. Thank you."

Memory flash: three youths, the pitiless smile and crazed eyes of the one called Braz, and the crackling of the lattice-blade.

Jana turned to Edralix. "What do you reckon?"

"I'm trying the obvious, first. Seeing if the crystal has neg images stored, and if they're different from the positives." As he spoke, his fingers danced through control gestures, and small display volumes shifted and whirled with cascading displays of code and data.

Jana looked at Yoshiko, and shrugged.

"That's OK." Yoshiko raised a tired grin. "I didn't understand, either."

"Sorry." Edralix looked back over his shoulder. "See—Let's say you take a holo still with one camera. When you view it, there's a virtual image the right way round—that's the one they used in the early days—and the real image, which you can walk around and is actually there, like this."

He gestured vaguely at the wide tableau of frozen dancers, of impaled Luculenti.

"We're with you so far," said Jana.

"Well, you see—The real image is reversed. Inside out, in fact. So what a holo terminal displays is a reversal of the original reversed real image."

"And the reversal is done by software?"

"Right. If the Maximilians' house system performs the calcs real-time when recording, then it's no good for us. If it stores the original and reverses it afterwards, maybe the editing was only done on the afterimage."

Yoshiko intently watched the code displays. She knew enough to see that the video-log's object interface was objecting to a contents scan, Edralix was overriding, using valid lower-level object-management codes to list the semi-autonomous objects within the log.

He began to mutter coding instructions.

Finally, he looked up.

"Got 'em."

"Well done," said Jana. "So there were two images, then?"

"No, that would have been too easy. But the editing algorithm wasn't perfect, partly because of nonunique solutions to the sum of Fresnel zone-plates over the original physical objects."

"Of course." Jana smiled.

Terminal in hand, Edralix got up and walked through the dancers, and stopped by the pillar where Rafael had stood.

"Where you view the pillar through the space which Rafael occupied, there's a difference in resolution from the original." He pointed, but the pillar looked the same to Yoshiko, no matter how she moved her head. "Partly because of the calculation resolution, and partly because this—" He indicated the frozen scarlet beam of light, passing the pillar and striking the wall. "—is intense enough to cause nonlinearities, which the editing model ignores."

Yoshiko stood up. "So where does—?"

A shadow was forming. A black man-shaped absence of light, blending to diffuse grey at the edges, standing by the pillar.

"I'm sorry." Edralix shook his head. "That's the best I can do. It's the same problem the editing ware had: multiple possible solutions to filling in an image."

"Well done." Jana gave a tight smile. "You've proven at least that the log was altered."

"Oh, yes. That was obvious."

"Describe him again." Jana's inky black eyes were intent on Yoshiko. "How he acted when Xanthia began to convulse."

The room was empty of recorded images now, and quite relaxing.

Yoshiko half closed her eyes, summoning up the memory. "Hooded eyes, body tight—I thought he was in agony, at the time."

"And now? What do you think now?"

"I saw the log image before it got edited out, remember? There was a look of, I don't know, hunger in his eyes. And satisfaction: half pain, half pleasure, you know?"

Jana let out a slow breath.

"Nothing that would hold up in court," said Edralix.

"No." Jana shook her head. "And we're talking about a crime that's almost literally unthinkable to Luculenti."

Yoshiko stared at her.

"Think of it from their point of view." Jana paused, considering her words. "They move through Skein the way a fish swims in the ocean. And their own minds are distributed across an array of internal processors called plexcores."

"But surely—" Edralix frowned. "That gives them all the more reason to be concerned, if someone can get through the safeguards on those interfaces."

"More reason, yes," said Jana. "But it's like doubting your own mind. If the interfaces are corruptible, how can you trust your own thoughts and dreams?"

Yoshiko looked from one to the other.

"Are they aware of their executing mindware? Day to day, I mean." An unbidden thought: *I could have asked Vin. But it's too late now.*

"No." Jana shook her head. "I would think that in Skein they just wish for a thing, and it's there. As natural as moving a limb: you don't work out the mechanics of the motion."

"I understand." Yoshiko thought. "I see what you mean about a psychological blind spot."

"Yes, but—" Edralix, sitting back in his chair, crossed his arms and stared at the ceiling. "Our friend Rafael is different, I bet. He's hacking into his own mindware, not to mention other people's. I'd bet he dives right down to low-level op-codes."

"Other people's? Plural?"

"He's right. We may not be sure what he's doing—" Jana's black eyes glinted. "—but why should we believe this is the first time?"

Yoshiko swallowed.

That suicide, what was her name? She closed her eyes, trying to remember.

There was a hand on her shoulder, and she jerked awake.

Embarrassing.

"Edralix will show you to your room."

"Thanks, Jana. But—"

"I made a call, while you were, ah, resting just now. I'm going to be staying on Fulgor for a while longer."

Yoshiko's body swayed as she stood up. "I don't know what—"

"We'll talk in the morning."

Edralix led her along a narrow hall. To one side, an open sliding screen led to a pine-floor dojo, with wooden bokken practice swords racked along the walls. Holostills of the legendary Dart, and his daughter Ro, discreetly occupied a corner.

Edralix stopped, instructing the building's system to give Yoshiko access to the residential apartments.

Looking at the empty dojo, she thought about those early UNSA Pilots, ordinary men and women with their brains virally rewired and eyes removed, bodies trained in spatial awareness through aikido and Feldenkrais movement, minds steeped in the scientific disciplines, sacrificing their sight for their careers.

"Such courage," she murmured.

"Yes." Edralix seemed to follow the direction of her thoughts. "Only really alive when they were carrying other people's cargo—" He stopped, as though embarrassed.

What a strange remark, thought Yoshiko, wondering if it were only her own tiredness which made it seem odd. Was that not how Pilots still were today?

Retaining one's eyesight, of course, was a nontrivial advantage over the old days.

"Here you are." Edralix waved a membrane into permeability. "Er—Sleep well."

Yoshiko, stumbling forwards as though drawn towards the bed, saw it rising up to meet her as she fell into blackness.

Violet fumes wafted from the tall tower's crown.

"Got it."

Perched on the escarpment's edge, the tower was both a forbidding sentinel and a monument to humankind's impudence. It was tall and narrow, surmounted by an ellipsoid control centre.

Behind Tetsuo, an Agrazzus scrambled down from a low crest, leaving behind a glowing blue chest. It had come from Tetsuo's backpack; he had not known what he was carrying.

From his hiding place, hunkered down behind a sorry-looking ragged bush, Tetsuo looked out at their objective.

Around the terraformer tower, a cloud of sparkling silver motes slowly coalesced.

"Twenty seconds." Kerrigan's voice was flat. "Go!"

The others burst from cover, and sprinted across the broken ground towards the tower's base.

Tetsuo, heart and lungs pumping crazily, staggered along behind them, cursing himself for taking the risk.

Seventeen seconds.

If the smartatom miasma self-healed, or the tower's system recognized the false all-OK signals being beamed to it, he would be fried.

Twelve seconds.

Not there yet. Nowhere near halfway.

Trust Dhana.

Ten seconds.

He stopped, slowing to a walk, chest heaving. He could not reach safety in time, no matter how hard he pushed himself.

Five seconds.

They were at the doorway now. Arcs of white light hurt his eyes, and he looked away.

Two seconds.

He should have stayed behind, safely hidden, until they managed to deactivate—

A raised hand: the OK signal.

The door was still intact, but the deadly defences were down. Dhana waved, and gave a cheery grin.

Tetsuo dropped to his knees and threw up.

When she awoke it was dark and cold, and she was half-lying on top of the bed, face down, her feet touching the floor.

Vin. Call Lori—

Wrist terminal was gone. Stolen.

Decades of training had deserted her . . .

Yoshiko pulled herself fully onto the bed, and the sheet wrapped itself snugly around as the mattress floated free on its lev-strips.

"*Vin*," she mumbled, and sank back into oblivion.

"Solid ceramic." Tetsuo rapped cautiously. "Really solid."

He leaned back out of the doorway. Looking up, it was like an artist's paintbrush dipped in a running stream: at the tower's apex, some hundred metres above, violet vapour still spumed into the winds.

"We are going in through the door, aren't we?"

Kerrigan, standing at one side of the arched stone doorway, looked at him curiously. "How did you think we were going to get in?"

"Never mind." Tetsuo shook his head. "So what's next? We fight our way up through fifty levels of warriors, each a master of a different deadly art?"

One of the Agrazzi sniggered. "You been inhaling some of them funny smokes Brevan has?"

Kerrigan looked away, trying not to smile.

"Well?" Tetsuo pressed his palm against the door. "Who's going to open—?"

[[[Begin: Module = Node089C.1067: Type = BinaryHyperCode Axes = 2
Execute
<superolateral net: element seventeen>.linkfile = IRprotocol.
Common.Gamma
End_Execute]]]

"You are," said Kerrigan.

Pain hammered into Tetsuo's head.

<<<MsgRcv DEVCOM284303; cause = device acknowledged command.>>>

"God, you bastards." Tetsuo screwed up his face in suffering, and pressed his fist against his forehead. "You bloody bastards."

Plumes of scarlet light blossomed in his vision. Slowly, one by one, he blinked them away.

The big ceramic door slid open.

"Sorry," said Kerrigan, with no trace of apology in his voice. "I had no idea it would be difficult."

Dhana pushed her way past Kerrigan, deliberately knocking him with her shoulder. She stopped inside the tower's entrance and looked around.

Tetsuo, sniffing and wishing he were less of a wimp, followed her inside. It was not his fault he had no tolerance for pain, but in this company it was embarrassing.

He did not look at Kerrigan.

Inside, an old stone staircase spiralled clockwise around a central shaft.

"Oh, my God."

Tetsuo looked at the steps to the left, leading up.

"You guessed it." Dhana grinned at him brightly. "See you up there."

She took the steps at a slow but steady jog. Tetsuo shook his head.

Brevan and the tallest of the Agrazzi slipped past Tetsuo, heading right, where the steps continued downwards.

Brevan winked at Tetsuo, then followed his companion down.

"Now what?" Tetsuo asked Kerrigan, who was pulling something from his pockets. "What are those?"

In each hand, Kerrigan held a sphere, which began to glow. Silvery light made his shock of white hair grow brilliant, and etched black shadows among his gaunt, narrow features.

"Something to make them sleep."

He smiled, a slow predator's smile, and loosed the spheres.

One flew upwards, coasting above the steps, while the other departed downwards to the underground levels.

"Come on."

One of the two remaining Agrazzi, the one called Avern, gave a thumbs-up sign to Tetsuo. Then Avern and his companion followed Dhana upstairs. Kerrigan began to climb after them.

"See you in a minute," muttered Tetsuo, as they disappeared around the curve. He started to trudge up the steps.

If he had not turned up, would this Luculenta sympathizer, Felice Lectinaria, have come along anyway? Or would they have climbed the tower's exterior and burned their way into the command centre? Or something equally crazy?

He moved upwards slowly, fatigue spreading through his thighs.

A hundred metres high, the tower. Ten metres diameter, the helical staircase inside. Maybe twenty five centimetres, each tread. Climbing through three metres or so to perform a revolution.

Five hundred steps. Travel distance of five hundred and thirty metres, if he kept to the centre of the treads. Eighty kilojoules of work, not much less than it would have been on Earth.

He stopped for a rest, then started upwards again.

Not much wear on the treads. Few people climbed up this two-century-old relic. Did no one come here any more, or did they just fly directly to the control centre at the apex?

Maybe they were all just light-footed, like Dhana, and danced up the steps like sprites.

Rest again. Then climb.

A series of periodic breaks and slow climbing. Seemed to stretch on forever.

Doorway. He stepped through the membrane, found himself in a shadowy well. The control centre's floor ran all around, just above head height.

He looked straight up. The domed ceiling was flooded with light, cool and inviting. He could do with a chilled drink.

Steps led up to floor level. More bloody steps.

I'm here, he wanted to call, but did not have the breath.

Ten more steps. Just ten . . .

A beam of light spat overhead with a sizzling crack.

Tetsuo froze.

"*Nobody bloody move!*"

A man's voice; tight with fear and anger.

"We're not doing anything." Kerrigan, his voice deliberately flat and calm. "You're in control, now."

"God damn right, I am. Now, you all back away from that console." Silence. "Move it!"

Shuffling sounds above, and some distant part of Tetsuo's mind noted that the sound was good cover, and he carefully climbed the last few steps.

Tetsuo came up behind a short man with cropped hair, the hood of his environment suit thrown back. The man was holding a graser rifle.

One of the Agrazzi was lying on the floor, face blanched, holding his shoulder where the jumpsuit was black and charred. Dhana and Kerrigan crouched beside him, looking concerned. The other Agrazzus merely looked sullen.

The man's rifle was aimed squarely at Kerrigan.

"You're in charge," Kerrigan said softly, not betraying Tetsuo's presence by the slightest flicker of his eyes. "What do you want us to do?"

There was a walk-in closet off to one side, filled with hanging env-suits. The man must have been in there, or right next to it, when Kerrigan's flying sphere had exploded and filled the place with gas.

Dispersed now, obviously.

"Just—" The man aimed at Kerrigan. "Shut up, OK?"

Tetsuo was peripherally aware of orange-clothed bodies slumped all around, but his attention was focussed on the man with the graser rifle.

Very short hair, fat neck, red and blotchy now with tension.

Target the neck. Wasn't that what Mother would do?

Tetsuo raised his hand to strike.

The man spun, sensing movement—

A wild fragment of memory, Mother to Akira, with a wooden practice knife: *Go for the weapon, son. Just keep attacking the arm and don't worry about getting cut, because you will unless they're amateur. Attack the limb until the functionality's destroyed and the weapon's dropped.*

—and then he was doing it for real, grabbing the rifle's easy-grip stock and jerking it up and grasping the man's sleeve.

Something struck his face, an elbow perhaps, and greenish-yellow lights swam before his eyes.

A crack of energy.

Tetsuo hung on to the man's sleeve with desperate strength, turning in a deadly dance, and then Dhana stepped neatly forwards and kicked the man straight between the legs and he dropped to the floor.

A deep groan issued from the fallen man. Hands jammed between his thighs, he was tucked into a tight foetal ball.

Dhana took the graser rifle from Tetsuo's suddenly feeble hands.

"What kept you, honey?"

Her eyes were very bright, her high cheeks flushed.

"Remind me—" Tetsuo shook his head. "—never to argue with you. Darling."

"What are all these people doing here?"

Nobody answered Tetsuo.

All around the great ellipsoidal room, orange-jumpsuited men and women were slumped on chairs and cushions, terminal pads scattered where they had fallen.

Tech types. He was sure of it. This place was more than an abandoned terraformer.

He stepped past the man whom Dhana had dropped. Sleeping now: a derm patch, swiftly applied by Kerrigan, stood out on the man's fleshy neck.

Waking up was not going to be pleasant for him.

Something beeped behind Tetsuo, as he crouched down beside

Kerrigan and Avern. Their wounded comrade lay still, eyes closed and ashen-faced. Ice-blue med-gel coated his shoulder.

"Hi, Brevan." Dhana had waved a display into life. "How are things with you?"

"All clear down here. You?"

She looked over at Tetsuo, who grimaced.

"One graser wound," she said to Brevan. "Vargred took a hit."

In the image beside Brevan, his Agrazzus companion looked concerned.

"He'll be all right," Kerrigan called. "Are the specimens there?"

"Yeah." The solemn Agrazzus turned, and stepped out of the display's view-field.

"We're checking them now." Brevan looked grim. "Looks like Felice was right."

Behind him, in the image, rows of cages held a bewildering mix of Terran species. A barn owl. A lynxette, prowling back and forth in its narrow confines. Furry forms curled up, sleeping.

"What about the test subject?" asked Brevan. "The human one, I mean."

An angry chimpanzee scolded them from its cage.

Behind Tetsuo, the other Agrazzus, Avern, called out, "I think we've got him."

He was examining a blond man slumped in a black control chair.

"Keep the link open," muttered Kerrigan, and went to join Avern.

With his thumb, he opened one of the unconscious blond man's eyelids, then the other.

From the holo display, Brevan said, "Tetsuo's met Federico Gisanthro, you know."

"Has he?" There was an indefinable look in Kerrigan's eyes. "What did you think of him?"

"Of Federico Gisanthro?" Tetsuo glanced at Dhana. "Bit of a hard case. I met him at a big trade exhibition. I never did work out what the head of TacCorps was doing there."

"Really." Kerrigan used both thumbs to keep the man's eyelids open. "Come over here, and see what you think."

Tetsuo walked over, and jerked to a halt.

The pale man's eyes were mismatched—one blue, one green—like Federico's.

"That's not Federico."

"But?" Kerrigan let go, and the man slid down in the chair like a deactivated doll.

"—But there's a resemblance, I agree."

"This is one of Federico's clones."

"You're kidding."

Tetsuo watched as Kerrigan ran some form of handheld scanner across the man's head.

"Oh, yes." A sour satisfaction tightened Kerrigan's drawn features. "There's no doubt."

"He doesn't look that much like Federico." And he obviously was non-Luculentus: no headgear.

"Isn't your mother a biologist?" said Kerrigan. "His DNA's identical; it takes a lot more than that to determine an organism, starting with the womb environment."

Different upbringing, right.

Federico Gisanthro had looked supremely fit, skin stretched taut across his face. This man looked softer, and his tunic bulged out to the rear behind one shoulderblade. Some sort of deformity.

Tetsuo frowned.

"Let's see what else we've got." Kerrigan picked up a terminal pad, and flicked through a series of tech-info displays. He seemed to know what he was doing.

"Do you know what this is all about?" Tetsuo quietly asked Dhana.

She glanced back at Brevan—he was still in the image, looking intense—and shook her head.

Brevan knew. He had been the first to mention Federico Gisanthro.

"There." Kerrigan looked triumphant. "There's his VSI code."

A blue pulsing space hung in the air.

VSI?

"Impossible."

The man had no headgear.

"Are you that naïve?"

"What do you mean?" Tetsuo reached up to touch the fine fibres rooted in his scalp. The LuxPrime pre-op tutorial-ware, part of his upraise preparation, had specifically mentioned this: the amp functions were replicated internally, but only as backup.

"Tradition. Nothing more."

Tetsuo looked at the pulsing display.

VSI. At least one plexcore.

"How would anyone know Luculenti are superior," added Kerrigan, "if they looked just like the rest of us?"

Dhana shifted her feet uncomfortably. Tetsuo wondered if she was going to kick Kerrigan. He rather hoped she might.

"Interesting." Kerrigan was still working the display.

Five silver clouds, linked by pulsing emerald flows.

"I think that one—" Kerrigan pointed at a cloud. "—is his organic brain."

"LuxPrime wouldn't—" Tetsuo bit his lip. "The legal max is three. Three plexcores."

"NMR scanner." Avern tossed a small device to Tetsuo.

Tetsuo caught it. "All right." He tuned a terminal to the scanner's output. "Let's see what we've got."

Two plexcores, embedded in the man's body.

Puzzled, he looked back at Kerrigan's display.

Five thought-domains.

The man's organic brain, two embedded plexcores, and—what were the extra two volumes?

For that matter, *where* were they?

"This is a TacCorps research project," Kerrigan said flatly. "Quite beyond their legal remit." He shut down his display. "And you're right, LuxPrime would not supply extra plexcores to anyone, for any reason."

Stolen, then?

Where would you steal a plexcore from?

"Grave robbers." Tetsuo gave a disbelieving laugh. "You're kidding."

"No." Kerrigan shook his head. "There are safeguards against that."

"What kind of safeguards?"

"You can't reinitialize a plexcore from a corpse. The core lattice destroys itself as soon as it's powered up."

Tetsuo looked at the display again, and frowned. Two extra centres of thought. Not plexcores.

"The only alternative to a plexcore," he said, musing, "is an organic—"

He ground to a halt, appalled.

Additional organic brains?

"Oh, God—" said Dhana.

Kerrigan was puffing open the unconscious man's tunic, and rolling him onto his side in the chair. He tugged the tunic down, revealing the man's upper back.

Over one shoulder blade, his skin was stretched out, almost translucent, over the bulging deformity—

Inside the bulge, something moved.

From behind Tetsuo, there was a retching sound. Dhana. The vomit-smell hit Tetsuo, but he could not turn to look.

Two large, grey eyes, completely blind, beneath the skin. A furless modified rat, slightly flexing its almost transparent body. The main arteries from its heart led directly into the man's torso: two bodies plumbed together into one.

"OK, Kerrigan." Tetsuo forced his voice to remain steady. "That's one of the extra processing centres."

"Looks that way." A grim smile.

Five processing centres, in the display. Two plexcores, two brains, and—

"So where's the other one?"

Wings spread, it soared. Tiny shifts of configuration: spreading feathers, as it rode the thermals.

The condor flew high above a sweeping range of purple ice-capped peaks.

Brevan's voice: "This is from a surveillance drone, set to follow the bird's flight."

He was piping up the image from the basement lab.

"The mountains are the Ranfidari Range," he added. "Three hundred klicks south-east of here."

Three hundred kilometres.

The unconscious man was interfaced with the condor's brain, as well as his embedded rat.

Impossible—

Tetsuo must have spoken aloud, for Kerrigan replied, "Not really."

The lab animals were bred—and engineered—for interfacing. That's why they were all Terran species, despite the terraformer's location at the hypozone's edge.

"The rat-implant—" The subcutaneous rat seemed to turn at Kerrigan's gesture, though the man remained unconscious. "—proved the interface could work. Locally, if you like." Kerrigan pointed at the condor in the display. "Then they added another, remote, brain to the nexus."

Tetsuo, speechless, shook his head.

Obviously, only a small part of the condor's brain was interfaced. Just a light touch, allowing the organism to function.

If a small, secret group inside TacCorps had gained some of LuxPrime's proprietary VSI tech—If they cracked the protocols completely, they could scan Luculenti thoughts, maybe even influence them . . .

"No, that's not it," Tetsuo muttered to himself. "Maybe that's a later goal."

To increase your plexcore nexus, to any size you want. Such vistas of intellectual potential . . . He felt a vertiginous sense of potential, poised for expansion. To grow your mind, without limit . . .

Wasn't that why he'd undergone the upraise?

But, but—

There were good reasons for the LuxPrime legal limit. The greater the nexus size, the greater the chance for transition effects, for the evolution of new patterns of thought, for *nonhuman* thought to occur.

And, always, the increasing overhead of communication flow between the plexcores—

"*Kuso!*" muttered Tetsuo. "*Merde!*"

Kerrigan looked grim, but said nothing.

Tetsuo clenched his teeth. "*Ikkene!*" He had really screwed up.

Why hadn't he seen it sooner?

Why would Rafael have been interested in sponsoring some ragged-ass Earther for upraise? Why, if not for exclusive comms-tech which could be put to such perverted uses?

Tetsuo turned away.

He stared out of the control-centre's window. In front, sparse green grass led to the dark Terran-species forest. To his left, the escarpment's edge. Beyond the sharp drop, roiling tan clouds indicated the start of the hypozone.

"Dear God—"

Bloody fool.

"—What have I done?"

Tetsuo's fingers flickered through rapid control gestures. Shards of light fell, blossomed into cubes and tesseracts: flowing text, rivers of colour and twisted volumes of state-space maps. Spinning icons inviting further options.

"I don't understand." Dhana was at his left shoulder. "What's this got to do with you?"

Tetsuo, intent, seated in front of the display, said nothing.

"There are two technologies at work here." Kerrigan, standing on Tetsuo's right, answered for him. "VSI tech, to link plexcores and brains together. And mu-space comms."

Tetsuo's speciality.

"Wait, wait." Dhana was insistent, wanting to understand. "Why mu-space comms? How is that involved?"

Tetsuo sighed, and turned his chair to face her.

"Look," he said. "You know you can stimulate a small portion of the brain and produce a sharp sensation: a clear memory of an event, a piece of music, even a smell."

Dhana nodded.

"OK, but actual thought isn't localized like that." Tetsuo started to point at a phase-space display, realized it wouldn't illustrate his point without a lot of explanation, and turned back to her. "Thought is spread out across a brain like a wave function. Not exactly holographic, but kind of."

"Uh, OK." Dhana's gaze flickered back to the still-unconscious man. "And if you have plexcores, a thought is spread out across brain-plus-plexcores."

"Across the nexus, right. Where was I?"

"Comms—"

"Well, yes. One component of that guy's nexus is the condor's brain—part of the condor's brain, anyway—and the condor's three hundred klicks away."

"OK."

"But at lightspeed, that's a microsecond comms delay each way. Which means—"

"—they're using mu-space comms," Dhana finished for him. "Instantaneous."

"Near as damnit."

"And . . . What?" Dhana's voice tightened. "You did consultancy for TacCorps?"

"No." Tetsuo's face was grim as he turned back to manipulate the image. "For my good friend, Luculentus Rafael Garcia de la Vega."

Akisu. Hacking, into the comms-ware. Tetsuo's fingers flew, and he gave instructions in a rapid-fire mutter, while instantiations of AI logic-trees branched like spreading ferns of glowing code through twenty holo volumes.

"Got it."

He pointed to a pale ovoid, representing the main driver procedure. Its shell peeled back, unfurled into a solid maze of code.

"There." His thumb and forefinger formed a circle, and the display zoomed in. "The documentation caption."

It read, *Copyright © ident: 400IA2.001.Tetsuo Sunadomari2472. All rights reserved.*

"Kerrigan?" Tetsuo asked softly. He could sense both Kerrigan and Dhana staring at the text.

"Mm?"

"How did you know my mother's a biologist? And that TacCorps were using my ware?"

A pause. Then, "Don't worry," Kerrigan said. "I don't think you're responsible for this."

"I should bloody well hope not."

There was a strained silence.

"Nice bit of negative publicity for TacCorps." Dhana's tone was thoughtful. "Going to give it to journalists before the demos?"

"During." Kerrigan nodded towards the display. "Tetsuo, can you download a copy of that image to a crystal, while we take some pictures of Federico's man, here?"

"Yeah." Tetsuo slumped in his chair, suddenly exhausted. "I guess so."

"Welcome—" Kerrigan gave a tight, wry smile. "—to the revolution."

Steam rose from Yoshiko's cup, curling lazily up through the shaft of late morning sunshine which poured through the wide window.

The window overlooked a pond, and the rest of the Sanctuary's grounds. Beyond the black iron railings, out on the green, children were running and playing.

"More?" asked Jana, and poured daistral from a jug.

They were seated in a pleasant polished-redwood dining area; it formed an interior balcony, overlooking the dojo Yoshiko had seen last night.

"Here you are." Jana blinked as she leaned into the sunlight, and handed Yoshiko the cup.

Jana looked more comfortable when she leaned back into comparative shade. Her triangular, slightly pinched face made her look like a slim feral cat, relaxed but alert.

Down below, in the clean wooden dojo, a practice mat was rolled up against one wall. Any lingering traces of exertion must be subliminal, but Yoshiko somehow knew that Jana and Edralix had been training hard this morning.

Yoshiko, on the other hand, had slept for sixteen hours. On waking, she had tried to call Lori: still unavailable. So was Septor.

Since then, she had sat here in a borrowed robe, sipping nutty daistral and eating dried fruit, trying to think of nothing.

Edralix climbed the stairs up from below, his gait athletic and springy. He sat by the window, pale skin glowing.

"Is this the one?" he asked, handing an infocrystal over to Yoshiko. "It was in your jacket pocket."

"Thank you." There was a slot on the low redwood table, and Yoshiko inserted the crystal. "Yes, that's the one."

The crystal from Tetsuo's house.

Swirling blue. The diagram of a Luculentus mind.

Stolen info?

"Oh." Blue galaxies of reflected light sparked in Jana's eyes. "That's interesting."

While Edralix adroitly manipulated the display, Yoshiko explained about Rafael. Vin had been lying, dead or dying, on Yoshiko's bed. Rafael had seen the diagram displayed on Yoshiko's bedside terminal, left in memory from previous use.

"He just stared at it, really coldly." Even the memory of it chilled Yoshiko. "He looked ready to kill. And his voice—"

No, not his voice. His eyes.

She had seen that inhuman, reptilian depth in his eyes, and known instantly that he was responsible for what had happened to Xanthia. And to Vin.

"Got it." Edralix was almost humming to himself. "Interesting, that someone's decrypted this completely."

A kaleidoscope of flaring light washed over them, as Edralix rapidly manipulated variables, flicking through choices of axes, selecting three or four parameters at a time.

"How many state variables are there?" asked Jana.

"Eighty-three primaries." He added, almost with relish, "That's recorded physical variables. There's an impressive list of derived functions, which is much greater. They're probably the sensible things to plot, as well."

A smile twitched across Jana's face.

"You mean this is going to take a while."

"Well—"

"If only my NetAgents worked in Skein—" Yoshiko held up her left hand. Her wedding band and the one remaining tu-ring, the one which had been too tight to remove, glinted in the light. "—I might have been able to analyse it myself."

Edralix froze the display, and leaned forward through a torn sheet of light, a strange attractor in an unlabelled phase-space, and looked at

Yoshiko's tu-ring. Its status light burned dull orange, as it had since her arrival on Fulgor.

"It's probably just a matter of protocols. Didn't they say anything about NetEnv devices at spaceport immigration?"

"No. Unless I missed it."

"Groundlings," Edralix muttered. "Er—"

"No offence," said Yoshiko, as Jana laughed.

"Um, here's some descriptive text, but—" He paused, as a tesseract of text opened up, sheets of glowing metallic green script in four orthogonal emulated dimensions.

"Don't worry." Yoshiko tried not to sound proud, for these Pilots could visualize many more dimensions than she. "I ken FourSpeak."

"Hmm. OK." Edralix was intent on the instructions now, his embarrassment forgotten. "Well, here goes."

The phase state display which sprang up was similar to before, but now revolving cubes of text and informational cartoon-graphics and InfoSprites floated and hovered among the pulsing sheets of light.

"That's better." Jana touched a sprite, and it began to talk about ion concentration gradients in a high crystalline voice, while supplementary script unfurled. "Now we can see what the pretty pictures mean."

They explored the diagram in minute detail. After twenty minutes, during which Edralix three times used another terminal to check technical explanations, they ground to a halt.

"That's it." Jana leaned back in her seat. "Next one, I suppose."

Jangling sheets of light tumbled and rearranged as an entirely new diagram, all silvery grey spaces and torn violet attractors, grew into being. A host of sprites and icons formed.

Yoshiko stared.

"How many variations are there? We could spend weeks checking every combination of parameters. Just what are we looking for?"

Edralix looked up at Jana, and shrugged.

Jana's eyes glittered.

"Something worth killing for," she said.

After three hours, they called a halt, and Jana fetched carbo-chews and more daistral while Edralix obeyed her instructions to relax.

"Have you flown solo yet?" Yoshiko asked, making conversation.

"Oh, yes."

Edralix tried to look casual, but a tiny golden spark of excitement flickered in his jet black eyes, and was gone.

"It must be wonderful." Yoshiko sensed the wistfulness in her own voice.

How marvellous it would be to see with one's own eyes the endless fractal dimensions of mu-space.

"Another standard year, and I'll be eligible for my own ship."

"You'll do well." Yoshiko hoped she did not sound patronizing. To get his own vessel so young, Edralix must be talented even by the Pilots' standards.

"Well— I might not take it."

He looked a little uncomfortable, so Yoshiko did not pursue the matter. She wondered, though, what he would do if he did not choose to fly.

She had heard rumours, through old family friends, that many Pilots were choosing not to pilot for a living, but to pursue other careers.

Having once seen mu-space, how could they ever stay away?

Edralix finished his daistral, put the glass aside, and powered up the display once more.

"I know." Jana tapped her fingernails against the table. "Why don't we try plotting mass against physical space?"

"Physical dimensions?" Edralix grinned. "How passé."

While the display swirled and coalesced, Yoshiko's thoughts grew grim. Whatever Rafael's crime, this was info which Tetsuo should not have.

She remembered the pain and embarrassment, when she was summoned to Tetsuo's school to be informed of her son's infotheft, hacking the local NetNode.

"Stop." Jana's voice drew her back into the present. "Go back. There."

Edralix whistled softly.

"How many plexcores does a Luculentus have? Two, three at most?"

Translucent parallelepipeds—"squidged bricks," as Tetsuo was fond of calling them—clustered around a central ovoid. The shapes were filled with a black and scarlet network of pulsing flows.

"Dear God."

Edralix swallowed. "One hundred and two."

"I don't understand." Yoshiko stared at the diagram, not believing what it told her.

"This is a Luculentus, with over a hundred plexcores."

"You're kidding—"

"Each of these—" Edralix indicated a parallelepiped block. "—represents a plexcore."

"A mind like this," said Jana, "is scarcely human."

"Is this a real person? Or, I don't know, a model? Speculation?"

"Real, I think." Edralix frowned. "These are real scan readings, from the VSI ware—"

"What is it?"

"It's the sheer size." Edralix stood up abruptly, and began to pace around the dining area. "What do we have here? Attotech?"

Yoshiko had heard the term: twistor engineering, at the lowest level of physical dimension, where even subatomic particles were huge. Attotechnology. Pure speculation.

"It can't be," she said.

"So what is it? Nobody can fit over a hundred plexcores inside a human body."

"A disembodied brain? In some kind of plexcore array?"

While they talked, Jana was manipulating the diagram, dragging down sprites and examining what they had to say.

"Not inside a body."

Edralix stopped. "What do you mean?"

Tiny digits glowed above the main arteries of neural flow.

"Those are distances." Jana's voice was grim. "In thousands of kilometres."

Edralix called up a sketch display, transferred info with a gesture from one diagram to the other, and ordered it to plot a physical configuration.

Only an extended sphere could fit the separations as shown.

"They must be scattered all over Fulgor."

Jana and Edralix looked at each other, and their Pilots' eyes were unreadable.

"One man's mind, spread through a hundred and two plexcores, across the face of the planet."

Yoshiko shook her head. That couldn't be right.

She touched a sprite. It displayed the distance between two neighbouring plexcores: nearly twenty thousand kilometres.

"The lightspeed delay must be—sixty-six microseconds, is that right?"

Jana's voice was very controlled. "That's why this needs mu-space comms to work."

"But—"

Tetsuo.

This was the connection to Tetsuo. Mu-space comms, subverted for use in VSI tech, so that a plexcore nexus could be expanded to such an extraordinary magnitude.

But everyone said LuxPrime was incorruptible.

"She's right." Edralix was blank-faced.

Yet a LuxPrime courier was killed at Tetsuo's house.

At my son's house.

"Wait a minute." Yoshiko stared at the two Pilots, and some of Edralix's strange remarks played back through her memory: how the original Pilots had been *"Only really alive when they were carrying other people's cargo—"* And he was considering not accepting the offer of his own mu-space ship.

So that's what the Pilots were up to.

"I understand now." Yoshiko looked from one to the other. "You're colonizing mu-space, aren't you?"

"It's obvious, in retrospect." Yoshiko's voice was strangely calm. "But we all have a blindspot, don't we? We think of Pilots as battling through, I don't know, a kind of wild raging sea. Glad to get back into real-space calm."

"It can be like that." A soft smile played about Jana's feline features.

"Well—An unenhanced human couldn't survive a second, conscious. But you're at home there, aren't you?"

Jana merely looked at Edralix. "I told you she was quick."

The intuitive leap had been obvious: mu-space comms gear could never grow really small, because of the energies involved in tunnelling through from one continuum to the other. But the great machinery could exist in either continuum.

If the hard work were done in mu-space, then real-space hardware could become small enough to interface with VSI tech. It only needed a transceiving film of smartatoms. It could be layered through a brain just like standard VSI, and would probably function better.

"We're renting comms facilities to the various LuxPrime subagencies which run Skein," Jana said.

"And that's how they're implementing the EveryWare/Skein gateway?"

Jana nodded.

"So this—" Yoshiko's mood darkened, as the implications came upon her. "—this Luculentus is using the same facilities."

"It's been in place a good while, getting ready. A skilful Luculentus could hide what's going on: the very architecture of the protocols means we can't monitor info-flow."

While they were talking, Edralix was pointing at sprites, opening up code-volumes, trawling through the documentation.

Yoshiko pictured vast floating cities in mu-space, in that endless fractal golden ocean among black spiky stars. Great structures, maybe whole worlds, which no one but the Pilots would ever see.

She brought her attention back to the moment.

"Object headers only," Edralix was muttering. "The actual guts of the code isn't stored here—actually, it's way beyond the capacity of one crystal—but header info of all the main driver modules is here."

One hundred and two plexcores, plus one organic brain: all one mind.

"So we can deduce what it does, even if we can't see the code?"

"That depends on how helpful the header info is. Right now, the objects refuse to talk to me. They're looking for MindSet validation codes, and I'm just trying to—"

"My NetAgents," Yoshiko interrupted. "They're developed in MindSet. Tetsuo used it, back on Earth, when he coded them up for me."

She held up her nonfunctional tu-ring.

"OK. Let's fix that ring." Edralix got busy. "You just need a protocol driver, and a translation engine."

"So how long will that—? Oh, thank you."

Yoshiko's tu-ring was glowing green. Operational at last.

The horse reared, hooves striking at the air. A samurai bannerman was mounted on its back; his banner fluttered in an unfelt breeze.

The scroll in his left hand was a sign that h-mail was waiting.

"Later," said Yoshiko. "I need kensei now."

The bannerman and horse disappeared.

Above her fist, a scruffy disreputable-looking samurai was sitting on a rock in the half-lotus position, cleaning his swords.

Musashi Miyamoto—or *kensei*, sword saint—was the most powerful of her NetAgents.

"Can you read this?" Yoshiko pointed at the glistening ovoid floating in front of Edralix, the representation of an object header.

"*Hai!*"

A text window grew into being on the ovoid's surface.

Edralix touched it, and a high sprite-voice sounded the text aloud.

"*Author: Tetsuo Sunadomari. Purpose: seventh layer protocol interpreter.*"

"No," whispered Yoshiko.

"Wait a minute." Edralix turned to the Musashi image. "Can you give me its provenance?"

Yoshiko nodded, giving permission to proceed.

"Hai." The swordsman pointed a sword at the ovoid. "Provenance: unauthorized copy of licensed original."

Yoshiko let out a shaky breath. "Who created the unauthorized copy?"

"Unknown."

It must have been someone good, to duplicate an object her son had designed.

Jana leaned forward.

"Who was the original copy licensed to?"

Musashi waited for Yoshiko's nod before answering: "Luculentus Rafael Garcia de la Vega."

Rafael.

Golden fire sparked in the obsidian depths of Jana's eyes.

"Gotcha."

Chapter Twenty-Seven

Small ant, antennae waving.
Lost. The floor is moonlit.
I watch the moons.

There were screams from above as an open-topped silver car was flung, tumbling and spinning, in a perfect parabola through the air.

It was time to increase his arsenal.

Hysterical laughter. Shrieks overhead, as mag-fields caught the car ten metres above the ground and slowed its descent.

I could show you some real excitement. Rafael's thoughts were grim.

The car was spat suddenly sideways, then corkscrewed upwards in a crazy trajectory while its passengers yelled again.

Rafael pushed his way through a queue of tourists and holiday-makers waiting to get on the ride. A little girl stared up at him with wide frightened eyes.

Pennants fluttered in the breeze.

As he passed a row of flagpoles, a great dragon popped into existence and breathed holo fire all over him, then faded into nonexistence with a cartoon grin.

Heart thumping, Rafael lowered his left arm. He had cocked his hand to arm the silver bracelet without even thinking about it.

He kept his fist clenched. That would cause the bracelet to remain powered up.

Tetsuo.

There was no way he could find Tetsuo before the proctors. Not physically.

Rafael crossed a footbridge over a small stream where model sharks swam. Holo tentacles reached up from the gentle waves to threaten children who walked near. None of them seemed fooled.

If Tetsuo was not dead, then sooner or later he would drift into Skein. Then, he would be Rafael's.

At the archery shoot, adults fired solid arrows at flying holo targets. For a moment, Rafael wondered how that could be safe. Then he saw a stray arrow freeze in midair and slowly fall to earth. Safety fields.

Did he want to plunder Tetsuo's mind? Rafael was not sure. He could as easily use his infiltration code to wipe Tetsuo's consciousness completely, without ever copying a thought or memory back to his own mind.

But subsuming Tetsuo would be one way of finding out everything he knew, while dealing with the threat.

The trouble was, Rafael had to strike through Skein, and to do that he needed more reliable, undetectable means of access: high-priority channels which would not log his activities. The sort of channels used by LuxPrime support teams, to dive straight to problem areas regardless of their physical location.

Tetsuo was Rafael's main supplier of mu-space tech, but Rafael had another source entirely for LuxPrime ware.

Beyond the fair's edge, behind gaily coloured tents, lurked a small establishment which obviously assumed its true identity only at night: the Oblivion Café.

Rafael took a seat at an open-air table, and paid for a glass of sparkling water by anonymous cred-ring.

In Skein, he surrounded himself with *a blank room, its walls softening to café au lait. Mirrored panels appeared, then a grey sofa, a potted plant.*

It was part of the game. To obtain the weapon he needed to ensure

Tetsuo's silence, Rafael would have to push his contact farther than he ever had before. The risk lay in pushing the man too far, which would be disastrous.

Back in Skein, he constructed a ghost-Rafael to sit upon the sofa. This was one way to minimize the risks: let him think that Rafael was calling from home.

Then, through the medium of his NetAngel, his ghost-Rafael, he opened up a SkeinLink to his source.

[[Captain Greflar Rogers, ident 5A27187]]

The ghost-Rafael crossed his legs, assuming a comfortable position on the non-existent couch.

<<<MsgRcv LUCCOM213887; cause = SkeinLink established.>>>

In the simulated holo display in Skein, the image of a florid-complexioned man grew into being: Captain Rogers, of the Bureau for Off-world Affairs.

"Rafael. How nice of you to call me at the office."

Meaning, he wished Rafael had called him anywhere but there.

"Still—" Rogers appeared to relax, realizing this was personal—not a recorded emergency call—and feeling confident in SkeinLink confidentiality. "I was hoping to get together with you, at some point."

"Can you meet me for lunch?" asked Rafael through his ghost-image. "I can be at the Aphelion Fair on Actrevnia Common in forty minutes."

Rogers glanced to one side, checking something.

"That's fine. I'll meet you at the fair."

"There's a place called the Oblivion Café, behind the archery shoot. It'll be quiet at this time of day."

"I'll see you there." Rogers' gruff voice was abrupt. "Endit."

In the ghost-room in Skein, Rogers' image winked out of existence.

Rafael kept a straight face in reality, while his NetAngel chortled. The man's attempts at manoeuvring Rafael were pitiful: about what one might expect from a Fulgidus bureaucrat whose ambition seriously outweighed his capabilities.

Rafael checked his bracelet. Still powered on.

He hoped he would not have to make use of it.

Sweet herbs dropped into the glass, colouring the water. Above him, the pale green sky wavered. A caramel-coloured cloud wobbled out of shape, then regained it.

There was an established pattern: Rafael had always turned up for his meetings with Rogers exactly on time. Rogers would not expect him to be here already, and so well prepared.

Rafael sprinkled more sweet herbs from the complementary packet into his drink, and leaned back in his chair. From his table, in the open, he could just discern the ripple of movement which led, like an awning overhead, from the café building behind him, to a dense copse of trees, a hundred metres away. Among the trees, a covered entrance led to the Actrevnia Common metrotube station, and to the network of underground scenic riverpaths which spread out from the city.

Rafael had visited the men's room on the café's second storey, waited till the corridor outside it was empty, withdrawn a long translucent rod from beneath his cape, pushed it through a window membrane, and placed it across the sill.

By now it would have spread out, a long five-metre-wide ribbon-shaped stretch of smartatom film, like an awning which joined the café to the dense stand of trees. In load-phase, it would be absorbing the ground-image below, and transmitting it, unchanged, vertically upwards.

Rogers' office was in Bastren East, the next district over from Actrevnia. He could walk here in fifteen minutes, but would probably get a taxi.

<<<MsgRcv RAFDEV995431; cause = smartatom film enabled.>>>

The film's main routine would be running now: from above, if a SatScan sweep were running, Rafael would be seen walking into the stand of trees. At Rafael's table, the image of a blonde-haired woman would seat herself, at the chair which he actually occupied.

He ordered a crinchnar from the table's terminal, a kind of open-topped spiced sandwich. He knew as soon as it rose through the table's delivery membrane that it was going to be unappetizing, but he chewed at it anyway.

A SatScan snapshot now would show a fair-haired woman, eating.

The food sat like lead in his stomach.

Remaining out of Skein, Rafael blanked his thoughts, and waited.

Rogers arrived five minutes late.

"Nice of you to come." Rafael kept his voice urbane, as he rose from his seat and motioned to the other man to sit.

Rogers flushed, though there had been no sharpness in Rafael's tone. "Sorry I'm late."

"I'm sure it was unavoidable. Drink?"

Rogers nodded.

A glass of sweetened sherry rose up—Rogers' favourite, already ordered by Rafael—and Rogers grasped the glass and half-drained it in one gulp.

"Very good." He sighed as he placed the glass down. "I needed that."

"Work must be very pressing at the moment. A lot of offworlders around, because of the conference."

"Yeah, well," Rogers nodded self-importantly. "A few robberies, but we're hopeful of apprehending the perpetrators real soon now."

"I'm glad. Tell me, Captain, do you think you might be able to help me with my latest venture?"

"I—don't know, Rafael. I honestly don't know."

"I can give you the specs." Rafael held out a crystal. "Here's the list of interface instructions I need to be able to call. It's quite low level. Engineering comm-channels in Skein."

Rogers looked at the crystal, but made no move to take it.

"You mind if I ask the purpose of this? What are you designing?"

"You don't normally bother with those details," Rafael said pleasantly, though every sense was on full alert. "Surely we can do business without getting into the boring tech stuff?"

"I'm sorry." Rogers swallowed. The movement caused his jowls to tremble, as though he had been slapped in the face.

"Well." Rafael paused, as though in thought. "It's a module that will contact a Luculentus through Skein, even if he's not actually logged on."

<<<MsgRcv RAFDEV995480; cause = surveillance miasma detected.>>>

A smartatom cloud, hovering above Rogers. Rafael's smartatom film would be preparing a gamma-ray burst.

Rogers said nothing, so Rafael continued. "Quite a useful concept, don't you think? Lots of applications. Soul-parents monitoring their offspring, for example."

"Are you sure that's all you're using it for?" The strain in Rogers's voice was obvious.

"Of course. What else?"

<<<MsgRcv RAFDEV995482; cause = countermeasures successfully invoked.>>>

"By the way, Captain—" Rafael smiled easily. "—Your surveillance cloud has been defused. I just thought you should know that."

The blood drained from Rogers' face.

"Just a precaution—"

"Why, Captain. What have you got to fear?"

"We—can't do business any more. That's what I came to tell you."

"Tsk, tsk." Rafael shook his head. "The prices I'm offering are increasing. Business is very good."

Rogers picked up the sherry glass, then replaced it without drinking.

"There's no contact." Rogers swallowed. "I've lost my contact."

"What do you mean?" Rafael closed his left fist around the crystal which Rogers had refused.

Sunlight glinted on his silver bracelet.

"My source in LuxPrime," said Rogers, "was a courier called Farsteen. And he's dead. Murdered. Don't you watch the NewsNets?"

"And he was your only source?"

"Didn't you hear me?" Rogers' voice was beginning to rise. He caught himself, looked around guiltily, then continued in a lower tone. "The man was *murdered*. LuxPrime pride themselves on being incorruptible. Maybe they found out about Farsteen, and did him in."

"I don't think LuxPrime employ hit squads."

"For God's sake—with their power, they can do whatever they want. It only takes one man to go over the bounds, you know?"

Like you, Rafael thought. *Just one man stepping outside the rules, for his own greed.*

"And you don't," he asked reasonably, "have any other contacts inside LuxPrime?"

"No. We—I—found out about some, er, incidents in Farsteen's past by accident. Sheer fluke."

"I see."

"You can't get any handle on a LuxPrime employee, not normally. You know that. That's why they've got that stainless reputation—"

"I know." Rafael shook his head. "You said 'we.' But no one else knows about you and me, do they?"

"God's sake, man. Do I look crazy? Of course they don't—"

Rogers looked surprised.

The bracelet tingled briefly around Rafael's wrist, and Rogers slowly slumped back in his chair. His corpse already had the toneless absence of the suddenly dead.

Rafael left before the inevitable smell rose.

What the hell was going on?

Under smartatom cover, Rafael made his way to the trees. He kept his gait slow, his manner pleasant, but inside he was spitting with the rage. In Skein, a thousand ghost-Rafaels were howling through dataseams, searching for connections between Captain Greflar Rogers and Tetsuo Sunadomari.

He sent the dissolve command to the antisurveillance film. Then he pulled up his cape's hood, drew on a smartmask to disguise his features, and walked through the copse and back out into the fair.

One link came back almost immediately: among the LuxPrime briefing-clusters which he had been sent as Tetsuo's sponsor, there was Tetsuo's immigration authorization, countersealed by Rogers' ident. So, on one occasion at least, they had met in person.

"Bad luck, sir." A girl spoke to an unlucky customer, pulling Rafael briefly from his reverie.

Farsteen.

Rafael had always been so careful to keep his tech sources apart, never hinting to Tetsuo that he was interested in LuxPrime ware, never letting Rogers infer that he might need mu-space comms capability.

Now they were linked, and the real tie was a dead LuxPrime courier called Adam Farsteen, whom Rafael had never heard of until his name was bandied about the NewsNets.

"Sir? Try your luck?"

Damn, and damn.

New tactics were required, now.

"Sir?"

Rafael realized he was standing in front of a coconut shy, no different from a Terran fair of centuries past.

"Of course."

New tactics.

Rafael took four wooden balls from the girl.

He threw the first.

[[Luculenta Lorelei Maximilian, ident 6654κ7•ϵ {sept5ΘΞ3}]]

Picturing Lori Maximilian's ideogram, he concentrated; a reply immediately returned.

<<<MsgRcv LUCCOM213886; cause = SkeinLink unavailable.>>>

Frowning, he threw the second ball. The soul-daughter, Vin. He had seen her on the bed, skull crushed, tended by those interfering Earther women. Was Vin dead?

[[Luculenta Lavinia Maximilian, ident 6654χ8•ϵ {sept5ΘΞ}]]

<<<MsgRcv LUCCOM213886; cause = SkeinLink unavailable.>>>

No reason code was appended; she could be alive or dead.

Third ball.

In Skein, he sent more NetAngels questing. A ghost-Rafael returned from a NewsNet search: the most severely injured partygoers had been flown to Medical Complex Gamma, here in Lucis.

Fourth ball.

Yoshiko Sunadomari. Tetsuo's mother. She, too, was a possibility. Perhaps as bait. Perhaps to die.

"Oh."

The girl was looking at him, stunned.

His first ball had whacked the coconut off its stand, and the following three had smacked into it one after the other as it fell to the ground.

Very slowly, the girl turned to fetch the coconut.

Another game he had won.

"Don't bother. I don't care for them, anyway."

He held in his soaring laughter as he strode away.

His strategy was clear. Strike first. Kill the mother, to draw the son out from hiding.

The concern on Yoshiko Sunadomari's face had been obvious. Concern for Vin Maximilian, whose whereabouts the ghost-Rafael had determined to high probability. Sooner or later, Yoshiko would turn up at the med-centre.

The bigger game was growing more interesting, and the stakes were getting higher. Absolute certainty grew in him that he would win again—as he always did. As he always would.

Win.

The bannerman, kneeling, offered her the scroll.

As soon as Yoshiko touched the icon, her h-mail queue opened: a string of three glistening teardrops.

"Would you like to be alone?" asked Jana.

A palm-up gesture to the first teardrop revealed the sender's name. Luculenta Felice Lectinaria.

"Not at all." Yoshiko smiled at Edralix. "You don't know what a relief it is, being able to use my own NetAgents."

Though Yoshiko had said she needed no privacy, Edralix got up to perform some task out of her sight, and Jana busied herself with replenishing the cups of coffee.

Yoshiko gestured at the second teardrop. Lori was the sender, so Yoshiko pointed to play that message first.

In text, it said Lori was staying at the med-centre where Vin was being treated. Medical Complex Gamma, Lucis City. A graphic showed the med-centre's location, by Accordia Square in the north of the city.

Vin wasn't dead.

Yoshiko shook her head, then pinched the bridge of her nose, to stop the sudden wavering of her vision. With the injuries Vin had sustained, wasn't death preferable?

After a while, Yoshiko felt able to open the other messages. She pointed to the one from Felice Lectinaria.

"Professor Sunadomari. It was a pleasure to meet you at the Aphelion Ball, despite the dreadful events of later that night."

In the display, the tall grey-haired Luculenta bowed her head.

"I thought you might be interested in this article," she continued. "It's not posted yet in Skein, but feel free to cite from it if you wish."

The woman's eyes looked directly at Yoshiko, very piercing in their intensity, and it was hard to believe this was a passive recording, without AI capabilities.

"Endit."

The icon was an owl whose head rotated ceaselessly from left to right. Yoshiko pointed, and it metamorphosed into a circle of nine translucent spheres, each containing a tiny moving scene.

Yoshiko worked her way through them one by one, watching intently as each unfurled its full-size image, its attendant text and graphs.

The first depicted a white-trunked tree, growing on a rocky hill in bright sunlight. Later spheres showed a small copse of the same type of tree, then a widespread bush. The bush spread runners along the ground; each clump of growth bore the same spear-shaped copper leaves as the tree.

Yoshiko read intently about both tree and bush: capillary pressures, mitosis rates, photoreactive activity plotted versus sunlight intensity and ambient temperature.

Finally, she sat back and sighed.

"Very interesting." Edralix was behind her, and his tone was ironic.

"Well, it is." Yoshiko pointed at the solitary tree, and its descendant, the bush with vinelike runners. "There are two different forms of the same organism. The bush adapts to the lack of shade caused by its parent, you see—"

She let out a sigh and shook her head.

"The thing is, Edralix—this is my work, you know?" Maybe too much so, thinking of how Tetsuo had turned out. "And if you're good at what you do, you practically are your work." She paused. "Like you and Jana."

"I know. I'm sorry." Edralix waved a hand awkwardly. "It's just, well, you met this woman at the Aphelion Ball, and now she's sending you stuff about a plant."

Yoshiko stared back at the display, as Edralix continued. "With all the other stuff that's going on, it just seems a little, I don't know, incongruous."

Yoshiko frowned. "Felice Lectinaria's obviously quite well known in the field," she said slowly. "But . . . you're right. Let's forget this, huh? Let's see what the third message was."

It was from Federico Gisanthro.

"We were going to meet, weren't we?" Federico's pale face was thin, with the strong ascetic look of a long-distance runner. "The events at the ball must have been particularly distressing for you. Please call me any time, or visit in person."

Yoshiko froze the display with a gesture.

"I forgot to mention," she said to Jana. "Federico Gisanthro's the head of TacCorps—" When the others nodded their understanding, she added, "He invited me to meet him today."

She explained how Lori had engineered their meeting, during the Aphelion Ball, and enlisted Federico's help.

"Very good." Jana sounded impressed.

Edralix started to speak, then closed his mouth.

Yoshiko waved at the display to continue.

"I'm at the TacCorps Academy today, Quatt'Day, and at Peacekeeper Central all day QuinzeDay. See you. Endit."

The display faded.

Jana sipped coffee.

"You'll need to give this Federico a copy of the video log."

"I know." Yoshiko sighed. "I guess I've been withholding evidence, haven't I?"

"Er—" Edralix looked diffident. "Jana? May I talk with you for a moment?"

Jana stood up. "Excuse us, Yoshiko."

Yoshiko waited until they had left. She stared out of the window, not seeing the pleasant grounds at all, but gathering her thoughts. Then she opened up a realtime call, and almost immediately her request was acknowledged.

Strange sense of vertigo.

To Yoshiko's left, below the balustrade in reality, lay the Sanctuary's dojo. In front, down the vanishing perspective of the preternaturally real holo display, lay a long training hall. Men and women in jumpsuits tuned olive green were warming up: butterfly jumps and flickflack somersaults.

Even in her youth, Yoshiko would not have trained like this.

"What do you think?"

Federico's gaunt image stood on the right, overlooking his agents. He was dressed in the same fashion, and his face was bathed in sweat.

"Lori told me you were interested in the fighting arts, Professor."

In front of Yoshiko, the agents paired up and began to spar. Boots thudded into ribs, elbows into jaws. Yoshiko saw one heavyset woman grab a smaller man by groin and throat and throw him bodily against a wall.

"What do you think?"

"Very impressive," Yoshiko said weakly.

An enormously muscled man at the side of the room barked an order. The agents formed groups: four against one.

"Go!" shouted the instructor.

The sparring grew fierce as the outnumbered single fighters tried to tangle up their opponents, punching and pushing them into each other's path.

The lights flickered out. In the darkness, bright pulses blazed like lightning, amid thunderous crashes of sound. The men and women continued fighting without pause.

"Battlefield conditions."

Battlefield? Yoshiko wondered. *I thought these were supposed to be law officers.*

The lights came up. The fighting ceased. Those who could stand to attention, did so.

"I gather your medics keep busy," said Yoshiko.

A dry chuckle from Federico.

"You've got that right." In the display, he turned his back to Yoshiko. "Guido? Perhaps a demonstration for our caller?"

The hugely muscled instructor stepped into the centre. He pointed to five of the biggest men, and they formed a circle around him.

Without warning, two of the men barrelled straight at Guido: one kicking at Guido's knees, the other throwing elbow strikes. Guido locked the kicker around the neck, and threw the convulsing man into the other attacker, and both men went down.

Guido took the attack to the other three, felling them quickly. Sweeping the last one to the floor, Guido dropped knees-first straight onto the man's chest, and there was an audible crack.

"Well, enough of that." Federico smiled pleasantly at Yoshiko.

The smile chilled her soul.

Guido came up to Federico.

"This is Professor Sunadomari." Federico gestured in Yoshiko's direction. "She practices the, ah, traditional arts, you know?"

Yoshiko wondered how much more Lori had told him about her.

"Flower or stone?" Guido's voice was as rough as she had expected.

Yoshiko had to think about what he meant.

"Flower, I guess."

Ornamentation, rather than rough stuff. *Dō*—disciplined path—more than *jutsu*, hard and practical.

"Anyway." Federico stepped in front of Guido, and the training hall became indistinct background. "This wasn't why you called, was it? I just thought you'd like to see TacCorps in training."

"Do they always train like this?"

"This is the Alpha Squad. They do."

In the shade beyond the image, Yoshiko could see that Jana and Edralix had returned. Edralix shook his head.

Yoshiko said, "I guess you don't have too much trouble, ah, subduing suspects."

"Not much." Federico smiled again. "You'll be happy to know I've already assigned two of my agents to the investigation, and Guido may be joining them."

"I—thank you."

Would Major Reilly appreciate the additions to her team?

"They will get results, I promise." His pale mismatched eyes looked intent. "You don't have any information, beyond what you gave to Major Reilly?"

"I'm sorry." Yoshiko shook her head,

"Be assured, we will do our utmost to find Tetsuo. Thank you for calling, Professor Sunadomari. Endit."

The display terminated, and Yoshiko let out a long sigh of relief.

"Bloody hell," said Edralix. "They don't mess around, do they?"

Jana stepped in front of the window. Sunlight created a bright nimbus around her unruly mass of black hair, her witchlike pointed face.

"You didn't give him the evidence."

"No," said Yoshiko. "I didn't."

•

"The thing is—" Yoshiko was explaining, "—Major Reilly wasn't really friendly, but she didn't try to intimidate me, either."

She tensed her muscles, relaxed. She was wearing a borrowed black jumpsuit, having freshened up, and felt ready for a training session.

"Well—" Jana's deep black eyes glanced at Edralix. "From Ed's political analysis, this Federico may be quite a potent force behind the scenes."

"He wasn't trying to help Yoshiko," Edralix said. "He was trying to keep her out of the investigation."

"Yes. That's just what he was doing."

That was what they had been discussing outside the room. Yoshiko had always known that Pilots kept their own intelligence services. It paid commerce to know what was happening among their clients' cultures.

Of course, no energy weapon had ever been transported from one settled world to another. On one level at least, the Pilots' intentions were overt, and patently benign.

"Are you going to give the video-log to Major Reilly?"

"That seems best. With Edralix's analysis, if that's OK?"

"Of course."

Jana leaned forward.

"There's something else."

Looking into her eyes was like falling through a black endless space.

"What?" asked Yoshiko, feeling suddenly fearful.

"This Felice Lectinaria—do you know her?"

"Her name's vaguely familiar, from the journals. I've been meaning to check."

"But you didn't meet her before the Aphelion Ball?"

"No. We only talked briefly. Why do you ask?"

"Because—" Jana's black eyes held distant golden sparks, threatening to flare. "There's more to her message, I think, than seems apparent."

"Oh." Yoshiko glanced at Edralix. "Encrypted info?"

"Not in that sense," said Jana. "I think she was being subtle, not knowing under which circumstances—in what company—you might receive her message."

A tree.

A bush, the tree's very different descendant.

"The second generation—" Yoshiko spoke slowly. "Grew up to be quite different from the parent."

"But it thrived." Jana's soft voice seemed to cut through the air.

"Yes, it did."

It had been her greatest fear. Only now, could she acknowledge it.

"Tetsuo's alive, isn't he?"

Ghostly images stalked the control room, walking among the fallen researchers like lost souls.

"You two go on."

Kerrigan bent over the holoprocessor, refining the decoy images. All around the ellipsoid control centre, a horizontal band had been tuned to transparency.

From outside—at least, from a distance—everything would look OK. As soon as the unconscious bodies were dragged out of sight.

"Come on," said Dhana. "It'll be easier going down."

"I should hope so."

Tetsuo followed. The walk downstairs was tedious, but not exhausting.

"You OK?"

"I'm not that unfit."

Dhana was out of sight. Rounding the turn, he saw that she was waiting for him.

"So why are you breathing heavily?" she asked.

"Because you're near me?" He made it a question.

"Yeah?" Dhana grinned. "In your dreams."

They carried on.

At ground level, Tetsuo steered well clear of the open doorway. No control signals blasted into his brain.

They continued descending, until they reached the basement level.

The kitten was dead.

"Oh, no."

It was the first cage they came to, among the rows of experimental specimens. Dhana gently took the small white body out. Dark crimson blood stained the tiny head around the implant incision.

"How could they?"

Tetsuo said nothing. He had heard both sides of this debate from Mother—live experiments were a last resort, but were used when other options were exhausted—and still had no answer.

He would never do this to an animal. He knew that much.

"Major Reilly, please."

"I'm sorry, that officer is unavailable at this time."

"Never mind." Yoshiko made knot-tying motions with her fingers, joining three bobbing crystalline spheres of light. "I have some info for her." The three objects were the Maximilians' video log, Edralix's analysis of the editing, and a copy of the Luculentus mind diagram. "Can you accept?"

"Go ahead."

The mind-schematic had been reconfigured so that the initial display showed the all-important physical dimensions, the vast number of plexcores forming the nexus. There was a short text addendum, explaining that Yoshiko had found it among Tetsuo's personal effects.

Yoshiko pointed, and the objects were gone.

"Info accepted. Do you wish to record a message?"

"No—I think it's self-explanatory. Thank you."

"You are welcome, ma'am."

As the display faded, Yoshiko dabbed a faint film of perspiration from her forehead.

"You did the right thing." Jana spoke from behind her.

"I hope so." She felt shaky but relieved. "At any rate, it's done now."

The capuchin, sitting on Brevan's shoulder, chattered away into his ear.

"I wish I knew what he was saying."

"Complaining, by the sound of it," said Dhana.

"The attrition rate has been awful. According to the logs, they've only just started surviving the interface."

The Agrazzus moved among the cages, making notes on his wrist terminal.

There were chimps and macaques. There were parrots and parakeets, ravens and owls. There were large lynxettes and tiny tabby cats.

"We have to—"

"No." Tetsuo interrupted Dhana. "No, we can't let them go."

"I can't believe you said that."

"They're better off here than in the wild. We're only just into the habitable zone."

"Subsonics." Dhana looked pensive. "We could drive them towards the forest."

"But if they were bred for research—"

"She's right." Brevan looked around. "TacCorps will shut this place down, as soon as they realize it's been discovered. The animals will be destroyed."

Tetsuo stared. There were so many of them. So many cages.

"Besides—" A wry smile flitted across Brevan's face. "—you won't win an argument with Dhana."

"Very funny."

"Yeah," said Tetsuo. "But he's right."

It was the last cage.

Two hours of wrestling the cages onto the loading bay's elevator disk, and taking them up to ground level a dozen at a time. The disk surfaced at the tower's base, close to the doorway.

There was an acrid tang to the air. Though Tetsuo did not need his resp-mask, they were close to the escarpment edge, close to the hypozone beyond the clifflike drop.

Wind whipped heather all about, and a flock of grey owls—released by Dhana from the previous load of cages—sensed the subsonics, and perhaps the stench of unbreathable atmosphere from the hypozone, and wheeled in the intended direction, heading for the dark forest.

"It'll bite you," Brevan warned, as Tetsuo opened the final cage.

A great white lynxette padded out, and looked up at Tetsuo with wide pale green-and-amber eyes. Its tufted ears were laid flat, in protest against the subsonics, but it made no move to leave.

The implant was a tiny scar on the back of its head.

"I wouldn't—"

But Tetsuo was already running the back of his hand along the lynxette's whiskers.

"Bloody hell."

Brevan looked at Dhana, who shrugged.

"Go," said Tetsuo.

It ran.

The white lynxette loped across the swirling heather, towards the forest.

"Get the cages out of sight." Brevan's voice was gruff.

Tetsuo rubbed his nose.

"This wind really stings, doesn't it?"

"Yeah." Dhana sniffed, and dabbed at her own eyes. "You guys."

The lynxette reached the trees, and was gone.

Chapter Twenty-Eight

Waving fields of silver
Moonlit grass. All is seen.
Moons shine, insects sing.

Blanched face, trembling hands. A crash had seemed inevitable.

"Are you OK?" Jana's slightly waspish voice cut into her thoughts.

"Oh, yes."

Yoshiko hid her amusement. The flyer had been manned—a tourist taxi—and the fellow had been scared witless at the notion of two Pilots for passengers, besides Yoshiko. He had dared to speak only to her. She had insisted on paying, and had tipped him generously.

"It's up ahead." Edralix, first out of the taxi-landing pagoda, pointed to a long black building on a low rise.

In the darkness, a plain orange holo floated over the med-centre's surrounding parkland.

LUCIS MEDICAL COMPLEX GAMMA

Vin was in there, somewhere. Yoshiko's amusement faded as quickly as it had arrived, and she shivered.

"Don't worry." Jana briefly touched Yoshiko's arm. "It can't be an emergency, if it's scheduled."

"No—you're right."

When Yoshiko had called the med-centre earlier, there had been a message waiting for her: an invitation to attend the med-centre's Neurological Institute at twenty five hundred hours, precisely.

Flanked by the two black-caped Pilots, Yoshiko slowly walked up the dark brick path which led to the main entrance. A small holo floated outside: an unravelling DNA double-helix surrounding a vertical tower processor, the ancient Hippocratic logo.

Small batlike flitterbugs darted back and forth around drifting glowglobes, attracted by the clouds of moths. The flitterbugs' erratic flight, hovering then flicking away, reminded Yoshiko of the hummingbird she had seen back on Ardua Station.

"Wait." Jana stopped, seemed almost to sniff the cold night air.

"What is it?" Yoshiko heard the nervousness in her own voice.

A flitterbug dipped down, flew past them, was gone.

Jana said nothing, black eyes questing in the darkness.

Trees rustled.

Edralix raised a hand as the flitterbug returned, arcing down towards Yoshiko—

Something flashed in Edralix's hand, and the flitterbug dropped onto the dark bricks with a soft splat.

Not a real flitterbug, at all.

"Ed—" Yoshiko stopped. A fluorescent blue fluid was leaking from the tiny body.

She reached down to examine the thing, but Edralix caught her injured arm, just above the cast.

"Smartvenom," he whispered.

"Quiet." Jana.

Normal night sounds. *Ignore.*

Yoshiko forced herself to breathe calmly.

Shadows. No movement in the darkness—

There.

A glint of silver.

"Look out!" Edralix pushed Yoshiko down, just as she started to move.

There was a crack of sound, and white fire lanced out of the trees towards them, but Jana had stepped into its path, whipping her cloak upwards.

A vertical shield of golden motes.

White fire splashed against sparkling gold. It spat and sprayed, but could not burst through.

"Come on."

Yoshiko got to her feet and sprinted for the main entrance, flanked by Jana and Edralix. No time to think. Heart pounding, mind reacting like an automaton, she just ran, while fire split the night behind her.

The Pilots' hands grasped her, almost lifting her up the last few steps, and then they were through. They nearly skidded across the polished pink granite floor.

"Peacekeeper emergency," Jana said urgently to the human receptionist, but the foyer's windows were already turning to impenetrable silver. "Someone's firing energy weapons out there."

"My God." The receptionist's face grew pale, as he waved open a display with fluttering hands. "You're not joking, are you?"

The impossibly handsome proctor appeared: the public face of the Peacekeeper AIs. "ProctorNet. Is this an enquiry or an emergency?"

Jana leaned over the receptionist's shoulder.

"Emergency. Get Major Reilly."

From the doorway, Edralix called back, "This is secured. The building system's very quick."

Small daylight-bright images of the grounds appeared in holo spheres above the reception desk—including fast-moving viewfields broadcast by smartbats—while three blank-carapaced drones skimmed into the foyer and hovered.

The med-centre's systems would already be interfaced with the proctors, Yoshiko thought. The entire building was sealed and under surveillance.

"What's going on?"

Yoshiko's heart thumped as she recognized the voice.

"Maggie! What are you doing here?"

"Same as you—I think. What is all this?"

"Someone's firing a graser outside."

"Not someone." Jana had appeared beside them, out of nowhere, and Maggie yelped in surprise.

"I don't—" Yoshiko began.

Jana interrupted. "It was Rafael de la Vega."

The receptionist twittered around them nervously, assuring them that the proctors would be here any second now. In fact, in one of the holo spheres above the polished desk, Yoshiko could see strobing blue rings sweeping across the dart-shaped outline of a flyer.

First priority—securing the grounds.

Maggie was looking agitated. She did not even have her videoglobe active.

"What's wrong?" asked Yoshiko.

"The Baton Ceremony. We've ten minutes before it starts."

"I don't understand."

"Why do you think we're here? Hasn't anyone—?" Maggie hugged herself. "Obviously not."

Yoshiko felt bewildered. She wanted to cry, to sit down and let her body tremble. But there was no time for that.

Edralix, tentatively, touched her shoulder.

"What is it, Edralix?"

From the corner of her eye, she could see Maggie growing pale. Sometimes, it was hard to remember how much in awe the Pilots were held.

"Oh, Edralix, this is Maggie Brown." Yoshiko performed the introductions. "Maggie, Pilot Noviciate Edralix Corsdavin."

"Er— Pleased to meet you, ma'am."

"Thank you, s—" Maggie, obviously about to call him "sir," stopped. She was at least half again his age.

Yoshiko felt a smile flicker across her face, despite the urgent manoeuvres she knew were taking place outside.

"Jana said—" Edralix looked in Jana's direction; she was by the desk, intent on the displays. "—we'll wait for the proctors. You two should go ahead."

"I—"

"Come on." Maggie, recovering her composure, took Yoshiko's uninjured arm. "We can't be late."

They saw Xanthia on the way.

The hushed grey corridor led past a membrane tuned to transparency. Inside, solemnly waiting on observation seats, were Maggie's son, Jason, and a fair-haired girl, maybe two years older. In her lap, she held Jason's toy monkey.

"That's Amanda." Maggie whispered, although their voices could not carry through the membrane. "Xanthia's soul-daughter. Her genetic daughter, too."

Beyond the seats, separated from the children by another membrane, Xanthia sat.

Xanthia's eyes were locked on infinity, and her pale bare arms clutched herself, as her upper body swung back and forth in endless metronomic repetition. There was no light of intelligence in those eyes.

Yoshiko could only stand and stare at what had once been Xanthia.

"Come on." Maggie's voice was gentle. "That's the ceremony up ahead." She pointed to the far end of the corridor, where Luculenti were gathering in a small antechamber.

From behind, a voice called them to a halt.

Major Reilly, accompanied by the Pilots and half a dozen dark-uniformed proctors, was hurrying towards them.

"You've an important ceremony to attend," Reilly said without preamble. "So I'm going to keep this short. You were fired at by Luculentus Rafael de la Vega, whom you suspect of having attacked Luculenta Xanthia Delaggropos—" Her eyes flickered to one side; she recognized the now-mindless Xanthia. "—through some sort of Luculentus communications channel. Is that correct?"

Yoshiko nodded.

"You saw him in the darkness?"

"No— I couldn't see a thing."

"But—" Reilly turned to Jana. "You could see him?"

"Yes," said Jana, and her eyes grew impossibly black.

"How well do you know him?"

"I have never met him. I saw a holostill, in a NewsNet item."

"I see." Reilly thrust out her square jaw pugnaciously, apparently unfazed by talking to two Pilots.

"Have you seen the video log?" asked Yoshiko.

"Yes. And that rather interesting diagram. Your son's role in this is still unclear."

"I—didn't have to hand it over to you."

Reilly looked hard at Yoshiko. "That's one reason I'm not pressing you on this."

Yoshiko swallowed.

"Major—" began Maggie.

"I know. You can make a full statement later." Reilly's voice was brisk. "Right now, you'd better get a move on."

Yoshiko did not move.

"We're still searching outside," Reilly continued. "When we find something—"

She stopped, seeing Yoshiko's frozen expression.

"Professor Sunadomari—Do you have any idea how many non-Luculenti get invited to a Baton Ceremony?" Her voice softened a little. "I'll wait for you."

"OK." Yoshiko swallowed.

"Come on." Maggie took her arm.

The group of Luculenti in the antechamber had grown bigger. Jana and Edralix followed, as Yoshiko and Maggie joined them.

No one, as far as Yoshiko knew, had invited the Pilots. There were surreptitious glances from Luculenti, but no audible remarks.

"Professor. Thank God you're here."

It was Septor, his face flushed and his stance unsteady, a half-empty glass in one hand.

"It's my privilege," said Yoshiko.

Up close, she could see that his eyes were watery and mildly bloodshot.

"Maybe you can convince her not to go through with it."

"Convince whom?" Yoshiko did not understand. "Of what?"

"Lori, of course," Septor said, and he was almost in tears. "She's too young. It's far too soon."

"Too soon?"

"Years too soon. She should live another decade, at the least."

"Live?" asked Yoshiko stupidly.

Septor gulped from his glass, as a grey-uniformed medical attendant came up to him.

"I'm all right," Septor said.

"I believe he means—" Jana's voice was soft. "—that Lori won't survive this Baton Ceremony, the passing on of memories. The soul-parent never does. Am I right?"

Septor looked away.

Yoshiko looked at Jana in shock. She was vaguely aware of Maggie standing open-mouthed beside her.

"I am right," said Jana.

There was no satisfaction in her voice.

Dark and cold: a thousand tonnes of black water above him, and acceleration's unseen hand pressing him back into his seat, and the memory of bitter failure in his mind.

Pilots!

Not like the damned coconut shy. This time the target had bodyguards. Two Pilots. Who could have expected that?

Should he have tried to shoot them, once his faux-flitterbug assassin had failed? Well, it was done.

Damn it . . .

He had run, drenched in sweat, while stars whirled and split apart in the night-sky above him—a smartatom spiral, spinning overhead, breaking up his image. Found a crowded plaza, configured his mask, and boarded a Pariduan shuttle.

Running from his prey. And Yoshiko was still alive.

Webbing clawed him back into the seat as the spit-capsule slowed, popped out of the tunnel's end, and screeched to a halt. Brilliance flooded the stark chamber.

Home. It gave him no feeling of security.

The lift-tube took him up to the lounge.

Had the Pilots seen him?

No matter. He had to establish his alibi firmly, on the assumption that they had. The windows depolarized at his unspoken command, and he looked out at the orange-lit Zen garden and saw himself walking in the moonlight.

No Skein ghost-Rafael, this, but a holo which was visible in reality: visible to SatScan and passersby alike.

The holo-Rafael turned at his command and walked towards the house. The false image had been perambulating right to the edge of the grounds—close enough to the neighbouring fishing lodge to have been logged by its surveillance system.

Rafael's spectral alter ego did not waver as it reached the lounge window and appeared to step through the membrane.

The holo-Rafael dissolved. Just one more piece of misdirection.

None of this was foolproof. An analysis of Rafael's home would reveal the top-of-the-range hi-res projectors hidden outside, and the tunnel which ran beneath Lake Darintia to a small villa on the Pariduan foothills.

He had to buy time, to shore up his alibi.

A ghost-Rafael directed the house drones, under smartatom cover, to remove the projectors outside. Simultaneously, a second Rafael under direct control opened a SkeinLink session with Septor Maximilian.

<<<MsgRcv LUCCOM213887; cause = SkeinLink established.>>>

"All my best wishes, sir," said Rafael in Skein, causing his image to bow formally. "Let us rejoice in this continuance, and give thanks for Lorelei's beautiful life among us."

"My thanks, Rafael." Septor replied as if by rote, his voice dead. "And Lori's, too."

"At this time, my thoughts are with you."

<<<MsgRcv LUCCOM213900; cause = SkeinLink revoked.>>>

He did not know the Maximilians well . . . but well enough to express his sympathy on the occasion of Lori's Baton Ceremony. Another small addition to the flimsy construct of his alibi.

Withdrawing from Skein, he felt its waves and eddies lapping at the edges of his consciousness. His questing NetAngels, his ghost-Rafaels, were like distant phantom limbs, sensed but autonomous.

A blaze of red, a howl of sound: emergency request. In Skein, a ghost-Rafael screamed into its master's mind, slamming its perceptions directly into Rafael's own, sharp and immediate:

THREAD ONE

<audio>

"Tetsuo?"

******

"Are you all right?"

THREAD TWO
<touch>
Resp-mask, tight
on face.

THREAD THREE
<voice>
******
"I don't—"

THREAD FOUR
<visual>
Her close-cropped
hair.
Mouth glistens as
she speaks.

And then it was gone, before his infiltration code could attempt a lock.

Luck. Bad luck. Tetsuo had entered Skein, just for a moment, as his mindware tried to integrate without proper supervision, test-running its linked modules.

Scowling, Rafael increased the instantiations of his NetAngel template, and a hundred thousand ghost-Rafaels prowled through Skein, searching for any sign of Tetsuo.

They would not stop questing, until Tetsuo was found alive, or proven dead.

Rafael exited from Skein. He had other problems to worry about.

Pilots.

Rafael's one vulnerability was the great size of his plexcore nexus—one hundred and two plexcores scattered across Fulgor, linked by mu-space comms, routed through the massive standard facilities rented out by the Pilots themselves.

Tetsuo's mother would have to die.

A wolfish smile spread across Rafael's face. He had just one weak spot, and Yoshiko had enlisted the help of the only people who could possibly attack it: Pilots.

It raised the stakes, yet again, of this ultimate game. It made life, and all his deaths, worthwhile.

"Good night, sweet Yoshiko." Grim amusement touched Rafael's voice. "And may flights of NetAngels sing thee to thy rest."

Vin's eyes were closed, as though in sleep. Her scarlet hair had been rearranged, to cover the shiny patch of repaired scalp above her left temple.

Vin—

Her chest rose slowly, and fell. Another shallow breath.

Atonal music muttered a low discord.

"This way," Grey tunic. A medical assistant, escorting Yoshiko and Maggie to their seats. Jana and Edralix were somewhere behind them.

Lori.

Lying on another couch, near Vin's, Lori's face bore the graven look of a Zen student in deepest meditation.

Feeling numb, Yoshiko sat down. All around her, Luculenti were taking their places among the rows of seats. The room was softly lit, its walls, floor and ceiling covered in soft grey furlike fabric. The atmosphere was hushed.

Septor, dressed in a formal grey and silver robe with white brocade and lace, made his way unsteadily down an aisle, and was escorted to a raised seat at the front, near the twin couches.

Motes of light. Shards of glass.

Panes of colour fell, broke up, swirled, rearranged their orbits, then slowly coalesced. Above the couches, a giant image of Lori's face grew into being.

"My first farewell," the image said, as its kind eyes directed their gaze at Septor, "is to you, my love. Farewell, and deep peace. May your soul-lineage be long and coherent."

Septor was still, but pain was etched into every line on his face, his shadowed eyes, the clawlike grip of his hands upon the chair.

"And to all of you, my friends—" Lori's image looked upon them. "—this is untimely soon for my passing onwards, but circumstances force us. You have each enriched my world, and I thank you for it.

"There is inorganic stardust, and there are layers upon layers of emergent phenomena, and there is human consciousness. Such wonder!

"I thank you for being my companions on the miraculous journey called life. I love you all."

The faces around Yoshiko were enraptured. What joy was Lori sharing with her peers? Yoshiko would never know.

Slowly, like stars before the dawn, the image faded.

Above Lori's couch, sapphire clouds depicted the glory of an inquisitive joyful mind. Over Vin, the tattered crimson-tinged remnants, rent here and there with darkness, of that bright and innocent soul.

Like the shifting of the tide, waves lapped into Vin's damaged mind, brightening its hue, as Lori's slowly ebbed. Yoshiko watched the flowing neural correlates of consciousness as one might sit at the ocean's edge. Processes migrated, calm and unstoppable. For how long? It felt like forever.

And then it was done.

Vin's aura was bright with shining life; Lori's was gone.

Gentle white-gloved hands touched Yoshiko's sleeve, then, and led her with all the other silent watchers from the room.

Only Septor remained, watching over the dark and lifeless remnant which had once been Lori. Rose and icy highlights bathed his face, reflections from Vin's mind-display, at which he could not bear to look.

"Who died?" Maggie's face was stricken. "Lori, or Vin?"

"I don't know." Yoshiko put a hand on Maggie's arm, comforting her. "Lori's body, for sure. But I think the Vin we knew was already gone."

The corridor's lighting was bright, almost obscenely harsh. Luculenti filed past them, heading outside to waiting flyers.

Jana and Edralix silently joined Yoshiko and Maggie. Together, they followed the Luculenti—past the observation room where Xanthia was held—back to the main entrance area. The huge windows were transparent once more, offering a view of armed proctors in the night, of their flyers hovering like patient bees.

A Luculentus, whom Yoshiko vaguely recognized from the Aphelion Ball, bowed to her.

"It was a good Passing." His smile was sad. "What more can one hope for?"

Yoshiko swallowed, unable to reply. The Luculentus nodded, and rejoined a group of his departing peers.

Tetsuo is one of these.

Major Reilly was waiting for them. They all sat down on a semicircular couch surrounding a low suspensor-table. Reilly waved away its offer of refreshments.

Jana leaned forwards. "Are you going to arrest Rafael de la Vega, Major?"

Reilly shook her head.

"He's got an alibi. SatScan and other surveillance places him elsewhere."

Golden fire glimmered in the obsidian depths of Jana's eyes. The blood drained from Reilly's face.

"I didn't say I believe the scans," Reilly said swiftly. "But I'm lacking what you might call admissible evidence."

The golden lights slowly died in Jana's eyes, and Reilly's relief was palpable.

"How did he know Yoshiko would be here?" asked Edralix.

"Hmm." Reilly looked thoughtful. "It was a reasonable assumption, if he had found that Lorelei or Lavinia Maximilian were here."

Lori. Vin. Everything was dreadful.

Yoshiko fought hard to concentrate on the conversation.

"I'll bet—" Reilly looked grim. "—he didn't count on two Pilots being here."

"I forgot to mention something." Yoshiko directed her remarks at Jana and Edralix, as much as at Major Reilly. "Someone planted smartatom bugs on me. I went to a place in Lucis yesterday, to get them swept."

"Successfully?"

"I thought so. Actually, they self-destructed as soon as they detected the scan."

"Oh, really?" Reilly's expression revealed nothing. "I wouldn't expect civilian tech to behave that way."

"This Rafael seems quite resourceful," said Edralix. "Perhaps he tried to find out what Yoshiko knew about her son's whereabouts. When she destroyed the bugs, he decided he had to silence her."

"Perhaps."

And then Yoshiko knew.

There are three timings in strategy, and this called for *tai no sen*—to wait for the attack, body calm and immobile, while the mind raced with possibilities.

Rafael, my enemy.

"Major Reilly—do you believe Rafael will try to kill me again?"

Reilly looked at her sharply. "That's a possibility. But we're obviously alerted."

"I wonder." Yoshiko spoke slowly. "Could you make that more obvious? Keep guards posted, whatever?"

"Standard procedure."

"Yes, but I was thinking of something, well, ostentatious. So that physical attack will be the last thing on Rafael's mind."

The area was quite deserted now. The Luculenti had left. The lone receptionist was bent over his desk, carefully ignoring them.

Proctors still patrolled the grounds outside.

Yoshiko turned to Jana and Edralix. "What do you know of Luculenti communication? Of what happened tonight, in the Baton Ceremony?"

Edralix cleared his throat. "Well—in general, they communicate by line-of-sight fast-comm links—which strictly speaking are not in Skein—or through Skein itself. Is that what you're getting at?"

"And the ceremony?"

"Deep scan. The elder passing on edited thoughts, memories, to her successor. The thing is, to scan that deeply, you're going to heisenberg the original into chaos. That's why the elder chooses to die."

"Chooses?" Yoshiko felt cold.

"Lori's physical death was caused by a euthanasia toxin. Self-administered, before the ceremony started."

"And if she hadn't taken it—?"

"You've seen Xanthia."

"Yes." Yoshiko let out a long, shaky breath. "Yes, I have."

Tai no sen. To wait for the enemy.

Yoshiko got up, and stood by the window. Her reflection was a pale and insubstantial ghost. The black night was real.

Wait for the enemy's commitment. Then counterstrike.

Finally, she rejoined the others.

"Lori made a suggestion." She forced her voice to remain steady. "Though she did not mean it quite literally—but there is an offworld quota."

A frown etched Jana's pointed features.

"I don't understand," said Reilly.

"Oh, no." Maggie stood up. "Yoshiko, you can't mean it."

"If Rafael can't reach me physically—" Yoshiko looked at Major Reilly. "—then he'll have to strike through Skein."

"A Judas goat," breathed Jana.

Reilly frowned.

Maggie said, "She's talking about upraise. Becoming a Luculenta."

"That's impossible."

"No." Jana's jet-black eyes glinted. "That's perfect."

Chapter Twenty-Nine

Black night's stars: silver
Flowers in inky fields.
Small as an ant: I'm waving.

Chasms fell away beneath him: sheer planes, steely grey ribbed with black, around which angular darts and polygons flew. A shower of crystal spheres flew past, and each contained a universe of visions, mathematical realms and seafaring vessels, poetry and picnics, music and—

"Tetsuo?"

Flicker: just inside the habitable zone, sitting on a fallen tree at the forest's edge. Morning mist steamed at the forest's edge.

"I don't—"

Turquoise info-waves crashed upon him, each a tumult of voices and white noise—so strange, these inconsistent fragments, as though he were missing something important—and twisted jangling constructs fell among the paths of his nervous system.

Then his mind twisted apart as the universe expanded: *blazing avenues stretching along twenty dimensions, more, all at right angles to each other, and he screamed inwardly as he tried to encompass impossible perspectives on endless data, shapes and communication-forms beyond simple primate comprehension.*

"Are you alright?"

Something . . .

Suddenly, it was there. Urgent and malevolent, an awful sense of presence, of something or someone terribly aware of all he was, of all the petty fears which made him Tetsuo. It reached inside him with protocols like pincers, with code-like claws, burrowing into the computations of his mind—

Out.

"Talk to me, Tetsuo." Dhana's small strong hands pulled off his resp-mask. A faint ammoniac whiff in the air, but otherwise fine to breathe. "What's going on?"

"Oh, God—"

Realms of data, questing phantoms . . .

"—I think I just logged on to Skein."

Dhana looked around urgently. "Keep your voice down."

<<<MsgRcv LUCCOM213900; cause = Skeinlink revoked.>>>

"Sorry." Tetsuo pinched the bridge of his nose between his fingers. "I won't do it again, if I can help it."

How could he explain? For a moment, he had existed in dimensions beyond human understanding.

"They're pitching the bubbles."

On a ridge overlooking a wooded dell, the air shimmered slightly. A disembodied hand briefly appeared behind it—one of the Agrazzi reaching through the smartatom chameleon-film for something—and a slightly shifted foreground image accompanied it: a dark circle, a hand appearing to reach into the dome-shaped disturbance. Then both hands were withdrawn, and the dome became quite invisible.

Tetsuo shook his head, feeling nauseated. Illusions in reality, nightmarish mindscapes in Skein. It was too much.

"Over here." Brevan beckoned.

Tetsuo stumbled twice as they walked, but Dhana was there to steady him.

Among the roots of a giant mossy tree, Brevan had set up a smart-atom bubble, still opaque. Kerrigan and Avern were inside already.

Tetsuo and Dhana ducked inside, then Brevan followed and sealed the gap, and spoke urgent instructions into his wrist terminal. Inside the tentlike bubble, nothing changed. Outside, Tetsuo hoped, light falling at every angle onto the bubble was partially redirected around it, and amplified and retransmitted in the original direction.

"I can't see the tower."

"Over there, between the forked trees."

"Got it."

They all watched the terraformer tower. Tetsuo's nerves grew steadier.

"Are you sure they're coming?" Dhana asked impatiently.

Kerrigan glanced at her." "Bound to be. Any—"

"There."

Hunched over, trying to get a better view, Tetsuo was acutely aware of Dhana pressed beside him, intent on the distant tower.

Predatory flyers slowly circled the tower.

"They're not landing."

"No. I think they're going to—"

There was no explosion.

A low hum, a buzzing which seemed to reach inside Tetsuo's guts, was accompanied by the merest puff of dust from the tower's base. Then, slowly, the tower crumpled and collapsed.

One flyer hovered over the settling dust. Blue lightning stabbed into a sequence of precise points amid the debris.

Then the flyers resumed formation, and steadily glided away.

"My God."

"What about the graser fire?"

Kerrigan looked grim. "Destroying the evidence. Including Federico's Luculentus clone."

Killing their own.

"Nice people."

Tetsuo looked around the faces in the smartatom shelter. Despite their words, none of them looked truly shocked. They had known TacCorps were this ruthless.

"You're bloody mad," he said. "All of you."

The dead girl sat up in bed and smiled.

"Yoshiko. Maggie." Lori's eyes looked out from Vin's sweet face. "It's good to see you."

Yoshiko's skin crawled.

"Vin?" she forced herself to ask. "Are—you all right?"

Scarlet hair, teenage face. Luxuriously appointed room: white and gold, carpet of mobile mandelbrots gently swimming, the med-scanners disguised as ornamental sculptures and decorative glass orbs. Morning sunshine poured through a skylight.

"Oh, Yoshiko." Those young features held an expression of ancient gravitas. "Perhaps you had better call me Lavinia."

"I—yes, OK."

Yoshiko and Maggie sat on faux Louis Quinze chairs, on either side of Vin's—Lavinia's—bed.

Yoshiko felt drained. She and Maggie had stayed overnight in guest rooms here at the med-centre—after Jana and Edralix had left—but sleep had not come easily.

Turning to Maggie, Lavinia said, "Yoshiko remembers Vin saying how much she hated her real name."

Dread crossed Maggie's face as Lavinia continued, "I recall saying those words to Yoshiko, on Ardua Station. But I also remember giving that name to my soul-daughter, when she was designated to me, aged eight."

"Lori?" Yoshiko tentatively asked.

"No, I'm not Lori." Lavinia shook her head. "But so much of Vin was lost, replaced with blank tissue and initialized plexcore lattice, that I am much more Lori than I should have been."

"I'm sorry."

"Don't be." Lavinia shrugged. "Whoever I am, this person you see was born because of what happened. *I am me.* How can I be unhappy that I exist?"

Yoshiko shook her head, and Maggie looked away. This was too much to grasp.

"Hurry now." Kerrigan's voice was abrupt. "Or we'll miss the rendezvous." Beside him, Avern and the other Agrazzus were helping their wounded—and glassy-eyed—comrade to walk.

Tetsuo paused, halfway up a leaf-strewn slope. A lone bird cheeped in a branch above his head.

"Good job he didn't say 'meeting,'" said Tetsuo in a stage whisper. "Wouldn't want to sound like an amateur."

Dhana snickered, then fell silent before Kerrigan's glare.

"You have a problem, Mister Sunadomari?"

"No, sir."

They forced a path among undergrowth, then headed downslope on soft ground. Among the tangled trees, Tetsuo caught a glimpse of white and orange.

A flyer, already landed and waiting for them.

A tall grey-haired Luculenta was there. While the wounded Agrazzus was put aboard her flyer, she conferred with Kerrigan and Brevan.

"Looks like we're honoured," murmured Dhana.

"You mean they're talking about me?"

"Who could blame 'em?"

Tetsuo, trying to think of a smart reply, realized that the Luculenta was walking towards them.

"I'm Felice Lectinaria." The woman's voice was very elegant. "I know Yoshiko."

Tetsuo felt the ground drop away beneath his feet.

"My mother?"

"... and they won't let me log on to Skein for ten bloody days!"

Maggie snorted with laughter, and the tension decreased.

Lavinia had chatted about her boredom in this room, her enforced abstinence from any form of interface. She revealed the sunny disposition of Lori or Vin, Yoshiko thought, and yet was neither.

Maggie sighed. "What about Septor? Shall we send for him?"

Journalistic instinct. Yoshiko smiled inwardly. Maggie's question had gone right to the heart of things.

The expression on Lavinia's face shut down.

"Relationships do not survive a Passing."

"But if you bump into him at a dinner or something—"

"Then we'll be exceedingly polite and formal with each other. There is a protocol which governs such occasions."

Yoshiko intervened before the silence grew awkward.

"What about young Brian?"

A flashing grin.

"He's not bad, is he?" For a moment, it was Vin sitting up in bed. "Can't dance, though."

Yoshiko remembered Vin and Brian in each other's arms, in the ballroom.

Lavinia's expression was suddenly stricken. "I—no, Lori—saw Xanthia. They say it's not my fault, but it was my ware, my safety routines which failed in the laser array."

"It wasn't your fault." There was cold fury in Maggie's voice.

"I don't agree. My house, my system."

"Haven't they told you anything?" asked Maggie. "Although—the med-centre staff can't know much about it, anyway."

"I'm supposed to rest." Lavinia's pale face was tight, and she shivered. "I don't deserve to live—"

Maggie's voice was low and fierce. "Whatever happened to Xanthia, it was Rafael de la Vega who did it."

"Who? Oh, yes. Rafael." Lavinia looked confused. "What could he do? Sabotage the laser array?"

Maggie looked at Yoshiko.

"We think," said Yoshiko softly, "he attacked Xanthia through Luculentus fast comms."

"What? But—There are LuxPrime protocols, safeguards." Lavinia was holding back tears. "And there were hundreds of us there, watching."

"Maybe that was part of the thrill. He could have used something like the scanware from, ah, Baton Ceremonies."

"He scanned Xanthia?"

"Or just initialized her mind." Maggie looked grim. "Scrambled it."

"But—"

"Here." Yoshiko dug in her pocket, then held out the infocrystal. "I don't know about the psychological effect of seeing this. If you're supposed to be resting—"

"Show me," said Lavinia, with an iron grimness neither Lori nor Vin had ever possessed.

"*Warning: stress levels indicate the patient needs rest. Visitors will please leave*—"

"Shut up!" Lavinia's voice was furious as she stopped the display, a hundred frozen dancers around Xanthia's tortured figure.

The med-centre system fell silent.

Yoshiko swallowed. She was not sure this was wise, but she could not have Lavinia torturing herself with misplaced guilt.

"Lavinia—" Maggie took Lavinia's hand, as once more debris fell and Yoshiko knocked Vin out of the way far too late, and Vin's head was a bloody ruin.

"I'm alright." Lavinia froze the display once more. "Federico Gisanthro moved fast."

"Yes." Yoshiko remembered the speed of his sprint across the ballroom floor, straight towards Xanthia. "He reacted very quickly."

"But I don't see Rafael at all. Where is he?"

"That," said Maggie, "is another story."

"I don't know much of this would be admissible in court." Lavinia pointed at the dark shadowy figure, the reconstruction produced by Edralix's analysis.

Maggie, who was also seeing this for the first time, said, "I remember him standing there. Rafael. That's just where he was."

"But your memory could be fooled, by virtue of seeing this. And the Pilots could have faked this analysis, more easily than someone could have edited my house-system's logs."

"You're playing devil's advocate, right?"

"Oh, Yes." Lavinia's face was grim. "In fact, Lori saw Rafael stumbling across the lawns towards the parked flyers. I—she—thought he was sick."

"Not too sick to hack into your house-system."

Yoshiko, who had been observing silently, said, "I don't know. Lavinia, before Lori gave me global authority to the system, weren't the proctors using it?"

"Yes, directing drones. Emergency access."

"There was a Luculentus, a big man, directing engineers—" Yoshiko cast her mind back. "He didn't seem overjoyed when you put me in charge."

"You're saying Rafael had an accomplice?"

"Looks that way. Perhaps Major Reilly can find out who he was."

Maggie shook her head. "How do we know we can trust her? If the accomplice was a proctor, I mean?"

Unsettled, Yoshiko got up from her seat, and paced across the room.

"There's a gym here in the med-centre." Lavinia's voice was amused. "I'm sure they'll let you use it."

"That's what I need, all right. To steady my nerves."

"We've got to know each other pretty well, haven't we?" asked Lavinia. "Considering what a private person you are, and—well, even I don't know who I am, right now."

Yoshiko stared at her. "That's right."

Maggie looked from Lavinia to Yoshiko, frowning.

"So," said Lavinia. "Why don't you tell me what's really on your mind?"

Yoshiko exhaled, calming herself. "First, let me show you the rest of what's on the crystal."

Billowing clouds of light called to mind the Baton Ceremony and Lori's demise, and Yoshiko shivered as though ice had enveloped her.

"Is he even human any more?" Maggie's face looked sickened. "Can we even imagine his thought processes?"

One hundred and two translucent blocks surrounded the central ovoid.

"We need to show this to someone at LuxPrime," said Lavinia. "A mind this size— Perhaps he truly did scan Xanthia, as in a Baton Ceremony, but taking absolutely everything that was her: all her thoughts, all her memories. Everything."

"How often—?" Maggie seemed on the verge of throwing up. "How many times has he done this before?"

"Many, perhaps." Lavinia's face was stony. "Though it's hard to tell. His mind has migrated across all the plexcores. You're right: his thoughts may no longer be remotely human."

"Haven't you people ever thought of this possibility?"

Lavinia shook her head, but said nothing.

"There's a dead LuxPrime courier involved in this," Yoshiko pointed out. "Perhaps Rafael had help in committing the unthinkable."

"Yes." Lavinia looked away. "That's just what it is. Unthinkable."

For a moment, she grew infinitely distant, then she turned back to Yoshiko and focussed on her. "Go on."

Yoshiko nodded at the diagram. "That's not all Edralix found." Yoshiko manipulated the display, and a sphere appeared, tiny nodes dotted across the surface, the joining arcs clearly labelled. "This shows physical separation."

"I don't understand."

"Rafael used my son's comms ware for this."

Maggie looked up. "What do you mean?"

"I understand." Lavinia sounded thoughtful. "Rafael's plexcores are scattered across the face of Fulgor." She turned to Maggie. "He would need instantaneous interfaces, to avoid lightspeed delays."

"Oh," said Maggie. "Mu-space comms. Of course."

"Actually," Lavinia continued, "with a nexus this size, even stacking all the plexcores together in one room would cause problems, without mu-space links. And they certainly wouldn't all fit inside Rafael's body as implants."

"Can Jana do anything?" asked Maggie.

"I don't think so." Yoshiko tried to remember what Jana had said about comms architectures. "Their systems aren't designed with eavesdropping in mind. I don't think they can isolate a particular individual's comms."

"So it's back to Plan A."

"What's Plan A?" asked Lavinia.

"Bait," replied Yoshiko, as Maggie simultaneously said, "A Judas goat."

"I'll call the LuxPrime tech who prepared the ceremony. He was very sympathetic." Lavinia spoke slowly. "There must be tracking ware, debugging modules, what have you. Yes, that's the way." She picked nervously at her lip. "If only integration didn't take so long. I'm not supposed to interface at all for a tenday."

"Er—" Maggie cleared her throat. "I don't think it was you that Yoshiko, had in mind."

"But she isn't a—Oh, I see."

Those young-old eyes seemed to bore into Yoshiko's soul.

Then, "I would be honoured," Lavinia said formally, "to sponsor you for upraise, Professor Sunadomari."

The words seemed to ring deep inside Yoshiko's soul.

Maggie stared into the diagram of Rafael's extended mind.

"Gotcha, you bastard."

Chapter Thirty

Sing songs to Mother.
Shine white hair, brighter than
Moons. There is no "I."

"*Not long now.*" The words sounded close by his ear.

Tetsuo jerked fully awake. He was on a sideways-facing bench seat in the rear of the flyer.

Up front, Felice Lectinaria turned back to look at him intensely. How had her voice sounded so near?

Felice turned to Kerrigan, sitting up beside her. They seemed to talk fiercely, but then Felice threw back her head and laughed.

"How are you do—?" Tetsuo started to ask Dhana, but she was scrunched up beside him, fast asleep. "Never mind."

Avern was watching over the wounded Agrazzus, now on a stretcher. Brevan and the remaining Agrazzus, seated opposite Tetsuo, were playing *go* using their wrist terminals.

No windows. Tetsuo stared up towards the front. Beyond Kerrigan's shock of white hair, he could see the Devindrani Mountains, blue-tinged and forested. Grey clouds smudged the darkening sky.

He sat back and watched the patterns of black and white stones floating between Brevan and his opponent, above a fine translucent grid.

Strategy. Tetsuo was not even sure why he was here. His only objective was to go along with the flow.

And to find out about Mother. So far, Felice had told him only that she was staying with friends. Luculenti friends.

The flyer dropped sharply in to land, flipping Tetsuo's stomach and waking Dhana.

"Can you wait a moment, Tetsuo?" called Felice, as the doors liquefied and the Agrazzi began to disembark.

Clean mountain air wafted in, clearing Tetsuo's head.

"All right."

Dhana winked back at him as she stepped out.

When everyone had left—besides the unconscious wounded man, whom Felice was taking elsewhere for treatment—the doors hardened and grew opaque, and the cabin lights grew dim.

"So what did you want to—?"

[[The eagle flew at him, wings beating, pinions tearing . . .]]

"My God!" He crossed his forearms in front of his face, just as the eagle vanished.

"Sorry," said Felice.

"Very funny." He wiped sweat from his forehead with his sleeve. "Why do you have a holoprocessor back here, anyway?"

"I don't, young man."

It had been a few years since anyone had called him that, and he laughed.

"So what did I just see?"

"Close your eyes."

<<kinaesthetic: freefall>>

<<proprioreceptive: strength in his outspread wings>>

<<video: below him, the Devindrani Mountains>>

Tetsuo snapped his eyes open, and jerked upright.

"The first image was a [public vision]. Had there been any other Luculenti present, they, too, would have seen the eagle." Felice's voice was soft, but every word dripped into his awareness with awful clarity. "The second was a <private send>: for your eyes—and every other sense organ—only."

"I guess the op worked, then."

"Yes. But we knew that, didn't we?" In the dim cabin, Felice's eyes seemed to shine. "Have you tried to log on to Skein yet? Tell the truth."

"No—But I nearly managed it, anyway."

He told her about the mind-twisting visions, the feeling of closeness with an observing malevolent spirit.

"Don't do it again."

"I wasn't planning to."

"I'm serious, Tetsuo. There are NetAngels questing through Skein for you right now, and they may not all belong to proctors. You have deadlier enemies."

Tetsuo pushed aside his growing dread: "There's no need to be mysterious. Just explain, in easy words."

"I will. Later. And I promise I will argue your case with the proctors." Felice held up a comms relay, which Kerrigan, no doubt, had given to her. "This is powerful evidence."

"Sure." Unauthorized copy though it was, Tetsuo's name was still on the ware's copyright. It could damn him more easily than it could clear him.

"Just don't get arrested in the meantime."

Knowing he was being dismissed, Tetsuo clambered out of the flyer.

"Stinking Rogavdarian!"

A small boy sprinted out of the undergrowth, followed by three bigger lads.

"I suggest," said Tetsuo, standing in front of the trio and sucking in his stomach, "that you return to camp."

Beside him, Dhana said nothing as they looked hard at Tetsuo. Then they turned away without a word, drifted back down a wooded path, and were lost from sight.

"So—" Tetsuo turned to the fugitive.

"Yeah? What do you want?" The boy spat. "A medal?"

Laughing, he ran off into the forest.

"Charming." Tetsuo shook his head. "What sept were the other three?"

"Segradorvedes, from their jumpsuit insignia." Dhana shrugged. "Your friend was a Rogavdarian."

"A stinking one, as I recall."

Side by side, they walked along the leafy trail. Once, an owl called. Shortly afterwards, two more skimmed between the branches overhead. Tetsuo shivered, recalling the specimens they had freed.

They came out on a ridge. Below them, the slopes arced down to the head of a wooded valley.

"These demos," Tetsuo said. "They're going to be peaceful protests?"

The evening sky was reflected in Dhana's eyes, glinting from smartgel or from incipient tears.

"Yes, they are."

"I hope—" Tetsuo looked downslope. "—I won't have to remind you later that you said that."

Down below in the encampment, a thousand skimmers moved like bright beetles, while the dark ants that were Shadow People milled among the rows of tents.

Their eyes held hints of dangerous knowledge, of unnerving sights which had stripped away their humanity.

Is he even human any more? That was the question Maggie had asked earlier, regarding Rafael. But now, seeing the piercing yet otherworldly stares of these three men, Yoshiko wondered how far down that path the LuxPrime techs themselves had ventured.

They wore ceremonial helmets, like pewter claws across their skulls, and their clothes were uniformly of burgundy and green. They should have looked ridiculous, but instead they appeared cold and hard and infinitely distant.

Yoshiko wore only a one-piece leotard-suit, which left her arms and feet bare. She shivered, though the chamber was not cold.

"Luculenta Candidate Sunadomari." A narrow-faced tech addressed her. "If you would, please—"

The waiting pallet floated in a column of amber sunlight, streaming from the crystal ellipse which formed the chamber's ceiling. In the shadows at the room's edge, Maggie stood by Lavinia's bedside, both of them intently watching Yoshiko.

Yoshiko climbed onto the floating pallet, and carefully assumed the lotus position. She unsealed the leotard, and slipped it down around her waist. She placed her hands on her knees, palms up, and controlled her breathing.

I don't want to do this.

It shone brilliantly in the sunlight.

She was too old to change. What if it altered her core personality, the very self she had built through decades of self-discipline?

The small cylinder, held by mag-fields, floated beside her pallet.

For Tetsuo's sake—

She shuddered as the cylinder, her plexcore, drew closer, and a kaleidoscope of shifting rainbows played across its surface: smartatom femtofactors coming to life, destined for brief but intense existence.

There is no pain.

It touched her bare stomach: searing heat and bitter cold; abrasive roughness that was silky smooth; shuddering joy and tearing agony.

It entered.

At some deep cellular level, she knew: femtofactors furiously pushed aside or tore apart the skin and fat, the interlaced tissue where abdominal muscles joined, as the plexcore insinuated itself among her organs. Skin healing, closing shut. The tendinous raphe, the seam between her stomach muscles, was reconstructed by femtofactors left behind as the plexcore bored deep inside.

She closed her eyes.

No pain.

Pushing aside where it could, tearing and rebuilding where it must, the plexcore sidled past blood vessels, the coeliac trunk, repairing damaged lymph nodes, and crawled upwards.

Extruding protein filaments to hold itself in place, the plexcore shunted into final position.

I will not cry out.

Among muscles, femtofactors repaired actin and myosin, rearranged the structural stroma proteins to their original configuration. In damaged nerves, they rebuilt neurofibrillae, reconstructed the cytoplasmic matrix of every injured cell.

As repair-femtofactors completed their tasks and died, deconstructing themselves, others directed the products harmlessly into Yoshiko's bloodstream, to the renal artery. The next time she urinated, fragments of billions of dead femtofactors would be flushed from Yoshiko's body.

Now it begins.

How could she know this? She felt, with a deep awareness, the insinuation of femtofactors along her neurons, as the interface construction began. Synaptic arrays formed across the end-feet of axons. The comms-substrate spread upwards, through hindbrain—rhombencephalon—and cerebellum, up into the deep structures of the brain, and onwards.

There was no single moment of transition, but at some point she realized the plexcore had powered up, and its VSI code was already exploring the network of her mind.

"We have success."

Yoshiko opened her eyes.

Vertigo. A dizzying sense of dislocation.

"The implant—" The LuxPrime tech's thin face seemed almost to float, disembodied, whitened by the shaft of sunlight. "—is successful."

A piercing whistle split the solemn atmosphere.

"Yo, Yoshiko!" At the room's shadowed edge, Maggie raised a triumphant fist. "Way to go!"

Everything glowed with an inner light: the smooth pallet, the soft fabric covering the floor, the techs' ascetic faces. The shadows, cloaking Maggie and Lavinia, held their own palpable warmth. Sitting in the sunlight falling from the skylight was like bathing in liquid gold.

"We won't be implanting headgear until later," said a LuxPrime tech. "The plexcore is partitioned for minimum functionality, and its basic integration will proceed very rapidly."

Every word seemed tinged with nuance and harmonics, complex and immediate.

The second man added, "You understand, it will be several tendays before we can enhance the plexcore, remove its internal partitioning."

"I understand." Yoshiko, still sitting on the pallet, pulled up her leotard and sealed it.

Her spine seemed to have grown straighter, her skin smoother and more sensitive. Even in lotus, she was preternaturally aware of her own balance, of the subtle perturbations and corrections in the pallet's levfield.

The timbre of her voice had subtly shifted, and she was more aware of her ability to control it. "I can log on to Skein, though?"

"Sufficiently, yes. Much of the Skein is configured for phase-space perceptions of five dimensions and upwards. But the rest is available to you."

"I—can't thank you enough for doing this. When Lavinia said she'd sponsor me, I thought the process would take days, at least."

The third LuxPrime tech stepped forward. He had been silent until now.

"My name is Dougan Farsteen." It did not need Yoshiko's new awareness to pick up the dark harmonics in his voice. "Whatever you need—" The man swallowed, and for a moment Yoshiko glimpsed nascent tears. "Whoever it was, we'll help you trap them."

The other two techs looked away.

There was a hint of questioning in his tone, also. Though using only voice, it was a Luculentus-to-Luculenta communication: a plea for more information, which he was certain Yoshiko held.

Lavinia had told LuxPrime of their suspicions, the possibility that Xanthia had undergone scanning as in a Baton Ceremony, from scanware which infiltrated LuxPrime defences. The likelihood that this was involved with Adam Farsteen's death.

She had said nothing about the attacker's presumed identity.

If LuxPrime suspected Rafael, they would immediately contact the proctors. But the hacking of the Maximilians' house system, and the smartatom bugs which had been planted on Yoshiko—"*I wouldn't expect civilian tech to behave that way*," Major Reilly had said—all spoke of peacekeeper involvement. Corruption among the proctors? They could not risk the possibility that Rafael might be warned, maybe even protected.

"Are you ready to proceed with the integration?"

"Yes."

Judas goat.

"As soon as we have interface, we'll present you in Skein."

Tethered to a virtual tree, waiting for the predator to strike.

"I'm ready."

THREAD ONE

<touch>

Smooth, wooden
floor. Naginata's
familiar haft.

THREAD TWO
<proprioreceptive>
Kneeling, sitting
back on her heels.
Pulse quickening.

THREAD THREE
<scent>
Citrus and pine.
Polished floor,
mountain air.

THREAD FOUR
<visual>
Facing her, the
stern warrior with
Yoshiko's face.

<<<MsgRcv LUXPRM888210; cause = SkeinLink modules installed.>>>

Leaping from the kneeling position, the warrior launched herself at Yoshiko, halberd whirling like a propellor. Yoshiko jumped back, retreating from the demon which bore her own face, beating the naginata aside with her own.

The warrior came in at an angle, cutting off a sideways retreat, forcing Yoshiko back along the polished dojo floor.

Outside, pine forests on mountain slopes lay beyond the opened screens.

The warrior kept coming: implacable, fierce, unstoppable as a hurricane.

It wasn't supposed to be like this.

Every counterstrike Yoshiko made was smacked aside, and the demon-warrior, the kami-Yoshiko, kept on coming. Its naginata's blade whipped past Yoshiko's throat, and she knew that she could die here for real.

Yoshiko was terrified.

Acknowledging her fear, admitting it to herself, she stood her naginata on end, and waited for death to strike.

"*Eeeee!*"

The shadow warrior struck and Yoshiko gave in to her fear, flinching and crouching, but the flinch became a spin and as the blade came at her she cut sideways to *kote*, against the wrist. Her crouch became a leap forward into a kneeling position and she struck in *kesa* style, all or nothing, no defence, thrusting forward and hooking up and her blade bit into her opponent's larynx and tore its life away.

<<<MsgRcv LUXPRM888220; cause = SkeinLink interface initiated.>>>

A wind howled across the formless void, and these were the words it spoke:

"Here is the extra code you will need."

[[[HeaderBegin: Module = Node728A.3219 Type = Quaternary-HyperCode: Axes = 256

Priority = absolute

Status = resident always

Concurrent_Execute

ThreadOne:<LuxPrime interface>.linkfile = LockChannelZero

ThreadTwo:<rhombencephalon channel>. linkfile = Lock-ChannelOne

ThreadThree:<intrapeduncular matrix>.linkfile = LockChannel-Two

ThreadFour:<thalamic/cerebral matrix>.linkfile = LockChannel-Three

End_Concurrent_Execute]]]

Modules that could hold infiltration code in an iron grip until Lux-Prime rescue came.

Night fell, black upon black.

Over an infinite silver plain of snow, the endless night grew a galaxy of stars. Meteors fell, comets blazed, and the stars rearranged themselves into words.

WE WILL PRESENT YOU NOW.

Great wings flapped in unison, and the chill draught took her breath away.

The three pairs of winged horses banked downwards, and Yoshiko's chariot—its huge dragonfly wings glinting where sunlight struck—followed their arcing trajectory.

Triumphant joy filled her as she glided in above a quicksilver road. Bordered by pillars of blue flame, it floated above a plain of gold and silver squares.

The chariot settled upon a hovering dais, and Yoshiko stepped down as chariot and horses became twisting columns of scented smoke which broke apart, dissipated, and were gone.

She stood alone, in a vast auditorium, and a hundred thousand upturned faces gazed upon her.

The voice came from everywhere, the vibrations of the universe itself.

"WE PRESENT TO YOU . . . LUCULENTA YOSHIKO SUNADOMARI.

"BID HER WELCOME TO OUR STRATUM."

The applause was deafening, a crashing roar of tidal sound.

Yoshiko bowed.

<<MsgRcv LUCCOM213900; cause = SkeinLink revoked.>>>

The three LuxPrime techs were bowing to her. Silently, they turned and filed out from the silent chamber.

The oval ceiling was a huge eye upon a green-tinged sky. The light it cast had shifted angle: hours had passed, though it might as easily have been seconds, or many years.

Accompanied by Maggie, Lavinia's bed moved across the floor, drawing close to the pallet upon which Yoshiko still sat.

"Luculenta Yoshiko Sunadomari." Lavinia was smiling, though tiredness webbed her face. "My congratulations."

"Not bad." Maggie winked. "Do I curtsy, or what?"

Chapter Thirty-One

Chrysanthemums in spring.
Memory fades, blooms shine.
Again, time to dance.

Black clouds, lit up by lightning. Winds howled across the blasted heath. A small straggle-haired crone bent over a steaming cauldron, whose glow cast her oriental features in deathly green.

There were wisps of random colour, vagueness replacing sharp outlines. Resolution failure. Losing focus.

Control. Concentrate.

"When shall we three meet again?" The crone leered. "In thunder, lightning, or in rain?"

"Nice one."

"Hush. Don't interrupt her."

A second witch, scarlet hair streaked with white: "When the hurly burly's done."

"Hey, I think I recognize that one."

"When Yoshiko has had her fun."

"So who could this be?"

The third witch performed a parody of a dance. "When Rafael's bad code can't run."

"Not me, for sure."

"Oh, really?"

Then the three old women joined hands over the cauldron and chanted, while the cold winds blew revenge.

"Fair is foul, and foul is fair:

"We'll catch the bugger anywhere."

<<<MsgSnd DEVCOM284700; cause = device termination requested.>>>

"Bravo!"

<<<MsgRcv DEVCOM284701; cause = device terminated on request.>>>

"Nicely done, Yoshiko."

Maggie and Lavinia clapped hands in mocking applause as Yoshiko withdrew from interface and the terminal powered down.

Yoshiko blinked, and rubbed her eyes.

"Very impressive." Lavinia lay back in her bed, looking weak but alert. "The LuxPrime guys went to town on device interfaces. But that's your natural imagination taking form in those images."

"Not bad for an Earther, eh?" Maggie said.

Yoshiko performed some neck rotations.

"Hard work, huh?" Maggie's hand made a short gesture towards her pocket, then stopped.

She was obviously dying to get her video-globe out, to capture a new Luculenta's first unsteady steps to interface.

"Go on, Maggie, for God's sake. If you want to record anything, that's fine."

"You mean it? I won't prepare a NewsNet item until—later."

"I know that." While Maggie readied her video-globe, Yoshiko turned to Lavinia. "Can I try editing ware? Amending the code in my mind?"

Lavinia's already pale face grew deathly white.

"Don't even think about it."

"But I can see the code, if I just kind of—"

"No." Lavinia's words held an icy intensity. "That's the danger, to look at the low-level code of your own mind. You're only aware of it now because you're still integrating. Later—later, movement through Skein, manipulating devices, forming images in fast-comm links, all become second nature. Like breathing."

As she mentioned breathing, Lavinia lay back, taking fast shallow breaths.

Maggie looked concerned.

"It's all right," Yoshiko said. "I get the message. I won't edit my own mindware. OK?"

Lavinia turned her head on the pillow to face Yoshiko, and smiled wanly.

Glass tears, floating.

"Isn't that your friend from Ardua Station?" Maggie pointed to the red-bearded image trapped inside a teardrop icon.

Eric Rasmussen. Forcing herself not to gesture, Yoshiko focussed intensely.

Nothing happened.

Lavinia, who had turned her head on her pillow to watch Yoshiko's attempt to check h-mail without gestures or voice, said softly, "Don't try so hard."

No—yes. The teardrop unfurled.

"Hi, Yoshiko." Eric tugged at his unruly beard. "Er—I decided to take leave. I'm going to be on Fulgor next Sez'Day. Perhaps we can meet up at some point? Er—Endit."

"Nice one," said Maggie.

When Yoshiko looked at her, she added, "Being able to access the message just by looking at it. That's all I meant."

There was a snort of laughter from the bed.

"Oh, good grief." Yoshiko pinched the bridge of her nose. "You two are a great help."

"We try to be."

"Come on, Lavinia. No, we don't."

"You're right. We don't."

Yoshiko sighed. "Can I just concentrate on getting the other message?"

"Don't let us stop you."

"Go ahead, Yoshiko. Say, Lavinia. Isn't today Sez'Day?"

"Now you come to mention—"

"All right, all right." What could she say? "Look, Eric's a nice guy, all right? But I hardly know him, and I've—other things to worry about."

"Sorry."

"Yes. Sorry."

Their apologies sounded unconvincing.

"So who's the other message from?"

"You think she's got *two* boyfriends? What a disgrace."

Yoshiko cleared her throat, and the heckling stopped. She turned her attention on the remaining teardrop.

Bright shards arranged themselves into a sharp-featured Luculenta crowned with grey hair. Felice Lectinaria.

"Luculenta Yoshiko Sunadomari: warmest greetings." In the image, Felice inclined her head in a regal bow. "I would like to offer my congratulations in person. I shall be at the Primum Stratum conference centre today, Sez'Day, in auditorium three alpha.

"Perhaps we can discuss the paper I sent you? Endit."

The image faded.

Maggie said, "She wants to talk about Tetsuo, doesn't she?"

Yoshiko was capable of receiving a realtime SkeinLink comm, but Felice Lectinaria would not have expected that, so soon after upraise. It was logical to communicate via h-mail.

Perhaps the LuxPrime techs should have given Yoshiko the ability to initiate a SkeinLink.

"What are you going to do, Yoshiko?"

"I guess— I'm going to a conference."

Maggie used her wrist terminal to check arrival times—Eric's shuttle was due to land in less than two hours—while Lavinia discussed tactics.

"Execute the lock-code, at the first hint of anything unusual."

"Right." Yoshiko's voice sounded more confident than she felt. The lock-code should stop Rafael's code from infiltrating her mind, but keep the comms-session locked so that LuxPrime techs could trace it back to him. But if they did not know exactly what Rafael's code did, how could they know their countermeasures would work?

"With luck," said Lavinia, "the code will execute automatically, without your even willing it. There's nothing to worry about."

Maggie flicked off her display. "I've ordered a taxi, Yoshiko. You can drop me off at the conference centre, meet Eric at the spaceport, and come back to the conference centre to meet Felice Lectinaria."

"Er—"

"Or I can come straight to the spaceport with you first, and we can both meet this Eric."

"Wait a minute." Lavinia held her hand up. "Yoshiko, just a simple addition to your code—"

```
[[[HeaderBegin: Module = Node38V7.2215 Type = TrinaryHyper-
        Code: Axes = 27
    Priority = absolute
    Status = resident always
    Execute
        contact = [[Luculenta Lavinia Maximilian, ident6654χ8•ϵ
            {sept5ΘΞ}]]
        LockChannelZero.append(SkeinLink(contact))
    End_Execute]]]
```

Lavinia, trembling, lay back.

"You're not supposed to interface." Maggie, concerned, looked around as though for help.

"I'm OK. Yoshiko—that will notify me, if your lock code activates."

"Thank you, Lavinia."

Maggie stood up, and straightened her jacket. The video-globe bobbed above her shoulder.

"I guess we should be going. Are you sure you'll be OK, Lavinia?"

"I'm in the biggest med-centre in Lucis City."

"That's a yes, then." Maggie leaned over and kissed Lavinia's cheek. "Take it easy."

"You, too."

Yoshiko and Lavinia clasped hands.

Maggie was the first to reach the door. She stepped through, with Yoshiko on her heels.

A giant figure stepped into their path, blocking their way.

Grey rain misted across the encampment.

"Watch out!"

It coated the dripping trees, turned the ground to mud, made everything slippery to the touch.

"I've got it."

Straining, Tetsuo hefted the wet crate up into the flyer's hold, earning respectful glances from his smaller Simnalari companions.

Dhana tapped on his shoulder. "Our flyer's about to lift."

"Right." He nodded to the Simnalari. "See you, guys."

"Cheers, Tetsuo."

Rain plastered his short hair to his scalp, and trickled down his smartgel-coated skin. Feeling strangely lighthearted in the cold, damp air, he and Dhana made their way across the churned-up ground to a battered old cargo flyer.

"You're settling in." Dhana peered at him from under her jump-suit's peaked hood. "You didn't have to help them."

"I know."

He helped her aboard, and scrambled inside himself.

"What are you doing here?" A youth, staring at Tetsuo's headgear.

Along the rows of seats, people turned to look.

Tetsuo nodded in Dhana's direction. "I'm with her."

"Oh, right." The youth looked at Dhana, and grinned. "That's cool."

Dhana snorted. "Can you keep the noise down?" She leaned back in her seat and closed her eyes. "Some of us need rest."

The youth winked, and turned to talk to his own companion.

Guido. That was the name. Yoshiko remembered seeing him, when she had called Federico. This was the man who had fought so brutally, injuring his subordinates.

"I'm very sorry, Professor." Beside her, a young man spoke. It was Brian Donnelly, the young proctor with whom Lavinia—Vin, then—had danced. "We're supposed to keep you under guard."

"We know that." Maggie's voice was sharp. "That's the whole idea. You're supposed to come with us—" She gestured down the corridor, where half a dozen more fit-looking men and women, all armed, stood watching. "—along with the rest of your people."

Guido shrugged his massive shoulders.

"You ain't goin' anywhere."

Yoshiko remembered: Federico had assigned TacCorps members to Major Reilly's team. It had not occurred to her that Federico's people might outrank the other proctors assigned to her.

Brian Donnelly looked thoroughly intimidated.

"You can't detain this woman," said Maggie, "She's a Luculenta."

"Can't see any pretty headgear."

"You—"

"Never mind." Yoshiko laid a hand on Maggie's arm. "Let's not argue with the man."

Guido breathed in, and tensed the great slabs of muscle in his chest, his massively swollen arms.

"Sensible move, ladies."

"Come on." Yoshiko led Maggie back inside.

Bright holo banners danced above the sea of bobbing heads, like orange ribbons caught in the breeze. Against the greyish sky, tainted with washed-out green, the letters fluoresced with unnatural clarity.

OUT OF THE SHADOWS

Like a human river, they flowed down the emerald slopes, heading for the extended buildings of the Primum Stratum conference centre. Widespread white wings, the building's hovering roof, glowed in contrast to the surrounding gloom.

Tetsuo looked back. On the ridge, a score of flyers was parked. Like flocking birds, more vessels were spiralling in to land.

"You OK?" Dhana squeezed his hand.

"Sure." At least the rain had not reached this far.

He had never been among a crowd this big. With an unsettling singularity of purpose, the marchers moved slowly but steadily along.

"Look."

Beyond the conference centre, an orbital shuttle was swooping in to land at Cicanda Spaceport.

Mother. It was an unavoidable reminder that she was here, on this world. She must be worried sick about him, and he had no way of contacting her.

A plaza lay before the conference centre. As the crowd's vanguard reached it, a small group of proctors came out of the building. One of them, Tetsuo thought, spoke briefly into a comm-ring.

Ragged cheers rose from the crowd, as the vastly outnumbered proctors disappeared back indoors.

Drops fell, spattering Tetsuo's forehead.

A wave of movement passed through the crowd, jostling Tetsuo, but he kept hold of Dhana. Her hand felt small in his, cold but electric.

Overhead, dark thunderheads were gathering. Only the faintest green bled through, like the juices from crushed grass.

Tetsuo looked up.

"Storm's coming."

Chapter Thirty-Two

Falling above mourners, white
Clouds cherish
Sunlight. There are fields to till.

This wasn't protection. This was house arrest.

Outside, Yoshiko's way was blocked by the worst of obstacles: a man twice her body weight, twice her strength. As highly trained as she was, but used to inflicting real and bloody damage on hard opponents. Ruthless, contemptuous of weaker beings.

Yoshiko had come across the type: the big psychopath who can take the discipline, who loves to cause pain. A bully who is most definitely not a coward.

She had no illusions. Guido would be as fast as her, but far stronger, harder, and more vicious.

"Maggie. Go out to the taxi. They won't stop you, on your own."

"But—"

"Please. If I'm not out in five minutes, could you go to meet Eric and Felice?"

"Of course." Maggie jammed her hands in her pockets, and frowned angrily. "We should contact Major Reilly. You're supposed to be under protection, not—"

Lavinia spoke weakly. "Yoshiko slipped away from their surveillance before. They want to keep track of her."

Maggie stared. "You think TacCorps planted the smartatom bugs on Yoshiko?"

"It's consistent, isn't it?"

"Not Rafael?"

"Major Reilly as good as told us— Bugs dissolving under scan. Not the way *civilian* tech should work."

"But Rafael—"

"Is to blame for—" Yoshiko glanced at Lavinia. "—what happened at the ball. But maybe not for editing the video-logs, for placing me under surveillance."

"Bloody hell."

Perhaps, too, Guido was under orders to intimidate Yoshiko, to make her crack, to spill everything she knew and guessed and feared. Mentally replaying her last conversation with Federico Gisanthro, she could see now the unresolved suspicion in his strange pale eyes, the hint of tension. He had known there was something Yoshiko was holding back.

A tidal rush of sound, her own blood circulation near her ears, overlaid her friends' conversation.

"Please go, Maggie."

"I—OK. What are you going to do?"

"I don't know."

Maggie left.

Was there nothing she could use as a weapon? Her naginata was at Lavinia's house. As for her tanto dagger—she'd given that to Eric on Ardua Station.

I'm scared.

She could visualize a big fist heading for her face—

OK.

Bigger and stronger. Contemptuous.

Think. Rethink.

Contempt—

Yes, I've got it now.

Rehearse. Consider all possible reactions.

"Yoshiko—" Lavinia, sounding far away.

She shut out her voice.

Important to keep the centre of gravity, the *hara*, as low as possible.

Yoshiko faced the door. Its surface rippled minutely, liquefied by her presence.

Now.

Guido, massive and frightening, glowered in front of her. His shoulders were the widest Yoshiko had ever seen.

"I told you—"

"No."

She stepped forward, left hand raised to ward him off.

His grip encircled her small frail wrist like an iron bracelet, heavy and unbreakable.

She was so very, very scared.

Ippon seiken.

Tears blurred her vision.

Right fist, centre knuckle protruding.

"Please—" Her voice caught in her throat.

"Leave her—" Young Brian's voice, cut off by a thud.

Don't look.

A huge force jerked her forward by her left wrist.

"Please, don't—"

Big open-hand strike heading for her temple.

Tension in the thumb. Hold the configuration.

Her body was soft, her knees bent in collapse.

Collapsing, and the blow missed, but the other strong hand still encircled her wrist.

Huge hand. Wide. Callused knuckles, protruding veins, black hairs covering sinews and muscle. The sinews' lines. Blood vessels' blue ridges.

Minute awareness. Time slowed down.

Back hand swinging towards her face. No avoidance this time.

Down.

The back of his hand, holding her wrist. Sinews and veins a map, showing her the way.

Strike down.

"Eeee!"

Now.

A lifetime's discipline lay behind the blow.

Her knuckle smashed into the back of Guido's hand. It struck precisely into the nerve point known as TW-3 and Guido dropped like a stone.

He fell on one knee and the snapping sound was like a slap in the face, and then he was lying on his side, cheeks drained of pallor, and the breath was rattling gutturally in his throat.

"My . . . God." It was young Brian, shaken, and ashen-faced.

"Are you all right?" asked Yoshiko.

"Yes—"

"I have to go."

"I—yes, OK." The other proctors were coming down the corridor, and Brian limped forward to meet them. He told them to let Yoshiko through.

"On Major Reilly's authority," he added.

Yoshiko looked back. "That man needs medical attention."

There were grim looks among the proctors, as one of them used her wrist terminal to summon help.

No one stopped Yoshiko as she pushed her way past them.

She was trembling in reaction, but forced herself to walk quickly to the main foyer. She paused briefly at the doors, remembering the graser fire from last night, then steeled herself and walked straight through.

Her skin crawled, but nothing happened.

Maggie waved from a hovering taxi. Yoshiko went down the broad steps to meet it.

"Wait." Brian's voice called from behind her. "I'm coming with you. Orders."

Yoshiko said nothing, but let him catch up.

They slid onto the seat beside Maggie. Immediately the ground dropped away beneath them.

"What happened?" asked Maggie. "How did—?"

"It was unbelievable." Brian stared at Yoshiko, awestruck.

The med-centre dwindled in size. Already, it looked like a child's toy.

"He saw only my weakness." In memory, it was as though Yoshiko had struck without volition, just letting it happen. "Not his own."

Cold and grey, the first wisps floated past, then storm clouds enveloped the taxi in darkness.

The vast atrium was eerily silent. Rows of glass display cases stood like military coffms, waiting to be shipped home.

"I don't like this." Brian's voice was hushed.

In plan view, the conference centre was a linked series of overlapping circles, beneath the hovering wings of the levitating roof. Their taxi had passed over a huge growing crowd of people, a demonstration of some kind, and over the visitors and delegates flocking to the conference here, on the Skein/EveryWare issue.

"Don't worry."

This part of the complex, obviously not booked for the conference, felt unsettling because of the contrast: empty, while thousands, maybe tens of thousands of people were milling around nearby. In here, dead silence.

"You shouldn't meet her alone."

"Don't worry," Yoshiko said again. "She wants to help. We can't risk frightening her off."

"You should at least have let Maggie come with you."

Yoshiko shook her head. "Someone had to meet Eric. And we're running late."

"Well, I'm not going to risk arguing with you." Brian gave a small, crooked smile. He took a black ring from his pocket, and proffered it. "Please take this. If you press the stud, I'll come running."

Grateful for his concern, Yoshiko slipped the ring on.

"Thank you, Brian."

"OK. It was auditorium three alpha, you said?" Using his wrist terminal, he pulled up a schematic of the conference centre. "It's up that way. I'll wait here for you."

As she walked up a curved and sloping hallway, tension prickled Yoshiko's skin.

Had she truly understood Felice's oblique message? Was Tetsuo really still alive?

He's all right. Don't worry.

It was Ken's dear voice, and for a moment she could see his gentle smile.

Oh, Ken.

To feel his fingertips brush against her cheek once more—

By the sweeping doorway, a holo glowed: 3α.

Yoshiko stepped through, into darkness.

"What's this?"

"Lower your head." Dhana slipped the ring around his neck. "A present."

All around them, a sea of people. Many thousands. Every now and then, a wave of motion would pass through the crowd, like a tidal force.

Dhana pressed a stud on the neck-ring. For a moment, everything blurred, and then Tetsuo could see clearly again.

"What is this?"

"A holo-mask. In case the proctors start observing." A wicked smile formed across her gamine face. "Actually, that's quite an improvement. I've always liked blond men."

"Very funny." Tetsuo noticed her shiver slightly as he spoke. "What's wrong?"

"The lip-synch's a bit off. It's kind of scary."

"Hush," said someone. "Proctors're comin'."

Tetsuo stood on tip-toe, using his height to see above the ocean of heads. Beyond the plaza, peacekeeper flyers were disgorging personnel whose jumpsuits were tuned to green, not dark blue.

"What's wrong?" Dhana held his arm and jumped up, trying to see.

"It's the TacCorps."

Shadows hung like bats in the cavernous darkness. Low shapes ranged across a floor so soft that all echoes were absorbed.

"Please don't move." The woman's voice played a glissando of fear down Yoshiko's spine.

Someone there. She touched something and spun, stepped triangularly and spun again.

No one attacked.

A seat. She was in an auditorium and had brushed against a seat, that was all.

Copper sparkles in the blackness overhead. Smartatom mist.

"Don't worry." Three metres above the floor, a cone of white light picked out Felice Lectinaria's haughty features. "I had to check for surveillance. I'm afraid your call-ring has been deactivated."

As she spoke, Felice descended through the darkness, and Yoshiko realized she was on a lev-platform, used by speakers to point out features on giant holo illustrations.

"I have to know—" Yoshiko was breathless. "Is Tetsuo all right?"

"He was fine when I talked to him yesterday."

"Oh, my God." Yoshiko grabbed a nearby chair, and sat down on its arm. "Thank you."

"I'm sorry. I didn't dare tell you more plainly, before now." Felice's tone was brisk, though sympathetic. "May I ask whom the call-ring was intended to contact?"

"A friend." Yoshiko looked up at her. "A trusted friend."

"One needs trustworthy friends, that's for sure." As the lev-platform alighted, Felice stepped off. "Many of mine are among the Shadow People."

"I'm sorry?"

"You saw the demonstration outside? They're representatives of many septs—clans and tribes, if you like—of minorities who live at the edge of what we consider the habitable zones. And often beyond that edge."

"I beg your pardon." Yoshiko's heart was thumping hard. "I know nothing of Fulgidi politics. I just want to know where my son is."

"He's with the Shadow People."

"Here? You mean he's outside, right now?"

"Oh, yes. I can't speak for his political commitment, but he has at least one special friend out there with him."

Yoshiko swallowed. "He's not under duress?"

"Absolutely not. And now, in return for that information—" Felice stopped, as though listening for something, then shook her head. "I want you to have this."

She held out a blue crystal. Yoshiko looked at it without moving.

"It's a comms relay," Felice continued. "A product of illegal research by TacCorps, using unauthorized copies of Tetsuo's ware."

"Why—?"

"I'm about to go public in my support for the Shadow People. There are NewsNet reporters all over the other sections of the complex, where the conference is being held."

Yoshiko accepted the crystal.

There was a scrape of sound, and she whirled, scanning the shadows.

"Don't worry." Felice smiled grimly. "The lev-platforms touch each other sometimes." She pointed to a group of disks suspended near the floor, like a giant child's mobile. "They frightened me at first."

Yoshiko looked down at the crystal in her hand. "Will this show that Tetsuo had nothing to do with that poor man's death? Adam Farsteen, I mean."

"No, but it's a start. A clone of Federico Gisanthro, a Luculentus, was interfaced with animal minds. Or rather, his mind was partially distributed across their brains, and you need mu-space comms to make that work, to remove the lightspeed delay." Felice smiled grimly and added, "We can prove that. We can also prove that your son's ware was stolen to do that job. From there, it's a short step to—"

"Stop. Stop right there." Yoshiko's thoughts whirled, and instinct told her to trust Felice. Rapidly, she said, "Rafael de la Vega has been infiltrating Luculenti minds—at least, Luculentae, female minds—and probably scanning them, absorbing them into his plexcore nexus."

"What? Rafael?" Those haughty features looked shaken. "You're talking about Xanthia Delaggropos. And Rashella Syntharinova."

"There are one hundred and two plexcores in Rafael's nexus," said Yoshiko, as a look of horror crept across Felice's face. "You're talking about research into the same kind of thing . . . "

The things Rafael had done. The nonhuman thing he might become. Felice obviously saw the implications immediately.

"But the TacCorps research was without extra plexcores." Felice was collecting her thoughts. "You can't just buy them from LuxPrime. Perhaps Rafael's found a way to stop them randomizing. I'm talking about grave-robbing—"

A soft, brushing sound. A foot sliding just above the carpet.

"Tell me about plexcores," said Yoshiko, but she was not listening to Felice's reply.

"After death, the plexcore is powered down, and buried. It's supposed basically to self-destruct if someone were to dig it up and try—"

There were two of them, at least. Possibly three.

"Felice!" Yoshiko whispered urgently. "Call for—"

A beam flicked out of the darkness, and Felice fell.

I can't initiate a SkeinLink.

"Guido's not too happy with you." A TacCorps agent, a grim-looking man, walked into the light, aiming a graser at Yoshiko. "In fact, he's rather pissed off."

Try anyway.

Like a child wishing evil ghosts away, Yoshiko concentrated on accessing Skein.

Nothing.

Another TacCorps agent, a short-haired woman, knelt by Felice and checked the pulse in her throat. The woman nodded.

Her colleague kept his graser trained on Yoshiko. He was crouched in a low stance, left hand outstretched, graser held in his right hand close to his body. Aware of Yoshiko's skills, neutralizing any chance of deflecting or seizing the weapon before he could fire.

Anger.

The third shadow moved. For a second, hope leaped as Yoshiko thought it might be Brian, but the figure was far too big.

The thing was to make them angry.

"The trouble with you—" Yoshiko started.

Getting closer.

Make some noise.

"*It's not fair!*" Yoshiko let all her fear and anger rip. "You bastards set my son up for murder and now you're trying to kill me and I just won't have it, do you hear? I JUST WON'T HAVE IT!"

The TacCorps man looked puzzled, then grim, and as his finger tightened on the firing-stud the shadow moved behind him and something dark and polished glinted as it hammered into the man's skull. He dropped like a stone.

The female agent near Felice was straightening up and aiming when Yoshiko grabbed her weapon's barrel and twisted and it fired into the agent's own torso and her face screwed up in pain as she fell.

"Yoshiko."

The woman was dead. Yoshiko had never used her art in anger before today, and now a woman was dead.

Something keened inside Yoshiko, a voice crying to the fallen woman to get up. But the body was an extinct shell, its eyes already coated with death's opacity.

"My God, Yoshiko."

The big bearish man was standing there.

"Oh, Eric."

Then her face was against his massive chest. Eric's strong arms enclosed her. He was warm and solid, infinitely comforting, and she felt safe at last.

A NewsNet broadcast? Irritably, Rafael put the NetAngel on hold.

Luculenta Yoshiko Sunadomari.

He had failed to kill her in person, and peacekeepers had descended in droves on the med-centre to prevent another attempt. Then she had made herself a prize, plump target. A Luculenta!

The NetAngel bleated another comm-request, and he quelled it once more.

He had never risked striking through Skein, for fear of being tracked through audit logs. Always, he had used untraceable line-of-sight fast-comm links. And yet, and yet—

Through Skein, he could subsume anyone, anywhere, without moving from his home.

A third request, and he nearly banished the NetAngel for good. A NewsNet retrieval was hardly likely to reveal his target. His NetAngels were supposed to prowl more promising infoseams.

Sighing, he gave the insistent ghost-Rafael his attention.

THREAD ONE
<video>
Aerial view:
Masses of Shadow
People, gathering.

THREAD TWO
<video>
Zoom and track:
Blond man, heavyset,
features wrong.

THREAD THREE
<video>
Overlay simulation:
The walk.
Superimposed Tetsuo.

THREAD FOUR
<audio>
Long-range pickup:
Girl: "I've always
liked blond men."

Tetsuo! Could it be—?

The simulation overlay pulsed red with an estimated match of seventy-three percent. Tetsuo should have disguised his walk, as well as his face.

If it really was Tetsuo . . .

For a second, the possible-Tetsuo bent close to the blonde-haired girl, and a portion of her cheek seemed to disappear inside the man's face. A holo-mask.

Alive. The only link to Rafael's use of comms tech.

Rafael had failed to kill the mother, but the real prey had crept out into the open, just the same.

Right out in the open.

For a moment, the unfairness of the situation overwhelmed Rafael, then he pushed the feeling to one side.

Focus on one thing: Tetsuo must die.

Quickly, before the proctors could get to him.

NEWS_NET_1:
"Twenty thousand
Shadow People, whom
many of us consider
mere legend, are
gathering here . . ."

NEWS_NET_2:
Phase.state(22)
Tactics.plot
Ramifications.graph

NEWS_NET_3:
<null>

NEWS_NET_4:
LoadTesseract

NEWS_NET_5
"This is Maggie
Brown, speaking for
NewsNet 5, on the
scene at the Primum
Stratum . . . "

Twenty thousand witnesses. Unless . . .

[[Luculentus Tetsuo Sunadomari, ident4001A2.001]]

<<<MsgRcv LUCCOM213886; cause = SkeinLink unavailable.>>>

Damn it. No response from Tetsuo's ident.

He might have risked it, striking at Tetsuo through Skein, but the dumb bastard was not capable of logging on. It was almost embarrassing, to be known as the stupid Earther's upraise sponsor.

What about the mother? Could Yoshiko have been upraised specifically to entrap Rafael? Unlikely. If LuxPrime suspected anything, the proctors would have descended upon him before now.

In any event, Yoshiko's death was now unnecessary. All he needed was to murder her beloved son, in front of twenty thousand onlookers.

Before his prey could fade back into cover, Rafael would deliver another virtuoso performance.

A dark sea, where waves of anger coursed, propagated through twenty thousand people. No, it was more than that: a giant organism, reacting fiercely as if by chemical instinct to the disturbance at its outer edge.

"*. . . disperse . . . immediate action . . . if . . . will not . . . peacefully.*"

The muted roar of muttered anger overlaid the proctor's warning.

Dhana stumbled, but Tetsuo caught her. Around them, a crush of people. The ranks were filling up from behind, as more came flocking down the slopes, past the quiet woods.

It was an organism, the crowd, and it curled around to trap the annoyance at its outer skin, the peacekeepers.

I don't like this.

An owl flew overhead, like a portent, and wheeled back into the forest.

Tetsuo held Dhana tightly. All around, people swirled. Only minutes ago, he and Dhana had been at the periphery of a peaceful gathering. Now, they were in the heart of a roiling mob, on the edge of chaos. The smallest disturbance, like a sky-borne dust particle precipitating a storm, would tip them over the brink.

There was a sweet scent, the tang of damp wild grass crushed by many feet.

"Out of the shadows!"

It became a battle cry, taken up by twenty thousand roaring voices.

"OUT OF THE SHADOWS!"

Anger became a tidal wave, and a tsunami of Shadow People fell upon the peacekeepers.

Escape. Now.

He dragged Dhana against the pull of the crowd, and for a moment fury blazed in her eyes. Then the fervent light faded, and she began to help him. They were two tiny organisms, swimming against the tide.

Milling bodies. They dodged and pushed and shoved, while collective adrenaline enraged the Shadow People's eyes and angry shouts were a swelling visceral roar of rage.

Suddenly, Tetsuo and Dhana broke free, were spat from the crowd's turbulence. The sudden absence of swaying, shoving bodies was shocking.

"Come on."

Reeling slightly, Tetsuo led Dhana to a sweeping buttress by the nearest building. They leaned against the hard grey wall.

"It's going to be awful, isn't it?" There was pain in Dhana's eyes.

Beyond, the mob still boiled and roared.

"Just wait here. I'm going to check something."

Around the buttress, an archway led inside. In the shadowed interior, a thin long-haired man was gesticulating at two big men who were blocking his way. TacCorps agents.

The man made a break for it, dodging the agents and running out. Then he stopped dead as lights sparkled in the archway and he dropped back, clutching his hand in pain.

Smartatom shield.

If that man could not get out, then neither could Tetsuo and Dhana get inside.

Unless . . .

Tetsuo reached up and pulled off the neck-ring, deactivating the holo-mask. For this to work, they would have to see his headgear, if they noticed him.

His heart was pounding, and the sweat of fear bathed his face, but he had to get Dhana to safety.

A faint shimmer in the air betrayed the shield's presence, as he drew close. If there ever was a time for him to take conscious control of his wild abilities, that time was now.

Do it. Do it.

Tears sprang to his eyes. Nothing.

Shuddering, he turned all his attention inwards, remembered the microwards, the terraformer tower, and dug deep inside himself, deep into his soul.

[[[HeaderBegin: Module = Node089C.1060: Type = BinaryHyper-Code: Axes = 16

Concurrent_Execute

<superolateral net: element fifteen>.linkfile = IRprotocol. Common.Alpha

<superolateral net: element sixteen>.linkfile = IRprotocol. Common.Beta

<superolateral net: element seventeen>.linkfile = IRprotocol. Common.Gamma

<superolateral net: element eighteen>.linkfile = IRprotocol. Common.Delta

End_Concurrent_Execute]]]

The shield wavered.

<<<MsgRcv DEVCOM284303; cause = device acknowledged command.>>>

Tetsuo stepped inside.

"— know my rights!" the long-haired man was shouting.

"You're not a citizen of this province, not even this world." Hard-edged, the TacCorps agent's voice. "You have no rights."

"Lucky we're here to protect you." The other agent.

"Look at my video-globes. Completely dead!"

Offworld journalist.

"Antisurveillance spray. Criminal elements in the mob. Come along, sir. For your own protection."

They wrist-locked him, then, and forced him farther into the building's interior. As they rounded a corner, the struggling journalist looked back, and just for a second his eyes met Tetsuo's.

Tyranny, they said. *And you're part of it.*

Then he was gone, and the hallway was silent.

The archway shields deadened sound.

Outside, a silent beam flickered through the gathering gloom. There were no screams, as the noiseless crowd broke apart, and became a panicking mob.

Dhana.

Attuned to him now, the shield let him pass. A roar of sound hit him. In the torrent of people, individuals tripped and fell, and were lost among the flooding mass of scared humanity.

She wasn't behind the buttress.

"Dhana!"

Beyond the mob, mirror-visored TacCorps agents on skimmers fired warnings, graser beams cracking through the air. Smartatom mists fell, anaesthetizing rioters who promptly dropped and were trampled. Elsewhere, hard-core demonstrators fought back with deadly miasmas of their own.

"Tetsuo!"

She was holding a small girl, pale and frightened, in her arms.

Tetsuo bulldozed a panicking man out of his way and grabbed Dhana and the child.

A graser beam licked out, and a TacCorps agent fell from a skimmer.

Immediately, a group of skimmers whirled in formation, and answering beams stabbed into the crowd.

"Come on."

He stood in the archway, deactivating the shield, and pushed Dhana inside.

In the crowd, a woman screamed.

"This way!" Tetsuo shouted. "Over here!"

They came running, their faces twisted by panic.

A flood of people passed Tetsuo. He hauled and pushed, helping the flow where he could, getting them indoors. It was only a trickle, compared to the vast mass of people panicking outside.

What was going on? Luculenti were not tyrants, though the effect of their existence might be oppressive. The Shadow People had real grievances. The Luculenti, and the Fulgidi merchants he had dealt with, were superlative negotiators. How could this breakdown happen?

"My daughter!"

He pushed a girl towards a stricken woman: a lucky guess. A tearful, joyful face, lost in the swirling mass of people.

Rain began to fall.

An elbow struck Tetsuo and he bent over, coughing, but he held position and the shield remained down.

He could no longer see Dhana.

Outside, a curtain of silver rain washed across the mob.

They came for him.

Skimmers arrowed above the dispersing crowds, heading for Tetsuo. On one of them, a tall man in TacCorps uniform was unhelmeted. For a moment, lightning flashed, and that ascetic face burned briefly white, and those mismatched eyes were pale and frightening.

Federico Gisanthro.

Was he the only reason for all this? Striking back, because the Shadow People were exposing his corruption? Or was he using this chaos somehow to strengthen his political power?

Run.

Dhana was somewhere inside. Crowds would be fleeing through the complex, through the heart of the conference centre. How many would escape to the grounds outside, to the tubeways and flyers which might take them into Lucis City proper?

"I'm sorry!" He spat rainwater from his drenched face as he moved into the open, and Shadow People stared at him with agony in their eyes as the smartatom shield reactivated.

Run. Now.

Briefly, he was running with a hundred other people, heading upslope with his lungs and heavy thighs burning, feet slipping on the muddy ground. Then he was on his own. Torrential rain lashed him, blocked his nose and blurred his vision.

Can't breathe.

Run.

Lightning flash.

For a moment, the trees ahead were lit up, stark against the dark forest beyond.

Safety. Just run.

The light was gloomy but Tetsuo thought a shadow moved across the ground. He pushed harder, lungs whining with a high-pitched wheeze, as something hard and massive smashed him between the shoulder blades, and wet grass slapped him in the face and blackness fell.

Chapter Thirty-Three

Spring rain, gently falling:
Shine through playful clouds,
Dance in golden sunlight.

The air was on fire. Golden clouds of burning light filled the auditorium. Black lightning spat. A thousand unseen demons howled. A great winged shape swooped upon them, talons raking, screaming as it missed.

Yoshiko and Eric ducked, clutching each other.

"What the hell—?" Eric, bewildered, still tightly grasped the sheathed tanto dagger.

Glassy blue all around.

Looking down, Yoshiko could no longer see her body, but felt a desperate hand grasping her arm.

"Eric?"

They were embedded in a glacier of icy light.

"What is this?" Eric's gruff voice wavered.

"*What is this?*" An echo. "*What is this?*" Moving. "*What is this what is this what is this?*" A mocking chorus.

Yoshiko took Eric's invisible hand and gripped it tightly.

They were in a pit of total blackness. Tiny stars began to twinkle, light years beneath their feet. Yoshiko locked on to the unseen spirit she hoped was Eric, and, swaying, they kept their balance.

"What are you doing with this man?"

The voice was Ken's, and Yoshiko let go of the invisible Eric's arm, and was lost.

Falling, through the dark.

Help me.

"Oh, no, my dear." A cold voice scraped the flesh from her bones. "No help for you."

She was lying on her back, and a whirlpool of grey mists endlessly spun.

From the rows of gravestones all around, decaying hands were thrusting upwards, clawing into wan cold light.

Help me.

A kind hand helped her stand.

"Oh, no—"

Ken's round face smiled at her.

Dear God. Give me strength—

"Oh, Yoshiko. How I've missed you." The voice which had been part of her, for most of her life.

—to do what I must.

The other half of her. The part which had been missing, torn relentlessly away.

"Ken," she breathed, and as he smiled she whipped the edge of her hand against his throat, smashing into the carotid sinus, and a very real and physical being dropped to the ground.

All around, illusory mists faded.

The auditorium grew visible once more. This time, all the lights came dimly on, and Yoshiko could see the massed ranks of comfortable seats—not gravestones—and the small collection of floating lev-platforms.

The redwood walls gleamed. Above, near the high ceilings with their dim skylights—dim because the formal wing-shaped hovering roof was suspended above the building—hung the laser array which had produced the illusions.

At her feet, the fallen Rafael, who had copied Ken's likeness from EveryWare—

It was Eric who lay on the ground, comatose, the useless dagger lying fallen beside him.

"Oops." The tall figure of Rafael, caped and hooded, was leaning against a wall at the back of the auditorium. "I think you made a wrong assumption, Yoshiko." His arms were crossed, and a beatific smile wreathed his lean and impossibly handsome face. "You don't mind if I call you Yoshiko, do you, Luculenta Sunadomari?"

"If you've—" Yoshiko stopped, centring herself. "Illusions won't help you now."

She opened a pocket in her jumpsuit, dropped in the blue crystal which Felice had given her, and sealed it. Then, slowly in case of blinding holo imagery, she knelt straight-backed and picked up the fallen dagger.

She glanced back. Felice and the TacCorps agents lay where they had dropped.

"Tetsuo's outside, did you know?" Rafael's words chilled her. "There's a bit of a riot going on out there, so I thought I'd find someplace nice and quiet. Rather serendipitous, don't you think?"

Yoshiko ignored him. This was no time for distracting words.

The short blade slid silently from its sheath.

"How quaint." Rafael's smile was gentle, almost loving. "Well, I've no time for tedious explication. Soon you'll see wonders such as you've never dreamed of, subsumed in the greater—"

Yoshiko advanced.

"That's interesting." His voice was silky, almost caressing. "You betray a distinct lack of surprise."

She jerked in reflex, though there was no pain.

<<<MsgRcv LUCCOM018772; cause = diagnostic requested.>>>

"No!" Yoshiko yelled.

```
[[[HeaderBegin: Module = Node728A.3219 Type = Quaternary-
        HyperCode: Axes = 256
    Priority = absolute
    Status = resident always
    Concurrent_Execute
        ThreadOne:<LuxPrime interface>.linkfile = LockChannelZero
        ThreadTwo:<rhombencephalon channel>.linkfile = LockChannel-
            One
        ThreadThree:<intrapeduncular matrix>.linkfile = LockChannel-
            Two
        ThreadFour:<thalamic/cerebral matrix>.linkfile = LockChannel-
            Three
    End_Concurrent_Execute]]]
```

Lines of code burned like golden fire in her brain, and she knew straight away that she had failed. The code was executing, locked on to nothing at all.

"Oh, dear." Rafael laughed gently. "I appear to have tripped some sort of code in your mind. What was it designed to do?"

"Lock you in place," said Yoshiko grimly. "Keep your comms in stasis until someone could get you."

"Tsk, tsk. That seems scarcely polite."

She raised her blade. "Just let me into your mind, Rafael. You'll wish you'd never started this."

"Yoshiko, Yoshiko. Well, since you ask so nicely—"

Cold paralysis stopped her dead.

Rafael's deep eyes seemed to have grown impossibly huge. Every detail of his face was perfect.

"Time," he said, and his beautiful words rolled over her, "to be reborn."

Cold fire burned in her veins.

Sounds whispered just beyond the edge of her awareness, calling to her. A wondrous light beckoned, from peripheral darkness where she could not see.

Yoshiko.

Oh, yes.

Come to me.

The words stroked her, burned her skin, inflamed her every nerve.

"*No*," a frail voice whispered weakly.

"Yoshiko—" Rafael became sternly commanding.

Chaos struck.

[[Swirling inchoate light, blinding in its brilliance.]]

[[Gut-wrenching ultrasonic screams.]]

<<audio_1: Run, Yoshiko.>>
<<audio_2: *Run, now!*>>

Felice.

With a glance back at the wounded Felice, who was raising herself up on one elbow, Yoshiko turned and ran.

Dodging seats, she sprinted past the collection of hanging lev-platforms. Then a low moan dragged her to a halt.

Felice, twisted body clutched in agony. Rafael, eyes glowing with dark malignance.

Yoshiko started to return, hefting her dagger, but a flicker of his eyes told her that Rafael was aware of her still.

Get out of here.

The lev-platforms.

She looked up. High above, dim skylights dotted the sloping ceiling.

OK, Luculenta. Let's see what you've got.

```
[[[HeaderBegin: Module = Node089C.1060: Type = BinaryHyper-
      Code: Axes = 16
   Execute
      do until ok_received
         <superolateral net: element++>.linkfile = IRprotocol.
            Common.genFn(lev,0;sts) repeat
   End_Execute]]]
```

A dozen lev-platforms leaped upwards, hurtled towards the ceiling, and smashed into it. Two of them crashed through skylights, and a torrent of falling glass and debris poured down with the suddenly lifeless platforms. Yoshiko crouched behind a row of seats as chunks of ceiling fell.

There was one functional platform left, bobbing lightly in the magnetic disturbance.

Yoshiko leaped aboard as her mind formed the instructions. There was time for one last glance at the dreadful tableau: Rafael's gaze locked on the dying Felice. Then the platform was flying upwards.

Ceiling.

Yoshiko dodged a jutting triangle of glass as momentum carried her up through the broken skylight. Whimpering, she threw herself off the platform a microsecond before it tipped and plunged back down inside.

The hard roof knocked the breath from her body, and she lay there stunned, bright green pulses flashing in her eyes.

Bulging eyes, rippled features: Tetsuo-*kami*, vengeful ghosts. It was his own inverted face, twisted in death. Mirror-visors, reflecting his fear.

Helmeted TacCorps agents surrounded him. Light shimmered gently across their weapons' transmission faces.

"No!"

Federico leaped down lightly from a skimmer, and the other agents drew back.

Tetsuo lurched to his knees, stood up in the mud, and wiped rain and dirt from his face. His momentary gratitude faded. Death was certain. His love for Dhana, forever unfulfilled.

Down below, the fleeing crowds were too busy to notice Tetsuo's fate.

Federico ran through the falling rain, inhumanly swift. Arms and legs pumped as he sprinted across the soaked grass, arrowing towards Tetsuo.

A planted weapon, sworn testimony that he had been about to bring it to bear. That was all it would take. Tetsuo would go unmourned to a killer's grave.

Time slowed.

Federico leaped high, leg cocked to deliver the necksnapping kick—

A flash of white.

—boot-edge thrusting—

Talons raked.

—and Federico fell, screaming.

Ripping teeth, scarlet blood.

"No!"

Tetsuo staggered forward, placing his body in harm's way as the agents recovered and brought their graser rifles to bear.

The rain ceased.

On Federico's twitching form, the white lynxette looked up at Tetsuo, amber eyes whirling with nameless emotions, as the air grew miraculously still.

The eye of the storm.

"You're both dead," said a visored agent, cold fury in her voice.

The last words Tetsuo would hear. He squeezed his eyes shut.

A soft whimper escaped him, beyond his control.

Death.

The ground shook, and the air exploded.

Huge bronze and silver darts in the sky: three vast mu-space ships, crashing into real-space. From tiny openings in the hulls, a thousand bubbles streamed downwards.

As each drop-bug hit the ground, an armed proctor leaped out and took up position. Here and there, among the masses of blue uniforms, black-jumpsuited figures moved.

Pilots.

The lynxette growled softly.

"*—name is Major Reilly.*"

Above the fallen Federico's wrist, a tiny holo image: a grey-haired square-jawed woman.

"*—down your weapons now, or face criminal charges. Luculentus Federico Gisanthro is relieved of command by executive order—*"

The agents standing around Tetsuo stiffened. He guessed they were seeing the same image, displayed inside their helmets.

Down below, proctors had contained the outnumbered TacCorps forces, who were already laying down their arms. Shadow People moved in a daze, aimlessly.

The agent facing Tetsuo pulled off her helmet, and dropped it to the ground. She stared coldly at Tetsuo.

One of the other agents tuned his visor to transparency, revealing a scarred and bearded face. He brought up a graser pistol, and targeted Tetsuo's heart. "Let's do—"

Graser fire spat, and the man fell.

"He was my best team leader." The unhelmeted agent laid her graser rifle on the ground. "Remember I did that."

"Looks—" Tetsuo's voice caught. "Looks like your people have all surrendered."

The TacCorps agents flinched as the lynxette padded up beside Tetsuo, but it sat on its haunches, and stared up at Tetsuo with unfathomable eyes.

"Pity," Tetsuo added. "I would have liked to see the Pilots in action."

•

Defeat swirled like ashes in Yoshiko's mind.

The way of the warrior is death. The first words of the Hagakure, the samurai code.

Pain stabbed through her grazed hands as she pushed herself upright. The flat roof was gravelled, one of seventeen vast interlocking circular roofs, at varying heights. Above her, smooth white ceramics blocked her view of the sky: the great wing-shaped hovering roof, held by mag-fields some two metres above the complex proper.

She took Felice's crystal from her pocket, and placed it beside her.

Way of the warrior. *Bushido.*

Yoshiko picked tiny stones out of her torn and bloody palms, and looked around. There were patches of moss and streaks of bird-dung, defacing the gravelled roof. A small fat Terran sparrow took off, alarmed, and arrowed away, its small wings a blur.

Later, in Hagakure: *if you are ready to discard life at a moment's notice, you and the* bushido *will become one.*

This high, the air was cold, but there was no draught. Though the hovering wing above blocked off the sky, still she was breathing fresh air, seeing every stone upon the roof with a preternatural sharpness. This was the living cosmos, and she was privileged to be part of it, for a while.

The thing was, to make her death count for something.

<<<MsgRcv LUCCOM213887; cause = SkeinLink established.>>>

<<video: Young face, scarlet hair.>>
<<audio: Yoshiko! What's happened?>>

"Vin! Lavinia . . ."

<<audio: Your lock-code executed, but terminated abnormally.>>

"He made it fail. Rafael did."

Sounds of disturbances, pandemonium, taking place on the ground where she could not see, drifted through the still, chilled air.

"He's coming for me, Lavinia. Break this link, or he'll get you, too."

<<audio: I've called Major Reilly. She was already on her way.>>

"It's too late."

<<audio: She's got Pilots with her.>>

Pilots?

On hands and knees, ignoring the pain, Yoshiko crawled to the roof's edge. Though gravel bit into her knuckles, she still clutched the tanto in her hand.

Green slopes. Down below, among a profusion of demonstrators who were dressed in every fashion imaginable, green-uniformed men and women were placing their weapons on the ground, as dark-uniformed proctors surrounded them. Here and there, Pilots moved among them.

If only she could call to them . . . but Rafael could strike through Skein. No time to get assistance, no way to seek escape.

<<audio: Major Reilly says, they've found Tetsuo. He's all right.>>

The world blurred.

A screeching sound, like ten thousand fingernails scraping slate, rose up from the smashed skylight, and Yoshiko knew immediately what it was. A lev-platform, wrenching itself from the crashed heap in the auditorium.

Rafael.

Desperately, she looked up. Like a gull's wings, the hovering roof spread above. Flimsily translucent areas suggested membranes which might lead to the upper surface.

"Lavinia?"

<<audio: I'm here.>>

"The Baton Ceremony code. I need to access it."

<<audio_1: You can't. The code's too dangerous.>>
<<text: Scanware. It's reserved for the ceremony.>>
<<audio_2: No one survives scanware execution.>>

"It's the only way. He's coming. Rafael."

{{{Priority obj_ident: ∞}}}

[[[HeaderBegin: Module = Node0000.00000: Type = n-way: Axes = unlimited
ScanWare.load
On_confirm( ): ScanWare.execute]]]

<<<MsgRcv LUXPRM000100; cause = WARNING: ScanWare ENABLED.>>>

She was on her own. The SkeinLink to Lavinia was cut without any warning, as the scanware took precedence in her mind.

<<<Source is Luculenta Yoshiko Sunadomari [[ident Terra: 98227A2]]>>>
<<<Specify target now>>>

"No." Her voice was cold.

Lines of code shimmered before her eyes. A true Luculenta swam in a beautiful universe of Skein, where images were summoned at a whim, information was absorbed without pain, and perceptions ranged through dimensions unknown to ordinary minds. But Yoshiko, who would never see those wonders, had to root among the nuts and bolts, the fabric of that other world.

She concentrated, and the underlying code changed and shifted, and then she breathed out, a long slow relaxing breath, as the editing concluded.

<<<Source is Luculentus Rafael Garcia de la Vega [[ident 7γ93Fϕ•ϵ {septΠΓΩ}]]>>>
<<<Target is Luculenta Yoshiko Sunadomari [[ident Terra: 98227A2]]>>>

Reversal achieved. Scanware loaded, and ready to run.

Execution time.

Molecules danced. Copper orbs, freed by old-fashioned sound, were carried along the broken expanse of lattice. Some were diverted to resonate in microcavities, finally lasing free. Sound and matter-waves converged, laying down nanofactors: metallic-hued arrays, rotating in time to soothing background music.

Behind the display, Rafael turned his face against the wall as his cape tuned to chameleon mode, while a team of proctors hurried by. As he waited, crouched, a ghost-Rafael came to him in Skein. The NetAngel deposited its find—a schematic of the conference centre, falling into place in Rafael's perceptions—and vanished.

Rafael trembled. Felice's bright and lovely mind sang in his cache, awaiting his loving attention, but he had to find Yoshiko before he could take time for integration.

When the proctors had gone, Rafael slipped out from behind the image, and its depiction of historical manufacturing techniques. Rushing now—for the lev-platform he had set to divert Yoshiko's attention would already be ascending—he stepped straight into the corridor wall, as the schematic in his mind's eye lit up, highlighting maintenance access-membranes.

A vertical shaft led all the way up. Swaying from vertigo, Rafael stepped onto the elevator disk which formed the shaft's apparent floor, and executed the command.

The disk whisked him upwards, slowing as it approached the membrane-ceiling. A brief sensation of dampness as he ascended through the membrane, and then the disk was level with the roof and he was in open air. He stepped off, and gravel scrunched underfoot.

No sign of the Earther woman.

Across the roofs flat expanse, nothing. Beyond, other roofs lay at lower or higher levels. Had she really jumped onto one of them?

"Yoshiko?" he called softly. "Where are you, Yoshiko?"

One metre above his head, the great wing-shaped hovering roof floated. Its underside was marred here and there with rusty streaks. Access membranes, leading to its upper surface, glistened softly.

There.

Just a tiny shift in opacity, but it was enough. A membrane, re-hardened no more than seconds ago.

Her courage was admirable.

Stepping beneath the membrane, he extended his arms, palms raised as though to heaven. A shaft of liquefied membrane flowed down to him, enwrapped him, and carried him upwards.

Ships.

Mu-space ships!

Rafael staggered slightly, as he stepped out onto the upper surface. All around, the broad wing-shaped expanse, the hovering roof, shimmered with rainbow hues. It was beautiful in its simplicity, a great curve of diffracted light high above the ground, and he was a tiny figure on its grand surface.

No Yoshiko. But, high in the storm-darkened sky, three mu-space vessels glinted, bronze and silver, unnaturally bright against the inky clouds.

A chill wind suddenly blew, and Rafael dropped to one knee, and pulled his cape about him. It was high, up here—far too high—and he felt suddenly exposed. He crouched lower, as the wind's force increased. It began to buffet him, and its slipstream tugged his breath away.

Damn the woman. Where was she?

And were the ships observing him?

Icy rain fell.

It plunged from the sky, dropped in torrents, and sprayed across the hovering roof like a field of metallic grass.

Wait—

<<MsgRcv LUCCOM213886; cause = SkeinLink requested.>>>

Yoshiko.

Love sang in his breast. Yoshiko was opening up herself to him.

Felice's soul seemed to cry with joy from his cache as he loosed her, subsumed her, and every thought and hope and dream of that bright mind, that joyful spirit, that childlike sense of wonder and enquiry, flooded through his being. He cried aloud as a maelstrom of fragmented images whirled through his extended mind.

Threshold. Power thrummed inside him, for his mind, spread across his Fulgor-wide nexus, had reached some new point of criticality.

Hold back, hold back. There was Yoshiko to deal with.

Her SkeinLink request shimmered in his soul.

A second mind, so quickly?

Yes.

Do it now.

Yoshiko must think she could lock him, while Felice's mind swirled through his, but she was wrong. This time, he was ready to defuse her lock code and plunge through her defences and strip her mind, like plucking petals from a flower.

Crouching on hands and knees, palms splayed upon the suddenly wet and slippery roof, Rafael squeezed his eyes shut against ricocheting rain, and focussed his thoughts.

```
[[[HeaderBegin: Module = Node12A3.33Q8: Type = Quaternary-
        HyperCode: Axes = 256
    Concurrent_Execute
        ThreadOne:<rhombencephalon channel>.linkfile = Infiltrate.
            Alpha
        ThreadTwo:<intrapeduncular matrix>.linkfile = Infiltrate
            .Beta
        ThreadThree:<LuxPrime interface>.linkfile = CodeSmash
        ThreadFour:<thalamic/cerebral matrix>.linkfile = Subvert-
            Array
        ThreadFive:<superolateral net>.linkfile = MindWolf
    End_Concurrent_Execute]]]
```

Rafael struck at Yoshiko, as thunder crashed and rain fell.

The white chrysanthemum.

A white globe of florets, floating in her mind's eye: in the absence of a death-poem, the last construct of her imagining, before her death.

<<<MsgRcv LUXPRM999999; cause = protocol breach; error is fatal.>>>

Yoshiko shuddered, as Rafael's code plunged into her.

Eyes flickering open, involuntarily. The blue comms-crystal was blindingly bright, as she directed her SkeinLink through its instantaneous relay.

Gravel biting into her knees. One ankle very sore: she had twisted it when she had dropped down to this lower roof, out of Rafael's line of sight.

The glowing crystal struck sapphire reflections from the steel, as she gripped the tanto dagger in both hands.

Something, at the edge of her awareness . . .

In samurai days, a woman would have bound her ankles to prevent immodesty in death, but Yoshiko wore a jumpsuit and her battleground was now. This was more than suicide, it was *ai-uchi*: striking simultaneously with the enemy; throwing away her life to take the enemy's own.

Rafael's code tore into her. She felt his dark joy, his cold power, the huge extent of his mind piercing into hers.

Blade, stinging her throat, as sweetly as a lover's kiss.

Be firm.

Be strong.

Never *give in.*

<<<WARNING WARNING WARNING>>>

<<<Scanware status = ready>>>

<<<Source is Luculentus Rafael Garcia de la Vega
[[ident 7γ93Fϕ•ϵ {septΠΓΩ}>>>

<<<Target is Luculenta Yoshiko Sunadomari
[[ident Terra:98227A2]]>>>

As Yoshiko cut into her own carotid artery, she centred herself, dug deep into her spirit, and visualized the invocation for her waiting scanware.

A simple symbol:

∞

The trigger.

<<<WARNING WARNING WARNING>>>
<<<SCANWARE EXECUTING>>>

Scanware, impelled by the infinity symbol, dragged Rafael's mind into hers. Offering herself, reversing the process of a Baton Ceremony, pulling a layer of consciousness through the comms-channel created by Rafael's own infiltration code. He dragged in her executing scanware, which ploughed through his extended mind and spewed it back towards her.

<<<<<<<<<<<<<<<interlock established>>>>>>>>>>>>>>>

((SOURCE ACTIVE))	((TARGET ACTIVE))
The bitch, what is she—?	Come on, Rafael. Come into me.
Scanning.	That's it. Show me everything.
You dare to scan *me*.	All the dark—
Get out! Get out!	Oh, God. Oh, dear God.

<<<<<<<<<<<<<<<<session initiating>>>>>>>>>>>>>>>>

Horror screamed inside Yoshiko.

Rafael's fear, or her own?

But then, but then . . .

That *other* she had felt, at the edge of her awareness, became scattered perceptions, tiny mind-fragments, tenuously connected . . .

There were hundreds of them . . .

Raw, and alive. Hundreds of minds: flying, running, burrowing, swimming . . .

There was a place for her. A tiny splinter of Yoshiko would live in each of them, every soaring bird and sprinting mammal, after she was dead.

<<<<<<<<<<<<<<<<<<<<executing>>>>>>>>>>>>>>>>>>>>

((SOURCE STATUS:
SEND))
<<audio: No! *No! NO!*>>
<<text: No! *No! NO!*>>
<<ideogram: twisted knot: chaos>>
<<video: bloody maelstrom>>

((TARGET STATUS:
RECEIVE))
"Too . . . late . . . Rafael . . ."

<<<<<<<<<<<<<<<<<<<executing>>>>>>>>>>>>>>>>>>>

There was an escape route. He could follow Yoshiko along the path to the scattered animals, but the connection would vanish when the scanware was done, and only scattered splinters of scarcely sentient awareness would remain among the hundreds of disconnected tiny brains. No consciousness at all. Everything that made him Rafael Garcia de la Vega would be gone.

Death sang amid the howling storm.

Some part of her was aware, then, of chill wind and distant motion; regardless, she drew her blade across her throat as surely as she drew Rafael into her dying brain.

Adrenaline's rush; blood in her mouth as her fangs bit into the kill; crisp air cutting cleanly beneath her soaring wings; a universe of pungent forest scents as she tracked her prey.

No! No! No! No!

Dirty, crawling animals. Links to the primitive, the disgusting . . . To all that he had grown beyond.

Damn you. NO!

Rafael's fear screamed, and her connection to the distant animals was lost.

Just her, then, and Rafael.

Everything stopped.

For a moment, the universe froze into icy stillness, as he locked his own mind.

Clever, clever . . .

Yoshiko, redirecting scanware, scanning his mind into hers. But Rafael was the greatest Luculentus of them all. His mind covered the face of Fulgor.

He *was* Fulgor.

He was the planet, and he was its god. No one, no one could stop—

A mind, across the face of the world.

Hold . . .

I will *not* give in.

<<<MsgRcv VEGCOM99998; cause = VSI failure imminent.>>>

Disintegration . . .

<<<MsgRcv VEGCOM99999; cause = VSI terminating immediately.>>>

He/she screamed as the blade's pain burned into her/his throat.

Don't—

The hand holding the knife—

Too late.

He was here, trapped inside Yoshiko. There was no escape.

Cutting her *own* throat. But he was here, too . . .

Yoshiko's will was unbreakable. The hand, set into motion, could not be stopped.

Spitting hatred, Rafael learned his final lesson.

Defeat.

RAFAEL:	RAFAEL:	RAFAEL:	RAFAEL:	RAFAEL:	RAFAEL:
Bitch!	I don't	Sweetness,	Storm, I	Not now,	Blackness
Just die,	want to	when	hate the	no it can't	coming
you		Xanthia			

SCAN_CHANNEL_ONE	SCAN_CHANNEL_TWO	SCAN_CHANNEL_THREE
00100X1X0011X00101X1	10X001X0X11X010X0X1	0X110X0XX101X01XX011
101XX101101X01XX0X1	X01XX101011X01001X0	10X0X01Xmother0X011X0
011X1110X11X0001X100	01Xblood01scentX01X011	X01XX011X010X0110X01
10Xnot my011X1never1X1	Xlike1X01copper001X1X0	01X0loveX010XX011X1011
01was my faultX101X0111	1X001X1X00X110X10X0	X1X0001X0X0XX11X010X
0101X0XX101010XX0X1	Xin0fulminatingX1X001X	0X0X1XIhateX010X110110
0XX11X00X1X0100XX01	01XX0110X0codeX1X011	10110X0X01X0XX10100X0
X0X011shadowsX0XX110	11XplungingX10XohyesX	01X01putrid0X11X01stink01
0X001010XX0110X0X101	X001Xinto10Xdeeper0011	0X110X101X001X01X10X0
X01please0X10X0010111	0X1X00X1X00X1XX0X11	X01101X0XXdeath0X1011X
1X110X0X01XXno0X10X	X0110X01deeper01XX101	01tearsX1XdoXnot01X0X11
01X00X0X11X01X001X11	1X010XX1X01101X011X1	X10pleaseX001stop00X01X1
1noXno1noXno1no1noXno	Xno1noXno1no0no1noXno	0noXno1noXnoXno1no1no0

<<<SCANWARE EXECUTION>>>

<<<life after death: love after love: hope beyond despair>>>

<<<LuxPrime>>>

Phase transition.

Rafael and Yoshiko becoming one . . .

Oh Ken. You should see this!

. . . one with the universe.

Perception: distinction versus pattern.

<<<die well>>>

Yoshiko/Rafael, thoughts spanning the Fulgor-wide nexus, fostering new modes of cognition, intuitively merging with the Tao Function's flow, the cosmic-connective wave-pattern, the dance of Shiva. All those lives. All that wonder.

She/he simultaneously saw:

— subquantum fluctuations, birthing particles in antichaotic simplicity,

— autocatalytic feedback: life itself arising,

— species' state-spaces' complicit intersection: parasitism, predation, and evolution,

— from a sea of bacteria, eukaryotic cells,

— from an ocean of people: love, economies, racial hatreds, cooperation,

— biospheres; stellar systems; galaxies and clusters; the Great Attractor,

— and, tantalizing, the overarching pattern, the self-awareness, the living thoughts of God Itself, the universe.

She/he did not know how, but silver rain drenched her/his distant self or selves.

Storm. Dying, dying, in the raging of the storm. Sweeping away the world.

Thunder crashed, for the very last time. Tears bade the universe farewell.

Lightning. Blade. Throat.

The storm howled and blessed water swept scarlet blood away; lightning flickered once and it was cold, cold, the chilly dark, and icy cold; oh, wait for me, my love; sleep now; as darkness falls and shadows come to rest and the cold, cold dark goes on forever; and we're at the end: goodbye my friends, goodbye, for love is all; and light, drawing back in all directions: black, inky black, final black, as all thought ends, all feeling fades, and the universe itself grows cold and silent.

Chapter Thirty-Four

Sunlight, till
Golden lightning flowers.
Dances. Summer storm: time again.

Sliding sideways through the air, amid the torrential downpour, it edged away from the clustered buildings with rainbows glittering across its surface. It spun, and arced slowly downwards, and crashed onto a plaza.

"My God." Dhana gripped his arm. "I think there was a man on that roof."

Tetsuo said nothing. A blast of static had shaken him: a random burst of control code. Whatever had generated it, the secondary effect must have been to shut down the lev-field generators of the conference centre's hovering roof.

Through the heavy rain, from here at least, no body was visible among the crumpled wreckage.

Inhaling, Tetsuo's breath was shaky. The scents of grass and mud were fresh in his nostrils. Life.

Beside him, the lynxette hissed.

"Shush," said Dhana. "It's all right."

Tetsuo's head swam. He had not asked her about the injured girl, the girl she had pulled from the mob. He did not even know how Dhana had found him.

The TacCorps agents, weaponless, were making their way down towards their surrendering comrades. They paused as a skimmer drew close, but it ignored them and they carried on.

The skimmer was heading towards Tetsuo and Dhana.

"Listen, I wanted to tell you—"

"Tetsuo, it's all right. There'll be time to talk, later."

Later. He had thought there would be no more time, none at all.

As the skimmer drew close, a woman jumped down and strode towards them. She pushed rain-soaked hair back from her grim features.

"My name's Maggie Brown." As she spoke, the video-globe above her shoulder bobbed closer. "I'm a friend of Yoshiko's."

"Who—?" Dhana stiffened.

"My mother?" Tetsuo felt suddenly sick.

"I'm sorry." Rain glistened like tears on Maggie's cheeks. "I'm afraid the news isn't very good."

Chapter Thirty-Five

Falling rain in spring.
Mourners coming in,
White as a chrysanthemum.

NEWS_NET_FIVE:
{[[Item: Luculentus on trial.]]}

AUDIO:
"There were more dramatic revelations today, as one of Fulgor's highest officials faces . . ."

AUDIO_2:
". . . found fifteen days ago, at the home of one Tetsuo Sunadomari . . ."

CLOSE_UP:
Decomposing corpse lifted from the ground. Proctors pull back the covering null-sheet.

TEXT:
Failing to recover the crystals, Farsteen, forced to accompany them, was brutally executed.

RECONSTRUCTION:
Camouflage-suited TacCorps agents drop from skimmers, and storm a fortified villa.

AUDIO_3:
". . . had been feeding proprietary LuxPrime technology to one Captain Rogers . . ."

CLOSE_UP_2:
Grim-faced, the pale Luculentus leaves the courthouse, surrounded by guards.

AUDIO_4:
". . . of all, it is alleged that Federico Gisanthro had full knowledge of Rafael de la Vega's activities . . ."

TEXT_2:
Almost certainly, the serial killer, de la Vega, was unaware of this surveillance.

AUDIO_5:
"The dead Captain Rogers intermediary between Farsteen and de la Vega, may also have been the source of Federico's . . ."

CLOSE_UP_3:
A hugely muscled man, sitting on a floating platform, taking the formal oath, to tell only the objective truth.

AUDIO_6:
". . . has come from former TacCorps agent Guido Valcento, who says Federico Gisanthro gave the execution order."

AERIAL_VIEW:
Swirling mob, TacCorps surrounding them. Graser fire lances into the crowd, as demonstrators flee.

TEXT_3:
One man, hoping to use illicit technology and civil unrest to further his own political ambitions.

AUDIO_7:
". . . This is Maggie Brown, at the Yudices Summi courthouse complex, for NewsNetFive . . ."

{{[brought to you by NewsNetFive]}}
{{[a division of Maximilian Enterprises]}}

Chapter Thirty-Six

White chrysanthemum:
Cherish its memory
Till it flowers again.

The words hung, glowing amber, above the shrine.

A gentle breeze carried the forest scents beneath a pale, clear green sky. Dark grasses sloped down to a wide, slow river. To one side, thick forest ended with a stand of proud birches, silver bark fairly glowing in the sunlight.

Their black capes swayed, tugged by the breeze. Kneeling, the two Pilots laid their wreaths, and stepped back from the white marble shrine.

Six Shadow People, led by Brevan, were the next to pay their respects.

The lynxette, crouched at Tetsuo's feet, flicked his tufted ears, but kept position. Dhana's grip tightened on Tetsuo's arm.

He read the poem's words softly, to himself. White chrysanthemum. Translated into Nihongo, it was beautiful.

Tetsuo had chosen it, for the shrine. It was a facet from one of the FourSpeak hypercube-haiku his mother loved to write.

<<audio: It was to have been my death-poem.>>

Tetsuo <sent> his reply:

<<text: I know, Mother. I know.>>

Yoshiko directed her skim-chair forward. It hovered slightly above the grass, and lowered itself before the shrine. Sunlight sparked sapphire highlights from the blue gel encasing her throat.

Sunlight. Flowers' scent. Wondrous life.

Though she could not speak until her throat was healed, she could communicate with her fellow Luculentus, her son.

Beside her, Eric, limping, took the chrysanthemums from her hand, and laid them at Felice's shrine.

Somewhere in Lucis, Rafael's funeral was being held today. There would be few flowers at that grave.

Rafael. Memory fragments: solitary childhood, traumatic Baton Ceremony, dark hunger, bright talent . . .

The skim-chair lifted and Yoshiko withdrew—slowly, so that Eric could keep pace—and they rejoined Tetsuo and Dhana.

Maggie, looking slightly flustered, composed herself, and laid a small, simple wreath. She had arrived late from the hearing, and only now went to stand beside young Jason. He was looking solemn beyond his years. Amanda, Xanthia's soul-daughter, stood with him, clutching his hand.

LuxPrime representatives, dressed in funereal white, laid their own wreath at Felice's shrine.

There was silence, as the mourners closed their eyes and bade Felice farewell, each in their own way. Then a young Luculenta with haunted eyes—Felice's soul-daughter, and the chief mourner—clapped her hands three times. The ceremony was over.

As people began slowly to return to the waiting skimmers, Jana and Edralix came over to Yoshiko, and bowed deeply.

When Jana straightened, her jet eyes glinted, black on black, like deep holes cut into the universe's heart.

Yoshiko started to rise from the skim-chair—she would not need it much longer, anyway—but Eric's hand on her shoulder stopped her. Instead, she inclined her head towards Jana, the nearest she could manage to a formal bow.

Yoshiko was alive because Jana had shut down the communications network of an entire world. Commerce, from the lowliest shop to the grandest corporate empire; education; government—all had ceased. Fulgor's heart had stopped beating.

Without any way to separate Rafael's comms from the rest, Jana had caused all mu-space comms to be closed down for five whole, endless minutes. Convinced of death's imminence, the Rafael-fragment in Yoshiko's mind had given up, disintegrated. All those other fragments, drawn into Yoshiko's suicidal determination, had been cut loose, each on their own, broken apart and terrified, adrift in hellish chaos.

Yoshiko could not imagine the politics, the frantic negotiations among the Pilots in their mu-space habitats, the humanity of those who would risk so much for one frail person. She knew only that her debt to the Pilots was one she could never repay.

Edralix winked.

The two Pilots gathered their capes around them and left. Yoshiko noticed the way other mourners fell back to give them room.

Maggie, walking up to Yoshiko's skim-chair, looked back at the departing Pilots and shivered.

"Sorry," she said. "I'm still not used to—Well, anyway. Guido sent you a message: *Flower bends, stone breaks.* Quite the poet, don't you think? He must have hit his head when you knocked him down."

Yoshiko, unable to speak, could only shake her head slowly, smiling.

Maggie added, "Petra—Major Reilly, I mean—sent her apologies. She's testifying right now."

Eric shifted his weight, easing his still-healing leg.

"Hey, Yoshiko. Are we ever going to go snorkelling? I'd like—My God!"

All eyes followed Eric's gaze.

The mourners froze.

Rustling, from the forest.

Eyes glinted among the shadows. Leaves trembled.

Movement . . .

The forest came alive with movement.

Realization swept across Yoshiko, but she could make no contact with them. The sparks of awareness, reflected shards of her own shared consciousness, were forever beyond her reach. The crystal relay, currently sitting in a courthouse, was dead.

In feline stealth, they crept forwards. With waddling bipedal gait, primate foreknuckles brushing the ground, they came. Rodent whiskers twitched. They advanced in slow unison, then stopped.

No one breathed.

The moment lasted forever.

Then a thousand eyes turned from the shrine, seemed to linger on Yoshiko, and looked away.

At Tetsuo's feet, the white lynxette stirred, then settled: home, now, was with Tetsuo and Dhana.

The animals disappeared, back into the forest's shade. Soon, the rustling faded and the trembling leaves grew still, as though they had never been here.

"Eric?" People started, as Tetsuo broke the silence. "Mother says, don't worry—" Tetsuo grinned, "—about the snorkelling."

"Sorry?"

"She says," added Tetsuo, as Yoshiko reached out to press Eric's hand, "there's always tomorrow."

"Wait." Dhana pointed. "Look, up there."

They came.

Five hundred pairs of wings split the air.

The flock wheeled in the clear green sky, and the arc they traced was the very curve of Ken's sweet smile. They cleaved the sky with the strength of collective purpose, then split apart and flew away in all directions, like freedom's promise borne on crystal winds, leaving yesterday's dreams scattered across the trail of time: waiting, waiting, to be dreamed again, on the day when love connects us all and those that are gone will sing again, and our tears will be of laughter, not of grief.

THE END

Acknowledgments

A paradox: writing is a solitary discipline; it is nurtured by the warmth and love of friends. To Yvonne, my wife, thank you for accompanying me on the path.

To the indomitable editorial director of Pyr, Lou Anders, thanks yet again for your energy and belief. And to the whole team at Prometheus/Pyr®, especially Peggy Deemer, a million thanks.

John Richard Parker, literary agent extraordinaire, continues to guide my steps, for which I am always grateful.

About the Author

JOHN MEANEY is the author of four novels—*To Hold Infinity*, *Paradox*, *Context*, and *Resolution*, the latter three titles comprising his critically acclaimed Nulapeiron Sequence. He also has numerous short fiction publication credits. His novelette "Sharp Tang" was shortlisted for the British Science Fiction Association Award in 1995, and *To Hold Infinity* and *Paradox* were on the BSFA shortlists for Best Novel in 1999 and 2001, respectively. His novella "The Whisper of Disks" was included in the 2003 *Year's Best Science Fiction: Twentieth Annual Collection*, edited by Gardner Dozois. His novella "The Swastika Bomb" was reprinted in *Best Short Science Fiction Novels 2004*, edited by Jonathan Strahan. His story "Diva's Bones" was reprinted in *The Year's Best Fantasy 5*, edited by David G. Hartwell and Kathryn Cramer. The Pyr® edition of *Paradox* was selected by Barnes & Noble as the number two science fiction or fantasy work in their Editor's Choice: Top Ten Novels of 2005. The *Times* called John Meaney "The first important new SF writer of the 21st century." Meaney has a degree in physics and computer science, and holds a black belt in Shotokan Karate. He lives in England. Visit his Web site at www.johnmeaney.com.